SOMEWHERE BEYOND ~~~~~~ ~~ ~~ the west, lightning struck. There was a crackling, an earth-shaking crash, and the leaden sky seemed to explode in a brilliant burst of light. For a few seconds, it was as though time stood still, while cattle, men, and horses were in shock. The longhorns recovered first. In a bawling frenzy of terror, they stampeded, the wind and rain at their backs. Riders drew their Colts, but the sound of gunfire was swallowed up in the fury of the storm.

"Ride!" Don shouted. "Ride for your lives!"

But his voice was lost in the roar of the wind and the rumble of thunder. He kicked his horse into a gallop, seeking to get beyond the far-reaching avalanche that was the running longhorns, hoping his comrades would follow. The rest of the riders gave it up, riding for their lives. Don looked back, and in a flash of lightning, he saw a riderless horse galloping ahead of the oncoming stampede. Wheeling his horse, he started back, but there was no time. In a brief flash of lightning, he saw a lone figure standing in the path of the thundering herd, his hands raised helplessly heavenward. Then the pathetic figure was gone, swallowed up under twenty thousand trampling hooves. . . .

THE OLD SPANISH TRAIL

Ralph Compton

St. Martin's Paperbacks

This is a work of fiction, based on actual trail drives of the Old West. Many of the characters appearing in the Trail Drive Series were very real, and some of the trail drives actually took place. But the reader should be aware that, in the developing of characters and events, some fictional literary license has been employed. While some of the characters and events herein are purely the creation of the author, every effort has been made to portray them with accuracy. However, the inherent dangers of the trail are real, sufficient unto themselves, and seldom has it been necessary to enhance their reality.

THE OLD SPANISH TRAIL

Copyright © 1998 by Ralph Compton.
Excerpt from *The Green River Trail* copyright © 1999 by Ralph Compton.

Cover photograph by Comstock Images.
Trail map design by L. A. Hensley.

For information address St. Martin's Press, 175 Fifth Avenue, New York, NY 10010.

EAN: 978-0-312-96408-5

Printed in the United States of America

St. Martin's Paperbacks edition / January 1998

10   9   8   7

This work is respectfully dedicated to my brother, the late James E. (Jim) Compton.

AUTHOR'S FOREWORD

In April, 1844, John Fremont introduced Americans to the Old Spanish Trail. Fremont was accompanied by Kit Carson, Alexis Godey, and others, and was heading east along the trail, bound for Missouri. Fremont had just concluded a reconnaissance of the West that had begun in St. Louis, continued northwest to Oregon, and then south to California. The eastward journey along the Old Spanish Trail included a formidable winter crossing of the Sierra Nevada, the Mojave Desert, and the torturous Great Basin. Fremont later published an account of the 1,200 mile journey.

Early Spanish explorers had used the route to reach the Colorado Plateau, following the Rio Chama to the northwest. While the trail seemed to wander through southwestern Colorado on its way to California, there was a reason. Due west of Santa Fe was the domain of hostile Hopi Indians. The Utes and Paiutes were bad enough—the Utes to the northwest beyond the San Juan Mountains, and the Paiutes somewhere north of the Grand Canyon, in northwestern Arizona.

While Fremont's published account brought the Old Spanish Trail national recognition, it had long been used as a trade route between Santa Fe and California. Antonio Armijo, a Mexican merchant, led the first successful pack train from Santa Fe to Los Angeles in 1829. His pack mules were loaded with woolen goods, and were traded at the missions for horses and mules. He then successfully drove his herds back across the same treacherous trail to Santa

Fe. A year later, William Wolfskill and George Yount traveled from Missouri to Santa Fe via the Santa Fe Trail. They
then rode northwest along the traditional Spanish route to
the Colorado Plateau, and from there southwest to Los Angeles. Thus began the glory days of the trail, although by
then it was centuries old. Travelers were forced to rely on
mules, for few wagons ever survived the journey. The trail
has been called "the longest, crookedest, most arduous
pack mule route in the history of America."

Apparently, the natural hazards and cussedness of the
trail were equaled only by the ever-changing unpredictable
climate. By day, men sweated under a merciless sun, while
at night they hunched over fires in heavy mackinaws,
woolen scarves protecting their ears. Little grew in abundance except cactus, and it seemed the hostile land had
much more than its share of scorpions and rattlesnakes.
Cougars prowled by night, and during scorching summers
there were grizzlies, ever-present threats to horses and pack
mules. Much of the mountainous terrain was shot full of
arroyos that flash-flooded during thunderstorms, and when
dry, provided abundant opportunities for Indian ambush.
And in the mountains there was often rain, hail, sleet, and
snow, all within a few hours.

About 1855, the Old Spanish Trail's heyday ended, for
Spanish and Mexican rule was no more. Gold-rich California had become a state, and with the opening of its harbors,
it was no longer dependent on overland trade. Ships came
from all over the world, bringing goods from England,
France, China, and Japan.

But like the Santa Fe and other famous trails, traces of
the Old Spanish Trail are still there, and with the exception
of hostile Indians, much of the land is unchanged.

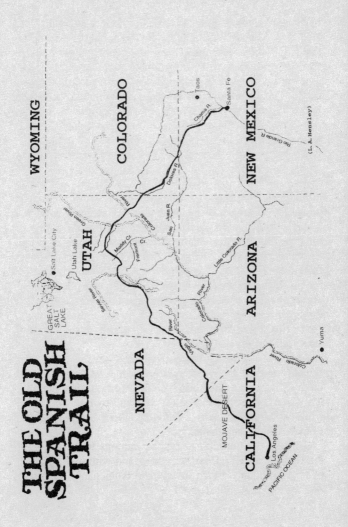

PROLOGUE

San Antonio, Texas. February 1, 1862.

*D*on Webb, Bob Vines, Jim Roussel, Les Brown, and Mike Horton had "learned cow" together, having been friends since childhood. While Webb hadn't told them why he wished to see them, they could read the excitement in his face, and they waited expectantly.

"Sorry I got no coffee," Webb said. "We got Mr. Lincoln's war to thank for that."

"Hell, if we're here to talk about the inconveniences of the war," said Bob Vines, "we got no flour for biscuits either."

Despite the grim reality of their situation, they laughed. Webb was twenty-five, while Mike Horton was a year younger. Bob Vines was twenty-two, Les Brown twenty, while the youngest—at eighteen—was Jim Roussel. All were dressed in Texas boots and range clothes with Stetson hats in various stages of disrepair. Belted around the lean middles of each was a Colt revolver. From the hip pocket of his Levi's, Webb produced a letter.

"Any of you wantin' to read this is welcome to," Webb said, "but for now, I'll just tell you what it says. It's from Warren Blocker, who moved to Santa Fe five years ago. He's somehow got himself a land grant, a new wife, and he wants five thousand head of Texas cattle. He's offerin' us thirty dollars a head, if we'll drive 'em there."

For a moment there was only stunned silence. Jim Roussel was the first to recover, and he cut loose with a Texas yell.

"My God," said Mike Horton reverently, "that's thirty thousand for each of us. Where in tarnation did Blocker come up with a hundred and fifty grand?"

"He didn't say," Webb replied. "He was goin' out there to do some mining. Maybe he struck it rich."

"I don't care if he got it stickin' up banks," said Les Brown. "Let's gather up the cows he wants and drive 'em there before he changes his mind."

"We got to get us an outfit together," Webb said. "For a herd that size, we'll need at least five more riders, and we've all got to eat."

"We can get the riders," said Vines. "Everybody's broke. Most of the northern trails are closed, and it may be just a matter of days until the Federals close the rest of them.* God knows when there'll be another cattle drive but for this one we're plannin', and there should be riders jumpin' at the chance to sign on. Eatin' may be a problem, though, unless we eat nothin' but beef."

"A man can't live on nothin' but beef," Roussel protested.

"That's what we're livin' on now," said Horton, "and as the war worsens, I can't see it gettin' any better."

"Neither can I," Webb said grimly. "For the kind of money Blocker's promisin', I'll eat prairie dogs from here to Santa Fe."

"I reckon all of us can agree on that," said Horton. "But what'll we do about a horse remuda? Every rider will need at least three horses."

"That may be a problem," Webb admitted. "I'll need another horse, and any riders who throw in with us will have to supply their own. We'd better start askin' around

*On April 19, 1862, President Lincoln proclaimed a blockade of all Southern states.

and see if we can come up with some extra mounts. How many horses do we have amongst us?"

"I got just one," said Jim Roussel, "but if I take along a few head of cows for my pa, I reckon he'll loan me two more."

"We'd all better go callin' on our kin," Mike Horton said, "but I purely hate promisin' money I don't have in my hands."

"So do I," said Bob Vines. "But times are hard, and they're about to get harder. Right now, a promise is better than nothing."

"We need riders and we need horses," Don Webb said. "Each of us must find one rider who has or can get three horses. Any questions?"

There were none, and when his friends rode out, Don Webb watched them go. Already a Texas convention was voting to secede, as the war came closer to home, and not one of them knew what the future held in store.

San Antonio, Texas. February 10, 1862.

Red Bohannon was near Don Webb's age and still lived with his aging parents. They all sat at the kitchen table as Webb explained his need for riders.

"Pa, what do you think?" Red asked.

"I think you'd be a fool not to go," said the senior Bohannon. "There's nothin' for you to do on this ten-cow spread, and with two-year-olds sellin' for less than three dollars a head, things can only get worse. I reckon I can spare you a couple of horses. Since all the trade's goin' to be shut off, there'll be no cash crops. I can use the mules to plant some corn and a garden."

Leading his two extra mounts, Red Bohannon rode to Webb's ranch. There they waited until the rest of Webb's companions arrived. Bob Vines was the first, accompanied by a young cowboy leading his two extra horses.

"This is Charlie English," Vines said. "Charlie, this is Don Webb."

"Howdy," said Webb. "The redhead here is Red Bohannon."

Within a matter of hours, Jim Roussel, Les Brown, and Mike Horton rode in, and with each of them was a rider leading his two horses.

"This is Arch Danson," Roussel said.

"Gents," said Les Brown, "this is Eli Mills."

"This ugly hombre is Felton Juneau," Mike Horton said.

Each of the new riders was a friend or relation of the man who had brought him, and Texans all, they wasted no time getting acquainted. They all gathered in Webb's parlor, sitting or hunkering where they could, while Webb told them the little that was known of the forthcoming drive.

"We can reach the Pecos River just east of Fort Stockton. That's two hundred miles, and from there to Santa Fe, it's three hundred more, but we can follow the Pecos all the rest of the way. I figure it'll be worth it for sure water."

"I hear there's quicksand in the Pecos," said Charlie English, "and once bogged down, a cow ain't got sense enough to back out."*

"That's what I've heard," Webb replied, "and we'll have to check it out for quicksand before the cattle are allowed to drink. We'll have some control over them, with sure water close at hand."

"I ain't one to horn in on another man's good fortune," said Felton Juneau, "but I got maybe a hundred head of two-year-olds I'd hate to leave behind. Is there any way I could include 'em in this drive? I'd be willin' to take pot luck in Santa Fe, anything over three dollars a head."

"I don't see anything wrong with each of you including a hundred head," Webb replied. "Why don't we put it to a vote?"

---

*In 1866, Goodnight lost 400 head at the Pecos River. (*The Goodnight Trail*, Book One)

The vote was quickly taken, with Vines, Roussel, Brown, and Horton nodding in agreement.

"I can't see a man leavin' his cows to just work for wages," said Bob Vines. "I'd say the butcher shops in Santa Fe ought to take five hundred head."

"I like the idea," Mike Horton said. "I feel some better about the drive, if we all have a stake in it."

"So do I," said Jim Roussel, "for several reasons. On a trail drive, a man signs on for wages and grub, but as all of you know, grub—except for beef—is in short supply. All of us may have to pitch in, taking payment at the end of the drive, along with wages."

"Fair enough," Red Bohannon agreed. "This is just the beginnin' of hard times, and nobody in Texas is flush. Pa had a good corn crop last year, and I can throw in enough corn meal to keep us in cornbread from here to Santa Fe."

"Bless you," said Don Webb. "Do any of you have kin who had a good crop of coffee beans last year?"

"Just a fair-to-middlin' crop," Arch Danson joked, "and we drunk it all ourselves."

They all laughed, despite the seriousness of their situation, and then they got down to business.

"Ever'thing seems to be comin' together, and I hate to mention it," said Felton Juneau, "but has anybody got mules and a wagon, or at least some pack mules?"

They had overlooked the obvious, and for a moment they looked at one another. Mike Horton eventually spoke.

"I reckon we could get a wagon, but that would take a rider away from the herd, and we can't spare one. What we really need is pack mules. No more grub and supplies than we'll have, two will be enough."

"Two or two hundred," said Red Bohannon, "it won't be easy. Pa let me have the two horses I needed, leavin' him only the mules. He'll need them to grow enough food just to stay alive, and I'm thinkin' that's goin' to be the same situation with everybody else."

"Whatever it takes," Don Webb said, "we'll need at least two pack mules. I'm asking all of you to pitch in and help find them. As for the cattle, we'll gather and hold them all here until we're ready to begin the drive. Bob, I reckon you, Jim, Les, and Mike will need help. What about the rest of you?''

Felton Juneau laughed. ''I could drive a hundred head in my sleep.''

''So could the rest of us,'' said Charlie English.

''Bring them here, then,'' Don Webb said, ''and then begin looking for those mules.''

San Antonio, Texas. February 17, 1862.

Charlie English arrived at the Webb place with a hundred and three two-year-olds and a mule.

''Bueno, Charlie,'' said Webb.

''I got the mule from kin,'' Charlie said, ''and it ain't all that good. I got him with a promise to pay, and I owe a hundred dollars.''

''It won't cost you anything,'' said Webb. ''For the mule and any supplies, I'll see that you're paid, right off the top.''

''I'm obliged,'' Charlie said. ''How about the others?''

''Red, Arch, Eli, and Felton have brought their cows,'' said Webb, ''but nobody's come up with a mule except you. Jim, Les, and Mike will be helping Bob Vines bring in his herd tomorrow. The day after tomorrow, the four of them will drive in Jim Roussel's herd, and finally, herds belonging to Les Brown and Mike Horton. I'm hoping, somewhere along the way, one of them will come up with another mule.''

''So do I,'' English said. ''I'm afraid this war's about to bust loose all around us.''

''It already has,'' said Webb. ''Yesterday, Texas troops took over the Federal arsenal, right here in San Antonio.''

* * *

The following day, Bob Vines, Jim Roussel, Les Brown, and Mike Horton arrived with the herd belonging to Bob Vines.

"Nine hundred and fifty," Vines said. "Best I could do."

"I may not have any more than that," said Jim Roussel.

"Then we may need that extra hundred head from each of our new riders," Webb said.

"I think we will," said Les Brown. "We cut out some scrub stock from Bob's herd, and Jim, Mike, and me aim to do the same with ours."

"Then I'll weed out some of mine," Webb said. "Hard up as we are, now that we have a market, we can't afford to deliver anything less than prime. Charlie brought us a mule. Do any of the rest of you have even a promise of another?"

"I can get one," said Jim Roussel, "but the asking price is a hundred and fifty dollars, which I don't have."

"The rest of us are in the same boat," Webb said. "See if you can get him with the promise to pay. That, and any grub and supplies you throw in the pot will come off the top, once we reach Santa Fe."

"I'll get him, then, and bring him along with my herd," said Roussel.

Each of the five new riders had more than a hundred head of acceptable two-year-olds, and when Webb, Vines, Roussel, Brown, and Horton had cut out the culls from their herds, there were 5,525 Texas longhorns ready for the trail drive to Santa Fe.

"Barring stampedes, I'm figuring two months for the drive," Don Webb said.

"It'll take a month for this bunch to become trailwise," said Mike Horton. "Don't look for 'em to do *anything* we want 'em to do, until then."

San Antonio, Texas. February 25, 1862.

"Head 'em up, move 'em out," Don Webb shouted.

Webb was riding point. Bob Vines and Jim Roussel were riding flank, while Eli Mills and Felton Juneau were at swing. Les Brown, Mike Horton, Red Bohannon, Charlie English, and Arch Danson rode drag.

"Damn," said Charlie, "I'd forgotten how much dust a herd can stir up."

His companions said nothing, for no sooner had they headed one bunch-quitter when a dozen more lit out down the back trail or for parts unknown. By the end of the first day, every man of them was exhausted and covered with dust from head to toe. Fortunately there was water, and after drinking, the unruly herd settled down to what little graze there was.

"God," said Les Brown, "I ain't lookin' forward to tomorrow."

"I ain't lookin' forward to *tonight*," Jim Roussel replied. "This bunch is so jumpy, the sound of a hoot owl is likely to send 'em skalley-hootin' back the way we just come."

Don Webb laughed wearily. "The good news is, we haven't come that far. Not more'n ten miles."

"I think we made one big mistake," said Mike Horton, who had ridden drag all day. "I know we have to make do with the riders we have, but we need at least two wranglers. Runnin' the horse remuda and the pack mules at the tag end of the herd is killin' us. The horses and mules have been raked with horns before, and they ain't about to get close to the cows. They're leavin' daylight between themselves and the herd, and them ornery cows is takin' full advantage of it. I've never seen so many bunch-quitters."

"That's gospel," Red Bohannon said. "Neither have I."

"I know," said Don Webb. "When the drag steers begin to slack off, it opens up gaps in the rest of the herd. The flank and swing riders have been catchin' hell too. But we'll just have to make the best of it until this bunch becomes trail-wise. Until then, the only relief you can expect is that you won't ride drag every day. Tomorrow, the five of you who rode drag today will take other positions, and the rest of us will take the drag. We'll swap every other day."

"Yeah," Bob Vines said, "but don't expect an easy ride. When the drag steers fail to take up the slack, all of them that's ahead will scatter like hell wouldn't have it."

"We're all worn to a frazzle," said Charlie English, "but skittish as this bunch is, we'll have to stand watch. Do we all ride?"

"No," Don Webb replied. "We're still close to home. We'll stand two watches, five of us at a time, the second watch taking over at midnight. If there's any trouble, it generally comes in the small hours of the morning, so I'll take the second watch."

"So will I," said Bob Vines. "In fact, why not have Jim, Les, and Mike join us? We're spearheading this drive, and if there's trouble, we ought to be there for the start and the finish of it."

"I can agree with that," Don Webb said, "as long as the rest of these boys don't feel we're takin' advantage of them."

Felton Juneau laughed. "Nobody has any advantage on a cattle drive. We all got the opportunity of bein' struck by lightning, throwed and gored durin' a stampede, or of just ridin' till we drop and can't get up."

Weary as they were, they all laughed. They built a supper fire, prepared their meager meal, and with only water to drink, sat down to eat. As dusk approached, Red, Charlie, Arch, Eli, and Felton saddled their horses for the first watch. Every man was armed with a Colt revolver and a Henry repeating rifle, and while they were only a few miles from their homes, they were taking no chances.

The weather held, and while nights were cold, there were no storms. Slowly the longhorns became trail-wise, settling down to the daily routine. Only when they were some fifty miles east of the Pecos River did trouble strike. Don Webb had ridden ahead, scouting for water, and when he returned, the rest of the outfit knew by his grim look that there was no water, or that it was too distant for the herd to reach by day's end.

"Nothing ahead of us but the Pecos," said Webb, "and it's every bit of fifty miles."

"Nobody sleeps tonight," Arch Danson predicted.

"There'll be some dewfall," said Les Brown. "Maybe that'll help."

"It won't come until late," Webb said, "and that may be too late."

The herd refused to bed down, and bawling their displeasure, began milling about. The night came, and with it a treacherous breeze from the west, bringing the tantalizing freshness of distant water.

"They're gonna run!" Mike Horton shouted.

"Maybe we can head 'em!" came the shout from Don Webb. "Let's ride!"

Some of them got ahead of the rampaging herd, but then had to ride for their lives because the thirsty longhorns wouldn't be stopped. It was all the desperate riders could do to save the horse remuda and the pack mules.

"I reckon we ought to be thankful the horses and pack mules didn't follow the herd too close," said Red Bohannon.

"I reckon," Don Webb said, "but sometimes the blessings just don't seem to equal all the trouble."

"What now?" said Jim Roussel, as they rested their horses. "We can't round 'em up in the dark."

"Why don't we get what sleep we can, and go after them at first light?" Mike Horton wanted to know.

"I reckon we might as well," said Don Webb. "The usual watch, so we don't lose the horses and pack mules."

There was some dewfall before dawn, and by noon of the following day, the riders had begun finding bunches of longhorns. Some of them were grazing, while others just looked westward, bawling like lost souls. By sundown, less than two hundred head had been found and herded together.

"Where's the rest of 'em?" Jim Roussel wondered.

"Maybe they've gone on to the Pecos," Charlie English suggested.

"Let's hope they have," said Bob Vines. "Let the west wind bring another whiff of that river tonight, and we'll lose the few we've been able to gather."

But they were able to hold the diminished herd, and late the next day they were within a few miles of the Pecos.

"We might as well drive them the rest of the way," Don Webb said. "Close as we are, they'll smell the water and be gone anyhow."

"I'm anxious to reach the river," said Les Brown. "Unless the rest of the herd's there, we're ruined."

Southwest Texas. The Pecos River, March 1, 1862.

Within four or five miles of the river, the portion of the herd they had gathered lit out for the water, the horse remuda and pack mules right behind them.

"Come on," said Don Webb wearily. "There'll be a moon tonight, and I want to see if we're still in the cattle business."

"Ah, hell, they'll be there," Arch Danson predicted. "Even a cow ain't dumb enough to leave water, and where there's water, there's got to be a little graze."

Reaching the river, the sight that greeted them was encouraging. The moon had begun to rise, and the east bank of the river was dotted with cattle. Even in the dim light from moon and stars, it was obvious that most of the herd had reached the river safely, and that few of them had strayed from it.

"I feel some better," said Bob Vines.

"I won't, until we round 'em up and run a tally," Charlie English said. "I don't have enough cows to lose any."

"I reckon that's why we're runnin' 'em under our own

brands, instead of a common trail brand,'' said Red Bohannon.

"Not exactly," Don Webb said. "We'd have lost a
month, trail branding 'em. If there's a loss, we'll each ab-
sorb part of it, when we reach Santa Fe."

"That's damned generous," said Eli Mills. "It's more
than I expected."

"Times are hard, and about to get even harder," Webb
said. "We're all Texans, and it's no time for one to take
advantage of another."

The following day, the riders began rounding up the scattered cattle. To their surprise and relief, only twenty head
were missing.

"We can follow the Pecos from here on to Santa Fe,"
Don Webb said. "Water should not be a problem."

"I never did read that letter," Mike Horton said. "I
reckon you know where this spread of Warren Blocker's
is."

"South of Santa Fe," said Webb. "He has a grant, so it
should be big enough that we can't miss it."

"With water, we ought to cover twelve, maybe fifteen
miles a day," Felton Juneau said.

"I think so," said Webb, "and we're about three hundred miles away. Without any more stampedes, and at ten
miles a day, we'll be there in another month. Warren said
his grant has its eastern border along the Pecos."

Santa Fe, New Mexico. May 2, 1862.

"This is easier than I ever expected," said Jim Roussel.

A newly painted sign erected beside the river said THE
WARREN BLOCKER GRANT.

"Don't crow too loud," Les Brown said. "We're not
there yet, and we don't have our money."

They crossed the Pecos at the next shallows onto what
they believed was the Blocker grant, but it was almost sun-

down before they saw any sign of life. A lone horse lifted its head and nickered.

"It can't be much farther," Webb said. "We'll be there before dark. Let's hold the herd here until I ride ahead and tell them we're coming."

Don Webb rode out, and what he discovered took his breath away. There was only the charred remains of what had once been a barn and a large log house. Beyond the barn, so new that grass had not grown over them, was what could only be a pair of graves. Slowly Webb turned his horse and rode back to meet the herd—

1

At the herd, Webb's companions waited anxiously. When he reported to them what he saw, there was a shocked silence. Mike Horton was the first to regain his voice.

"You sure we're at the right place?"

"You saw the sign pointin' this way," said Webb.

"I reckon this is a fool question," Jim Roussel said, "but where do we go from here?"

"Santa Fe," said Webb. "It's clear enough what happened, and somebody had to bury Warren and his wife, so we'll go callin' on the county sheriff. Then we'll have to find some hombre that can afford five thousand Texas longhorns. Red, why don't you ride with me. The rest of you take the herd back along the river and wait for us."

Wordlessly the rest of the riders obeyed, as Webb and Bohannon rode upriver toward Santa Fe. They had no trouble finding the sheriff's office. The lawman sat at a desk cleaning his Colt. He got to his feet when they entered.

"I'm Don Webb and this is Red Bohannon."

"Sheriff Carpenter. What can I do for you?"

"Not much, I'm afraid," said Webb. "Warren Blocker was a friend of ours, and we just came from his place. What was left of it. What can you tell us?"

"Not a lot," Carpenter replied. "Couple of sheepmen found 'em, and they was dead and buried a week, before I heard about it. I took a posse out there, but the trail was cold. A dozen riders headed south, and we lost 'em when they split up. Renegades, I'd say."

"Maybe," said Webb, "but why single out the Blockers? We saw only one horse, and not another head of stock anywhere."

"Money," Sheriff Carpenter said. "The Blockers came from southern Arizona, and first thing they done was deposit forty thousand dollars in the local bank. It was no secret that Blocker had made his fortune in mining, and just a few days before his place was raided, he took thirty-five thousand out of the bank. I reckon I shouldn't speak ill of the dead, but it was a foolish thing to do."

"Under the circumstances, I'd have to agree with you," said Webb. "Thanks for the information."

"Sorry I couldn't be of more help," Sheriff Carpenter said.

Webb and Bohannon closed the door behind them and stood on the boardwalk looking around.

"Come on," said Webb. "I see a livery sign, and that's usually where most livestock is bought and sold."

The livery barn was large, and the office door was at one corner, in the front. Above the door was a sign that read LIVESTOCK BOUGHT AND SOLD. JORDAN WINKLER, PROP.

"Come in," the big man said, easing his chair down to its front legs. "I'm Winkler."

"Webb and Bohannon," said Don. "We have Texas cattle to sell. Prime, two-year-olds and under."

"How many?" Winkler asked cautiously.

"Fifty-five hundred," said Webb.

Winkler whistled long and low, shaking his head.

"Folks around here don't like beef?" Red Bohannon asked.

"Not that much of it, friend," said Winkler. "This is sheep country. Most folks around here are third and fourth generation Mexican, and they was livin' here while this territory still belonged to Mexico. They're mostly mutton eaters. Them that's partial to beef is them that's come here from Missouri and Texas. I'll take two hundred head, twenty dollars per.''

"Thirty dollars," Webb said.

"Twenty," said Winkler. "No more."

"Twenty-five," Webb countered.

"Twenty," said Winkler.

Webb sighed. "Two hundred head, twenty dollars a head."

"I'll want a bill of sale," said Winkler. "When can you have them here?''

"In the morning," Webb said. "Do you have pens?"

"No," said Winkler, "just a corral, and it's full of mules. Just drive the cows here, and I'll have some riders to take charge of them."

"One thing more," Webb said. "Do you know of anybody, anywhere, who might buy the rest of our herd? We'll sell at twenty dollars a head.''

"Ellerbee and Sons in Los Angeles will take them," said Winkler, "and they'll pay lots more than twenty dollars. Couple of years back, they bought three thousand head of sheep from here. Send 'em a telegram, ask if they'll buy, and ask for a quote."

"Thanks," Webb said. "Where's the telegraph office?"

"Take a left out of here, and it's a block up the street," said Winkler.

They were almost to the telegraph office when Bohannon spoke.

"You forgot to ask how far it is to Los Angeles, and how we're to get there."

"I didn't forget," Webb said grimly. "We got no choice but to go, even if it's three thousand miles. You reckon Texas cowboys can't take a herd of longhorns where Mexicans drove three thousand damn sheep?''

Bohannon laughed, and they paused outside the telegraph office, pooling their meager resources to pay for the telegram. They entered, and taking a yellow form and a pencil, Webb wrote out the message: *Have 5,000 head prime two-year-old Texas steers. Stop. If buying telegraph quote.*

"We'll wait for an answer," said Webb, as he paid for the telegram.

"Might not have it 'fore tomorrow," the telegrapher said. "We close at six."

"Then we'll wait till six, and if it hasn't come, then we'll be back tomorrow," Webb said.

"Tarnation," said Red, when they left the telegraph office, "ever'thing's ridin' on that telegram. We're in one hell of a mess if they don't answer. Denver's God knows how far to the north, *Mejicano* land's to the south, and the war's comin' to Texas."

"That telegram's got to pay off," Webb replied. "While we're waitin' for an answer, we can maybe learn something about the trail to Los Angeles. Let's find out if there's a newspaper in town."

The Santa Fe Chief occupied a small office across the street from the jail, and when the Texans entered, an elderly lady looked at them over the tops of her spectacles. Don wasted no time.

"Ma'am, we have some cattle we aim to trail to Los Angeles. We've heard other stock has been driven there, and we're needin' some directions."

"You're talking about the Old Spanish Trail," she said, "and there's twelve hundred miles of it. We used to print a map when it was in regular use. Perhaps I can find one."

One entire wall of the office was lined with shelves, each of them sagging under a load of what obviously were back issues of the newspaper. Eventually she presented them with a yellowed edition of the newspaper.

"There's a full-page map in here," she said.

"We're obliged, ma'am," said Webb. "What do we owe you?"

"Nothing," she said, with a grim smile. "You'll hate me before you reach Los Angeles."

Thirty minutes before the telegraph office was to close, a reply came from Ellerbee and Sons in Los Angeles. It said: *Buying at sixty dollars a head. Stop. Confirm delivery date.*

Speechless, Webb and Bohannon left the telegraph office, pausing to read the brief message again.

"Lord Almighty," said Bohannon, "that's three hundred thousand dollars for the five thousand head. I ain't believin' it's possible for a bunch of hard-scrabble Texans like us to get our hands on that kind of money. Not with the country at war."

"California's a hell of a long ways from the war," Webb said, "and it ain't that many years since they discovered gold. They got the money and we got the cows, and if some joker gets overly interested, we're from New Mexico, not Texas."

"That's sound thinking," said Bohannon. "It'd be just like the Federals to take our herd or the money."

"Not as long as I'm alive and with a gun in my hand," Webb said.

"After Ellerbee's quote of sixty dollars a head, twenty dollars don't seem like much," said Bohannon, "but it'll be enough to keep us in grub from here to California."

"I reckon," Webb agreed, "but that presents another problem. Enough grub for ten of us over twelve hundred miles purely won't fit on two pack mules. We'll need four more."

"Winkler has a corral full of 'em," said Bohannon, "and when he pays us for the two hundred cows, we'll have money."

"I reckon we'd better see him and arrange to buy another four mules," Webb said. "He may have the pack saddles too."

Again Winkler was leaned back in his chair, looking as though he likely hadn't moved since they'd last seen him.

"We're much obliged to you," said Webb. "Ellerbee's agreed to buy the rest of the herd. Now we're needin' four more pack mules to see us through to California."

"I can't help you," Winkler said. "I've almost never got any for sale, and I got none now."

"You got a corral full of 'em," said Bohannon. "You can't bear to part with at least four?"

"If they was mine, I'd sell you the whole damn bunch," Winkler said shortly. "I took 'em on for a couple of days, feedin' 'em for a gent name of Starnes. Him and his riders is takin' 'em south, to sell in the minin' camps. You'll have to talk to Starnes. He's at the Santa Fe Hotel, and he's tight as the bark on a tree."

"Thanks," said Webb. "We'll talk to him."

Webb and Bohannon found Henry Starnes at the hotel, and he listened to their plea.

"That bunch of hee-haws will bring a hundred and fifty dollars apiece in the mining camps," Starnes said, "and I won't sell for a penny less."

"But you're still a long way from the mining camps," said Webb. "A hundred apiece."

"Forget it," Starnes said. "You're wasting my time."

"Then maybe this will interest you," said Webb. "We have a herd of Texas steers, all two-year-olds or less, and prime. We've been quoted sixty dollars a head for them in the mining camps. We'll swap you three of them for one mule."

Starnes laughed. "You're a long way from the mining camps. If I was interested and I liked the looks of your herd, I might swap. One mule for four cows."

Webb swallowed his anger. Starnes was taking unfair advantage, and there was nothing they could do but accept.

"The herd's downriver maybe ten miles," said Webb. "Why don't you ride down there with us? Winkler's buying two hundred head. We can drive yours here along with his."

"If they're good enough for Winkler, they're good enough for me," Starnes said. "I'll swap with you at Winkler's in the morning. I'll expect a bill of sale."

"You'll have one," said Webb shortly, "and we'll expect one from you."

Webb and Bohannon mounted their horses and rode south along the Pecos. When the rest of the outfit saw them coming, they gathered around. First, Don told them of the quote from Ellerbee in Los Angeles, and emerging from what had seemed like certain defeat, they broke into a round of cheers. Their jubilation knew no bounds when they learned of the sale of two hundred head to Winkler, but there was anger on every face when they were told of the expensive trade for four additional mules.

"Damn it," said Bob Vines, "we'll have money comin' for the two hundred head. We'd have been better off, just payin' the hundred and fifty dollars per mule."

"I didn't think so," Webb said, "because Winkler's only payin' twenty dollars a head. I know two thousand dollars sounds like a lot, us all bein' broke, but we can spare the cows and I reckoned we'd need the money for grub."

"You done exactly the right thing," said Jim Roussel. "I don't care how long and hard this Old Spanish Trail is, long as we got plenty of grub. Maybe we can buy coffee too."

"There's two mercantiles," Red Bohannon said. "I saw 'em."

"Once we've collected from Winkler," said Webb, "I think each of us should have fifty dollars for personal use. The rest will be used for supplies and grub. Anybody object to that?"

"That's more than fair," Charlie English said. "I don't remember how long it's been since I had fifty dollars I didn't owe somebody."

They all shouted their agreement, and while there was still daylight, they gathered for a look at the map of the Old Spanish Trail.

"Don't look all that bad," said Mike Horton, "if it's anywhere close to right. There's a lot of rivers. At least through most of Utah Territory."

"I been to the High Plains a time or two," Felton Juneau said, "and in the mountains there's always springs."

"Let's hope that's the case between here and California," said Don Webb. "There'll be mountains aplenty."

"I can't imagine that much territory without Indians," Arch Danson said. "I think we'd better do some askin' around, before we go lopin' along that trail."

"We will," said Don Webb. "Red and me had a lot to do, all in one day. Now that we have some money comin' in Santa Fe, the pack mules that we need, and a buyer in Los Angeles, we can start lookin' at some other things."

"Maybe one of them other things can be a pair of wranglers," Les Brown said. "I'd use my fifty dollars toward payin' 'em, just to get the pack mules and the horse remuda away from the drag steers."

"We'll consider that," said Webb. "Let's see what's left, after we've bought supplies."

Next morning, shortly after first light, the outfit had cut out two hundred and sixteen head from the herd.

"Mike, Red, Charlie, and me will drive 'em into town," Webb said. "The rest of you stay with the herd. Once we've collected our money, all of you will have a chance to ride in, to take care of personal needs and to help decide on supplies we'll need for the drive on to California."

When Webb and his companions reached town with the herd, the livery was open for business and Winkler was waiting for them.

"They are prime," said Winkler. "Wish it was so I could afford more of 'em."

"I reckon it's just as well you can't," Webb said. "After that quote from Ellerbee, we couldn't afford to sell 'em to you. There's two hundred and sixteen. We traded sixteen of them to Starnes for four mules."

"I told you he was tight," said Winkler. "There's fifty of the varmints, and he tried to talk me into grainin' the lot of 'em for three days, at ten dollars a day."

"That reminds me," Webb said. "We don't know what the graze is like along this Old Spanish Trail, so we'll need grain for our horses and mules. How are you fixed for that?"

"Just had a supply train in from St. Joe," said Winkler, "so I got shelled corn. But you'd better make a deal for it before Starnes moves out. He'll be needin' a lot of it for his mules."

"Then let's finalize our deal for the cows," Webb said,

"and we'll go ahead and pay for some corn. We've had our share of troubles already."

By the time the Texans had swapped bills of sale with Winkler and had collected their money, Henry Starnes and two of his riders were looking over the herd.

"Satisfied?" Webb asked.

Starnes nodded, producing a bill of sale for four mules. In turn, Webb handed him a signed bill for sixteen head of steers. Starnes' two riders entered the corral with lead ropes and led out four mules.

"The lead ropes are not included," Starnes said.

"I didn't reckon they would be," said Webb. "We have our own."

Winkler looked at Starnes in disgust, but Starnes seemed not to notice. His riders were cutting out his sixteen head of cows.

"You're supposed to have those mules out of my corral today," Winkler said. "When?"

"Soon as the rest of my outfit gets here," said Starnes shortly. "I'll be needin' grain."

"I've already sold most of it," Winkler said with some satisfaction, "but you're welcome to what's left."

Winkler had three riders in charge of the cattle, and he spoke to them.

"Keep them bunched here until those mules are gone. Then herd them into the corral and give them some hay."

"Winkler," Webb said, "before we take these mules back to camp, do you have have pack saddles?"

"I have four," said Winkler. "By the time folks get here, they generally have their pack saddles. Not much call for them, so you can have them all for twenty-five dollars."

"We're obliged," Webb said. "We'll take them."

"Now," said Mike Horton, when each mule bore one of the newly purchased pack saddles, "why don't we stop by one of the mercantiles and and see if they have coffee? I think we all deserve some."

"We can do better than that," Webb said. "We'll get some coffee, some tinned fruit or tomatoes, and maybe a side of bacon. We're all needin' a good feed.''

Reaching the store, they were elated to find all the items they sought, and with typical Texas fervor, they bought thirty pounds of coffee beans and a two-gallon coffee pot.

''I know we ain't but three hours away from breakfast,'' said Red Bohannon, ''but there wasn't any coffee. Why don't we try again, when we get back to the herd?''

Don Webb laughed. ''You're readin' my mind. Let's ride.''

Their breakfast fire had long since burned out, but a new one was quickly kindled when they rode in with their purchases.

''Pass me a sack of coffee beans,'' said Bob Vines, ''and I'll get 'em ready for the pot.''

''It's been so long since we've had coffee, I hope you ain't forgot how,'' Jim Roussel said.

''Of course not,'' said Vines scornfully. ''I take off my sock, fill it with beans, and then smash 'em with the butt of my Colt.''

They all laughed, recognizing it for the cowboy humor that it was, and when the coffee was ready, they filled their tin cups and drank the scalding brew.

''I've drunk nothin' from this cup but water for so long, it don't know what coffee is,'' Red Bohannon said.

Using pointed sticks, they broiled rashers of bacon over the open fire, washing it down with tinned tomatoes.

''Here's a tally book and a pencil,'' said Don Webb. ''I'll pass it around, and all of you can write down what you think we'll need for the trail. Don't bother with flour, bacon, coffee, or beans, because all those are things we know we'll need. Now I'm going to hand each of you fifty dollars. We'll ride into town, five of us at a time, today and tomorrow. The day after tomorrow, we'll buy our supplies and grub, and the next day, we'll take the trail west. Visit the saloon for a few drinks, if you like, but don't stash a bottle in your saddlebag. There'll be no drinking on the trail.''

"We'll need a couple of gallons to treat wounds or snakebite," Les Brown pointed out.

"For that, but nothing more," said Webb.

"Bueno," Bob Vines said. "I'll find us a snake."

"Then you'd better save enough for a gunshot wound," said Don Webb, "because I'll shoot the first hombre that shows up drunk after we leave Santa Fe."

Bob Vines, Jim Roussel, Les Brown, Arch Danson, and Eli Mills rode into town in the early afternoon. Despite their joking about the whiskey, they avoided the saloons, going to the mercantile instead. There they purchased socks, tobacco, hard candy, and ammunition for their Colts and Henry rifles. Only then did they pause at the Silver Dollar Saloon.

"I'd like to sit in for a few hands of poker," Jim Roussel said.

"You'll end up broke," said Bob Vines.

"No," Roussel insisted. "I'll risk one double eagle. If I lose that, I'm out. Generally I'm lucky. I once won a hundred dollars."

"I reckon the rest of us can stand a beer or two," said Vines. "By then, you'll likely be broke."

The saloon was doing a thriving business. Many of the patrons, by their dress, were obviously miners, but the occupations of the rest were questionable. Their Colts were tied-down, their hats and boots looked new, while their clothing and their hands showed not a sign of toil. The Texans stood in the gloom surveying the saloon and its inhabitants.

"I don't like the looks of most of this bunch," Bob Vines said. "Some of them look like they could have been involved in the robbery and murder of the Blockers."

"But we don't know that," said Roussel.

There were several poker games in progress, and at that moment, a man kicked back his chair and bowed out. Three of the five remaining participants were of the stripe that Bob Vines had suggested might be renegades. One of them sported twin Colts. Roussel took the empty chair and dealt himself in. Bob, Les, Arch, and Eli each ordered a beer and took a nearby table where they could watch the game. Roussel quickly lost three pots, but he then took a fourth, fifth and sixth, putting him a few dollars ahead. Bob Vines caught his eye, but he grinned triumphantly, shaking his head. He won three more pots, and with a snarl the big man with the *buscadera* rig kicked back his chair and got to his feet.*

"I don't like the way you play, kid. I think you got somethin' up your sleeves besides your elbows."

Just for a second there was dead silence, and his antagonist already had a gun in his hand when Jim Roussel shot him. He tumbled over backward, upsetting his chair. Two of the other men at the table, obviously his companions were on their feet, clawing at their Colts.

"Don't," said Bob Vines coldly.

Vines, Brown, Danson, and Mills all stood there with leveled Colts.

"Somebody get the sheriff," the bartender shouted.

Jim Roussel remained where he was, and the duo who had been about to draw their guns sat down, their murderous eyes on Roussel. The sheriff's office was nearby, and soon Sheriff Carpenter arrived. He knelt beside the man Roussel had shot and found him dead.

"It was self-defense, sheriff," the house dealer volunteered. "He had his gun in his hand before the young gent drew."

"What about it, barkeep?" Sheriff Carpenter asked.

"The man called him a cheat," said the barkeep. "It was a more than fair fight."

"I reckon he's with you," Sheriff Carpenter said, his eyes on the four Texans who still held drawn guns.

"He is," said Bob Vines quietly, "and if you have no objection, we'll be on our way."

"Not until I get your names," Sheriff Carpenter said. "I don't doubt the self-defense claim will stand, but there'll

*A buscadera rig is right and left holsters, to accommodate two guns.

be an inquest in the morning. You'll have to be present.''

Despite the tragic turn of events, Roussel insisted on collecting his winnings. The five of them left the saloon, but as they mounted their horses, the two friends of the dead man stood on the boardwalk watching them.

"I got me a strong hunch this ain't over," said Arch Danson.

"I have an equally strong hunch you're right," Bob Vines replied. "I reckon the sooner we're out of this town, the better off we'll be."

"Damn it," said Roussel angrily, "a Texan don't run."

"A Texan bleeds like anybody else when he's shot in the back," Bob Vines said grimly.

"God," said Les Brown in awe, "I didn't know you was that sudden with a Colt."

"I can take care of myself," Roussel said.

"I'm not so sure of that," said Vines. "The hombre you shot has at least two friends, and there may be more. Remember, the Blockers were robbed and murdered by renegades, and they got away unidentified. That may be part of the same bunch hanging around the saloon."

Don Webb listened grimly as Roussel told him what had happened at the saloon. Bob Vines, Les Brown, Arch Danson, and Eli Mills added their assurance that the fight had been in self-defense.

"I don't question your need to defend yourself," Webb said, "but I do question your judgment, sitting in on a game with armed men who look suspicious."

"They were well-dressed," said Vines, "and none of them—includin' the one that Jim shot—looked like they'd ever done an honest day's work."

"There's still time for Red, Mike, Charlie, Felton, and me to ride into town," Webb said. "I think we'll do some of our buying today, the rest tomorrow, and leave here the day after tomorrow. Under the circumstances, I'll feel better when this town is behind us."

"Bob, Les, Jim, Arch, and me still have to ride in for that inquest tomorrow," said Eli.

"True," Don Webb said, "but you'll be there for that, and nothing more. I want all of you to return here immediately. Mike, Red, Charlie, Felton, and me will then take all the mules to town and buy the rest of what we need."

"I don't like bein' treated like a prisoner in this camp," said Roussel sourly.

"You'll like being shot in the back even less," Webb said, "but don't get the idea all my concern is for you. The hombre you shot may be part of a vindictive bunch that will gun down any of the rest of us, just on general principles."

"Sorry," said Roussel, not sounding sorry at all. "I reckon I didn't think of that."

"Well, by God, it's time you *started* thinking," Webb said angrily. "If you want to risk your hide, that's your business, but when the rest of us may be bushwhacked for a fool thing you've done, then it becomes *our* business. We're an outfit, and we'll have to stand together."

Webb, Horton, Bohannon, English, and Juneau rode into town. First they went to the wagon yard, where they bought enough canvas to protect the supplies the four extra mules would carry. On impulse, Webb led them to Winkler's place and asked the liveryman a question.

"We're in need for a pair of wranglers to tend our horse remuda and pack mules on the trail. Do you know of a couple of gents who might hire on?"

"Maybe," said Winkler. "Dominique and Roberto. They're Mexican. Brothers, and you can't tell 'em apart. They're from California, and they're good with horses. They're here in town somewhere. Check with me tomorrow, and I'll see if I can round 'em up."

Without incident, the five Texans returned to their herd, and there was considerable rejoicing when Don Webb told them of the possibility they might have wranglers for the mules and the horse remuda. It wasn't quite dark when the first watch went on duty, and from somewhere across the river, came the thunder of rifles. Riders seized their Henrys, but the shooting ended as suddenly as it had begun.

"Anybody hit?" Webb shouted.

"One slug parted my hair," said Charlie English.

"I'm not sure they intended to hit us," Mike Horton said. "There's plenty of cover, and they could have attacked before dark."

"I have an idea who they are," said Webb, his eyes on Jim Roussel. "This may be just the start, and it's a long way to California."

2

Hernandez and Doolin—the men who had fired on the herd—rode north of Santa Fe a few miles to a secluded cabin. In back of it was a corral and lean-to that provided shelter for the horses. Unsaddling their mounts, they loosed them into the corral with the other animals. The ten men within the cabin had already eaten and were drinking coffee from tin cups when Hernandez and Doolin entered. Griff, the leader of the bunch, spoke.

"Where's Pickford?"

"Dead," Hernandez replied. "He started a fight over a poker game, and the young gent he drawed against was chain lightning with a pistol."

"Damn it," said Griff, "I've warned all of you to shy away from gun trouble in town. That's all it'll take to get the law interested in us. Did the sheriff question either of you?"

"No," Hernandez said, "but he took our names. There's an inquest tomorrow, and we got to be there."

"The sheriff's no fool," said Griff. "He'll start to wonderin' how Pickford was able to drop a bundle in a poker game when he's been hangin' around town for months without a sign of work. Then he'll start lookin' slanch-eyed at everybody else of the same stripe. We got to ride out of here, pronto."

"Hell," Doolin said, "I got a woman here."

"There's women other places," said Griff callously. "We've worked this territory dry anyhow."

"We got more'n thirty-five thousand, our last job," Oliver said, "and the law ain't got a clue. Ridin' south, like we done, and splittin' up, it's all been blamed on renegades from south of the border."

"Them of you wantin' to stay here will just have to take your chances then," said Griff. "I've stayed alive by not pushin' my luck. I'm going back to Los Angeles."

"Then I reckon I'll stay on for a while," Doolin said. "The hombre that gunned down Pickford is part of a outfit that's got a herd of Texas steers south of town, on the Pecos, and there must be five or six thousand. They'd be worth fifty dollars a head in the mining camps."

"Damn," said Oliver, "they'd be worth a pile. But how did you know about 'em?"

Doolin said nothing, and it was Hernandez who spoke.

"After Pickford was shot, we follered them five hombres," Hernandez said.

Griff was glaring at him suspiciously, and he was glad he hadn't mentioned that he and Doolin had fired on the camp. After a prolonged silence, Quando spoke.

"Might be reason enough for us pullin' out of Santa Fe. If we can get our hands on that herd and drive 'em to the mining camps, we'd be set for life."

"Maybe that's where this outfit's takin' 'em," said Fedders. "This is mostly all sheep country around here. When they move out, we could foller along, lettin' 'em do most of the work. Then when we're far enough from Santa Fe, where there's no law lookin' at us, we can ambush that bunch and take the herd."

"Not bad reasoning, as far as it goes," Griff said, "but you couldn't unload that many cows in the mining camps south of here if every miner bought three."

"Maybe not," said Doolin, "but there's mining camps all over Nevada."

"And except for the Comstock, every damn one is hard-scrabble," Griff said. "We was through most of 'em."*

"Well, hell," Doolin said, "it was just an idea."

"Maybe a better idea than you think," said Griff. "I can't believe that bunch brought a herd this far, without some hope of sellin' 'em. Tomorrow I aim to ride in and maybe find out where they're headed."

"You think we can take the herd then," Doolin said.

"I don't see why not," said Griff, "if there's a market. I want you and Hernandez to be there for that inquest tomorrow, but ride out when it's done. The rest of you are to stay here until I learn something more about this trail herd."

Santa Fe, New Mexico. May 6, 1862.

"Those of you who have to be in town for the inquest, go ahead," said Don Webb, "and when it's finished, come on back here. You'll stay with the herd while the rest of us ride in and load up with supplies and grub."

The five of them saddled their horses and rode out, aware that Webb's caution was intended to prevent further trouble in town. While nothing more had been said to Roussel, he knew his standing had diminished. Not because he had defended himself, but because he had taken part in a poker game in a strange town among strangers. The youngest rider in the outfit, he silently vowed to be more cautious in the future and to redeem himself in the weeks and months ahead. They dismounted before the sheriff's office half an hour before the appointed time for the inquest.

"It'll be held at the court house," Sheriff Carpenter told them.

So as not to attract undue attention, Griff waited until time for the inquest to begin before riding into town. Knowing Winkler to be the most likely buyer of livestock in

*Development of the Comstock Lode began in 1859, and over the next thirty years, more than six hundred million dollars in gold was taken from it.

Santa Fe, he stopped there first. The adjoining corral was full of longhorn cows and Griff used them as an excuse to question Winkler.

"I heard there was a passel of longhorn cows bein' sold," said Griff. "You buyin' all of them?"

"No," Winkler replied. "Just two hundred."

"Where's the rest of 'em? I might be interested in some, if the price is right."

Winkler laughed. "It won't be. They've had an offer from a dealer in Los Angeles for three times what I paid."

"Just my luck," said Griff. Elated, he mounted his horse and rode away. He had all the information he needed.

"In view of the testimony by witnesses," the judge said, "this court accepts the plea of self-defense. Case dismissed."

Sheriff Carpenter waited until the five Texans had left the court house. He then spoke to them quietly.

"Do you gents aim to be here awhile?"

"No," Bob Vines said. "We'll be leaving tomorrow at first light."

"I don't aim to seem inhospitable," said Carpenter, "but it might prevent more trouble. We know Pickford had at least two friends and maybe more. The court's accepting a plea of self-defense likely won't impress them."

"We're considering that," Vines said, "so we're leaving a mite earlier than we intended to. Texans don't run from a fight, but we can't see having more gun trouble when there's nothing to be gained by it."

"That's a wise decision," said Sheriff Carpenter approvingly. "I wish more hombres on the frontier felt that way."

Vines and his companions rode back to the herd.

"The few supplies we already have will have to go into our saddlebags," Don Webb said. "I want all six mules with empty packsaddles."

When each mule bore a packsaddle, Webb and his four companions saddled their horses and headed for Santa Fe, leading the pack mules.

"We might as well go to Winkler's for the grain," said Webb. "Then we'll know how much more we'll have room to take with us."

"Good thing you went ahead and bought your grain," Winkler said. "Starnes didn't get as much as he wanted."

"Then he's lucky he ain't got as far to go as we have," said Red Bohannon. "Was you able to find them two Mexican wranglers for us?"

"Dominique and Roberto," said Winkler. "They was in town last night. Been layin' around a sheep camp with some friends of theirs, and they seemed interested in goin' to California. Especially if they're bein' paid. I told 'em to be here this mornin', and I'm surprised they ain't. They'll be along, I expect. How much longer will you be here?"

"Until tomorrow at first light," Webb said. "We're south of here, on the Pecos."

"I'll send 'em along," said Winkler. "There was another gent here a while ago, asking about your herd. Talked like he was interested in buying."

"He didn't tell you his name, I reckon," Webb said.

"No," said Winkler, "and I didn't ask. He seemed disappointed when I told him you've got a buyer for your herd in Los Angeles."

When they had loaded their grain and headed for the mercantile, Red Bohannon spoke.

"I got my doubts there's anybody around here interested in Texas cattle, even if we'd sell at twenty dollars a head."

"What I was thinking," Charlie English said. "He didn't have to tell the varmint where we was goin' from here."

"No," said Webb, "but it won't make any difference. It won't take a Comanche scout to follow a herd the size of ours."

"I reckon we'll have to keep a close eye on our back trail," Felton Juneau said.

"Friends of the varmint Jim Roussel shot," said Mike Horton. "I wish he wasn't a long-time *amigo*. We could string him up."

Webb laughed without humor. "Jim's pistol-pullin'

likely had something to do with it, but if they're interested in the herd, we couldn't have escaped them. Thieves are drawn to plunder like buzzards to a carcass.''

In a somber mood, they reined up before the mercantile.

''The way things is goin','' said Bohannon, ''one of us had best stay out here and keep watch as we load the mules.''

''Do that,'' Webb said. ''The rest of us can tote out the supplies and grub. Last thing we need is for some hombres to ride off with our mules.''

The five of them spent two hours arranging and re-arranging the loads, balancing them to lessen the strain on the mules.

''We'd best buy two or three tins of sulfur salve,'' said Charlie English. ''A packsaddle can rub a mule raw before you know it.''

''You're right,'' Webb replied, ''and we were about to forget that.''

When Webb returned from the store, he had three tins of the salve and eight quart bottles of whiskey.

''I see you're familiar with the ways of pack mules,'' said Felton Juneau.

''Considerably,'' Webb said. ''Never tote anything in gallon jugs. Bust a jug and you've lost a gallon. Bust a bottle and you've only lost a quart.''

''*Si,*'' said Arch Danson, ''and never load 'em all on one mule. I've seen the varmints hunker down and roll with a packsaddle.''

When the mules had been loaded and the packs secured, they mounted their horses and headed for the herd. As they departed, Griff watched with more than casual interest and with considerable satisfaction. He then rode away to join his companions to the north of town.

''Well,'' said Doolin, when Griff arrived, ''what did you learn?''

''All I needed to know,'' Griff said. ''They have a buyer for the herd in Los Angeles and that's where they're bound. Some of 'em just left town with six loaded pack mules.''

"They'll likely be takin' the trail tomorrow then," said Hernandez.

"I expect they will be," Griff said, "but we don't have to be in any hurry. In fact, I'm plannin' for us to stay maybe a week behind them. We can't have them spot us on their back-trail, because they'll know why we're there."

"Yeah," said Ibanez, "and if they're goin' the way I expect 'em to, there'll be places for an ambush every hundred yards."

"The Old Spanish Trail," Rodriguez said. *"Montañoso."** *

"It's hell with the lid off," said Griff, "but when the time comes, that'll work to our advantage. There's no better place in the world for an ambush."

"Includin' Pickford's, we got only two extra horses," Kenton said. "That won't be near enough to pack grub for all of us. That herd's likely to be on the trail three months."

"We can fix that easy enough," said Bullard. "All we got to do is find us a sheep camp where they got horses, and take 'em."

"Not until we're ready to ride," Griff said. "If the law comes lookin' for horse thieves, we'd better be long gone. We'll load our pack horses here, not in town. We'll ride in, two of us at a time, until we got all the grub and ammunition we need. We don't want anybody knowin' there's a bunch of us aimin' to ride out. That sheriff is nobody's fool, and we can't afford for him to get curious as to what we got in mind."

When the Texans returned to the herd with their loaded pack mules, Dominique and Roberto were there. Winkler had been right. The two of them were identical, right down to their dress. Their trousers were black, with tight legs, while their matching vests were gold embroidered. Black, polished high-heeled riding boots and wide-brimmed sombreros completed their attire. They seemed not more than

---

*Mountainous.

a year or two out of their teens, and they swept off their sombreros to greet the new arrivals.

"The Señor Winkler send us," said one of them.

"Wranglers," Webb said.

"*Si,*" they replied in a single voice.

"You look so much alike," said Webb, "how are we to know which of you is which?"

They looked at Webb in a manner that implied they were willing to forgive him of his ignorance. Finally one of them spoke.

"When you call Dominique, Dominique come. When you call Roberto, Roberto come. *Comprende?*"

The outfit laughed uproariously, while Dominique and Roberto only looked confused.

"From here to California, a hundred dollars for each of you," said Webb.

"*Si,*" they replied in a single voice.

But then either Dominique or Roberto said, "No cook."

That got the attention of the Texans.

"Tarnation," Mike Horton shouted, "can you cook?"

"*Si,*" they replied.

Bob Vines laughed. "I think we're missin' something here. For a hundred dollars each, we're gettin' a pair of wranglers. If they're expected to cook, the ante goes up."

"*Si,*" said the Mexicans with straight faces.

"How much?" Webb asked. "Another fifty dollars each?"

"*Si,*" they replied.

"If they can cook," said Bob Vines, "I'll pay 'em out of my share."

"No," Webb said, "if they can handle our horse remuda and the pack mules on the trail and do the cooking as well, then we'll all pay them. Not an extra fifty dollars, but a full hundred dollars extra. Does anybody object to that?"

"My God, no," said Mike Horton.

The rest of the outfit quickly shouted their approval. Webb looked at the Mexican duo, and with wide grins, they nodded their approval. Nothing more was said, and when it was time to begin supper, Dominique and Roberto attacked the chore with the enthusiasm and skill that soon convinced the Texans they were about to get their money's worth. They had bought a second two-gallon coffee pot, and well before supper was ready, there was plenty of hot coffee. The meal, complete with sourdough biscuits, was something to remember.

"We owe Winkler for sending Dominique and Roberto to us," Mike Horton said.

"I agree," said Don Webb, "as long as they can do their job as wranglers and still have the strength and ambition to cook like they did today."

"No reason they can't," Red Bohannon said. "All they got to do load and unload the pack mules, and see that the horse remuda and the mules keep pace with the herd. If they wasn't doin' that, it'd be that much harder on the the rest of us, and we'd still end up doin' our own cooking."

"It's hard to argue with that," said Webb. "They're off to a good start, and none of you is any stronger for them than I am. A man can live with a hard trail if there's good grub along the way."

"Damn right," Charlie English said, "and when it comes to cookin', I reckon the only incentive any of us has had was to keep from starvin'."

While it was still light enough to see, Don Webb opened up the yellowed newspaper to the full-page map of the Old Spanish Trail. The rest of the outfit gathered as close as they could, and they were encouraged, for the map was well drawn, complete with rivers.

"It looks good at the start," said Bob Vines. "There's a river flowin' in to Santa Fe from the northwest. Looks like it goes all the way to the San Juan Mountains."

"I'm looking beyond the San Juans," Webb replied. "It says Ute Indian Territory. And over there in southwestern Utah, it says Paiute Indian Territory. Could be a double dose of trouble."

"From what we've heard," said Red Bohannon, "the

trail's not been used all that much in recent years. Maybe the Indian situation has changed.''

''About like it's changed in Texas,'' Felton Juneau said. ''The Comanches are worse than ever.''

''Maybe Red's right,'' said Webb. ''We'll likely have to find out for ourselves and just be prepared. From this map, I'd say we'll be well beyond the San Juans before we reach Ute territory.''

''That's the way to stay alive in Indian territory,'' Bob Vines agreed. ''Just expect one of 'em behind every rock, bush, or tree.''

After breakfast, Dominique and Roberto loaded the pack mules while the rest of the outfit saddled their horses.

''Head 'em up and move 'em out,'' Don Webb shouted.

The herd lurched into motion. The riders headed them to the south of Santa Fe. Dominique and Roberto expertly moved the horse remuda and the pack mules in behind the drag, and the herd soon reached the Rio Chama, which flowed in from the northwest. At that point, with the leaders following the river in an orderly fashion, Don Webb rode far ahead. Fifteen miles later, he turned back, having seen nothing but some bear tracks. Their first day was far better than any of them had expected, but the herd had become trail-wise before reaching Santa Fe. Supper was excellent, and the outfit looked with favor upon the two young Mexicans, for their performance on the trail had been more than adequate.

''I'm purely gonna miss this river when we leave it,'' said Les Brown. ''There's nothin' like having ready water at the end of the day.''

''Enjoy it while you can,'' Don Webb said. ''From the looks of the map, we'll be seein' some long dry stretches. We'll just have to hope there are springs and maybe streams that somebody didn't think was worth mentioning.''

The night was divided into two watches. Red, Charlie, Arch, Eli, and Felton took the first, while Don Webb, Bob Vines, Jim Roussel, Les Brown, and Mike Horton changed with them at midnight. But they were not disturbed. The elevation was such that they could see the distant lights of Santa Fe.

Griff had ridden to the western outskirts of Santa Fe, and watched from a distance as the herd crept northwest, along the Chama. Satisfied as to the direction they were traveling, he mounted and rode back to the cabin. Oliver and Seeco had arrived just ahead of him with the first load of supplies from the mercantile.

"They're takin' what used to be the Old Spanish Trail," Griff said, when he entered the cabin. "Give 'em a week, and we'll follow."

"*Bueno,*" said Doolin. "Where do you reckon we should bushwhack them and take the herd?"

"In the Mojave Desert," Griff said. "The cattle will be thirsty and ornery, keepin' the riders busy. Once we got control of the herd, Los Angeles ain't that far."

"I like that idea," said Quando. "It'll be hell keepin' all them varmints bunched along them mountain trails, with so many draws and arroyos where they can run."

"Quando," Griff said, "tomorrow you and Lennox will ride to Santa Fe and bring back another load of grub and supplies. I'll have a list ready."

"I'm sick of settin' on my hunkers around here," said Lennox. "Can't we stay there at least long enough for a few drinks?

"No," Griff said. "We're ridin' out of here before we attract any more attention. Stay out of the saloons, and when you're done at the mercantile, get out of town."

"If I'm any judge, we're in for some rain," said Red Bohannon, while the outfit waited for supper.

"I've been rained on before, and I can take that," Charlie English said. "It's lightning that purely scares hell out of me. My daddy was struck and killed while herdin' cows."

"It's always a threat," said Bob Vines, "and that's when

riders are most vulnerable. It's during storms with thunder and lightning that we have to be in the saddle.''

"I ain't familiar with this country," Eli Mills said, "and I was hopin' we'd have a few days on the trail without a stampede. That won't be likely, with thunder and lightning.''

Rays of the setting sun flared red along the western horizon as they ate, and by the time the first watch was saddling up, there were jagged fingers of distant lightning.

"It's still a long ways off," said Webb. "It's unlikely it'll reach us before sometime tomorrow or tomorrow night. Maybe it'll rain itself out before it even gets to us.''

He avoided the obvious, for every man knew that when the elements threatened, all of them would be in the saddle until the danger was past. The herd was strung out along the river, nipping at what graze there was. After several hours, the riders on the first watch reined up, resting their horses.

"Besides the cookin', I'm glad we took on them Mexican wranglers," Arch Danson said. "They're keepin' the mules and the horse remuda separated from the herd at night, givin' us at least some hope that if the herd stampedes, it won't take the remuda and mules with it.''

"I was thinkin' the same thing," said Eli Mills. "They're a mite young, but I'd say they been over the mountain a time or two. They both got Henry rifles in their saddle boots.''

Time dragged on, and it was near midnight when the silence was broken by the bawling of terrified cows. The uproar had begun among the grazing herd that was nearest the area in which Dominique and Roberto had secured the horse remuda and the mules.

"Charlie," Red shouted, "you come with me. The rest of you try to calm the herd.''

Within seconds, Don Webb and his four companions had thrown aside their blankets and were in their saddles, joining Arch, Eli, and Felton as they sought to prevent a stampede. But before Red and Charlie reached the scene of the disturbance, there were two blasts from a rifle. The horses and mules hadn't been disturbed, and the bawling of the cows had ceased. Both Mexican wranglers were mounted, their rifles in their hands.

"What in thunder happened?" Red asked.

"*Gigantesco Oso,*"* said one of the Mexicans.

"You hombres handled him just right," Red replied. "Gracias."

"A grizzly come across the river," Red said, when he and Charlie had ridden back to join their companions. "Dominique and Roberto convinced him he didn't want one of our cows after all."

"Fast thinking on their part," said Bob Vines. "I reckon we could afford to lose a cow to the bear, but the varmint might have stampeded the rest of the herd, the horse remuda and the mules."

"This may be just a taste of what we can expect as we go on," Don Webb said. "There may be cougars as well. We can't let the quiet deceive us. We'll have to ride continuously from one end of the herd to the other."

"We'll have to do better than that," said Red. "We kind of felt like the herd was safe enough on that side next to the river, when we should have kept 'em shy of it enough for us to ride a circle."

"He's right about that," Charlie said. "The bear come from across the river, and it was a near miracle that Dominique and Roberto was able to drive him back the way he come. If he'd run through the herd, they'd be scattered from here to yonder, the horse remuda and mules along with 'em."

"I'm ashamed of myself for not having thought of that," said Don Webb. "Feel free to choose yourselves another trail boss if you want."

"Oh hell," Charlie said, "none of the rest of us thought of it either until the bear showed up. We all just had some valuable experience without it costing us."

*Gigantic bears.

"We won't make the same mistake again," said Webb. "It's time for the second watch anyway, and we'll move the herd back far enough from the river for us to circle it."

"Bueno," Red replied. "And as long as the herd's bedded down along the river, we'll start the first watch by movin' 'em back, so we can ride a circle."

Webb and his companions rode along the river bank, forcing the longhorns well away from the water. For the rest of the night, the riders circled the herd and there was no further disturbance. With the dawn came a light breeze from the west, bringing with it the smell of rain.

"Maybe we'll luck out and it'll come before dark," said Jim Roussel. "Lightning don't seem near as fearsome in daylight."

"No, but the thunder does," Felton Juneau said, "and that's mostly what sets the herd to runnin'."

They took the trail as usual, following the river, and the rain started shortly after the noon hour. But the storm had diminished, and while there was rain, the thunder failed to reach a level that would frighten the herd. Lightning flickered, but without the dark of the night for a back drop, it had little effect. The drive continued, for the wind had died and there was no driving rain tempting the longhorns to turn their backs to the storm. Skies had cleared to the west, and the rain ceased well before sundown.

"That wasn't bad," said Eli Mills. "Maybe the trail ahead won't be so bad after all."

Mike Horton laughed. "Give it a few more days. It'll live up to our expectations."

He didn't know just how right he would be . . .

3

❦

$\mathcal{A}$pproaching Santa Fe from the south, two strangers rode in. After some hesitation, they approached the sheriff's office and dismounted. They were a salty pair, each with a tied-down Colt. Sheriff Carpenter eyed them with interest when they entered.

"We're lookin' for Wiley Pickford," the older of the two said.

"Wiley Pickford's dead," said Sheriff Carpenter. "What's your interest in him?"

"I'm Ben and he's Curt. Wiley is our youngest brother. What happened to him?"

"He started a fight in the Silver Dollar Saloon and was gunned down," Carpenter said.

"Who done it?" Ben demanded.

"A gent name of Jim Roussel," said Sheriff Carpenter, "and the fight was more than fair. Your brother called him a cheat and drew first. There were witnesses, including a couple of Wiley's friends, and the court ruled it self-defense."

"We ain't satisfied with that," Curt growled.

"Leave it alone," snapped Sheriff Carpenter. "Wiley Pickford was drunk, and whiskey has a way of clouding a man's mind. From what I learned, he had lost a pile of money at the poker table, and then he made the mistake of losing his temper."

"We ain't here for no Bible-thumping," Ben said. "Where can we find this Jim Roussel that done the killing?"

"He's no longer here," said Sheriff Carpenter. "He's with a trail herd, and they started west a week ago."

The Pickfords left the sheriff's office without a word.

"We didn't get the names of them hombres that was with Wiley when he was shot," Curt said, as they mounted their horses.

"Won't make no difference," said Ben. "We want that varmint that's with the herd, and if they ain't been gone but a week, we won't have no trouble follerin' 'em."

"Then we'd better go to the mercantile and load up on grub," Curt said.

"We ain't in a hurry," said Ben. "A herd of cows won't cover that much ground, and we want that bunch far enough from town that the law don't get involved after we've paid off this Roussel for killin' Wiley."

"I'm almighty tired of this place and not bein' able to ride into town," Doolin said.

"Yeah," agreed some of his companions.

"All of you just shut the hell up," said Griff. "I'm *segundo* here, and I say we'll wait another week before we ride, and it won't be into town."

"Hell," Bullard growled, "at least let one of us ride in and bring back some whiskey."

"Maybe I will," said Griff. "But none of it goes with you when we ride after that trail drive. It was Pickford bein' drunk that got him killed and likely aroused suspicion toward the rest of us."

Southwestern Colorado. May 17, 1862.

"We're nine days out of Santa Fe," said Don Webb. "It's time we had a look along our back trail. When we reach the foothills of the San Juans, we'll find us a high point and see if anybody's following.''

"I reckon you're expecting company," Jim Roussel said.

"I am," said Webb.

He said no more, nor did he need to, for it had been Roussel's gunplay in town that had triggered their suspicions. When breakfast was over and the pack mules were ready, the herd took the trail, approaching the foothills of the San Juans. Before the end of the day, the elevation would be sufficient for Webb to see for many miles along their back trail. They milled the herd at noon, taking time to rest the horses. Webb spread out the map.

"Looks like this river plays out somewhere before we reach the San Juans," Bob Vines said. "Could be a water problem."

"Since we're not sure," said Webb, "I think we'll bed down the herd wherever the river ends, even if it means a short day's drive. That will allow me to get an early start in the morning, looking for water."

"I don't see anything on that map but rivers," Mike Horton said. "There must be some springs and lesser streams."

"Maybe," said Webb, "but this territory's new to us, and we can't be sure. Besides, as I scout ahead for water, I'll be looking for Indian sign. Indians will know we must have water, and what better place for an ambush?"

"Yeah," Red Bohannon agreed, "and if the herd's thirsty, they'll be the most ornery and hard to handle as we approach water."

It was an indisputable fact of trail driving. They moved on, and as they drew nearer to the San Juans, the river began to diminish. Two hours before sundown, Webb signaled the riders to mill the herd. Here they would bed down for the night, lest the next water be too distant for the herd to reach it. Once the herd had settled down, Webb swapped his tired horse for a fresh one from the remuda.

"Mind if I ride along with you?" Red Bohannon asked.

"Saddle a fresh horse and come along," said Webb.

They rode away toward the foothills.

"I reckon Roussel's a mite put out that you didn't ask him to ride along," Red said.

"He's young and he'll get over it," said Don. "He about halfway thinks I'm holding a grudge for that shooting in Santa Fe, and he's looking for me to prove otherwise."

"Which you don't aim to do," Red replied.

"No," said Don. "He's already been weaned, or he should have been."

They rode on, eventually reining up near a stone outcropping.

"There's a hump that must go up thirty feet," Red said. "Maybe we can reach the top of that."

"I aim to try," said Webb, "and then you can take a look, but one of us will have to stay with the horses. We haven't seen any Indian sign, and that's when they're the most dangerous."

Red remained with the horses. Don managed to find enough finger- and toeholds to reach the top of the huge stone monument. The sun to his back, he had an excellent view of the river for many miles. But squinting his eyes into the distance, he saw nothing that aroused his suspicions.

"See anything or anybody?" Red asked.

"Nothing," said Don. "When I get down, you can take a look."

"My eyes ain't that much better than yours," Red replied. "I can't see sweatin' my way up and down that rock for nothing. Supper should be near done by the time we get back to camp."

They mounted their horses and rode back to the herd.

"Anybody trailin' us?" Bob Vines asked.

"I reckon not," said Don, "but that don't mean they won't. They'll know the herd can't travel more than a few miles a day. They have plenty of time."

The herd again took the trail at first light, and when they had settled down to their usual gait, Don Webb rode on ahead, seeking water and watching for Indian signs. While the trail hadn't been in use in recent years, there was still plenty of evidence of past use, for rocks had been chipped and dislodged by many hooves. To Webb's surprise, the trail took an unexpected direction, winding somewhat to the south, along a lower elevation. He had ridden not more than a dozen miles when he came upon a stream, and a few hundred yards beyond that, another stream. He followed the second one to the southwest, and the two soon joined.* There were no Indian signs, and elated, he crossed the second stream and continued riding west. Eventually he turned back, content with his discovery. He had found these uncharted streams, and it was proof enough there might be others. The rest of the outfit, upon hearing his report, shared his enthusiasm.

"Another twelve miles then," said Bob Vines.

"No more than that," Webb assured him, "and there's pretty good graze between the two streams. The trail—what I've seen of it—seems to follow the southern perimeter of the San Juans. The territory may get mean as we go deeper into it, but the presence of water where we expected little or none is a promising sign. Texas longhorns can take a hell of a beating, if they have water and a little graze."

It was a truth that none of them disputed, and with renewed vigor, they pushed the herd on. Having had water and some graze the night before, the longhorns offered little resistance, and the drive reached water well before sundown.

"Good water," said Les Brown, "but this don't seem wide or deep enough to be called a river. Maybe that's why the map don't show it."

"Maybe not," Red Bohannon said, "but hombres ridin' this trail don't give a damn if it's a river or a spring branch. What we need to know is where we can find water. These varmints that draw maps has got a lot to learn."

*Tributaries of what is now the San Juan River.

"*Si,*" said one of the Mexican wranglers who had been listening. "*Dos rio oeste.*"

"Two *more*, west of here?" Webb asked.

"*Si,*" said the Mexican. "Dominique and Roberto come this way. *Dos año.*"

"Two years ago?" Red asked. "To California?"

"*Si.* Drive sheep."

"That must be the sheep drive Winkler was tellin' us about," said Red. "Three thousand of the wooly varmints, and if they made it, our cows can."

"Are you Dominique or Roberto?" Webb asked.

"I am Dominique."

Without fanfare, Don snatched the Mexican's sombrero, drew his Colt and shot a hole through the crown of the hat. He then returned it to Dominique's head.

"I'll buy you a new hat when we reach California," said Don, "but between here and there, I want to know which one of you is which. Do you know of other water that may not be on the map?"

"*Si,*" Dominique said.

"Then I'll be talking to you or Roberto before we begin each day's drive," said Don. "*Comprende?*"

"*Si,*" Dominique said.

Roberto had heard enough of the conversation to know what Webb was asking, and he nodded his agreement.

"Who ever would have expected that?" said Bob Vines. "I'd bet neither of them is even eighteen, and they've already been down the trail from Santa Fe to Los Angeles."

"I reckon we struck gold when we hired them two," Red Bohannon said.

"I'm beginning to think so," said Don Webb. "It'll be a godsend, having some idea how far we are from the next water. I'll still have to scout ahead for Indian sign, but maybe we won't be facing any dry camps."

The following day, once the herd was moving, Don Webb again rode west. Not quite fifteen miles distant, he came upon another stream, and beyond that, yet another. Just as Dominique had predicted.

"The water's there," Don told them, when he reached the herd. "About the same as the streams we reached yesterday. They may not qualify as rivers, but they're runnin' deep and the water's clear."

"*Si,*" said Dominique and Roberto.

"Gracias," Webb said. "I'll talk to the two of you tomorrow before we move out."

Before taking the trail the following morning, Don Webb talked to the two Mexican wranglers about how far they must travel to the next water.

"The next river on this map is the Colorado," Don said, "and it's too far."

"*Si,*" said Dominique. Kneeling, he drew a line in the dirt. "*El rio.*"

"The Colorado?"

"*Si,*" the Mexican said. He then drew a second line, angling it away from the first in a manner that coincided with the direction in which the drive was traveling.

"There's a runoff from the Colorado," said Webb.

"*Rio,*" Dominique insisted, shaking his head.*

"River, creek, whatever," said Webb, "there's a stream forking off the Colorado."

"*Si,*" the Mexican said.

"I've heard of that," Bob Vines said. "Sometimes what begins as overflow from some major river becomes a lesser river in its own right. But I reckon it didn't impress whoever drew our map."

"I'm about ready to trash the map and depend on Dominique and Roberto," said Webb.

When the herd had taken the trail, Webb rode out to learn how far they must travel to reach water. Fifteen miles later, he came upon a dry stream bed, and there was enough of

*The Dolores River. It forks off from the Colorado in southeastern Utah, and the Old Spanish Trail follows it for a few miles prior to the crossing of the Colorado.

a trail remaining to assure him that others must have followed the stream. Another mile and he reached the point where the water played out. It simply disappeared into the deep crevice between a pair of giant boulders. Beyond, however, the water deepened, becoming what could well be a river. Webb rode on another half a dozen miles, and the ancient trail continued to follow the stream. Although it was still early for the grass to green at higher elevations, there was some graze. After a distance that Webb judged to be fifteen miles, there was a bend in the trail that led west, where the stream angled in sharply from the north. Webb rode back to meet the herd, again with good news.

"The river's there," he told the outfit. "Maybe twelve or thirteen more miles. There's some graze, and I rode what I reckoned would be a day's drive, before the stream bends to the north."

"So there's a good chance we can reach the Colorado without a dry camp," said Red.

"I think so," Don said. "Tomorrow I'll ride on to the Colorado."

"*Malo rio*," said Roberto, raising both hands over his head.

"High banks," Felton Juneau said.

"*Si*," said Roberto. "*Mucho alto*."

"If sheep crossed, our cows can," Don said. "Can you and Dominique show us where the sheep crossed, Roberto?"

"Many sheep die," said Roberto.

"I don't like the sound of that," Bob Vines said.

"Neither do I," said Webb. "We'll have a look at the sheep crossing, but we may have to improve on it. High banks can't go on forever."

"Don't be too sure," Mike Horton said. "I've never been to Utah, but I know hombres who have, and there's some almighty deep canyons."

"According to the map, we'll have to cross the Colorado at some point," said Webb, "and we'll have to water the herd. If they can get down one bank, then we'll find a way to get them up the other.''

Charlie English laughed. ''That's what I like most about Texans. They'll tackle hell with a hatful of water, if there's no other way but through it.''

''Yeah, but they've never done anything about the weather,'' said Eli Mills. ''From them clouds over yonder, I'd say we're in for another storm. What do you aim to do about that, Don?''

''I'm hoping we can reach water and get the herd bedded down for the night,'' Webb said. ''Then I aim to get wet, along with the rest of you.''

By the time the herd had been bedded down and the outfit had eaten supper, there was a rumbling of thunder.

''Tarnation,'' Arch Danson said, ''don't it ever just rain in this part of the world without thunder and lightning?''

''*Nunca*,'' said Dominique.

''We've been almighty lucky, so far,'' Don said. ''If there's thunder and lightning, we'll all be in the saddle for the duration.''

''That's the bright side of trail driving,'' said Charlie. ''You never have to worry with tryin' to sleep during rotten, miserable weather, 'cause you're always in the saddle, trying to keep the damn cows from runnin' off the edge of the world.''

They all laughed, for it was a truth to which they could relate. Even before the sun had gone down, the sky had begun to darken and the thunder rumbled closer. Without a word being spoken, every rider saddled a fresh horse, preparing for the worst. The herd had been moved far enough from the river for the riders to circle it, and even in the twilight they began doing so.

''The trouble with lightning is that you never know where it'll strike,'' Les Brown complained. ''Let it strike to the west, and the herd runs east, but if it strikes to the west, the varmints will stampede to the east.''

But there was little time for conversation as the thunder drew closer and lightning raked the western sky with jagged yellow fingers. But as the storm worsened, not a drop of rain fell, nor was there any wind. In the terrifying calm, a cow bawled, until finally there was a melancholy chorus, lamenting like lost souls. Thunder shook the earth and as one, the longhorns lurched to their feet.

"Get ready," Webb shouted. "Another rumble like that, and they'll light out."

But the thunder died away, and suddenly the terrible silence was broken by what could only be described as an explosion. Lightning struck with a blinding flash, shattering a huge boulder within yards of the herd upstream. A dozen steers died, while shards of rock like stone shrapnel struck others. Like a fearful, bawling avalanche they broke into a run back the way they had come only a short time before. Riders tried in vain to head them, only to have their horses scream and rear after being raked by horns. Dominique and Roberto were in their saddles, riding madly, but their valiant attempt to save the horse remuda and the mules was futile. The thunder of hooves was soon lost in the rumble of thunder.

"My God," said Arch Danson, "I never seen lightning strike that close."

"Me neither," Eli Mills said. "If it had hit a few seconds sooner, we'd have lost half the outfit."

"I just hope them stampedin' varmints didn't trample our packsaddles and grub," said Mike Horton. "Dominique? Roberto?"

"They've been down the trail before," Don Webb said. "The packsaddles are all right."

"*Si,*" said one of the wranglers from the darkness.

"Well, we can't start the gather in the dark," said Les Brown, "and there's no rain. I'm for startin' a fire and boilin' some coffee."

"That'll serve as a beacon for any Indians within fifty miles," Bob Vines said.

"I'll risk it," said Mike Horton. "Besides, my horse got raked by a horn, and I'll need some light to doctor him."

"Likely more than one horse was raked," Don Webb

said. "As for Indians, there's no way to trail a herd without them knowing where we are. Some of you try and scare up enough wood for a fire for at least long enough to check out our horses and boil some coffee."

Only two or three of the horses had escaped being raked by lethal horns, and while the riders were applying sulfur salve to the wounds, Dominique and Roberto filled both coffee pots and got them on the fire.

The thunder had died away and there was only an occasional flicker of lightning. Still there was no rain.

"I've never seen a storm like this," Red Bohannon said.

"There was likely rain somewhere to the west," said Don Webb. "It just rained out before it got to us. We'll have to keep watch over our horses, but two of us at a time, two hours each should be enough. Let's turn in, get what sleep we can, and start our gather at first light."

Santa Fe, New Mexico. May 20, 1862.

Ben and Curt Pickford saddled their horses and rode west, along the Rio Chama.

"We ought to catch up to 'em in maybe four days," Curt said. "You thinkin' of bushwhackin' 'em?"

"Why should we?" said Ben. "All we want is the bastard that shot Wiley, and I want him to know why we're gunnin' him down. He ain't gonna know that, if he's shot in the back or gunned down from ambush."

"Texas cattle means Texas riders," Curt said, "and I never knowed a Texan that didn't side his *amigo*. Even if he had to stomp his way into hell and fight the devil."

"Maybe," said Ben, "but I'm countin' on their Texas pride workin' in our favor. There ain't a Texan alive that'll admit he needs help, even if he's got to die with his boots on."

"So we're goin' to call him out," Curt said. "Which of us is gonna face him?"

"I will," said Ben. "If he bores me, then it's your turn."

"Wiley wasn't no slouch with a Colt," Curt said, "and from what the sheriff told us, he didn't have a chance."

"From what the sheriff told us," said Ben, "Wiley was also drunk. That slows a man down. I don't aim to be drunk."

"Me neither," Curt said, "but I can't help wonderin' about this Jim Roussel. Suppose he outguns the both of us?"

"Then we'll be joinin' Wiley in hell," said Ben.

Dominique and Roberto had breakfast ready before first light. The outfit ate hurriedly, and leaving the Mexican wranglers to watch over their supplies, they rode east in search of their stampeded herd, horse remuda, and pack mules. They found the horse remuda and the mules first.

"Thank God they don't spook as bad or run as far as longhorns," Red Bohannon said.

"Red, you and Charlie drive them back to camp," Don Webb said. "Have Dominique and Roberto doctor any of them that's been raked by horns. Then ride back and join us for the gather."

The horses and mules were soon gathered and on their way, while the rest of the outfit rode in search of the longhorns.

"Tarnation," said Felton Juneau, "I hope they ain't rememberin' the last water on our back trail. That's a good seventeen miles."

"They watered yesterday, before the storm," Don said. "It'll take half a day of sun to dry 'em up enough to search for water. Then they may return to where they last watered, and that's in our favor."

"I hope you're right," said Eli, "but my optimism is just shot all to hell where cows is concerned."

They still hadn't found any cows and had stopped to rest their horses when Red and Charlie caught up to them.

"We told Dominique and Roberto to drag them dead steers well away from camp," Red said. "Where's the cows you gents was gonna gather?"

"We decided not to look for them until you and Charlie was with us," said Don. "We reckoned you wouldn't want to miss out on the fun."

Santa Fe, New Mexico. May 21, 1862.

"Tomorrow we ride," Griff said. "If anybody's got business in town, let's hear it now. I don't want no whining, once we're on the trail."

"You said no whiskey, but we won't have nothin' for snakebite or gunshot wounds," said Bullard.

"I didn't say we wouldn't have whiskey," Griff said. "I meant there won't be no bottle passed around. The whiskey will be in my saddlebag, and nobody samples it until I see a snake or some bullet holes. We should have ammunition and grub aplenty. We forgettin' anything else?"

Nobody said anything.

"Then we'll ride out at first light," said Griff.

The riders were two-thirds of the way back to their old camp before they began seeing the stampeded cattle.

"I was afraid of that," Bob Vines said. "They're closer to the water at our old camp, and that's where we'll find most of them."

"That's better than if there was no water for fifty miles," said Charlie. "Then we'd have to ride god knows how far in every direction."

"That's right," Don agreed, "and since most of the herd may be back yonder at the forks of that river, we'll ride there first. Any cattle between here and there, we can add to the gather on the way back."

It was the sensible thing to do, and when they reached their old camp where the two streams forked, they found great bunches of grazing steers.

"Maybe we won't lose more than a day," said Mike Horton. "Looks like they're mostly all here."

"Well, let's hope they've had a blessed plenty to drink,"

Bob Vines said, "because we're a day's drive away from
the water they ran away from. It'll take some time, roundin'
'em up and headin' 'em back that way."

"They'll be back there tonight, however long it takes,"
said Don Webb grimly. "They'll be thirsty, and if there's
any wind from the west, they'll smell the water ahead."

"Damn right," Charlie English said. "That run they
took last night spoiled our day, so if they run again, we'll
make sure it's in the right direction."

Most of the longhorns were scattered along the river, and
were quickly gathered.

"Let's run some tallies," said Don. "We can't quit this
gather until we've found all or most of them. Everybody
count, and we'll take the lowest tally."

Several hours later, when they compared tallies, Felton
Juneau had the lowest.

"Forty-five hundred ain't near enough," Don said. "The
question is, can we make up the difference between here
and camp?"

"Let's five of us hold what we've got," said Bob,
"while the others ride ahead and see how many can be
added. That way, we'll have some idea of how many more
are missing."

"I'll buy that," Don said. "Take Jim, Les, Arch and Eli,
and see what you can do. When you feel you've gathered
all you can, a couple of you stay with them, while the
others ride back to help us trail these ahead to join them."

Two hours later, Arch and Eli returned.

"We found six hundred head," said Eli.

"Counting the two hundred and sixteen we left in Santa
Fe, and the dozen dead, we've got enough to consider this
gather done," Don said.

"We didn't ride all the way back," said Eli. "There may
be some that'll remember the water ahead, and drift back
there."

"You're right," Don said. "But if they don't, we'll go
with what we have. Let's get them moving or supper will
be almighty late."

4

*I*t was almost dark when they reached camp with the herd. Dominique and Roberto had seen to it that the horses and mules had been watered and were well out of the way when the thirsty longhorns arrived.

"We were almighty lucky there was water close on our back-trail," Bob Vines said. "If there hadn't been, we might have been a week roundin' up the herd."

"Next time, we may not be so fortunate," said Don Webb. "Keep the varmints back far enough from the water for us to circle the herd."

The night was peaceful, and the outfit was ready to take the trail when they saw two riders approaching along the back-trail. They reined up and dismounted.

"Who are you and what do you want?" Don Webb asked.

"Ben and Curt Pickford," one of the strangers shouted, "and we're callin' Roussel, the varmint that gunned down our brother Wiley."

"The court ruled the shooting self-defense," said Webb. "Leave it alone."

"We ain't leavin' it alone," Ben said.

"If they won't have it any other way, I'll face them," said Roussel.

"If that's how you Pickfords want it," Webb said,

"Roussel agrees. But the rest of us aim to see that you do it one at a time. Who goes first?"

"Me," said Ben.

He began walking, his right hand near the butt of his Colt. Roussel began walking to meet him, as the rest of the outfit moved out of the line of fire. Curt Pickford was careful to keep his hand well away from his weapon, for the eyes of Roussel's companions were on him. When Ben was within forty feet of Roussel, he went for his gun. Roussel seemed in no hurry, not reaching for his Colt until Ben had begun his draw. But Ben never fired his weapon, for Roussel's lead slammed into his arm, just above the elbow. Ben dropped his Colt and stood there dumbly, as blood dripped off the tips of his fingers. Finally, with his left hand, he seemed about to reach for his fallen weapon.

"Ben, no!" Curt shouted.

"Leave it lay, Pickford," said Roussel. "I didn't want to shoot your brother any more than I wanted to shoot you, but if you come after me again, I'll kill you. Both of you ride out while you can."

"We're goin'," Curt said hastily. "Come on, Ben."

Curt's voice trembled, and it seemed to get through to Ben. Using his left hand on the saddle horn, he managed to mount his horse. Curt then mounted and led out. Ben followed and they rode back the way they had come.

"You should have killed the varmint," said Les Brown. "we'll have it to do later on. Next time, the varmints will bushwhack us."

"Maybe," Roussel said, "but it all seemed so foolish."

"Jim's right," said Don. "The first killing may have been unavoidable, but this one sure wasn't. This hombre was so slow, my old granny could outdraw him."

"Them two slipped up on us," Red Bohannon said. "When we take the trail again, I'd say we ought to see if there's anybody else about to surprise us."

"You're right," said Don. "It'll give us a chance to be sure the Pickfords don't get the idea of doubling back, gettin' ahead of us, and settin' up an ambush."

"That wasn't exactly what I had in mind," Red replied. "I can't imagine us bein' there in Santa Fe without some varmints takin' an interest in this herd."

"Neither can I," said Bob Vines. "It's just a question of when they come after us."

"Anybody with that in mind won't be in any hurry," Don said. "They won't have to be too bright to know we're bound for California, and if they have plans for the herd, I can't imagine them tryin' to take it until we're a lot closer."

"Makes sense to me," said Charlie. "Let a bunch of dumb Texans do most of the work, and then when we're within hollerin' distance of Los Angeles, they'll try to take over."

"That bein' the case," Red replied, "it's all the more reason we need to know if they're trailin' us. Then before they come after us, we'll go after them."

Webb laughed. "You're readin' my mind, Red. Once we know we're being followed, we'll go after them long before they come after us. Once the herd's moving, I'll ride back for a look at our back trail."

When the herd settled down, Red moved into the point position, allowing Don to ride along the back trail. He had to ride a considerable distance before finding a vantage point from which he could view the area they had traveled the day before. All he could see was the two faraway dots that had to be the Pickford brothers. Don mounted his horse and caught up with the herd.

The Pickfords had stopped just long enough for Curt to bandage Ben's wounded arm.

"I ain't done with them," Ben snarled.

"Next time you call out Roussel, you'll be by yourself," said Curt. "Neither of us is any match for him with a pistol. Wiley's dead and gone, and us bein' gunned down won't change nothin'."

"I wanted him to know who we was and why he was bein' gunned down," Ben said.

Curt laughed and Ben swallowed his anger. They rode

on, and when they reached the stream where they had camped the day before, they dismounted to water and rest their horses. Suddenly a cold voice spoke from a nearby thicket.

"Turn around, keepin' your hands where I can see 'em."

Careful to obey the command, Ben and Curt turned around to face a cocked Colt. The hombre who had the drop on them was armed with two Colts, the second one holstered and tied-down on his left hip.

"We're headin' for Santa Fe," said Curt. "You got nothin' on us."

"You wasn't headin' for Santa Fe yesterday," the man with the gun said, "and it wasn't no hoss fly that bit your amigo on his gun arm and took his pistol. Now the two of you start walkin' downstream."

The outfit had made their camp well away from the trail, beneath a stand of trees that would dissipate the smoke from their fire. Eleven men rose to their feet, their hands near the butts of their Colts. Griff spoke.

"What you got there, Hernandez?"

"Them two that's been ahead of us, I reckon. Looks like they met up with the bunch they was after and was persuaded to ride back to Santa Fe. Leastwise, they say they're goin' there."

"Who are you," Griff demanded, "and why was you trailin' that Texas outfit?"

"Ben and Curt Pickford," said Curt, "and our business was personal."

"Haw, haw," Quando said. "If you was goin' to rustle the herd, I reckon you must of done somethin' wrong."

"It ain't none of your damn business," said Ben.

"I think it is," Griff said, drawing his Colt. "Now you tell us the straight of it, or I'll bust your other arm."

"One of that outfit gunned down our brother in Santa Fe," said Curt sullenly. "We was out to avenge him."

"Ah," Griff said, without sympathy. "You was outgunned and run off with your tails between your legs."

"We ain't finished with them," said Ben.

"They already got that Texas bunch watchin' their back-trail," Hernandez said. "I say we ventilate the both of 'em, before they foul things up any worse."

"Not so fast," said Griff. "We can't trail that bunch all the way to California without them knowin' we're followin' them. While these gents ain't no better with a pistol than Wiley was, I'd gamble they can drive cows and hold their own in a bushwhacking."

"Damn right we can," Curt said. "We want satisfaction, and if we can't have it in a fair fight, we'll take it any way we can get it."

Griff laughed. "Maybe you should throw in with us. We aim to take that herd, and we can't do it with any of that Texas outfit alive."

"We want only one man," said Ben. "If we join you in ambushing the outfit and taking the herd, what's in it for us?"

"A thousand dollars for each of you when we sell the herd," Griff said.

The Pickfords looked at one another, careful not to betray their thoughts. There was no doubt they were being offered a pittance, but the alternative might well be a couple of hunks of lead. Ben's arm needed time to heal, he needed a Colt, and they must consider some means of bettering their lot.

"We'll ride with you," Curt said. "We're wantin' vengeance, and we'll take it any way we can get it."

"Bueno," said Griff. "But you got to be patient. We don't aim to take over the herd till it's near Los Angeles. If you ain't had breakfast, there's grub."

"We didn't bring much grub," Curt said. "We wasn't plannin' on trailin' 'em all the way to California."

"We got enough," said Griff. "There's coffee on the fire. Bullard, break out a slab of bacon from one of the packs."

"I didn't have nothin' but bandages to fix Ben's arm," Curt said.

"I got whiskey in my saddlebag," said Griff. "You'll

need to pour some of that on the wound, and if there's fever, he'll have to drink a slug of it later on.''

There were some black looks directed at Griff when he handed Curt one bottle of the whiskey that had been off limits to the gang. But Griff seemed not to notice, and Curt doused the bandage on Ben's upper arm with almost a third of the whiskey. The rest he returned to Griff. The outlaws sprawled on their bedrolls, sipping coffee, apparently in no hurry. Ben slept while Curt eyed the outfit with caution and distrust.

Following the appearance of Ben and Curt Pickford, there was no more difficulty as the herd moved on toward the Colorado. When the outfit gathered for supper, Don spoke to them.

''Tomorrow, I aim to ride on to the Colorado. Keep the herd movin' at a good gait and maybe we can reach the river by tomorrow night.''

The following morning, before the herd took the trail, Don spent some time with the Mexican horse wranglers, questioning them about the Colorado. Dominique and Roberto drew lines on the ground, and by the time Webb rode out, he had some idea where the banks of the river might be low enough and the water shallow enough to cross the herd. But he had ridden less than five miles when, topping a ridge, he found himself facing more than a dozen mounted Indians. Before he could make a move, his horse nickered and one of the Indian ponies answered. Wheeling his horse, he kicked it into a gallop. Behind him, he could hear the thump of hooves and the screeching of Indians. There was a light breeze out of the northwest, and hoping his distant partners would hear, Don drew his Colt and fired three times. There was no answer, and he rode desperately on, knowing he could not reach the herd in time . . .

''Mill the herd!'' Red Bohannon shouted, reining up and waving his hat.

"Why?" Bob Vines asked, reining up his galloping horse.

"Three shots somewhere ahead," said Bohannon. "Don's in trouble."

Vines wheeled his horse and galloped away, knowing that seconds counted. The rest of the outfit—except for the Mexican wranglers—soon came on the run, Vines in the lead. There were no questions, for they could hear the distant rattle of gunfire. Don Webb was fighting for his life . . .

"You've done your best, old fellow," Webb said to his heaving horse. Drawing his Henry rifle from the boot, he tumbled out of the saddle, taking cover within a scattering of rocks. None of them were more than knee-high, forcing him to go belly-down. It was poor cover at best and would suffice only for as long as it took the Indians to surround him. He could hear their shouts of glee as they began to circle, saving their arrows for the finish that seemed only minutes away. But suddenly there was a clatter of hooves and the roar of rifles as Webb's Texas companions bought into the fight. Webb scrambled to his knees and began firing at the retreating Indians. Les Brown had caught up Webb's horse and passed him the reins.

"I'm obliged," said Webb. "They took me by surprise, and I thought sure I was done for."

"You're almighty lucky Red's got dog ears," Bob Vines said. "He heard your shots, but nobody else did. We just took his word, ridin' like hell until we heard you shootin' at the varmints."

"We'd better get back to the herd," said Don. "It'd be just our luck for them to use me to draw the rest of you away, and then start a stampede."

There was no sign of the Indians, and the herd was grazing peacefully.

"They may give us hell from here on to the Colorado," Mike Horton said. "With that many in a scouting party, there may be a camp close by."

"I won't be surprised," said Webb. "But are they Utes or Paiutes?"

"If our map means anything, they're Utes," Bob Vines said. "We shouldn't run into the Paiutes until we're almost out of Utah Territory."

"It's gonna be almighty risky for one man to separate himself from the rest of the outfit," said Charlie English. "Don, I reckon you'd better not get more than a mile or two ahead of the herd, as long as we're in Ute and Paiute territory."

"Like hell," Don said. "We got to have water, and that means somebody's got to ride ahead. I'm trail boss, and that somebody is me. I've fought Comanches and still have my hair, and I can't see the Utes and Paiutes bein' any worse."

"We're fairly certain the Colorado's not more than a day's drive ahead," said Bob Vines, "so why don't we just push the herd as hard as we can and get there before dark?"

"I reckon we can do that," Don Webb said, "but why ride all around a problem, when we know we'll have to face it sooner or later? Just keep the herd movin', and Indians or no Indians, I aim to ride ahead to the Colorado."

Nobody argued with him, and after saddling a fresh horse, Webb rode out.

"He's Texan to the bone," said Charlie English.

"Yeah," Red Bohannon agreed. "Sometimes I think they ain't completely satisfied unless they're down to their last handful of shells and surrounded by Indians or outlaws."

"Thank God for 'em," said Bob Vines. "It was that kind of men that raised the stars and stripes over Texas."

With Bohannon riding point, they soon had the herd moving again, every rider listening for the distant rattle of gunfire that meant Indian trouble.

Webb rode cautiously, his Henry rifle ready, avoiding any cover that might conceal a band of Indians. But as he had suspected, it seemed they didn't expect him to again ride ahead of the herd, following his narrow escape. His confidence grew as he rode on, and his horse soon quickened its gait, for the wind brought the distinctive smell of water. When he finally reached the Colorado, he looked upon it in awe, for the banks were even more forbidding than he had expected. His thirsty horse was struggling to get to the water, as impossibly distant as it seemed.

"Damn it, horse," said Webb, "you'd break your fool neck gettin' down there. We got to find a place where the bank ain't straight down."

Webb rode southwest along the river, seeking a place where it was possible to reach the water. Dominique had insisted that a herd of sheep had watered and crossed somewhere to the south, and with that to encourage him, Webb rode on. He had ridden at least five miles before he reached the place he believed the Mexican wrangler had recalled. Sometime in the past, there had been a rock slide. Huge boulders had tumbled into the river, leveling the bank and filling the river bed to the extent that the water was shallow. Webb rested his horse, and when the animal could safely drink, led him to water. While the one bank had been reduced to the extent that the herd could get to the water, they still must climb the opposite bank. Shaking his head over that improbability, Webb rode back to meet the herd, and found them nearing the end of the diminishing stream they had been following. He waved his hat, signaling the outfit to head the lead steers and mill the herd. When the longhorns had settled down, the outfit joined Webb to hear what he had to report. Quickly he told them.

"We don't dare take 'em on to the Colorado without some means of gettin' them down to the water and up the opposite bank," Webb concluded. "Way it looks right now, they'd smell the water and stampede. They'd run right off that high bank and we'd lose the whole damn herd."

"I'd suggest levelin' that high bank down some," said Bob Vines, "but we have no tools for digging. All we have is an axe."

"I've been thinking about that," Webb said, "and it might be enough. While that other bank is almighty steep, there's plenty of rock along the rim. Suppose we were to cut some heavy poles, and using them for leverage, started a rock slide?''

"Sounds like our only hope," said Mike Horton.

"We'll have to leave the herd here, where there's water and graze," Webb said, "and as much as I don't like the idea, we'll have to divide the outfit. We'll need some strong backs to pry those boulders loose, and even then, we don't know that we can."

"Then let's start today," said Jim Roussel.

"I aim to," Webb replied. "We'll try to make do with four men. Bob, I'm leaving you in charge of the herd. Jim, Red, and Charlie, you'll come with me. If we don't finish the job today, we'll swap places with some of the rest of you tomorrow."

With Red carrying the axe, they rode out. This certainly was no time to divide their forces, and strong on the mind of every man was the possibility that hostile Indians might attack one or both parties. But there was no help for it, and they were determined to complete the task as quickly as possible. When the four men reined up, Webb's three companions looked doubtfully at the opposite bank.

"This can't be the place Dominique claims them sheep crossed," Jim Roussel said."

"I know that," said Webb, "but we don't know how far downriver that is. What we *do* know is that we can't drive five thousand longhorns along this river for any distance, without some or all of the varmints goin' over the bank, however steep it is."

"Even if we can level that bank down some, we still got a problem," Charlie said. "All them cows will be scramblin' for water at the same time. Some of 'em will have to drink and be drove across to the other side, to make room for the others. Not more than five hundred of 'em at a time, I'd say."

"One damn problem at a time," said Webb. "We got one thing on our side. The herd's got water where they are, and when they get here, they won't be half dead with thirst.

I'd say your idea is possible, and that's how we'll do it. We'll drive them here five hundred at a time, after we're sure we can water and cross that many, without the varmints killin' themselves or gorin' one another.''

"Before we can do anything else, we have to get ourselves and our horses over to that other bank," Jim Roussel said, "and we can't do it here."

"No," said Don Webb, "but we can get our horses down to the water from this side. We'll ride along the river bed until we find a break in that opposite bank."

They had no idea how far they might have to ride, and while none of them spoke of it, the danger was obvious. Leading their horses down to the water, they mounted and rode in single file, Don Webb leading. They had ridden only a few yards when an Indian arrow thudded into the riverbank just above Don's head. Another grazed his horse and it reared, nickering in fear and pain. While Don sought to calm the horse, Jim, Red, and Charlie had their Henrys in action. The attackers were on the high northwest bank of the river, and as they attempted to loose more arrows, deadly lead from the rifles cut them down. Out of the saddle, Don managed to turn his frightened horse back the way he had come, allowing his companions to fire without fear of hitting him or his mount. As suddenly as it had started, the attack ended, no damage having been done except the painful gash along the flank of Don Webb's horse.

"Red," said Don, "let me have your horse and you take mine. The three of you get out of here and ride along the bank, keepin' watch. I'll continue downriver until I find a place where we can get the horses and ourselves up the opposite bank."

The trio returned to the point of the rock slide and led the horses out of the river. Red took a tin of sulfur salve from Don's saddlebag and applied a generous amount of salve to the bloody furrow in the horse's flank. The three of them then mounted and rode along the river bank, while Don continued riding along the river bed.

"Up yonder," Charlie said, pointing. "I'd bet that's where the sheep crossed."

The depth of the riverbanks diminished until Don had no difficulty leaving the water, without having to dismount.

"We'd be a bunch of damn fools, making a crossing of our own, with this one already here," said Jim Roussel.

"Maybe," Don Webb conceded, "but this is nearly ten miles downstream from where the old trail crosses. We'll still have to get the herd down here before they smell water."

"We've been headin' straight for the river," said Charlie. "From where we are now, we can ride back to the herd, breakin' a trail. Then we can drive the herd to the southwest, comin' at the Colorado from an angle. The banks are low enough along here for most of the critters to drink all at the same time."

"That'll work, I reckon," Red Bohannon said, "but it'll take us at least ten miles out of our way on each side of the river. That's two days lost."

"That's what's bitin' at my tail feathers," said Don, "but there's no help for it. Had we made our own crossing, the outfit would have been divided, and we've just seen what that can lead to. We'd better get back to the herd. We don't know that they weren't attacked."

"I reckon we ought to pay more attention to Dominique and Roberto," Jim Roussel observed. "That crossing's a mite inconvenient, but it beats hell out of anything we could have done with an axe."

While Red and Charlie agreed, they said nothing, for Don Webb didn't seem in the least impressed with Roussel's opinion. Webb led out and the others followed, riding at an angle such as Charlie had suggested until they reached the herd.

"We thought we heard shots," said Bob Vines. "Indians?"

"Yes," Don Webb replied. Quickly he told them of the attack and of the crossing they had discovered.

"Is where sheep cross," said Dominique.

"It's a good crossing," Webb conceded, "although it's a good ten miles downriver. We figured out a way to drive straight to it, and after we've crossed the Colorado, we'll have to get back on the trail. It'll cost us maybe two days."

"But we might have spent that much time and more, trying to level that riverbank," said Les Brown. "Besides, it would have divided the outfit, givin' them Indians a chance to cut some of us down."

"I'm considering that," Webb said, with some irritation. "We'll stay here tonight, and after a good watering, we'll drive the herd all the way to the Colorado. We should be able to water them and get them across the river before dark."

"That'll be a good move," said Bob Vines. "I'll feel some better after we've crossed the Colorado. Up to now, we've faced only a few Indians here and there, but I can't shake the idea that somewhere along the way they'll attack with a force that'll boggle our minds."

But the Utes had other plans. An hour before sundown, twenty-five of them reined up their horses a hundred yards west of the camp. An Indian who obviously was the chief rode forward making the peace sign, but the unbelieving eyes of the Texans were on the bedraggled captives who were forced to walk along behind him. There were seven white women, and behind each of them, a knife in his hand, was an Indian brave. The captives were in rags. The oldest didn't look more than twenty-two or-three, while the youngest two might still have been in their teens. The mounted Indian reined up and began speaking rapidly in Spanish.

"I can't understand him," Don Webb said.

"Me neither," said Felton Juneau. "I know some Spanish, but I can't figure him out."

The Indian had become silent and looked angry. The only sound was the sobbing of one of the captives.

"Dominique," Webb said, "see if you can understand him."

The Mexican spoke a few words of rapid Spanish, and suddenly the Indian again began to talk. He included gestures toward the captives, and at one point, the oldest of the seven was brought forward. Her yellow hair was matted and dirty, and her tattered dress had been ripped off well above her knees. There was a large purple bruise on her cheek, and her left eye was swollen shut. Upon command from the chief, her Indian escort seized her ragged skirt, raising it well over her head. She wore nothing beneath it. Every Texan in the outfit had a hand on the butt of his Colt, when the spokesman for the Indians again became silent. Facing Webb, Dominique spoke.

"He wishes to trade, señor. He wishes two horses for each of the señoritas."

"That's impossible," said Webb angrily. "We don't have enough horses, as it is. Tell him we'll swap him cows."

"For the love of God," cried the yellow-haired woman, "save us!"

"We will," said Webb, "but we can't do it his way."

Dominique had told the Indian what Don had said, and the Ute spoke rapidly, angrily, shaking his head.

"He no want cows," Dominique said. "He no get horses, the señoritas die *mañana*."

"No horses," said Webb.

Dominique repeated Webb's response and the Indian shouted a command. Immediately the braves forced the weeping captives back the way they had come. Each of the women was thrown belly-down over a horse, and with an Indian mounted behind them, they were taken away.

"By God, them was white women!" Red Bohannon roared. "There's some killin' needs to be done, and I aim to do it."

"I'll be right behind you," shouted Charlie English.

There was a chorus of agreement from most of the others. To quiet them and get their attention, Webb drew his Colt and fired in the air. Finally they were quiet, and he spoke.

"In case none of you noticed, that bunch outnumbered

us considerable, and there may be six times that many close by. We'll take those white women away from them, but we can't light out after them in broad daylight. Now settle down and listen.''

5

Nobody had to remind them their situation was precarious, that they were but few in number and far from home. On the frontier, men found a way to do what needed doing.

"We won't have much time," Felton Juneau said. "They know we ain't of a mind to do any tradin', and they won't fool around. They'll likely come after us in the mornin' before first light."

"Not if we make our move tonight," said Don Webb. "We must find their camp, learn how strong they are, and where they're holding those captives."

"Any one of us can do that," Mike Horton said. "We're all Texans, and we've had to fight Comanches all our lives."

"Then you'll be ridin' with me," said Webb. "We'll start just before sundown. The rest of you be settin' on ready when we return."

Nothing more was said, and when the time came, Don and Mike saddled their horses and rode out.

"They're almighty confident," Mike said. "We could follow their trail in the dark."

"I don't doubt they have the numbers," said Don, "but overconfidence can go against a man. The last thing they'll expect is for us to attack."

"I'd feel better if the herd was across the Colorado,"

Mike said. "If this bunch is anything like the Indians I'm accustomed to, they won't take kindly to us snatchin' captives from under their noses."

"We'll have to come up with a plan that'll buy us some time," said Don.

They had ridden almost fifteen miles to the southwest before the smell of wood smoke warned them of the nearness of the Ute camp. It was almost dark when, leaving the horses and taking their Henrys, they managed to find enough cover to observe the camp without being seen. It was strung out along the west bank of the Colorado, where a dozen or more cook fires burned down to coals. There were three teepees.

"Thunderation," Mike said, "there's more than a hundred of 'em, not countin' women."

"The captives must be in one of those three teepees," said Don, "and we need to know which one."

But they waited for almost an hour without learning exactly where the captives were.

"We know they're in one of the teepees," Don said, softly, "but we might stay here all night without ever learning which one. We'll just have to raise enough hell to bust into all three of them. It's time we was gettin' back to the herd and decidin' how we aim to do it."

The rest of the outfit, except for Dominique and Roberto, had their horses saddled.

"Unless you're thinkin' otherwise, we figured some of us oughta stay with the herd," Bob Vines said.

"Good thinking," said Don. "We're up against more than a hundred Utes, and there's no way we can pull this off unless we outsmart them. They're maybe fifteen miles to the southwest, along the west bank of the Colorado. Three teepees, and since we didn't see any of the captives, they must be in one of them."

"Ten-to-one odds," Jim Roussel said. "That's better than they had at the Alamo."

"Unless somebody has a better idea," said Don, "I think five of us will try and rescue the captives, while the others stampede the horses. The rescue will probably be the most dangerous, so we'll depend on volunteers. I'll be the first.''

''I'll ride with you,'' said Charlie English.

''Me too,'' Mike Horton said.

''Count me in,'' said Red.

''Me,'' Felton Juneau said.

''That's it then,'' said Don. ''Bob, you'll be in charge of stampeding the horses. Jim, Les, Arch, and Eli will be riding with you. The horses are strung out along the river, to the north of the Indian camp, and there may be sentries. It's important that you stampede them all, not allowing any of the Utes to catch a mount, because after this is done, we still have to get the herd across the river and out of Ute territory. That means those horses must be run far enough to keep those Utes afoot for a week or more.''

''Leave it to us,'' said Bob, ''and you gents had better watch your step, because we'll stampede the herd right through the Ute camp.''

''Bueno,'' Don said. ''Are we forgetting anything?''

''Yeah,'' said Jim Roussel. ''Once you've rescued them females, they'll all be afoot. The horses in our remuda are already bein' worked to death.''

''He's right,'' Bob said. ''Before we run those Indian ponies too fast and too far, we'd better rope seven of them for those women to ride.''

''That'll make your part of this a little tougher,'' said Don, ''but I'll admit that I can't think of anything better.''

''No matter,'' Bob said. ''It's got to be done, and the only choices we have are some of those Indian ponies.''

The cattle were grazing peacefully and would be on their own until the outfit returned. Dominique and Roberto would see to the horse remuda and the pack mules. With Don and Mike in the lead, the Texans mounted and rode out. Don and Mike reined up where they had left the horses before, and the ten of them proceeded on foot. Those who had not seen the Ute camp wanted a firsthand look at what might become a very perilous undertaking. After a few moments of observation, they crept back to their horses.

"Too dark for you to see much," said Don, "but you could see the three teepees and the grazing horses."

"Give us enough time to get in position beyond the horse herd," Bob said. "I reckon you aim for us to stampede the horses before you make your move?"

Don laughed softly. "You know it, amigo. Since they're on the other side of the river, we'll all have to cross somewhere to the north of them. The best place is where we aim to cross the herd. When you've stampeded their horses from here to yonder, you may have to circle back to there just to get across the Colorado."

"So will you, to escape with the captives," said Bob, "but that shouldn't be a problem, if we stampede the horses south, right through the camp. Let's ride, gents."

They were some five miles north of the Ute camp when they crossed the Colorado, and while they were still a mile away from the grazing horses, Bob Vines and his companions dismounted. They crept ahead on foot, each man holding the muzzle of his mount, lest one of the animals nicker and reveal their presence. Three hundred yards behind them, Don and his men advanced in similar fashion, awaiting the start of the stampede. It came suddenly, with shooting and Texas yells. With the river on one flank and the shouting, shooting cowboys behind, it wasn't difficult to run the frightened horses right through the Indian camp. Foremost in the mind of every Ute was the need to capture one of the horses from the fleeing herd, leaving only the squaws to defend the camp. The five men who hoped to rescue the captive women came galloping on the heels of those who had stampeded the Ute horses. Don, Red, and Charlie were swinging their lariats, and each dropped his loop over the exposed poles at the very top of one of the teepees. In an instant the trio of shelters were snatched away, revealing the female captives. Three had been concealed in the first teepee, and two in each of the others. But they were not alone. There had been two Ute squaws in each of the teepees, and armed with knives, they ran screeching toward the five Texans as they dismounted. Two of them came after Don, and as he slugged one, the other drove a knife into his upper left arm. Quickly he subdued the second with a blow from the muzzle of his Colt. Several of the captive women wrestled with the squaws, fighting for possession of the knives. But other squaws had thrown themselves into the fray, and there was a dozen of them on the ground before the Texans were able to reach the captives.

"Look out," Red Bohannon shouted. "Some of the varmints got horses."

Four of the Utes had managed to catch horses from the fleeing herd, and they all came whooping back with lances in their hands and killing on their minds. Quickly the Texans shot them off their horses, and thinking fast, Red and Charlie caught the rope bridles of two of the animals.

"Good," said Don. "We'll need them."

Without a word, Don seized one of the youngest of the women and set her astraddle of the Indian pony. But before the rescue could proceed, the oldest captive—the woman with the tangled yellow hair—sprang to the saddle of Don's horse and kicked the animal into a gallop. But Charlie English was after her in an instant, catching the horse's bridle and leading it back. Sobbing and cursing, the frantic woman clawed at Charlie's face, as he lifted her out of the saddle.

"Wait your turn, ma'am," Charlie said. "You're not the only one."

Each of the two youngest women was placed on one of the captured Indian ponies. The other five captives were each riding with one of the Texans. Don made it a point to choose the yellow-haired woman who had made off with his horse. The seven horses were barely out of the Ute camp when there were frantic shouts from downriver.

"Damn," Felton said, "Some more of 'em caught horses."

"We'll try to outride them," said Don. "At least as far as the river crossing."

There was no moon, and the pursuit soon fell away to silence, allowing the Texans to slow their tiring horses to a walk. Reaching the place where they would cross the Colorado River, they reined up to rest the horses. Jim Roussel and Les Brown were leading the two Indian ponies on which the youngest captives rode. Suddenly the woman sharing Don's horse spoke.

"Will you allow me to change positions? The saddle horn is ruining my behind."

One of the other women laughed and Don said nothing, as she eased herself around.

"We goin' to wait on the others?" Red Bohannon asked.

"No," said Don. "When the horses have rested a little, we'll go on."

They crossed the Colorado, taking the long way back to the herd. Drawing near, they reined up, as a voice spoke from the darkness.

"*Quien es?*"

"*Tejanos,*" said Don.

They rode on toward a soft glow. Dominique and Roberto had dug a fire pit, allowing them to have a fire without it being seen from a great distance. There was the distinctive fragrance of boiling coffee. The Texans lifted their female companions to the ground and dismounted. Red and Charlie then helped the two youngest women off the captured Indian ponies.

"Thank you ever so much for saving us," said one of the girls in a trembling voice. "My name is Ellie Andrews."

"I'm Millie Nettles," the second girl said.

"Hold off on the introductions until the rest of our outfit gets here," said Don. "Have some coffee."

Silently Roberto and Dominique filled tin cups with coffee, while the five Texans stood near their saddled horses, listening. At the first sound of approaching riders, they spread out into the darkness, and Mike Horton issued a challenge.

"Bob Vines and *companeros,*" a voice said softly.

The five Texans rode in, leading seven captured Indian ponies.

"Where in tarnation you hombres been?" Red demanded. "We was about ready to go lookin' for you."

"Where do you reckon?" said Eli Mills. "Them damn Indian ponies run like a bunch of wild turkeys. Especially when they been stampeded."

"You didn't stampede all of 'em," Charlie English said. "Some of that bunch caught up horses and come after us."

"Sorry," said Bob Vines. "We did the best we could."

"That was plenty good enough," Don Webb said. "Were any of you hurt?"

"One of the squaws nicked me with a knife," said Don.

"I fix," Roberto said. "Where?"

"Left arm," said Don.

Dominique built up the fire and the coffee pot was replaced with another pot filled with water. Roberto came with the medicine chest as Don removed his shirt.

"What about tonight's watch?" Bob asked. "You want us all in the saddle?"

"No," said Don. "We'll go with the usual watch, but when you sleep, don't shuck anything but your hats. It should take those Utes a couple of days to catch their horses, but we can't take any chances. They've lost face, and I don't expect them to take that without a fight."

"Before we begin the first watch," Bob said, "we ought to introduce ourselves to these ladies and learn something about them."

"Names only, for tonight," said Don. "Everything else can wait until we get the herd across the Colorado. Ladies, why don't you tell us your names? Then I'll introduce us, and we'll find you some blankets so you can bed down for the night."

"I'm Rose Delano," the woman said, who had ridden away on Don's horse.

"Sarah Miles," said another of the women.

"Ellie Andrews," one of the youngest girls said.

"Millie Nettles," said another of almost the same age.

"I'm Molly Rivers," the fifth one said.

"Wendy Oldham," said the sixth.

"I'm Bonita Holmes," the last one said.

Quickly Don introduced himself and the rest of the outfit. Dominique and Roberto removed their sombreros and bowed.

"I reckon all of us can contribute a blanket or two, so these ladies don't have to sleep on the ground," said Don. "Dominique, I'd like for you and Roberto to picket these Indian ponies. I reckon we'll have to do that for a while, so they don't get homesick for their friends and go lookin' for that Ute camp."

"I suppose this is not a good time," Bonita said, "but may we have something to eat? For weeks, the squaws fed us nothing but corn mush, and only a little of that."

"I'm ashamed of myself for not having thought of that," said Don, as Roberto wrapped a bandage around his wounded arm. "Red, you and Charlie picket those Indian ponies, so Dominique and Roberto can fix the ladies some grub."

When the newly acquired horses had been picketed, Red and Charlie joined the first watch. Bob Vines had collected an extra blanket or two from each man, and he presented them to the women. But what they most yearned for was food, and they ate hungrily all that Dominique and Roberto had prepared. The coals in the fire pit were kept alive only to provide coffee during the night. The Texans saw that the women spread their blankets near the fire, so that the riders on watch could see to their safety. The riders on first watch circled the camp, pausing occasionally to speak to one another, their conversation centering on the women they had rescued from the Utes.

"I reckon the two oldest is Rose Delano and Sarah Miles," Charlie said. "They'll both be good-lookin' females when they've had a chance to fix their hair and clean up some."

"I'd like to get to know 'em better before we get to California," said Arch.

"You don't know that they'll be goin' on to California with us," Eli said.

"I'm fair-to-middlin' sure they won't have any choice,"
said Arch. "For sure, we can't take 'em back to Santa Fe."

"But they may have families there," Eli said. "Maybe
husbands."

"We're a long ways from Santa Fe," said Red. "It's
more likely they're all from California. That's somethin'
we'll have to learn after we've had a chance to talk to
them."

The watch changed at midnight, and conversation among
the riders dealt almost entirely with the seven women so
recently rescued.

"That Ellie Andrews is no older than I am," Jim Roussel
said. "I aim to get to know her before we get to California."

"I kind of feel the same way about Millie Nettles," said
Les Brown. "That leaves the oldest ones for Don, Bob, and
Mike."

"You young roosters are taking a lot for granted," Don
said. "Ellie and Millie may be young, but on the frontier,
many a woman younger than either of them will be married
with children. Don't waste your time speculating until
we've learned more about them."

"That's good advice," said Bob, "but when will we
have time for that? We'll be lucky if we can get the herd
across the Colorado before some of those Utes catch their
horses and come after us."

"We should be able to get the herd across today, with
time to spare," Don said. "If we do, then we'll be able to
question these women before supper."

"We're assuming they'll be going on to California with
us," said Mike. "Suppose some or all of them are from
Santa Fe?"

"We managed to rescue them from the Utes," Don said,
"but we're under no obligation to return them to Santa Fe.
Taking them with us to California won't be easy, and if
they get there safely, I don't feel any more obligation to
them than that."

"We have only those Indian ponies and no saddles,"

said Mike. "We'll be in plenty of trouble if any of them can't ride."

"We'll cross that bridge when we get to it," Don said.

The night passed quietly. During a hurried breakfast, Don had something to say to the seven women.

"I realize we need to talk, to learn more about you, and we will, but now is simply not the time. We stampeded the horses belonging to those Utes, and before they're able to find them and come after us, we must get this herd of cattle across the Colorado River. We're expecting to do that today. Maybe there'll be some time for us to talk before supper. We have only the Indian ponies for you to ride, and no extra saddles. Is that a problem for any of you?"

To Don's relief, none of them spoke, and he continued.

"When we're ready to take the trail, some of us will help you to mount. You'll follow the herd, keeping up with the drag riders."

"It's my turn to ride drag," said Jim Roussel.

"I don't think so," Don said. "You're a flank rider. Red, Charlie, Arch, Eli, and Felton are riding drag. Remember, it's important that we keep the herd bunched. When we reach the crossing, I want them tight, without any gaps. I want every pair of horns proddin' the critter that's ahead, and don't allow any of 'em to stop and drink. There'll be time enough for that, once they're across."

Before the herd moved out, the riders helped the women mount the Indian ponies. To Don Webb's relief, the seven riders fell in behind the drag, as ordered. Don rode ahead, seeking high ground from which he could observe the back trail, but he saw nothing to alarm him. The seven poorly mounted women were keeping up with the drag riders and the herd was moving at a faster than usual gait. Reaching the crossing without difficulty, the lead steers were driven into the shallow water and the others followed. While a few tried to pause and drink, they weren't desperate for water, and so were driven across without delay. When they were bunched along the far bank, some of them began nipping

at newly green grass while others made their way down to
the water to drink. Sundown was almost two hours away.
The riders unsaddled their mounts and helped the women
to dismount, while Dominique and Roberto unloaded the
pack mules and lighted supper fires.

"Now," said Don, "we have some time before supper.
Let's talk."

The seven women gathered around, and with their ragged, tattered clothing in mind, carefully seated themselves.
The Texans hunkered down facing them, each group silently observing the other. When nobody spoke, Don took
the lead.

"We're bound for Los Angeles with these cattle. About
all we can do for you is take you there. I'm sorry we don't
have some clothes to offer you, but it's hard times back in
Texas, and most of us have only what we're wearing."

"They took our shoes and underclothes and burned
them," said Wendy Oldham.

"You're fortunate it's summertime," Don said, "but at
night it gets almighty cold here in the mountains. Indians
or not, I reckon we'll have to keep a fire. Where are you
ladies from, and how were you captured by the Utes?"

"We weren't captured by the Indians," said Rose Delano. "Renegades raided our mission school, near Los Angeles. We were taken from there and sold to the Indians
more than three months ago."

"All of you are from California then?" Don said. "Do
you have kin there?"

"No," said Rose. "The mission takes in the homeless.
Sarah and me were there for ten years."

Bonita Holmes laughed. "Not all of us were homeless.
The mission takes in wayward ones who have nowhere else
to go, whose kin have had enough of them. There's no
walls, but it's a prison, just the same. We worked like
slaves in the field from dawn to dusk and all we got was
our food and the little that we wore. The Indians didn't
burn *all* our shoes and underclothes, because some of us

had none. Some of us were near naked when we were taken by the renegades."

"It's the truth," Ellie Andrews cried. "You won't take us back there, will you?"

"Shut up, both you you!" shouted Rose.

"I won't shut up," said Ellie bitterly. "You and Sarah held the rest of us while we were whipped and beaten."

"It's the truth," Bonita said. "They were favored because they helped control the rest of us. I'll show you what they did to us."

She stood up, raising her tattered skirt high, and there was nothing beneath it to hide the brutal scars from her waist to her knees. Momentarily shocked speechless, there was no mistaking the hostility in the hard eyes of the Texans as they glared at the two older women.

"I had nothing to do with that," Rose said angrily.

"Nor did I," said Sarah. "She was like that when she came to the mission."

"She was not, nor was I," Molly Rivers said.

She stood up and lifted her shirt, revealing the same ugly scars.

"There's more," said Ellie, as she and Millie got to their feet.

"That's enough," Don said hastily. "We believe you."

"Damn right we do," said Jim Roussel, "and if you're sent back there, it'll be over my dead body."

There was a thundering chorus of agreement from the rest of the outfit, while Rose and Sarah looked frightened. Don Webb saw the fear in their eyes and spoke to reassure them.

"Quiet. You ladies have my word that none of you will be forced back into a life where you were mistreated and beaten. Are all of you of age?"

"Yes," said Ellie. "Millie and me are the youngest, and we'll both be nineteen our next birthday."

"Good," Don said. "We're a long way from California and there'll be plenty of time for us to talk again. Just remember what I promised. Now let's get ready for supper.''

The five younger women seemed glad it was over. They scattered toward the two cook fires, the cowboys following. Don Webb found himself looking into the pale faces of Rose and Sarah, and it was Sarah who spoke.

''I'm twenty-four years old, and Rose is twenty-three. We disgraced our kin and they disowned us. The mission is the only home we've ever had, and we were forced to subdue the younger girls. We have scars too. Do you want to see?''

''No,'' said Don hastily. ''I don't know what to say to either of you, except that I hope, once you reach California, that you won't return to the mission.''

''I doubt that we will. Terrible as the experience with the Indians was, we learned from it, didn't we, Rose?''

''Yes,'' Rose said, so softly that Don almost didn't hear. She said no more, and Don Webb didn't wish to hear any more. He turned away from them and joined the rest of the outfit near the supper fires. Not surprisingly, all the five younger girls were enjoying the attention of the cowboys. But sundown came, and it was time for the first watch to begin. There was a chill wind from the northwest, forcing the girls to retire to their blankets for warmth, but that didn't affect Jim Roussel. He sat next to the blanketed Ellie and continued talking.

''He ought to be sleeping,'' said Bob Vines. ''Come the second watch, he'll be nodding in the saddle.''

''He does,'' Don said, ''and I'll swat him with a doubled lariat.''

Don rolled in his own blankets, trying to get some sleep before the start of the second watch, but Mike Horton was next to him, and Horton wanted to talk.

''What do you think of Rose and Sarah?''

''I don't know,'' said Don. ''What am I supposed to think?''

''Do you think they had something to do with beating the younger girls?''

"Yes," Don said, "but I think they were beaten themselves. From what Sarah told me, she and Rose have scars too."

"Did you see them?"

"No," said Don, "and I didn't want to. I wouldn't stand by and watch a dog take that kind of beating. Seeing scars like that in human flesh makes me want to kill somebody."

"It kind of grabbed me the same way," Mike said, "and that's why I was asking what you thought of Rose and Sarah. I was watching them while the girls was showin' the scars on their behinds and blaming Rose and Sarah."

"I'll be careful not to tell anybody," said Don. "You've got to be the only Texan alive who would be watching the faces of two females wearin' clothes while there's a girl showin' her bare bottom."

"Go ahead and laugh, damn it. I'm serious."

"I know you are," Don said. "Don't mind me. Go on and talk. I'm listening."

"It was somethin' in their eyes. They didn't say nothin', but somethin' in their eyes made me feel sorry for them. I believe they done what they was accused of doin', but I believe they're ashamed of havin' done it. Ain't that worth something?"

"I think so," said Don. "Why?"

"I just wanted somebody to tell me I'm not crazy. I'm gonna talk to Rose and Sarah. You reckon they're asleep?"

"I doubt it," Don said.

Mike said no more. Leaving his blankets where they were, he got up and vanished in the darkness.

6

❧

"*I* have a strong hunch those Utes will be findin' their horses today if they haven't already," Bob Vines said, as the outfit gathered for breakfast.

"I have that same feeling," said Don. "I want all of you—the drag riders especially—to keep your eyes on our back trail. At the first sign of riders, sing out. I'll ride ahead to learn how far we are from the next water, and I'll be looking for Indian signs as well."

Don unfolded the map, and as many as could gathered around to study it.

"It looks promising," Mike Horton observed. "The next river flows into the Colorado a few miles to the south, and it forks not far from where we'll cross. Looks like we'll follow that south fork quite a ways before the trail swings back to the southwest."*

"I aim to ride beyond the forks," said Don. "If the map's even close to right, we'll be able to reach water before sundown."

The herd took the trail and Don rode on ahead. Red, Charlie, Bob, Les and Mike rode drag. Don's order strong on their minds, they constantly watched the back trail. The herd, well-watered, behaved, allowing the drag riders an opportunity to talk. Rose Delano, feeling comfortable with

*The Green River.

Mike after their talk the night before, guided her horse alongside his. He tipped his hat to her, and she spoke.

"Do you believe those Indians will come after us?"

"Yes," said Mike, "if they can find their horses before we get too far ahead of them. I haven't had any experience with the Utes, but if they're anything like the Comanches, losin' their horses is a considerable blow to their pride. They'll want to get even."

Rose shuddered. "I was hoping they would give up and leave us alone."

Seeing them talking, Sarah Miles had ridden close enough to hear their conversation.

"Will they attack while we're spread out like this?" Sarah asked.

"I don't know," said Mike, "but it will be to their advantage if they can get close to us before we know they're there. That's why Don wants us to watch the back trail. If we see them soon enough, our rifles can cut them down before they're close enough for their arrows to hurt us."

"I hate the thought of them being killed," said Sarah, "but they abused us terribly. It scares me half to death to think of what they might do if they were to capture us now."

"I think they'll kill any of you as quickly as they'll kill any of us," Mike said. "All we can do is try to get them before they get us."

With that same thought in mind, Don Webb rode cautiously. While they had a clear view of their back-trail, the herd had to travel between distant buttes and pinnacles of rock that lay ahead, any one of which might provide cover for the Utes to launch flank attacks. Going out of his way, Don rode wide of all such cover, but nothing disturbed the tranquility of the land. In the vivid blue of the sky, buzzards drifted effortlessly, and there was no other sign of life. Don rode on, and when he reached the river, he followed it south until it forked. There were tracks of deer and the occasional paw prints of a grizzly. More frequent were the lesser paw prints of what Don recognized as cougars. After resting his horse, he watered the animal and started back to meet the herd. But long before he reached it, he heard a shot. Reining up, he listened, and it was quickly followed by two more. It was all the warning a frontiersman needed, and he kicked his horse into a fast gallop.

The drag riders continued watching the back-trail, and it was Red who first saw the approaching Indians. Drawing his Colt, he fired three times. Riding point, Jim Roussel began to head the lead steers, causing them to circle. The flank and swing riders joined him, and the herd soon was milling. The riders then galloped their horses along the back-trail, joining their comrades who had been riding drag. Aware of the approaching danger, Dominique and Roberto were driving the remuda horses and the pack mules around and beyond the herd of longhorns.

"Not more than a dozen of them," Charlie observed, "and they know full well we can see 'em coming. Wonder what they have in mind?"

"Who knows?" said Bob Vines. "If some of them have somehow gotten ahead of us, I'd say they might be planning an attack from two directions. Don will have heard the shots. If he's found any sign up ahead, that'll tell us something."

Near enough to see that there was no immediate danger, Don had slowed his horse to spare the heaving animal. By the time he had reined up and dismounted, the Utes following them were much closer.

"It was me that fired the shots," said Red. "Not enough of them back there to do us any damage, but I reckoned all of us should come together and maybe get a handle on what they're plannin' to do."

"Exactly what you should have done," Don said. "I doubt they've had time to get ahead of us, for I found no sign. I purely don't understand why some of 'em are trailing us, unless they aim to get on our nerves."

"They can get close enough in the dark to stampede the

herd," said Mike Horton. "It's a way of slowing us down, forcing us to split up."

"Except for the Comanches, I've never heard of Indians attacking at night," Les Brown said.

"I don't think what Mike's suggesting is considered an attack," said Don. "Old Indian superstitions bother them only if there's a chance of them dying in the darkness, and they can stampede the herd without any danger to themselves."

"I think we'd better all stay in the saddle every night until this threat is behind us," Bob Vines said. "These coyotes can sneak in, stampede the herd, and be gone before we're able to get astraddle of our horses."

"We'll push on to the water," said Don. "It's not that far, and we'll arrive well before sundown. There'll be time for all of us to get a little sleep before dark. Like Bob says, we may all be in the saddle every night until this Indian threat is behind us."

The herd moved on and the Utes followed, being careful to stay out of rifle range. Don rode well ahead of the drive, steering them wide of any cover that might have aided the enemy in setting up an ambush. They reached the river and settled the herd down on the graze between the two forks. Tomorrow they would follow the south fork until the old trail veered away from it.

"All of you from the first watch get as much rest as you can," Don ordered. "In two hours, you'll swap places with those of us on the second watch. By then, it'll be suppertime, and after we eat, we'll all be in the saddle until first light."

It would be an exhausting ordeal, trailing the herd all day and standing watch all night, and the riders from the first watch stretched out, their heads on their saddles.

"That seems terribly hard, riding all day and being in the saddle all night," said Sarah Miles.

"Hard as it is, it's nothing compared to havin' to gather a stampeded herd," Mike said. "At best, trail driving is a hard life."

After supper, the herd was bunched, and aware of the possibility of a stampede, the Mexican wranglers had separated the horse remuda and the pack mules from the longhorns. Yet all the animals were grouped so that the riders could circle them, half the outfit riding clockwise and the others riding the other direction. It was as near-perfect a defense as they could devise, and there was nothing to arouse their suspicions until the early hours of the morning. After moonset, the darkness seemed all the more intense, and suddenly there was the patter of hooves and the frightened nicker of a horse. It came galloping between the bunched longhorns and the gathering of the horse remuda and pack mules. There was a rope around the animal's neck, and trailing behind it was the hide of a fresh-killed cougar. Try as they might, none of the riders reached the horse in time, and the combined smell of cougar and fresh blood brought instant disaster. The horse remuda and the pack mules stampeded first, despite all the efforts of Dominique and Roberto to restrain them. Right into the herd of restless longhorns the riderless horse ran. The herd came to its feet as one, and with a terrified bellow, stampeded after the horse remuda and the mules. There was no holding them, no heading them, as they galloped madly westward. The riders were ready for an attack, but there was none. The sound of the stampede diminished until there was only silence, seeming more profound than ever.

"Damn them," Charlie English said. "We wasn't able to even fire a shot."

"Nothing to shoot at," said Don wearily, "and muzzle flashes would have provided an an excellent opportunity for them to shoot arrows into some of us."

"At least the varmints all stampeded west, along the south fork of the river," Mike Horton said. "When they're tired runnin', they won't scatter from here to yonder, huntin' water. We won't be a week roundin' 'em up."

"No," said Don, "gathering them may not be that great a problem. The real problem will be gathering 'em without the damn Utes picking us off from cover. All of you catch a couple of hours' sleep, keepin' your rifles handy. I'll stand watch until first light.''

''I'll split the time with you,'' Bob Vines offered.

''No,'' said Don. ''There's not that much time.''

Don settled down near the packsaddles and found Dominique and Roberto awake.

''We no sleep,'' one of the Mexicans said.

When the first rays of approaching dawn feathered the eastern sky, Dominique and Roberto had the cook fires going and the coffee boiling. Every rider was awake, lest the Utes defy their gods of superstition and attack, but there was no sign of the Indians.

''Not enough cover,'' said Red. ''The cowardly varmints.''

''Not so much cowardly as smart,'' Don said. ''If you was facing Henry rifles, and all you had was a bow and arrows, you'd be as cautious as they are.''

Hurriedly the outfit finished breakfast and saddled their horses.

''We're forgettin' somethin','' said Mike Horton. ''These seven women are here, along with our packs and supplies. If a dozen Utes come skalley-hootin' in here, Dominique and Roberto wouldn't stand a chance.''

''I'm aware of that,'' Don said. ''You and Red will stay here. Come noon, you'll swap out with two other riders.''

The eight of them saddled their horses and rode west along the river.

''Since we'll be here a while,'' said Rose Delano, ''and we're right here beside the river, I need to wash myself. My hair is filthy.''

''So is mine,'' Sarah said.

''I don't know,'' said Mike doubtfully. ''I wish you had talked to Don about that.''

''Yeah,'' Red added. ''Them Utes can be all around us before you know it. You'd have to find you a place that's private, and we can't allow you out of our sight.''

Rose laughed. ''We haven't had a shred of privacy in

months. Why should the lack of it bother us now? We'll
do our washing right here.''

"Then go ahead," said Mike. "We'll turn our backs
until you're done."

"Oh damn," Bonita said, in feigned disgust. "If we
won't have an audience, then I just won't bother."

They splashed around for half an hour, while Mike, Red,
Dominique, and Roberto were careful to keep their backs
turned.

The Texans had traveled not more than three miles when
they began seeing longhorns, but there was no sign of the
horse remuda and the pack mules.

"We can gather the herd later," Don said. "I reckon
we'd better go looking for the horse remuda and the pack
mules first. The varmints have had time to round them up,
if they started at first light."

They didn't have to ride far before finding the tracks of
unshod horses. The Utes *had* cut out the horses and pack
mules and had driven them south. The trail was fresh, and
the Texans followed it until the terrain became rough,
shrouded with brush and outcroppings of rock. Don reined
up, his companions surrounding him.

"I'm ridin' west a ways and then south," Don said.
"Bob, I want you to ride east for maybe half a mile and
then turn back south. The rest of you continue to follow
the trail, but be slow about it. That bunch knows we'll be
followin', and I'd bet my old granny's rockin' chair that
some of them will double back with ambush on their minds.
If you see any sign of it, Bob, ride on back. I'll do the
same, and we'll decide how best to turn the tables on
them."

Don rode west, and after turning back to the south, expected to find tracks of Indian horses, where one or more
riders had doubled back with an ambush in mind. But there
were no tracks. A mile or so distant, having again ridden
south, Bob made a similar discovery. They had guessed
wrong, overplayed their hand. The Utes had counted on that

as a means of dividing the riders, and before Don and Bob could join their comrades, the Utes attacked. There was a rattle of gunfire, and it ceased as suddenly as it had begun. Don and Bob reached the scene of the attack to find Jim Roussel and Arch Danson on the ground, each with an arrow in his thigh.

"The varmints come at us from two directions," Charlie English said. "Scared hell out of our horses, and by the time we calmed them, we didn't have any targets. The shots we fired was just wasted."

"They disappeared like smoke," said Les Brown.

"How many of them?" Don asked.

"Maybe ten," said Les.

"We'll still have to recover the horses and mules," Don said. "Arch, you and Jim will have to ride back alone if you're able. Are you?"

"I am," said Arch, "but that leaves only six of you against all of them. Besides those that jumped us, there had to be others watchin' the horses and mules."

"He's dead right," Jim Roussel said. "Why don't we just tie our bandannas above these wounds to stop the bleedin' and all of us ride on?"

"No," Don said. "The two of you will ride back and see to those wounds. The rest of us will go after the horses and mules. Now mount up, both of you, and ride."

Reluctantly they did so. The rest of the outfit continued following the trail of the horses and mules.

"From here on," said Don, "we won't split up for any reason. We'll be outnumbered two to one or more, and it'll take our combined efforts just to come out of this alive."

"The range of our Henrys is greater than that of their bows and arrows," Bob said. "If we can't defeat them, maybe we can make it hot enough that they'll give up the horses and mules."

"That may be our only chance," said Don. "If we get too close, there's a possibility we'll ride into another ambush. Let's see if we can get within rifle range without havin' them bushwhack us again."

Eventually there was a cloud of dust against the blue of the sky, and after topping a rise, they could see the horses and mules half a mile ahead. Sixteen mounted Indians were shouting and pushing them onward.

"Let's ride," Don shouted. "Soon as we're in range, rein up and drop as many of them as you can."

Every man knew it was a calculated risk, for if they didn't reduce the odds quickly, the Utes could turn on them. Drawing their Henrys from their saddle boots, they kicked their horses into a gallop. Their greater numbers inspired the Utes to fight instead of run, but while still out of range of Indian arrows, the Texans reined up and began firing. A first volley dropped six of the Utes, and before giving up the cause, four more fell. The six remaining kicked their horses into a gallop, riding for their lives.

"That's how it should have happened to start with," Don said. "Then Jim and Arch wouldn't have been wounded. Me and my bright ideas."

"Not your fault," said Charlie English. "If we'd been up against Comanches, they'd have left maybe four riders with the horses and mules, and the rest would have doubled back for a bushwhacking. These damn Indians has got a different set of rules."

"That they have," Bob said. "Let's gather those horses and mules and get back to camp while we can."

"Yeah," said Felton Juneau. "There was more than a hundred Utes in that camp when we stampeded their horses. There could be another bunch attackin' our camp while we're after the horses and mules."

It was a possibility none of them wanted to consider, and they quickly headed the horses and mules back the way they had come. They all heaved sighs of relief when they reached camp and found there had been no attack. Jim Roussel and Arch Danson already had their thighs bandaged, a fire was going, and there was a tangy odor of fresh coffee.

"How bad are the wounds, Mike?" Don asked, immediately after dismounting.

"Flesh wounds," said Mike. "Neither arrow hit bone, and it wasn't too hard drivin' 'em on through."

"Bueno," Don said. "We'll have to count on Arch and Jim to help defend the camp, so the rest of us can begin gathering the herd."

"Tarnation," said Arch, "you need us in the saddle, not laid up here in camp."

"We likely won't have a fever before sometime tonight," Jim said. "Maybe not then."

"Anything you do may make the infection more difficult to heal," said Don. "Both of you will stay right here, keepin' your rifles handy. So will Mike and Red. The rest of us will begin gathering the herd, doing the best we can."

The six of them rode out, following the path of the stampede, and soon began finding groups of grazing cattle.

"Let's follow this stream as far as we can find any cattle, and work our way back from there," said Don. "We can gather those nearest our camp on the way back."

They rode on, wary of anything that offered the slightest cover, until they no longer found any of the stampeded herd.

"There's plenty of 'em along this fork," Bob said, "but if I'm any judge, there won't be more than half the herd."

"That means the others may be up yonder along the north fork," said Don, "leadin' me to wonder why. There's water here, along with fair-to-middlin' graze."

Bob laughed. "Don't ever try to puzzle out the ways and the wanderings of a cow. In the dark, some of 'em may have got into the river, run out on the other side and just kept going. As we ride back, let's keep an eye on that far bank for tracks."

Soon as they began finding grazing cattle, they bunched them together and drove them back toward camp.

"There's where a bunch of 'em crossed the river," Bob said, pointing.

"We'll gather all we can on this side, and move 'em closer to camp," said Don "Then we'll cross the river and ride to the upper fork. With any luck, we'll find the rest of them there."

There was no more than two hours of daylight remaining when they bunched the longhorns along the river, near their camp.

"Maybe we ought to run some tallies and see how many we're missing," Les suggested.

"I think we should gather the rest of them," said Bob. "Then if we're still shy some, we can start fresh in the morning."

"I'm inclined to agree with Bob," said Don. "If we luck out, and find the rest of them along the upper fork, we can rest easy. But if we're still missing a large number, we may have some tracking and serious brush-beatin' ahead of us. I don't favor stayin' here any longer than we have to. The longer we're delayed, the better the chance those Utes will find the rest of their horses, regroup, and come after us."

"Lookin' at it that way, I reckon we'd better ride to that upper fork and get busy," Les said.

Leaving the longhorns bunched near their camp, the Texans crossed the south fork of the river and rode north. Reaching the north fork, they were encouraged to find reasonably good graze and very little cover suitable for an ambush. Eventually they came upon bunches of grazing longhorns. While the graze wasn't substantial, it was adequate.

"Still not all of them," said Don. "We'll ride on until we don't see any more of 'em, and start pushin' them toward camp."

When they could see no more cattle, they turned back.

"I hope we can gather enough without followin' this north fork any farther," Bob said. "On up yonder, the bank gets downright brushy, and there's some upthrusts of rock that would hide men on horses."

"I saw that," said Don. "Time enough to concern ourselves with that after we've taken some tallies. If we don't have time before dark, we can first thing tomorrow."

But when they neared camp, they found Red and Mike mounted, waiting for them.

"Keep that bunch separated," Mike shouted. "We've already run tallies of them that's already here."

"Bueno," shouted Don in reply. "We'll have time to tally these before dark."

Quickly they headed and bunched the longhorns, and every rider began counting.

"I tally fifteen hundred," Bob said.

"Fifteen-fifty," said Don.

"Sixteen hundred," Charlie English said.

"Fifteen-twenty-five," said Eli Mills.

"Fifteen-sixty-five," Felton Juneau said.

"Fifteen-seventy-five," said Les Brown.

"We'll take the low count of fifteen hundred," Don said. "Now, Red, we'll see just how good you and Mike are. What's your tallies?"

"Thirty-one hundred," Red replied.

"Thirty-one-twenty-five," said Mike.

"Forty-six hundred, total," Don said, "and we can't live with that."

"We could run 'em all together and everybody take a new count tomorrow," Les said.

"We could, but we're not going to," said Don. "We'd still be lacking more than we can afford to lose, and we'd have lost the time spent taking another count. Tomorrow at first light, we're ridin' back along that north fork, beatin' the bushes."

"I just hope we don't scare up any two-legged varmints with bows and arrows," Felton said.

"So do I," said Don, "but if we do, it's the luck of the draw. We're not leavin' here without another four hundred head, if we have to fight every Ute in the territory."

While they had their misgivings, nobody disagreed, for they were all Texans. One of them had taken a stand, and his comrades could do no less. They drove the second gather of longhorns in with the first, bunching them near camp. Dominique and Roberto had the horses and mules gathered on the other side of the camp, near the river. Mike and Arch were sleeping, and supper was underway.

"Somebody's been in the river," Don said, his eyes on the still-wet hair of the women.

"I gave them permission," said Mike.

"It's dangerous, any of us being separated," Don said.

"No," said Mike. "They wasn't more than ten feet away. We turned our backs."

"They did," Bonita said, "although we told them they didn't have to. For all the time we were with the Indians, we weren't allowed to wash ourselves."

"She's right," said Rose. "It would have been worth any sacrifice we might have had to make."

"Rose and Sarah cleaned and bandaged the wounds, after I removed the arrows from Jim and Arch," Mike said.

"Bueno," said Don. While he still didn't care that much for the two older women, Mike Horton seemed to look upon them favorably. For that reason, Don Webb would give them the benefit of the doubt.

"With Jim and Arch wounded, that leaves four of us for each watch," Bob said. "That is, unless you want us all in the saddle all night."

"We'll stay with four men per watch," said Don. "We had everybody in the saddle last night, and we accomplished nothing, except we didn't lose the horses we were riding. All of you, when you sleep, leave your horses saddled and picket them. I think there's more to it than these Utes wanting to get even. They want our horses and mules. Starting tonight, we'll cross-hobble all the pack mules and every horse in the remuda."

"Bueno," said Dominique and Roberto.

Don noted with approval that Rose and Sarah were testing Jim and Arch for fever at regular intervals. After supper, Dominique and Roberto left one coffee pot on the coals as the riders on the first watch saddled their horses.

"Some of us on watch can see to Arch and Jim during the night," Don said, mostly for the benefit of Rose and Sarah.

"No," said Rose. "It's the least we can do. Those of you on watch have more than enough responsibility. Sarah and me will place our blankets next to them, and when they become feverish, we'll give them whiskey, just as Mike told us to."

"We're obliged," Don said. In an odd sort of way he was pleased that these women had seemed to respond to the confidence Mike Horton had in them. He silently promised himself that when the opportunity presented itself, he would talk to Mike about these strange females. But tonight they were short-handed.

"Jim and Arch are feverish," Mike said. It was near midnight, as he and Don saddled their horses for the second watch.

Don didn't ask whether or not they had been given whiskey, for that would have implied a lack of confidence in Rose and Sarah.

"Rose is twenty-three, one year younger than me," Mike volunteered.

"That's not too old," said Don.

"It is for a woman," Mike said. "Sarah's a year older than that."

"I notice it hasn't discouraged you all that much," said Don.

"They've been through hell, since they was young girls," Mike said. "I'm considerin' that. Once they've had a chance to clean up, and are dressed up, I think any man would be proud of them."

"I don't doubt it for a minute," said Don. "I think I know of at least one that will be."

7

The second watch circled the herd for two hours before stopping to rest their horses. "I'm almighty tired of the saddle," Bob said. "I think I'll see how Arch and Jim are gettin' along."

Bob found the two awake. Rose had just given Arch whiskey, and Sarah was trying to get Jim Roussel to down some of the brew.

"No . . . more," said Jim, coughing. "I . . . I'm not a drinking man."

"I'm pleased to hear that," Sarah said, "but you must become one, until that fever lets you go."

Dutifully he swallowed another dose, and within minutes he was snoring.

"If he lives through this," said Bob, "we'll never have to worry with him hanging out in saloons."

"My sympathy is with him," Sarah said. "The stuff smells terrible."

"Him and Arch will be all right in a day or two," said Bob. "I wanted to see how they were getting along, but mostly I wanted to be free of that saddle for a while."

"Try riding without one, with only the ragged end of a skirt between your behind and the backbone of an Indian pony. Those poor beasts are just skin and bones."

"Sorry," Bob said. "I'd forgotten you're so poorly mounted. We can't find saddles for you and the others, but we can fold some extra blankets and maybe that will help some. I think we'll have to begin feeding those Indian horses a ration of grain, even if it runs us short. They won't make it to California on the kind of graze we've had.''

"I don't mean to seem ungrateful, after all you've done for us," said Sarah, "but when I think of returning to California . . .''

"All I know is what I learned from Mike after he talked to Rose," Bob said. "I reckon there's not much for you to go back to."

"Oh God," she said, trailing off into a sob.

"If you'd like to talk, I'm a good listener," said Bob. "We need to know somethin' of your life there, and what you aim to do once we reach Los Angeles."

"I don't know," Sarah said. "I truly don't know. I'd as soon go back to the Indians as to return to the . . . the mission.''

"Is it a real mission, the kind the Spanish established in California?"

"My God, no," said Sarah. "Perhaps it once was, but now it's no more than a prison. The sisters—Agatha, Birdie, Elvira, and Mert—aren't sisters at all. We were forced to endure their preaching on Sunday, and they used God as a threat of eternal damnation.''

"If it's not a real mission, what purpose does it serve? How does it survive?"

"It's called a home for wayward girls and women," Sarah said. "In truth, its a dumping ground for girls whose families don't want them. My mother died when I was seven, and a year later, my father left me at the mission. That was sixteen years ago, and I haven't seen or heard from him since."

"My God," said Bob. "Maybe he was in touch with them and they didn't tell you."

Sarah laughed bitterly. "Oh, he was in touch with them. He sent money every month until I was of age. They told me, using that to torture me. They said he didn't want me, that I was evil, that I was bound for hell.''

"You believed that?"

"Of course I did. What else could I believe? My only kin had left me there because I wasn't wanted. I lay awake wondering what I had done that made me so evil, wondering if I could do anything to redeem myself."

"You were beaten, like the others?" Bob asked.

"Yes. I was beaten because I was full of the devil. That's why Rose and me. . . . why we whipped the younger girls. We were told that they were afflicted the same as the rest of us, and if we didn't whip them, we were given their beatings."

"Your daddy was paying for your keep and you still were forced to work?"

"In the fields," said Sarah. "We worked from the time it was light enough to see until it became so dark we couldn't see. You can't imagine how hard that was for those of us who had been beaten the night before. You may not have noticed, but I walk with a limp. My left leg was broken during one of those beatings, and it grew back crooked."

"Damn them," Bob said. "You had no medicine, no doctor?"

"No. The bone was never set. But I was one of the lucky ones. Some of the younger girls never survived those beatings. Some mornings, after a beating, one of the beds would be empty."

"You never saw the girl again?"

"No," said Sarah. "The dead ones were buried somewhere near the mission."

"How many were there, besides the seven of you?"

"Nine more," Sarah said, "and they were all younger. The same renegades who took us took them, but they weren't brought into the mountains with the rest of us."

"What happened to . . . the sisters?"

"We never found out," said Sarah. "We were taken away just before dawn, and when I looked back, the mission was burning."

"They may have been burned alive then."

"Perhaps," Sarah said, "and if they were, it serves them right."

"After all you've been through, I can't understand . . ." At a loss for words, his voice trailed off.

"Why I'm still sane? I'm not sure that I am."

"That wasn't what I meant to say," said Bob. "I can't understand how you can speak of it so calmly, as though you were watching it happen to someone else."

Again she laughed bitterly. "You expected wild, hysterical tears?"

"I reckon," he conceded. "You're a woman."

"I am now. But it all started when I was a child of eight. Then there were tears, but I learned they were useless. The sisters took savage satisfaction in seeing us cry, because it was proof enough that their discipline was having its effect. I vowed never to cry, whatever they did to me, and I didn't. Not even when my leg was broken. Now there are no tears left."

"The others . . ."

"The others are just as hard, full of hate, and shy of tears as I am," Sarah said.

"Did the Utes . . . abuse any of you?"

Again she laughed. "Oh, that? There was only one thing they could do to us that had not been done, and they tried it. We fought them like mad dogs, and they gave up on us. Why do you think they were willing to swap us for horses and mules?"

"Rose didn't sound all that tough, when she cried for help. We suspected the Utes had pretty well had their way with all of you."

"Rose—and all of us, for that matter—feared only one thing. When the Indians were unable to get horses and mules for us, we were afraid they would find us useless and kill us. After all we've been through, we wanted to live."

"It was hell on us, watching them take all of you away," Bob said, "but there was no way we could live with such a trade. If we had met their demands, they would have taken our measure and decided we were afraid of them. Then we would have had a battle on our hands.''

''You don't think you will now, after killing so many of them and taking back the mules and horses they had stolen?''

''Maybe,'' said Bob, ''and maybe not. We gunned some of them down when we rescued you and your friends, and we accounted for ten of the sixteen that had made off with our horses and mules. Indians bein' superstitious, they sometimes back off from a fight they believe has gone sour. It's considered bad medicine, and they can give it up without losing face.''

''So you think they might have done that.''

''All of us are hoping they have,'' Bob said, ''but only time will tell. We must be ready to fight if they won't have it any other way.''

''I wish we could help you, but at the mission, they never allowed us to get our hands on any kind of weapon. Not even a dull knife. Any of us firing a gun would be out of the question.''

''That won't matter,'' said Bob, ''because we have no extra weapons. Now I reckon I'd better get back to circlin' the herd.''

''I feel better having talked to you,'' Sarah said. ''I've been so long without so much as a kind word, a sympathetic voice . . .''

''I've enjoyed talking to you,'' said Bob, ''even if a lot of it was hard on you, thinking back to those early years. I feel like I know you better, and that under all that rawhide toughness, there's a flesh-and-blood female just waitin' to be set free. We'll talk again, if it suits you.''

''It suits me, Bob Vines, and I'm flattered. Perhaps I'll begin feeling and acting like a flesh-and-blood female.''

There was soft laughter from the darkness, and Bob suspected that Rose had listened to most or all of their conversation. But he didn't care. There was a lightness to his step and an unfamiliar excitement in his heart as he returned to his waiting horse. His three comrades had long since resumed circling the herd. A rider approached, and from the darkness, Don Webb spoke.

"We've been some worried about Arch and Jim. You've been gone long enough to have dug graves, buried 'em, and preached a sermon."

"Sorry, daddy. I should have asked your permission. I've been talking to Sarah."

Don laughed. "You've been staking your claim."

"Maybe," said Bob. "Does that bother you?"

"No," Don replied, "but she's nearer my age than yours."

"Long as it don't bother you," said Bob shortly. "I flat don't care if she's old enough to be my granny."

He mounted his horse and rode away, Don Webb's quiet laughter following him in the darkness.

There was no evidence of the Utes during the night, and among the riders there was some optimism during breakfast.

"Them Utes may be thinkin' of us as bad medicine," said Mike Horton. "We nailed ten of the sixteen that rustled our horse remuda and pack mules."

"Maybe," Don conceded, "or they may just be waiting for the rest of their bunch to find their horses and join the fight. We want another four hundred cows, but I don't aim to trade anybody's scalp for them. All of you ride with your guns handy and take care not to get separated."

Jim Roussel and Arch Danson were awake and sweating.

"We ever do another cattle drive," Roussel vowed, "I'm buyin' the whiskey for snakebite, arrow, and gunshot wounds. What you been pourin' down us is the vilest stuff I've ever laid tongue to. How much did you spend, twenty-five cents a quart?"

"A dollar for all eight quarts of it," said Don with a straight face. "Keeps a man from gettin' snakebite, arrow, and gunshot wounds too often."

"Why don't we ride along the south fork of this stream?" Les said. "There may be some cows drifted down, lookin' for better graze. If we don't find any, we can always ride on up to the north fork and go from there."

"It's worth a try, and not out of our way," said Don. "We'll do it."

But the effort was wasted, for there were no more cows along the lower fork.

"Good try," Mike Horton said. "Now we got to do it the hard way. The varmints have dug into the brush up yonder along the upper fork."

Reaching the upper fork, they rode cautiously. Surprisingly, they found no longhorns in the brush, for it was shaded and there was little graze. When the brush diminished and the bank was again clear, they began finding grazing cattle.

"Praise be," Don said. "Looks like we'll find more than we expected."

They rode on, until they could see no more cows. Then they started back, gathering as they went, until all the wanderers were in a bunch.

"I believe we have more than enough," said Don, "but let's run some tallies."

Each of them began counting, and when they were finished, they reviewed their totals. The highest count was six hundred thirty, and the lowest count six hundred twenty-five.

"Six hundred twenty-five it is," Don said. "With what we've already gathered, we have five thousand two hundred and twenty-five. We've done well."

"In more ways than one," said Bob. "It looks like the Utes have decided we're all bad medicine. This would have been an ideal time for them to strike."

"I've been listening for shots," Les said. "With only four men in camp, and two of them wounded, I thought they might go after the mules and the horse remuda again."

"I don't think so," said Don. "They've learned what these Henry rifles can do, and the cover is a mite skimpy. Four men with repeating rifles could cut down a tribe of Utes."

Elated over their good fortune, they headed the newly gathered herd south. There all the cattle were bunched along the river.

"You found enough then," Red Bohannon said.

"Yes," said Don. "We have five thousand two hundred and twenty-five."

"Then we can move out anytime," Mike said.

"Not until Jim and Arch are able to ride," said Don.

"Jim and Arch are ready to ride," two eager voices shouted.

"Then we'll take the trail at first light tomorrow," said Don. "All of you get what rest you can."

While Jim and Arch still limped, they were on their feet, if for no other reason than to prove their trail worthiness. But they had much more than that in mind. Life on the trail being highly unpredictable, the pair used their daylight hours wisely. Roussel devoted his time to Ellie Andrews, while Arch Danson made a play for Bonita Holmes.

"Don," said Red, "you'd better get busy. There's not enough of these gals for us all to have one."

"Thanks," Don said, "but I have one waitin' for me in San Antone. The rest of you ugly varmints had better move in while you can. When this bunch reaches California and gets all fancied up, you might not have a chance."

"That's the God's truth," said Red. He started by tipping his hat to Molly Rivers and flashing her a Texas grin. He then hunkered down beside her, and as only a Texas cowboy can, soon had her laughing.

"Mike," Felton Juneau said, "what have you been sayin' to Rose Delano? When we took her from the Utes, she looked like she'd been dragged by the heels through a briar patch. With nothin' to do with but river water, she's done somethin' to her hair. It looks like polished copper."

"I believe that's called washing," said Horton. "You might try it with yours."

"Hell, I ain't woman hungry," Juneau said. "I got me a gal in San Antone that don't mind the smell of horse and cow sweat."

It prompted Horton to look closer at Rose Delano. She definitely *had* done something to her copper hair, and Mike wasted no time complimenting her.

"My God," said Bob Vines, "this looks more like a Sunday school picnic than a trail drive."

Sarah Miles laughed. "What's wrong with that? You're sitting here with me. It's as new to the others as it is to me, having a man just sit and talk. Look at Rose. This is the first time I've ever seen her hair looking like that. What do you suppose happened?"

"I reckon Mike Horton grinnin' at her had something to do with it," Bob said. "All of us are taking advantage of this time, and it may be what Don had in mind. Something tells me the worst part of this trail drive is ahead of us. We may not have time to sit and talk like this again."

"I truly hope we do," said Sarah. "For the sake of the others, as well as my own."

"Whatever happens along the way," Bob said, "none of you should worry about reaching California. I don't mean to seem . . . forward. I just want you to know . . ."

Words failed him. Leaning forward to look into his eyes, she spoke softly.

"I *do* know, and I thank you."

Millie Nettles was talking earnestly to Les Brown, while Wendy Oldham laughed at something Charlie had said. Bob Vines grinned in appreciation. If all these women lived to reach California, their days of captivity and fear were over.

Southern Utah. June 3, 1862.

"Head 'em up, move 'em out," Don shouted.

The herd again took the trail, with Don scouting ahead. The women, while they had no saddles, had learned to assist the drag riders in heading bunch-quitters. The horse remuda and pack mules followed, with Dominique and Roberto keeping them as near the drag as they could. Once the herd had settled down, Don galloped his horse ahead, anxious to see how much farther the trail would follow the lower fork of this unknown river. Despite the fact they had seen nothing more of the Utes, he looked for any sign. After a little more than twelve miles, the trail turned southwest, away from the river.

"We'll have water for tonight, horse," Don said, "and we may have time to see what's ahead for tomorrow."

Don rode southwest, following the trail, and soon came upon a river flowing south.*

"Tarnation," said Don aloud, "the trail follows this river from the north."

It was enough, for one day, and Don rode back to tell the outfit of their good fortune.

"That is good news," Bob said. "Water for today, as well as tomorrow."

"Once we leave this river," said Don, "I figure it's maybe twelve or thirteen miles to the point where we reach the one flowing in from the north."

"But you don't know how far the trail follows that one," Mike said.

"No," said Don. "I figured water for two days was enough. Once we reach that river flowing from the north, I'll ride from there. Tonight, before supper, we'll have another look at that trail map."

The drive moved on, and when they reached the southerly bend in the trail where they must leave the river, they bedded down the herd. When the horses were unsaddled, the pack mules unloaded, and supper underway, Don spread out the trail map. He found the river that flowed in from the north.

"According to the map, the trail bends away from it some," Don said, "but not enough to get us off course."

"Looks like we'll be followin' it for a pretty good distance," said Bob. "Maybe we can get a second day's watering before we have to leave it."

*The Sevier River

"Maybe two days beyond that, we'll be gettin' into Paiute country," Charlie said. "That is, if this map's for real."

"No reason why it shouldn't be," said Red. "It said there was Utes, and they was there for real."

"We'd better count on it," Don said. "Dominique?"

The Mexican left the supper fire and leaned over Don's shoulder, as he pointed to the word on the map. For a moment, Dominique said nothing.

"*Indios*," said Don. "Paiute."

"*Si,*" Dominique said, comprehending. "*Indios. Malo.*"

"I reckon that answers our question," said Don.

"Maybe we can drive north of the old trail and miss them entirely," Jim Roussel said.

"Not without getting into Nevada's Great Basin," said Don, "and God only knows what the water situation is there. The old timers—probably the Spanish—who blazed this trail knew what they were doing. We can't afford to pioneer a new route, with five thousand thirsty cows dependin' on us."

The Colorado River. June 3, 1862.

Griff and his renegade outfit had no trouble finding the place where the longhorns had crossed the river.

"One of us ought to ride ahead and see where they are," Doolin said.

"One of us will, when the time comes," said Griff, "and I'll be the one to decide when the time comes. Get too close, stir up some dust, and they'll spot us on the backtrail."

"Hell, there's more of us than there is of them," Bullard said.

"That means nothing, if we're bushwhacked," said Griff. "Now damn it, all of you just settle down and let me do the thinking."

"That's what bothers me," Ben Pickford said quietly.

"All we want is to avenge Wiley, and we got to ride with this bunch all the way to California."

"It was that or have them ventilate us," said Curt, "and we still don't know that they won't. It ain't gonna help Wiley none if both of us gets gut-shot."

"No use whinin' now," Ben said. "We drawed the cards and we got to play 'em to the finish."

"I reckon," said Curt, "but this has all the earmarks of a busted flush."

"You Pickfords cut out the whisperin'," Griff shouted. "This is my outfit, and you got anything to say, you say it loud enough for ever'body to hear."

The outfit settled down along the Colorado, waiting.

Southwestern Utah. June 4, 1862.

"There's a storm buildin'," Felton Juneau said.

Nobody could argue with that, for there were dirty smudges of gray along the western horizon. The evening sun set behind a bank of gray clouds, reaching mile-high fingers of crimson into the blue of the sky. When darkness fell, the wind rose, coming out of the northwest, bringing the smell of rain. Golden shards of lightning danced nervously through the darkness, while distant rumbles of thunder seemed more imagined than real. The outfit had reached the point where the trail swung south along the Sevier River, and while there was plenty of water and decent graze, the longhorns were restless. Two or three started bawling and others joined until there was a bizarre chorus.

"My God," said Rose, "what's wrong with them? It sounds like the end of the world."

"They believe it is, every time a storm comes," Don said. "And if it's anything like the last one, we may all be sharing their feelings. Jim, I have a job for you, Les, and me. We're goin' to cross-hobble the pack mules and the horse remuda. Dominique and Roberto would do it, but I've told them to get supper ready as quickly as they can.

Spooky as the herd is, we may have to begin circling them before dark.''

It proved to be a wise decision, for the riders barely had time to eat. Some of the longhorns were on their feet, refusing to graze or lie down, bawling their frustration. Red, Charlie, Bob, and Mike finished eating first. Saddling their horses, they began circling the restless herd as the threatening storm moved ever closer. Quickly the rest of the outfit joined their comrades, seeking to calm the herd. Dominique and Roberto were with the pack mules and the horse remuda, which Don had ordered moved across the river. All the horses taken from the Utes had been crosshobbled and were with the remuda horses. As the riders circled the bawling herd, Sarah got near enough to Bob's horse for him to see her in the gathering darkness.

"If I can be of any help, I'll get my horse," she said. "I'm sure the others will too."

"No," said Bob. "Bless you for offering, but it's too dangerous. All of you should be across the river, with the hobbled horses and mules."

"Please be careful," she cried.

He leaned from the saddle, tilted her chin and kissed her. Then he was gone.

"Get ready," Don shouted against the rising wind. "They're gonna run."

Thunder had become a continuous rumble, and while the lightning wasn't striking, it lit up the darkened sky with an eerie glow. Before one flash faded, another flickered to life. The riders continued circling the herd, nervously pondering the direction the herd might stampede, knowing it would be influenced by the thunder and lightning. The thunder grew louder until it seemed to come from everywhere, literally shaking the earth. The longhorns were suddenly on their feet, and with a bawling, thundering commotion that threatened to drown the fury of the storm, they stampeded south, along the river. The riders tried to head them. A horn raked the flank of Don Webb's horse, and he was thrown into the path of the stampeding herd. Risking his own life, Red Bohannon galloped his horse into the path of the rampaging longhorns. With only seconds to spare, Webb leaped up behind Red and they escaped being trampled. All their efforts were futile, and by the time a drenching rain began, the sound of the stampede had been swallowed by the rumble of thunder. Les Brown rode in, leading Don's horse. A flash of lightning revealed a wicked gash along the animal's left flank.

"Sing out," Don shouted.

One by one, they called out their names, proof that they were alive. As suddenly as the storm had arisen, it was gone. The rain became a drizzle before ending entirely. Even as the thunder rumbled away, there were breaks in the clouds and a few timid stars were visible in the purple sky. A half-moon crept out from behind the clouds as the dejected cowboys led their horses back to where their supper fire had been.

"Were any of you hurt?" came Sarah's anxious inquiry from the darkness.

"No," said Bob, "but we lost the herd again."

"Damn near lost Don," Charlie said, "if Red hadn't been close enough to go after him."

Neither Don or Red said anything, for men who often faced death every day seldom spoke of the near misses. Suddenly there were flames from one of the fire pits where Dominique and Roberto had prepared supper. They had covered the coals with enough dirt to protect them from the rain, and now they had resurrected the fire and had hung one of the coffee pots over it.

"Coffee," said Roberto cheerfully.

"Bless you," Don said. "We're all wet and cold."

There soon were flames from the second fire pit, and Dominique hung the second pot on to boil.

"Where in tarnation did they find dry wood in the dark, after a rain?" Les wondered.

"Some of us rounded it up while they were cooking

supper," said Rose, "and they put it under the canvas, with the supplies."

Don Webb laughed. "Even without a herd, this is a *muy bueno* outfit."

8

"*T*he herd stampeded south, and at least for a while, that's the direction we'll be taking," Don said, as the outfit finished breakfast. "We'll load the pack mules, take the horse remuda, and go after them."

"Bueno," said Bob. "Accordin' to the map, the trail don't exactly follow this river, but it's close. If the herd sticks to this river, we should be able to round 'em up, and then by turning slightly southwest, hit the trail again."

"The map says this river runs south almost to the Grand Canyon," Charlie said. "That means we'll soon be in northern Arizona Territory, and Paiute country."

"So be it," said Don. "Like the Utes, they're just another problem we'll have to overcome."

With only the pack mules and horse remuda, their progress was rapid as they followed the stampeded herd. As they had hoped, the longhorns had continued running south along the river. Even though the trail soon veered away from the river, the map indicated that by driving west, they would soon be on the trail again a few miles farther south.

"It'll be worth drivin' west a few extra miles to get back on the trail," Red observed. "The varmints ain't likely to stray too far from water, and it'll make our gather easier."

"Makes you wonder why the Spanish didn't blaze this trail alongside the river as far south as they could," said Mike Horton.

"I have an idea why they didn't," Don replied. "Followin' this river due south should take us right into Paiute territory considerably quicker than if we followed the old trail."

"If the Paiutes are ornery enough to come after us," said Eli Mills, "we'll have to face them sooner or later. What's the use of puttin' it off?"

"Eli has a point," Bob said. "If something's got to be done, delayin' it won't make it any easier."

"With that in mind," said Don, "we'll ride until we first begin finding cows. There we'll leave the pack mules and the horse remuda. From there, I aim to scout ahead, looking for any sign of Indians. If the Paiutes are of a mind to make trouble, the stampede will have told them we're coming."

"Then let's just go ahead gathering cows," Jim Roussel said, "and fight the Paiutes if and when we have to."

"No," said Don. "If they're gonna be ornery, we need to know so some of us can be handy with our rifles, when they come to take our pack mules and horse remuda."

"It worked out pretty well when Jim and me was wounded," Arch said. "Mike and Red stayed in camp, and with four repeating Henrys, we could have raised considerable hell if the Utes had bothered us. But I reckon it was harder on the rest of you, gatherin' the herd."

"Not near as hard as having the Utes attack an unprotected camp," said Don.

Well after they had left the Old Spanish Trail to follow the stampeded herd along the river, they began seeing bunches of grazing cattle. Don waved his hat and they all reined up.

"Here's where we'll make camp," Don said. "I know it's still early in the day, and we'll likely have time to round up some of the cows, but I aim to ride ahead a ways, lookin' for Indians. The rest of you stay right here until I do some scouting."

"There'll be more than enough guns to protect the camp," said Charlie. "Suppose I ride with you?"

"Come on then," Don said.

They saddled fresh horses and continued riding south, following the river. There were more and more grazing longhorns, but after several miles there was only an occasional animal.

"That ain't near all of 'em," said Charlie.

"No," Don agreed, "and it makes no sense that most of them stopped running while the others kept going. There must be a reason."

There was. Tracks of a large number of longhorns led off to the southeast. Don and Charlie dismounted, and leading their horses, they studied the ground.

"They was bein' driven," Charlie said. "Horse tracks. Unshod horses."

"I reckon that answers our questions about the Paiutes," said Don. "Let's trail them a ways and see if we can learn how many there were."

Leading their horses so as not to disturb the existing tracks, they began studying the ground.

"Fresh tracks," Charlie said. "Maybe a dozen horses, and lots more cows than we can afford to lose. Do we keep followin' 'em?"

"Not in daylight," said Don. "They'll be expecting us. In fact, I suspect that's why they took the cows. If we go looking for them, they can bushwhack us, or while our forces are divided, they can take our pack mules and the horse remuda. We'll gather as many cows as we can, and after dark we'll find their camp."

Don and Charlie returned to their horses and rode back upriver, pushing ahead of them the cows that grazed along the river. As they neared their camp, there were more and more longhorns, until there were finally too many for just two riders. They rode on, and reaching camp, quickly told the rest of the outfit what they had discovered.

"Red, Mike, Arch, and Jim will stay here to defend the camp," Don said. "The rest of us will ride downriver and gather all the cattle grazing there. We'll drive them as near as we can, and tonight we'll go looking for that Paiute camp."

The cattle were easily gathered before sundown. After driving them as near the camp as possible, the riders ran tallies. The shortest—and the accepted one—was 4,200 head.

"Damn," said Felton Juneau, "they knew what they was doin'. Ain't no way we'll take a loss like that."

"Hell no," Red Bohannon agreed. "Not if there's five hundred of the varmints."

"I expect there'll be a bunch," said Don, "and it won't be easy getting our cows back. Once we find their camp, maybe we can figure a way of doing it without getting ourselves shot full of arrows and scalped."

"My God," Sarah said, "is there no end to Indians in these mountains?"

"We shouldn't have any more Indian trouble if we can get past the Paiutes," said Bob, "but they're a tribe we don't know anything about."

"We'll have supper early and put out the fires," Don said.

"How many of us are ridin' after the Paiutes?" Jim Roussel asked.

"Not more than two of us," said Don. "We don't dare leave the camp unprotected, and until we know how many Paiutes we're facing and where they are, there isn't much we can do. Charlie and me will find the camp. Then we'll ride back, and we'll make some plans. I want all of you to keep your weapons handy while we're gone. They may be counting on us doing exactly what we're about to do."

While none of them complained, all the women seemed fearful of what might lie ahead. Charlie spent some time with Wendy Oldham, obviously attempting to reassure her. Supper was ready well before sundown, and the fires were put out.

"There'll be a moon later tonight," Charlie said.

"We'll be going well before then," said Don. "Soon as it's dusky dark, we'll saddle our horses and ride."

"How will you follow them in the dark?" Bonita asked.

"We know the general direction they were riding," said Don, "and they'll have a fire."

That ended the conversation. The riders said nothing more, lest the women become even more frightened, and when it was dark enough, Don and Charlie saddled their horses. Wendy was nearby, and before mounting, Charlie took her hand. Don led out and Charlie followed.

"That young lady thinks highly of you, Charlie," Don said.

"I aim to ask her an important question once we reach California," Charlie said.

Back in camp, Ellie Andrews had a serious question for Jim Roussel.

"Is it true that you shot a man in Santa Fe?"

"Yes," said Roussel. "It was him or me. He claimed I cheated him at poker and drew on me. Who told you?"

"That doesn't matter," Ellie said. "Were you cheating?"

"No," said Roussel angrily.

He said no more, and when the silence grew painful, Ellie spoke quietly.

"I'm sorry. I didn't mean to pry. It's none of my business."

"I'm hoping it will be, when we reach California," he said, more kindly.

"What . . . do you mean?"

"I mean I'll give up the saloons, gambling, and hell-raising," he said. "That is, if you'll have me."

"And if I won't?" said Ellie, in a devilish tone.

"Then I reckon I'll have to spend all my time in saloons, at the poker table, gunning down any hombre that'll draw on me. Without somebody to care, I'll likely just go plumb to hell," Jim replied.

"But I care," she said.

"How much?"

"Awful much. More than I ever cared for . . . any man," said Ellie.

"Oh?" he replied, raising his eyebrows. "There have been other men?"

"Oh no," she cried. "I'm just nineteen, and I was taken to the mission when I was six. I've never so much as spoken to *any* man. Until you."

Roussel laughed. "Then you don't know what a unwashed, unsavory gun-totin' bunch of varmints we are."

"But you said you'd change, if I . . . I'd have you."

"You never said you'd have me," Roussel teased.

"I can't imagine why you would want me," she said. "At the mission, they told me I was awful, that I was ugly. Under this dress, I have scars all over me."

"Where you were beaten," said Roussel. "Why?"

"Because I cried, and I cried because I felt so alone."

"There's nothing ugly about you, even with your scars," Jim said. "I want you, and I promise you'll never be alone again."

"Then you can have me," said Ellie, "but I must tell you I'm ignorant in so many ways and I don't know how to be a woman. I never had anybody to teach me."

"I'll tell you a secret," Jim said. "I'm a year younger than you, and I . . . I've never been with a woman. I reckon there's a lot to learn. Maybe we can get the hang of it together."

She laughed. "I'm willing to try."

Don and Charlie soon reached the place where the Indians had begun driving the stolen cattle toward the southeast. There they slowed their horses to a walk, and not until they had ridden almost ten miles was there any sign of the Paiute camp. Then faintly they heard the barking of a dog. Both men dismounted. Lest the horses nicker and give them away, they must continue on foot.

"Careful," Don said softly. "The wind's at our backs."

It was a disadvantage, for they were approaching a camp where there were dogs. One of the animals might betray their presence while they were afoot, a great distance from their horses. Suddenly Don stepped on a dead branch and it snapped. Both men froze, for in the still of the night, sound carried. They paused for several minutes, not daring to move, listening. But there was only the wind, and they continued their slow progress. The dog barked again, much closer, and again they paused. It seemed they were at the foot of a slight rise, and as they topped it, there was a pinpoint of light in the canyon below.

"If they're expectin' us," Charlie whispered, "there'll be lookouts."

"That's why they have a fire," said Don softly. "They want to lure us in close enough to capture us, and that's why we're not goin' any closer. Let's get back to the horses."

Reaching their horses, they rode back upriver, neither of them speaking. There would be time enough, once they reached their camp. When they were near, they reined up.

"Don and Charlie ridin' in," Don said.

Quickly they dismounted and unsaddled their horses. Nobody said anything, waiting, and eventually Don spoke.

"We found their camp, and it may be even larger than we thought. They have a fire, so that means they're not afraid of us. In fact, they're hoping we'll come close enough for their sentries to take us."

"May be a permanent camp," Charlie added. "They have dogs, so there may be squaws and young 'uns too."

"It won't be easy gettin' our cows then," said Mike Horton.

"No," Don said. "They're in a kind of canyon, and you can bet they'll have lookouts on the rims. I doubt even another Indian could get in there in the dark. We'll have to get lots closer than Charlie and me were tonight, and we'll have to do it in daylight. We'll have to see where the cattle are before we can figure a way of taking them and getting ourselves out of there alive."

"They'll expect us to follow their tracks and those of the cattle," said Bob. "We'd best circle around and approach them from another direction. That way, maybe we can take them by surprise."

"I aim to be close enough to see that canyon at first light," Don said. "I reckon they'll expect all of us to come ridin' in, and they'll be waitin' to wipe us out to the last man, so that's the one thing we dare not do. Our only chance may be for one of us to get into that canyon and stampede the herd right through that Paiute camp."

"That would get them out of the hands of the Paiutes," Eli Mills said, "but then they'd be scattered all to hell and gone. It's a shame we can't get to the canyon rims with our rifles and gun down the whole bunch, leavin' the cattle undisturbed."

"You're dreamin', Eli," said Charlie. "There may be a hundred or more Paiutes. Enough shootin' to wipe them out would scatter that herd all over Arizona Territory."

"If the shooting didn't, the smell of blood would," Don said. "We'll have to see exactly what we're up against and plan accordingly, but killing them all isn't the answer."

"I'm glad," said Rose Delano. "It sounds so . . . brutal and barbaric."

"I know," Don replied, "but no more brutal and barbaric than what they likely have in mind for us. Anyway, all we want is the rest of our cows, and the less killing we have to do, the better off we'll probably be."

"That's the gospel truth," said Bob. "Some Indians are vindictive, wanting revenge for their dead. They might trail us for a hundred miles, picking us off one at a time."

"I understand your thinking, Don," Jim Roussel said, "but where is it written that *you* have to go into that canyon and stampede the herd? Why not me?"

"The rest of you voted me trail boss," said Don, "and a lot of responsibility goes with it. Are you bucking for the job?"

"No," Jim said, "but as partners, all of us should be willing to share the danger."

"I've never doubted the willingness of any of you to share the danger," said Don, "but in this case, there'll be more than enough danger for everybody. I'm countin' on that bein' a box canyon, and after I've stampeded the cows, the Paiute horses, or both, I'll be almost totally depending on the rest of you to see that I get out of there alive.''

"I reckon we can do that," Arch said. "If you aim to stampede the horses along with the cows, that leaves the Paiutes afoot."

"It all depends on where the horses are," said Don, "as well as where the herd is. In a box canyon, obviously the camp should be nearest the open end, preventing the live-stock from wandering away. If that's the case here, our only hope is to stampede the herd and the Paiute horses right through the camp. We'll just have to wait and see where the camp is, in relation to the horses and the herd."

"All of us will be ridin' at first light then," Jim Roussel said.

"Every rider except Dominique, Roberto, and the la-dies," said Don. "They'll remain here with our horse re-muda and pack mules. After I've had a look at the canyon in daylight, I'll get back with the rest of you long enough to decide what action we must take. Now it's well past the time for those of us on the second watch to get what sleep we can."

But there would be little sleep for the women. Red, Char-lie, and Arch were part of the first watch, and since there was only the horse remuda and the pack mules, the men were afoot, leading their horses. Molly Rivers quietly joined Red, while Wendy Oldham sought out Charlie. Arch was speaking softly to Bonita Holmes. Felton Juneau and Eli Mills kept their distance, allowing their comrades some privacy.

"Kinda leaves you out, don't it, Felton?" said Eli.

"Not as much as you," Juneau said. "I got me a gal back home."

"Got me one," said Eli, "and I'm countin' on enough dinero from this drive to take her before a preacher. I'm bettin' some of these hombres left one behind too. They're taking advantage of the present company for a little sport."

"I'll make believe you never said that," Juneau replied, "and was I you, I'd not say it too loud or too often. You'll end up with your ears beat down around your boot tops."

But the rest of the cowboys hadn't heard. While those who would take the second watch slept, Red, Charlie, and Arch were very much occupied.

"Bonita," said Arch, "you got nothin' to worry about. All of us has fought Comanches in Texas since we was old enough to hold and sight a long gun."

"I can't help worrying," the girl said. "I've never had anybody to . . . to worry about, and I'm just so afraid . . . something will happen. I wish you'd just let them have the cows."

"No way I'd agree to that, if there's a thousand Paiutes," Arch said. "All I own is just a hundred cows, and my share of the loss would cost me every one. It's the same with Eli, Felton, Red, and Charlie. We all got to have the money from the sale of our few cows because it's hard times in Texas. I aim to go back in style, not hungry and broke as the day I rode out."

Red had just had a similar conversation with Molly Rivers.

"Six thousand dollars," said Holly. "I never dreamed there was that much money in all the world."

"There is," Red assured her, "and it's waitin' in California. When we ride home to San Antone, I aim to *be* somebody, not that poor, ragged bastard, Red Bohannon."

"I like the part about riding home," said Molly. "It's just that I've had so little, for so long, I can't believe there's anything more. If anything happens to you, I'll still be the same ragged Molly Rivers I've always been."

"Nothin' will happen to me," Red said. "Just you don't worry."

But the fear she was about to lose all she seemed to have gained was strong on her mind. But she wasn't alone. The same fear stalked Wendy Oldham.

"Charlie . . ." said Wendy.

"What?" Charlie inquired.

"I . . . I don't really know what to say. About tomorrow, I . . . I'm afraid."

"Don't be," said Charlie, taking both her hands in his. "Some of those are our cows, and we purely can't afford to lose 'em. They're the difference between us ridin' back to Texas flush or broke and hungry."

"Wherever you go, I want to go with you, and I want you alive. Even if we are broke and hungry."

The second watch took over at midnight, and Don Webb found himself pretty much alone. His four companions were attempting to ease the minds of their worried women.

"Damn it," Don said, when he finally had a chance to speak to Bob Vines, "that bunch of females acts like all of us are goin' to be strung up at dawn. They weren't as spooked when we were up against more than a hundred Utes."

Bob laughed. "There's been considerable water gone under the bridge since then, pard. These ragged ladies have tied what's left of their lives to a bunch of Texas cowboys, and they're not of a mind to lose any of us. Can you blame them, knowing what they've been through and the little they've had?"

"I reckon not," Don said. "It's just hard to get used to all this doom and gloom on a trail drive. Every man of us knew when we left Santa Fe that this would be hell with the lid off. Now, before we see even a single Paiute, we have this bunch that already has us scalped and shot full of arrows."

"Don't let it get to you," said Bob. "When the time comes, every one of us will back you till hell freezes. You know that."

Feeling guilty about leaving Don alone on watch, Bob had left Sarah long enough to talk to Webb. He returned to Sarah.

"He's angry with us, isn't he?" Sarah said.

"Not really," said Bob. "He's just not used to . . . well . . . this situation on a trail drive."

"He's said very little to any of us," Sarah said. "Does he have a woman of his own?"

"Back in Texas," said Bob. "Most Texans wouldn't feel that a trail drive is the place for a woman."

"Do you feel that way?"

"Under normal circumstances, yes," Bob said. "But there's nothing normal about all of you being held captive by the Utes, and us taking you away from them. There's not a man in Texas—even a killer or thief—who would have left any of you captive. We could only take you with us, and we did that, but it's created a situation that's a mite uncomfortable. Not only do we have to concern ourselves with staying alive, we're forced to consider what will become of all of you, if something *should* happen to us."

"We're a burden to you," Sarah said.

"I haven't lied to you," said Bob, "and I won't. You— and the others—are a burden only to the extent that we fear something will happen to you when we're unable to protect you. Every man fears something or somebody may harm his woman when he's not there to defend her, and that's not just on a dangerous journey such as this. Many a Texas woman has been taken captive or killed by outlaws or hostile Indians. We would have the same fears for you, if all of us were home in Texas. But here on the trail, the danger is much greater. Do you understand?"

"Yes," Sarah said. "It's not your fault that we're with you on this trail drive, no more than it's ours. But we have much for which we should be thankful. If all of you hadn't come on this drive, and if we hadn't been captives of the Utes, then none of us would ever have met. Does that make a difference to you?"

"Yes," said Bob, "and hard as this drive is on us all, it's worth it. I've been trying to recall the women I know back in Texas, and I can't think of a one that measures up to you. If not for this drive, I'd never have found you."

Mike Horton had been trying unsuccessfully to calm the fears of Rose Delano.

"Suppose all of you are killed when you raid that Indian camp," Rose said.

"We're Texans," said Mike. "We won't be."

"But suppose you are?" Rose insisted.

"Then you'll have to make do with a Paiute brave," said Mike angrily.

Rose said no more, and the silence grew long and painful.

"I'm sorry," Mike said. "That was uncalled for."

"Not really," said Rose. "I wanted you to promise me something that would take all the worry from me, and you couldn't. It's me that should be sorry, because I only fear what will happen to me, if something should happen to you. I am so selfish."

"With good reason," Mike said, "and I can't blame you for that. I only wish I could tell you that nothing will go wrong, that we'll take back our cows and all of us will come through it with our hair still in place. I can only tell you that all of us have been through the fire more than once, and that we expect to come through it this time. But I can't go any farther. Only God can get beyond that."

"You've said and done all I have any right to expect," said Rose. "Instead of unloading all my fears on you, perhaps I should get back in touch with God and say some prayers for all you."

"Bueno," Mike replied. "That'll do more good than all the worry."

The night passed uneventfully, and the outfit gathered for breakfast before first light. While they were saddling their horses, Don told them what he had in mind.

"Instead of riding in from the southeast, as they'll expect, we'll circle around and ride in from the west. I'll find the way to reach the box end of that canyon, study the situation, and get back to you. Any questions?"

There were none, and they rode south along the river. They passed up the beaten path where the cattle had been driven away to the southeast, and when they were five miles to the south, Don led them eastward. Frequently they reined up, listening. There was no wind and eventually they heard the distant bark of a dog.

"All of you remain here with the horses," Don said quietly. "I won't make any moves until I've come back and told you what I have in mind. Then we'll all work together to get our herd and get out of here alive."

Carrying his Henry, Don was soon lost in the brush and pinnacles of rock that thrust up from the rugged terrain. He paused often, listening, and once he heard the dog bark again. He moved on, careful to avoid any dead branches, loose rock, or dried-out pine cones. Eventually he could see what he believed was the box end of the canyon, for there was an outcropping of rock that rose out of the earth like the prow of a ship. Carefully, looking to left and right, Don crept forward. Reaching the stone parapet, he dropped to hands and knees. A rock that had looked solid suddenly rolled away, causing a clatter. Don paused, holding his breath. Hearing nothing, he continued, removing his hat as he neared the crest of the rock. Reaching it, he peered into the canyon below.

"My God," Don breathed aloud.

The cattle were near the box end of the canyon, just as he had hoped. Beyond them, next to the Paiute camp, were the horses. Don estimated there were close to two hundred. The Paiutes had their cook fires nearest the entrance to the canyon, along a stream. There was sandy floor from one end of the canyon to the other, with virtually no graze, and Don sighed with satisfaction. He had seen enough. Quickly he retraced his steps, making his way back to his comrades. He spoke quickly, allowing them no time to ask questions.

"There's nearly two hundred horses, and they're between our herd and the Paiute camp. There's water in the canyon, but no graze. Before the sun is noon-high, those longhorns will be hungry, ornery, and hard to hold. We have time on our side."

"They'll have to take their horses out to graze," said Bob.

"That's exactly what we're goin' to be waiting for," Don said. "Then we'll scatter them from here to yonder. That should draw the rest of them out of that canyon and allow us enough time to go after our herd."

9

"*T*hose Paiutes must have expected us yesterday or last night," Bob Vines said. "They'll know they can't hold the longhorns much longer, and I can't imagine them driving all that bunch of ornery critters out to graze and then driving 'em back."

"You bet they won't," said Don. "That's too much like hard work. They herded them into that canyon to start with only because they expected us to come after them. We just complicated things for 'em by not showing up soon enough."

"There's a possibility they took the horses out to graze during the night," Charlie said. "That could complicate things for us."

"That would be more difficult in the dark, with a chance some of the horses might be lost. If we're still waitin' at sundown and they haven't taken the horses to graze, then I'll have to agree with you. But we won't have to wait much longer. The longhorns will be givin' 'em hell pretty soon," said Don.

Within minutes, as though fulfilling a prophecy, the longhorns began acting up. There was distant bawling of a few, growing in intensity as the others joined in.

"They'll soon be gettin' the hell out of there pronto," Mike predicted.

"That means the Paiutes will have to move their horses

or risk having them caught up in a stampede," said Don. "Come on. We'll have to dismount and lead our horses the last few hundred yards."

As the Texans drew nearer, the dismal bawling of the longhorns became louder. There was an even greater din, as some of the dogs joined in with a barking chorus. Don reined up, his companions following suit. They all dismounted, taking their rifles, and made their way on foot to the head of the canyon. With the furor going on below, there seemed little chance they would be discovered. The longhorns had been pushing and shoving, and some of the horses were being raked with horns. Already there was a fearful nickering, as the Paiutes struggled without success to get ropes on their mounts. The Texans grinned at one another. This bunch of Paiutes was learning what might become an expensive lesson.

"It's goin' even better than I expected," Don said softly. "They'll have to drive all the horses out in a bunch, and as soon as the last horse is clear of that canyon, we're gonna be right on their heels. Bob, I want you to take Jim, Les, Mike, and Felton with you. Get to the far rim of that canyon pronto, making your way to the shallow end. Red, Charlie, Arch, Eli, and me will follow the near rim, comin' together with the rest of you near the shallow end. We're going to run those horses so far, the Paiutes won't find them for a month. Let's ride."

The Paiutes had their hands full. Every one—from the youngest to the oldest—who owned a horse was trying to separate their animals from the bawling, kicking longhorns. Wounded horses nickered in pain and in fear, and many Paiutes were carrying or dragging to safety their unfortunate comrades who had been raked with savage horns. Finally most of the horses were headed toward the shallow end of the canyon, the Paiutes running after them, lest they stampede. But several of the animals, in haste and in fear, ran through the ash-concealed coals of burned-out fires. Crying in pain, they broke into a gallop, the rest of the herd following. By the time they streamed out the shallow mouth of the canyon there was no stopping them. Except for those gored by the restless longhorns, every one was caught up in a full-fledged stampede. The frustrated, shouting Paiutes were left behind and on foot, and they soon discovered to their dismay that their problems were just beginning. Thundering down the canyon in a bawling fury came a thousand head of longhorns intent on destroying anything or anybody in their path. Paiutes who were near enough, ran for the mouth of the canyon, while others attempted to climb the walls. Squaws dropped cooking pots, and seizing their young, ran for safety. Some were trampled as they tried to scale the canyon walls. When the last of the horses were out of the canyon, the Texans were right behind them, shouting and shooting. They ran the herd for miles, fanning out and scattering them. Finally, their own horses exhausted, they reined up.

"I hated to see the longhorns run," said Bob, "but wasn't it almost worth it, seeing the Paiutes gettin' a good dose of trail-drivin' revenge?"

"Almost," Don said. "But some of the squaws and young 'uns may have been trampled."

"I know," said Bob. "I'd hate that, even if it wasn't our fault. Where do we go from here?"

"We'll circle back to the far end of that box canyon," Don replied. "We'll keep out of sight, so the Paiutes can remove their dead. When we're sure they've all gone in search of their horses, some of us will start beatin' the bushes for our cattle."

The Texans rode wide of the canyon, coming in near the box end. Dismounting, they crept to the rim. The scene below was ghastly. Three horses were dead, and a fourth lay thrashing and squealing in agony. On the sandy canyon floor, nine braves lay sprawled, unmoving. Beyond them, in the wreckage of the camp, lay the bodies of five squaws. Most tragic of all, beside each of them lay a dead child. While it had not been of their doing, the Texans were touched. Don Webb had removed his hat and bowed his head. When his companions sneaked looks at him, there

were tears on his dusty cheeks. By ones and twos, some of
the Paiutes drifted back into the canyon and began removing their dead.

"Bob," said Don, "I want you, Jim Les, Mike, and Felton to return to our camp while the rest of us begin searching for our cows. I think these Paiutes will go after their
horses before they try anything else, but we can't be sure.
They were big losers, and their medicine's all been bad."

"If we aim to follow that river south a ways, we could
drive the rest of the herd a mite closer," Bob said. "Any
of the cows you're able to gather, you won't have as far to
drive them."

"That might be wise," said Don. "Go ahead and move
them downriver, maybe another five miles. Whether we do
or don't gather the rest of the herd, we'll see you before
sundown."

Bob and his companions rode north, while Don and his
riders again circled the canyon to pursue their stampeded
longhorns.

"None of us got a scratch," Bob reported, when the five
of them returned to camp. "All the Paiute horses stampeded. Unfortunately, our cows stampeded with them. Don
and the others have gone in search of our herd. We're
gonna move our camp five miles downriver."

"Oh, I'm so glad none of you were hurt," Sarah cried.

None of the others said anything, but the relief was in
their eyes. Quickly the riders bunched the herd, while Dominique and Roberto loaded the pack mules. Within an hour,
the outfit had the herd moving downriver. Several miles
beyond where the Paiutes had first driven the cows away
from the river, they headed the herd and settled them down
on what graze there was.

"Them longhorns will be gettin' thirsty and lookin' for
water," said Charlie. "I wonder which way they go, when
the time comes?"

"Perhaps they'll return to the canyon where the Indians
were holding them," Rose said.

"No way," said Charlie. "There's the smell of death. They'll never return there."

Reaching the shallow end of the canyon, Don and his riders reined up.

"We can't ride too far too fast," Don said. "While that bunch is armed only with bows and arrows, I don't doubt they'd take time in their horse-hunting to kill and scalp us. We'll keep to the open as much as possible."

"While we were stampeding those horses, we didn't cross a stream of any kind," said Red, "and we know the varmints won't be goin' back to that canyon. Question is, where will they go in search of water?"

"We had those horses a good distance ahead of them," Don said, "so I don't figure they ran too far. With any luck, maybe they've angled off to the south, so we can follow them without catching up to the Paiutes. Let's see where the tracks lead us."

Less than a mile beyond the mouth of the canyon, the cow tracks turned south.

"They've slowed down," said Eli.

"They're more hungry than thirsty," Charlie said. "Maybe we can round 'em up before they get a hankerin' for water."

Within another mile, they began seeing grazing cows. But the graze was skimpy, and there was rarely more than two or three animals grazing together.

"We'll gather as we go," said Don, "so we don't have to come back this way."

They rode on, following the erratic tracks.

"They're driftin' west, back toward the river," Arch said. "I never would of believed a cow was that smart."

"They're not," said Don. "The graze gets better, back toward the river. They're drawn toward that."

"Let's hope it don't draw that bunch of horses, with the Paiutes following them," Arch said.

"Not likely," said Red. "We must have run them a good fifteen miles, and there's got to be water ahead of them that's closer than this river to the west of where we are.''

They continued following the tracks, and it soon became obvious that the cows were indeed headed toward the river where the rest of the herd waited.

"Look at their strides," Charlie said. "They ain't even botherin' to nip at the little bit of grass along here. They know there's somethin' better ahead."

Red laughed. "Yeah, like water. There's a little breeze in our faces, and that's all it'll take to get the interest of a cow. They've had three hours of sun, and when a longhorn gets thirsty, the varmint just naturally forgets all about graze."

"That's the truth," said Don. "We've found less than a hundred of them, and from the tracks, I'd say we'll find the rest of them somewhere ahead, maybe along the river."

Bob and his riders, as a precaution, circled the herd they had just brought downriver. Suddenly and distinctly there was the distant bawling of a cow somewhere to the south.

"Can that be one of our bunch?" Jim Roussel wondered. "When they lit out of that canyon, they were headin' east, after those Paiute ponies."

"True," said Bob, "but we were right behind the horses, keepin' them running. Those longhorns didn't have anybody drivin' 'em, and once shy of that canyon, they might have run another direction. Maybe south. The wind's out of the west, and one whiff of this river could have 'em headed back this way. The rest of you stay here, while I ride downriver and see."

Bob hadn't ridden more than five miles when he sighted grazing cattle. Others were in the water, drinking.

"Horse," Bob said aloud, "Don and the boys lucked out. Let's get back to camp."

Less than three miles east of the river, Don and his companions had no trouble with the hundred or so they had gathered, for the longhorns knew there was water ahead. Their thirst wasn't yet stampede-strong, but it was sufficient to keep them trotting at a faster than usual gait.

Red laughed. "Look at 'em go. This has to be the easiest gather in the history of trail-driving."

"Don't crow too loud too soon," Don cautioned. "We're gettin' our herd back, but we don't know that those Paiutes won't coming looking for us once they catch their horses."

"Maybe they will," said Red, "but I reckon they've learned one thing. You don't take a bunch of Texas long-horns hostage and hold 'em without graze."

"Or water," Charlie added.

Soon they were within sight of the line of green that marked the banks of the river. The cows broke into a gallop, thrashing through the brush and into the water. Along the banks, other longhorns grazed.

"I'd bet my hat they're all here," Don said. "Let's ride downstream and work our way back. Maybe we can gather them all and reach camp in time for supper."

They rode along the river until they could see no more grazing cows on either bank.

"Red, you and Charlie cross over to the other bank," said Don, when they were ready to ride upstream.

While Red and Charlie found only a few cows along the opposite bank, they drove all of them across the river until there was a single herd. After not quite two hours, they bunched their gather in with the rest of the herd.

"That should be all of them," Don said. "Let's run some tallies."

The low count was 5,200.

"We can live with that, I reckon," said Bob.

"There may be a few more downriver," Mike said, "if this river's good for another day's drive."

"We'll have another look at the map," said Don, "and in the morning I'll ride ahead far enough to decide what we should do."

They spread out the map and studied it, paying particular attention to the river along which they traveled.

"Look there," Bob said, pointing. "This stream that we're following goes on south, but almost joining it is another that flows west, toward Nevada Territory.''

"Then what we need to know," said Don, "is where we leave this river to reach the fork in this other one. Once we're on it, the trail follows it right on into Nevada."*

"*Si,*" Dominique said.

When Don spread out the map, Dominique and Roberto were always there, quick to agree or disagree with its claim. The outfit had learned to appreciate their knowledge of this old trail.

The Colorado River. June 6, 1862.

Griff and his band of renegades had made their camp alongside the Colorado where the bank was low enough for them to reach water and to water their horses. Except for easy access to the water, it was a poor location, for the opposite bank was a jumble of rock and shallow arroyos that permitted the Utes to conceal themselves while creeping close enough so that the outlaw camp was within range of their arrows. Having had their horses stampeded and their comrades slaughtered by the white man, the Utes thirsted for revenge. At first light, they struck.

"Indians!" Doolin shouted, dropping the coffee pot. An arrow had buried itself in his shoulder.

Seeco, Fedders, and Ibanez were struck by the deadly barbs before any of the renegades could fire a shot.

"Shoot, damn it!" Griff shouted.

The renegades *were* shooting, but their position was poor, while the Utes were loosing their arrows from cover. When gunfire from the defenders became too heavy, the Indians retreated, vanishing like smoke.

"They're gone," said Griff. "Hold your fire."

"You've been through these mountains before," Hernandez said accusingly. "Why didn't you warn us about Indians?"

---

*The Virgin River, which flows into the Colorado near the Grand Canyon.

"Because I've never been attacked by Utes," said Griff angrily. "They must have come out on the short end of a fight with that bunch of Texans."

"Tell it to Seeco and Ibanez," Hernandez said. "They've rode their last trail."

Both men lay on their backs, arrows buried deep in their chests. Fedders had an arrow in his left thigh.

"All of you take the horses half a mile west of the river," said Griff. "We'll set up our camp there, get some fires going, and some water on to boil. Those arrows will have to come out of Doolin and Fedders."

"Seeco and Ibanez deserve to be planted where the varmints can't get at 'em," Bullard said. "Don't you aim to bury 'em?"

"Find a shallow arroyo and cave it in on them," said Griff. "That is, unless some of you feel like digging somethin' more decent with a spoon or Bowie knife."

His attitude was callous, unfeeling, but his comrades expected nothing better. Bullard and Rodriguez took the horses belonging to Seeco and Ibanez and went looking for a place to bury them. Griff and the rest of the bunch took the remaining horses and their supplies well beyond the river, where there was no convenient cover for another attack by the Utes.

"Quando," Doolin said, "you've had experience with arrows. Will you drive this one on through?"

Quando laughed. "What's it worth to you?"

"It might be worth me doin' the same for you sometime," Doolin snarled.

"Quando, if I tell you to drive that arrow through, you'll do it," said Griff.

"I don't want his damn hands on me," Doolin said, through clenched teeth.

"I'll take care of it," said Hernandez, "after I'm done with Fedders. I'll need a bottle of that whiskey, Griff."

"All kinds of volunteers," Quando sneered, "when they can get their hands on a bottle of redeye."

"Quando," said Griff, "shut up."

Quando laughed but said no more. He stood at ease, his right hand near the butt of his Colt, but Griff ignored him. From his saddlebag he took a bottle of the whiskey and handed it to Hernandez. Uncorking it, Hernandez passed the bottle to Doolin, who downed half of it. When Fedders took his turn, he drank the rest.

"No more," Griff said, "unless they come down with fever."

"That'll slow us down, them bein' wounded," said Kenton.

"Three or four days, maybe," Griff replied, "but it won't make any difference. We're on the trail of a herd of cows, and for us, time ain't a problem. Besides, them of you that gets in a hurry, there's somethin' you better keep in mind. We ain't free of Indians by a jugful, and the next hombre sweatin' an Indian arrow might be you."

They went about moving their camp, every man with his rifle handy. Suddenly there was a thump of hooves, as Bullard and Rogriguez returned at a fast gallop. They swung out of their saddles, and there was a bloody gash along the left flank of Bullard's horse.

"Indians," said Rodriguez.

"Damn," Lennox growled. "You coyotes ride out to plant Seeco and Ibanez, and come back bringin' more Indians."

"We didn't have time to plant Seeco and Ibanez," said Bullard. "The same bunch that cut down on us was just waitin'. Arrows was flyin' ever'where."

"Hell, I can understand you leavin' Seeco and Ibanez, them bein' dead," Quando said, "but why did you leave their horses an' saddles? We could of used them."

"We had to ride like hell, just gettin' away with our hair," said Rodriguez angrily. "If them horses and saddles mean all that much to you, then you just mosey on out there and get 'em."

Some of the men laughed and Quando's hand dropped to the butt of his Colt, the look on his face ugly.

"Go ahead, Quando," Bullard said, his thumbs hooked under his gunbelt.

"Yeah, Quando," said Rodriguez. "I ain't never liked you, and the more I see of you, the less I like you."

"I don't like a damned one of you," Griff said, "but for the time being, I need you all. I'll kill the first man pullin' iron."

Slowly Quando relaxed and the standoff was avoided.

Northwestern Arizona Territory. June 7, 1862.

"I'll ride ahead and see how much farther we can follow this river without losing the Old Spanish Trail," Don said. "Keep your rifles handy and watch the back-trail. We don't know how soon some of those Paiutes will find their horses."

Once the herd was moving, Don rode downriver. The map indicated that the river flowed into the Colorado somewhere to the south. Far from that confluence, however, they must again travel west, if they were to follow the old trail. Don rode what he believed was fifteen miles, as far as the herd could travel in a day, before riding west in the hope of again finding the trail that would lead them to Los Angeles. After riding at least a dozen miles westward, he came upon a stream that was on the map but was unnamed. The map indicated that the old trail followed the stream for a distance into southeastern Nevada. It was enough for the time being, for they were assured of water for two days. Don rested his horse, watered the animal, and then rode eastward until he reached the river the drive was following. He then rode north until he met the herd. He waved his hat, pointing south, a signal that they were to continue. He rode ahead of them, and when he reached the place where they must turn west to return to the trail, he signaled a halt. The riders headed the longhorns, bunching them along the river. After supper, before time for the first watch, Don told them what he had discovered.

"From here, it's maybe a dozen miles west, where we'll pick up the old trail again. As the map seems to indicate, the trail follows an unnamed river a ways into Nevada, where we'll be crossing its southern tip into California."

"We're not that far from California then," said Rose.

"No, we aren't," Don agreed, "but it's a long hard ride from there to Los Angeles, and our map don't show a stream anywhere between western Nevada and Los Angeles. But it does show the Mojave Desert."

"*Si,*" said Roberto. "*Desierto. Malo.*"

"Do you and Dominique know where there's water in the desert?" Don asked.

"*Si,*" said Roberto. "*Rio abajo desierto.*"

"River under the desert," Bob said.

"*Si,*" Dominique agreed.

"You can find it then," said Don.

"*Si,*" Dominique said.

"Per'ap," said Roberto.

Don looked uncertainly from one of the Mexicans to the other. Dominique and Roberto conversed for a moment in rapid Spanish. Finally both of them nodded to Don.

"You can find it, then," Don said.

"*Si,*" said the pair in a single voice.

"I hope they know what they're talking about," said Sarah.

"So far, they've been more dependable than the map," Bob said. "If there's water under ground, there's likely just a few places where it will surface. Even then, the water may be poisoned with alkalai and undrinkable."

"How do you know if it's poisoned?" Sarah asked.

"By tasting it," said Bob. "Trouble is, if the cattle are thirsty, they'll stampede toward the nearest water, and we won't be able to hold them."

"After bringing them this far, they could drink poisoned water and die," Sarah said.

"They could," said Bob. "Our only hope is that Don, with help from Dominique and Roberto, can guide us to clean water."

There was little conversation that night, as they all contemplated the dread desert that lay ahead. Nobody bothered with the map, for it showed no water from southwestern Nevada all the way to Los Angeles.

"There'll be time enough to concern ourselves with the crossing of the desert when we get there," Don said. "Dominique and Roberto seem sure of themselves."

There was no disturbance during the night, and none of the outfit was aware that anything was wrong until they arose at first light.

"Ellie, Millie, and Bonita are gone," said Rose, her voice trembling.

"Gone!" Don all but shouted. "They've been told not to wander at night."

"But they did," said Rose. "They must have."

"The damn Paiutes have them," Jim Roussel shouted. "Let's saddle up and go after the varmints."

"Nobody's going anywhere, until we know for sure," said Don.

"But they've got Ellie," Roussel groaned.

"They also have Millie and Bonita," said Les Brown. "You ain't goin' nowhere without me and Arch."

"Quiet, damn it," Don said. "Bob, you and Mike begin circling the camp clockwise. Red, you and Charlie circle from the other direction. Sing out when you find any sign."

The rest of the women huddled together, nobody saying anything. Dominique and Roberto had begun breakfast as though nothing out of the ordinary had happened.

"Hell, *all* of us should be lookin' for signs," said Roussel.

"With all of us trompin' around, there wouldn't *be* any sign," Don said in disgust.

Red and Charlie made the discovery.

"Indians took 'em over yonder near the water," said Charlie. "Crossed the river with 'em, where they had horses waitin'. Six of the varmints, and they rode north."

"We can't leave the camp unprotected," Don said.

"Five of you will have to stay here, while the rest of us trail those Paiutes and rescue the girls."

"I'm goin'," Roussel bawled. "They took Ellie."

"I'm goin' too," said Les Brown. "They have Millie."

"I got to go," Arch said. "They got Bonita, and I aim to kill some Paiutes."

"Wrong," said Don. "None of you are going. The last damn thing we need is a bunch of hotheads ready to kill at the drop of a hat. It's the surest way to have the Indians kill all three of the girls. Bob, Mike, Red, and Charlie, you'll ride with me. The rest of you keep your rifles handy and your eyes open. If six of them have found their horses, there's a chance the others have. This could be a trick to draw some of us away, while the rest attack the camp."

"Damn you, Don Webb," Roussel shouted, "you can't—"

"I can, and I have," said Don. "I'm trail boss. Now shut up."

He didn't like it, but he said no more. Les Brown and Arch Danson looked equally grim, but they kept their silence, as Don and his companions saddled their horses and rode across the river.

"Oh God," Sarah moaned, "I hope they can rescue the girls alive."

"If they don't," said Jim Roussel, "I'll personally wipe out every damn Paiute in this territory."

"Like hell," Les Brown said. "Some of them belong to me."

"And me," said Arch.

Nothing more was said. They settled down to await some word from their comrades, hoping for the best and fearing the worst.

10

The Paiutes had taken Ellie, Millie, and Bonita silently by seizing the girls, a hand over their mouths, and clubbing them senseless. When the three of them came to, they were far upriver, each belly-down over a horse on which a Paiute rode.

"Ellie, Millie!" Bonita cried.

A blow to the back of her head stunned her, and before her companions could answer her desperate cry, they too were struck. When Bonita again regained her senses, she went for the Paiute's bare leg, sinking her teeth into it. The Indian reacted violently, and threw her head-first from the horse. Her head struck a stone, and before she could move, the Paiute had dismounted. He seized her, threw her belly-down over the horse, and mounted behind her. Seeing her mistreated, Ellie and Millie began screeching and fighting. Suddenly all the Paiutes reined up their horses and dismounted. One of them took each of the girls by her hair, and the three of them were dragged to the ground. Their hands were forced behind their backs and their wrists were bound with rawhide. Their ankles were bound in a similar fashion, and each of them had a wad of dirty cloth stuffed in her mouth. They were then flung belly-down over horses, Paiutes mounting behind them. The barking of dogs marked their arrival at the Indian camp. They were dragged off the horses, their gags removed, and then they were thrown into a teepee. The flap was closed behind them.

"Damn them," said Bonita. "At least they could have untied us. My arms and legs are asleep."

"I'm afraid that's the least of our problems," Ellie said. "After what happened to them in the canyon, what will they do to us?"

"Arch will come after me," said Bonita. "Don't you think Jim and Les will be coming after you and Millie?"

"I suppose they'll try," Ellie said, "but Don's the trail boss. He may not allow them to come after us."

"That's what worries me," said Millie. "He was always telling us not to be up walking about after dark, and we disobeyed."

"We only went to the river for a cool drink," Ellie said. "How were we to know these damn Indians would be lurking there?"

"We'd better be thinking about what we can do to help ourselves," said Bonita. "After we've been used by these Indians, I'm afraid our men won't have us."

"Oh God," Ellie said, "they'll use us and then kill us."

"They may kill me," said Millie, "but they won't use me. I'll give them hell."

"So will I," Bonita vowed. "I'd as soon be dead as to live like a squaw."

"I suppose we'll soon know what they have planned for us," said Ellie. "They're getting awful noisy out there."

All too soon, one of the Indians entered the teepee. With his knife he slashed the raw-hide bonds binding Bonita's arms and legs. He forced her to her feet and she fell, for her legs were numb.

"*Esposa*," said the Indian, seizing her again. "*Esposa de Mirlo.*"

With one brawny arm about Bonita, he drew aside the teepee flap and stepped outside.

"Oh God," Millie said, "I remember one of those words from our time with the Utes. *Esposa* means 'wife,' I think."

Bonita was led to a roaring fire, and in the shadows surrounding it, she could see the grim faces of many Indian braves. The Indian who had dragged her out of the teepee took her by the hair, forcing her to stand in front of him, facing the multitude.

"Mirlo," said her captor, loudly enough for them all to hear. *"Esposa de Mirlo."*

One of the Indians, whom Bonita believed might be the chief, left the circle, stepping forward. He spoke.

"Esposa de Mirlo muerto." Pointing at Bonita, he spoke again. *"Esposa de Mirlo."**

"Esposa de Mirlo," the rest of the Indians shouted in a single voice.

The Paiute—whose name was Blackbird—took that for tribal approval, and throwing Bonita over his shoulder, he disappeared into the darkness.

Oso Pato—Bear Paw—entered the teepee where Ellie and Millie fearfully awaited their fate. Millie's bonds were quickly severed and the Paiute forced her to stand, but her feet and legs wouldn't hold her, and she would have fallen if he hadn't supported her.

"Esposa," said Bear Paw. *"Esposa de Oso Pato."*

"Don't let him take you, Millie," Ellie said. "Fight him."

"I'll try," said Millie, with more courage than she felt.

Bear Paw led the girl before the assembled Paiutes and the same ritual was performed. He then flung Millie over his shoulder and set out for his teepee.

Lizard—Lagarto—entered the teepee where only Ellie waited.

"Esposa," the Paiute said. *"Esposa de Lagarto."*

He forced Ellie out of the teepee ahead of him, taking her before the tribe. For a third time the assembled Paiutes shouted their approval. Taking Ellie over his shoulder, Lagarto disappeared in the darkness. Mirlo, Oso Pato, and Lagarto had lost their wives because of the bad medicine brought upon them by the white man. Now it was only

---

*"Wife of Blackbird dead. Wife of Blackbird."

fitting that the whites should pay. Three Paiute braves had taken white squaws. There would be more . . .

Don, Bob, Mike, Red, and Charlie had no trouble following the trail. It led north, along the river.

"We know one thing for sure," Charlie said. "They're expecting us. They didn't bother trying to hide their trail."

"That's bad news in more ways than one," said Red. "By the time we find their camp, they'll have had the girls long enough to ruin them."

"Maybe not," Don said. "Those women are young, but they're tough. We took them from the Utes, after they had failed to take them as wives. I don't look for the Paiutes to be any more successful."

"I think you're right," said Bob. "Trouble is, the Paiutes could slit their throats before we can figure a way to rescue them."

"Indians are inclined to torture captives before killing them," Don said. "It's not a very pleasant thought, but it could buy us some time."

"We'll likely need some time," said Charlie. "We got maybe ten hours of daylight, and I can't see us making any moves before dark."

"It all depends on the situation," Don said. "If the girls refuse to become squaws, then the Paiutes may not waste any time. We could find ourselves facing a showdown long before dark."

It was the small hours of the morning, and pitch dark in the teepee to which Mirlo took Bonita. Sliding her off his shoulder, he dropped her on the bare ground with a force that rattled her teeth. While she couldn't see him, she felt his groping hands. Doubling her fist, she swung hard, smashing his nose.

"Ugh," Mirlo grunted. "Ugh."

Bonita came off the ground scratching, clawing and kicking. The Paiute was off balance, and when he tumbled over on his back, Bonita was astraddle of him. It was a near perfect position, and she drove her knee into his groin. Before he doubled up, she drove the knee in a second time. Rolling away from him, Bonita got to her hands and knees and started slapping the sides of the teepee, seeking the closed flap. Not finding it, and desperate, she slammed her bare foot against the base of a lodge pole. It was torn loose, and Bonita took advantage of the small opening. Ramming her head through, she was almost free, when she was seized by rough hands. She kicked and fought, but the two squaws outside were too much for her. A third squaw opened the flap, and Bonita was flung back inside the teepee. Mirlo had recovered somewhat, and she felt his hand on her face. Bonita sank her teeth into one of his fingers. Doubling his other fist, the Paiute slammed it into the side of her head. Bonita was barely conscious, but managed to roll away from him. Feeling stones beneath her—a fire ring—she seized one and swung it with both hands as hard as she could. There was a dull thud as it connected with the Paiute's head, and there was only his labored breathing. Feeling carefully, Bonita found the teepee's flap, and she tore through it in such a fury the squaws couldn't stop her. But a pair of Paiute braves did. Laughing, they dragged the kicking and clawing girl back toward the teepee, only to see Mirlo emerging on hands and knees. He spoke rapidly, angrily, and their laughter ceased. The braves dragged Bonita back toward the fire, the bloodied Mirlo following.

Oso Pato had an equally hard time with Millie Nettles. The Paiute began shouting so violently at the girl, that several men of the tribe entered the teepee and removed her. Oso Pato approached the fire, his face and bare chest a mass of bloody scratches. His left leg seemed stiff, and he walked with a limp.

"*Cobarde*," someone shouted. "*Oso Pato cobarde*."

The last thing any Indian wished to be called was a coward, and Oso Pato turned on his tormentors in a fury.

"*Gato*," Oso Pato shouted. "*Diablo gato*."*

---

*Devil cat.

Under the watchful eyes of the Paiutes, Bonita and Millie
were stood side-by-side near the fire. It seemed they were
all waiting for something, and it wasn't long in coming.
The screams from Lagarto's teepee were not screams of
terror, but of anger. Finally there was a thrashing about that
threatened to collapse the teepee, and eventually Ellie
crawled out, unmolested. Finally, Lagarto emerged, clearly
reluctant to face his comrades, some of whom were laughing openly.

"Esposa de Lagarto?" the chief asked.

Dejectedly, Lagarto shook his head. Blood oozed from
many scratches on his face and chest, and his right thumb
was twisted in an unnatural position. Two braves seized
Ellie and stood her beside Millie and Bonita.

"I suppose none of us made it as wives," Bonita said.

"No," said Millie fearfully. "Now they have something
else in mind for us."

"I'm afraid I know what it is," Ellie said.

Three stakes, head-high, had been driven into the ground,
a few yards from the fire. The Paiute whom they believed
was the chief pointed to the three of them and spoke in a
thunderous voice.

"Torturar."

Half a dozen screeching squaws rushed forward, two of
them seizing each of the scared women. The three of them
were backed up to stakes to which their wrists and ankles
were bound with rawhide. With slender branches, all the
squaws gathered around them, lashing their backs, arms and
legs. They could only close their eyes and take the beating.
When it was finally over, it seemed they were ignored. The
fire had burned down to coals, and but for three squaws,
the Paiutes had disappeared.

"They don't intend to burn us at the stake," Bonita said.

"Not yet," said Millie.

"That comes later," Ellie said. "They've given up on
us as squaws."

"I'm dying for water," said Bonita.

"I made some while they were whipping us," Millie said.

"So did I," said Ellie. "I think that was the purpose of the whipping. They wanted to humiliate us."

"Well, I don't feel humiliated," Bonita said. "That Paiute tried to take me, and I gave him more than he expected."

"I think we all did that," said Millie, "but a lot of good it's going to do us, if we die at the hands of these savages."

"We're not dead yet," Bonita said, "and the longer we stay alive, the better our chance of being rescued."

"Nobody will miss us until dawn," said Ellie, "and I can't imagine them sneaking up on this bunch of Paiutes in daylight. They're camped right out in the open."

"I know it seems hopeless," Millie said, "but I thought it was hopeless when the Utes had us. There was as many or more of them as there is in this bunch."

"These men we're hoping will rescue us are Texans," said Bonita. "If there's a way to save us, they'll think of it."

Among those left with the herd, the mood was grim. Jim Roussel, Les Brown, and Arch Danson paced the riverbank, cursing the Paiutes. The four women said little, and when they talked at all, it was among themselves.

"I have confidence in them," Sarah said. "When we believed all was lost, they were able to rescue us from the Utes."

"It's not that I don't believe in them," said Rose. "There are so many Indians, I fear that nothing can be done until after dark. God knows what will happen to Ellie, Millie, and Bonita by then."

Again a barking dog alerted the Texans they were nearing the Indian camp.

"We'd better shy away from the river," Don said. "They may be camped alongside it."

"There's a ridge over yonder," said Bob. "We should

be able to see for three or four miles without being seen."

They crossed the ridge, riding along the far side until there was sufficient cover for them to approach the crest of it afoot without being seen. From there they were able to see the river, including the portion where the Paiutes were camped.

"Damn them," Charlie said, "the girls are tied to stakes. This don't look good."

"In a way, it's better than I expected," said Don. "From the looks of things, those Paiutes didn't waste any time trying to take advantage, and if they had been successful, the girls wouldn't be tied to stakes. With the bringing in of captives, the Paiutes have likely been up most of the night. They're getting some rest before continuing their sport."

"They know we'll be coming," Charlie said, "yet all I see is three squaws."

"You're forgettin' they have dogs," said Red. "That pack would be barkin' their heads off before we could get within hollerin' distance."

"There's an arroyo over yonder beyond their camp," Bob said. "If we were to conceal ourselves there, we'd be within rifle range, and we'd have a better view than from here."

"We're going to consider that," said Don, "but unless it runs well beyond the Paiute camp, we can't get into it without being seen."

"It had better be deep enough to hide the horses," Mike said. "We get too far from our horses, and that bunch can ride us down, even against our Henrys."

"All we can do is try," said Don. "We'll ride downriver until we're out of sight of the camp. Then we'll ride east and see if we can work our way into that arroyo."

But when they left the river, riding east, there was no arroyo where they had hoped it would be.

"It doesn't extend down this far," Bob said. "It may be a dead end."

"We can go a little farther north," said Don. "We'll have to leave our horses here, and I'm not one to leave them unwatched this close to an Indian camp. The rest of you remain with the horses, and I'll do some scouting on foot.''

It was the sensible thing to do, and Don was soon lost in the underbrush. There was a light wind out of the west, and eventually he smelled wood smoke. The Paiute camp was coming alive, and whatever they had in mind for Ellie, Millie, and Bonita might not be long in coming. To Don's relief, he soon came upon the blind end of the arroyo. It was deep enough to conceal men and horses, but the horses couldn't be taken into it until it became more shallow. To lessen his chances of being seen or heard, Don made his way down the rim to the canyon floor, where there was an abundance of sand and little else. To his dismay, when the arroyo's rims became low enough to get the horses into it, the Paiute camp was entirely too close. Don hurried back to his companions.

''This arroyo doesn't shallow down soon enough,'' Don said. ''We'll have to leave the horses here and take our chances afoot.''

''Bad news if they discover us,'' said Bob, ''but what other choice do we have?''

Nobody said anything, for they all knew the answer. Tying their horses securely, they took their rifles and slid down the rim into the arroyo. They halted where the rim was just high enough for them to stand upright and view the Paiute camp. Some of the squaws had switches, whipping the three bound captives.

''Damn them,'' Mike Horton said. ''I'd like to shoot them down, women or not.''

''I know how you feel,'' said Don, ''but it's too soon for us to make our move. They're suffering now, and they may have to suffer a lot more, before we can set them free.''

''We're in big trouble, if they just decide to burn them at the stake,'' Charlie said. ''All of us would be dead before we could get to them. Even if by some miracle we were able to free them, we'd never make it back to our horses.''

"We can't get our horses into this arroyo," said Bob, "but we can bring them a lot closer. There's plenty of cover beyond us, to the east."

"There's also a west wind," Don said. "Bring our horses in line with that Paiute camp, let them smell the Paiute mounts, and you're just asking for one of ours to nicker. I know we're risking our necks, but our horses stay where they are."

Sudden activity in the Paiute camp captured every man's attention.

"They're goin' somewhere," said Mike.

"Damn right they are," Charlie said. "They're ridin' downriver, and there must be fifty or more."

"My God," said Bob, "they figure we've had enough time to split our forces, and now they're headin' for our camp."

"So are we," Don said. "Nothing is likely to happen here until they return."

They ran along the arroyo until they were well away from the Paiute camp. Then they quickly scaled the rim, mounted their horses and rode south.

"From which direction do we ride in?" Mike asked.

"It won't matter," said Don. "There'll be enough of them to surround the camp."

"Indios!" Dominique shouted.

The Mexican wranglers were the first to begin firing at the approaching Paiutes. But the Indians reined up just shy of rifle range, split their forces and began moving left and right, in an ever-widening circle.

"Tarnation," said Jim Roussel, "there's enough of 'em to surround us."

"Just what they got in mind," Felton Juneau said, "and they aim to taunt us into wasting as much ammunition as possible. Don't shoot until you know they're in range."

"By then, they'll be close enough to rush us," said Eli Mills. "Hell, they'll come at us from ever' direction. Five of us can't shoot that fast or that accurate."

"Maybe not," Les Brown said, "but we got to try."

"Come on, you bastards!" shouted Arch Danson.

"Dear God," Sarah cried. "There are so many of them."

"They must have been waiting for Don and the others to ride away," said Rose.

There was absolute silence, for Dominique and Roberto had ceased firing, realizing the Paiutes were still out of range.

To the north, Don and his companions had heard the few shots, and reined up, listening. But the silence seemed more ominous than the gunfire, and they rode on.

The Paiutes continued to advance, and suddenly with a whoop they came galloping in from four sides. Just as quickly they withdrew, for the defenders poured forth a withering fire. But their respite was short-lived, for the Paiutes attacked again, withdrew, and then attacked a third time. But suddenly, beyond the ranks of the attacking Indians, there came the rattle of gunfire. Horses galloped away riderless, and the remaining Paiutes kicked their mounts into a mad gallop, seeking to escape with their lives.

"Rein up," Don shouted to his companions.

Nobody spoke. They rode on into camp.

"Lord Almighty," said Felton Juneau, "you gents are a welcome sight."

"Anybody hurt?" Don asked.

"No," said Jim Roussel. "Where's Ellie, Millie, and Bonita?"

"Where the hell do you think?" Charlie English demanded angrily. "It wouldn't have been any help to the girls if we'd set up yonder watching that Paiute camp while half the varmints rode down here, shot all of you full of arrows and took your scalps."

Roussel was about to shout an angry response when Don stopped him.

"The girls are alive," said Don. "There may be nothing we can do until dark unless the Paiutes force us to make

our move. It's unlikely they'll hit you again, because they
lost pretty heavy. Reload your weapons and be ready for
anything. We have to return to our position and do what
we can to rescue the girls.''

Les Brown seemed about to explode with anger, but
Rose Delano quieted him. Quickly Don and his companions
wheeled their horses and rode away. Avoiding the river,
they rode northeast, reaching the close end of the arroyo
they had so recently departed. There was a distant wailing
in the Paiute camp, testimony to the effectiveness of Henry
rifles.

"Let's go," said Don. "God knows what effect this will
have on the captives.''

"Could be bad news," Red agreed. "Maybe half that
bunch that rode south didn't come back. The others are
likely in a killing mood.''

Leaving the horses, the five of them crept up the arroyo
to their former position. The sight that met their eyes wasn't
encouraging. The three captives had been stripped naked
and squaws were lined up in two long rows, facing one
another.

"They aim to kill them," Bob said, "but they'll have
some fun with them first. They'll have to run the gauntlet.''

"Them damn squaws has got clubs heavy enough to
break an arm or leg, or crush a skull," said Charlie. "Them
three women won't ever live through that.''

"They'll have to," Don said. "It's the only chance they
have. The way those squaws are lined up, the girls will be
running this way. They have to reach this arroyo, and it'll
be up to us to see that they do. We'll have to see that those
Paiutes lose interest in everything except these Henry rifles.''

"Shoot to kill then," said Mike.

"Yes," Don said. "We have no choice, but we won't
shoot the squaws. While the men won't take part, they'll
be close enough to watch, and they'll also be within rifle
range. They're already gathering, and I'm gambling that
one holding his horse is the chief or medicine man. He'll

mount the horse for a better view, and when he does, I'll shoot him off it. That'll be the signal for the rest of you to cut loose. Make every shot count. After the first couple of volleys, our targets will be coming after us."

"We'll have a chance, as long as we can shoot," said Red, "but when the girls get here—if they do—we'll have to run for our horses. That's all the time the Paiutes will need. They'll mount up and ride us down."

"We're not going to give them that chance," Don said. "I want you to bring all of our horses up here, as near the canyon rim as you can, but keeping them under cover. Then come on and join us in time for the shooting."

"As you pointed out a bit earlier," said Bob, "with our horses that close, one of them could nicker, giving us away."

"I haven't forgotten," Don said, "but we're now in a position where it's well worth the risk. The wind's died down some. Get goin', Red. We don't have much time."

Ellie, Millie, and Bonita had watched fearfully as a great number of Paiutes had ridden downriver, for they believed they knew where the Indians were going. But within no more than two hours, less than half the Paiutes had returned, and some of them were wounded. Mirlo, Oso Pato and Lagarto were among those who had not returned, and the others seemed to blame the captives. Squaws threw sticks and stones at the three helpless women bound to stakes.

"Now they'll kill us for sure," Bonita cried.

"Not for a while," said Millie. "They have something else in mind."

The three cringed when a squaw approached with a long knife. Wordlessly, she cut the rawhide thongs that bound the three captives to the wooden stakes. Two other squaws, each armed with knives, approached the first. Each of them seized one of the girls, and with deft strokes of their knives, they stripped the captives naked. The braves looked on, while the squaws laughed and jeered. Bonita, Ellie, and

Millie were allowed to stand there just long enough to regain the feeling in their feet and legs. Then they were prodded to the upper end of the two lines of squaws who had
begun gathering. Some of them had only switches or heavy
sticks, but a few had clubs or lances. One of the squaws
seized each of the naked captives by the hair, halting them.
One of the squaws grunted, pointing down the corridor between the lines of those who waited in anticipation.

"Dear God," said Bonita, "they're going to make us
walk through there. They'll beat us to death."

"Maybe not," Millie said. "I'll be running, not walking,
and if I can get my hands on one of those clubs, I'll crack
some heads."

"So will I," said Ellie angrily. "Don't give up, Bonita."

But before the terrified women could be forced through
the gauntlet of vindictive squaws, a shot rang out. The Paiute chief toppled from his horse, and for a moment, the
Indians were shocked into immobility. Like echoes of the
first, other shots rolled like thunder through the stillness,
and Paiute braves fell to rise no more.

"They've come for us!" Ellie cried. "Run!"

Evading the squaws with their clubs and sticks, the
women ran frantically toward the distant arroyo. But the
braves had taken up their bows and were loosing arrows at
the fleeing women. Bonita screamed. One of the deadly
barbs had buried itself in her left thigh, and when the leg
gave way, she fell. Hearing her cry, Ellie and Millie paused,
looking back.

"Come on!" shouted a voice from the arroyo. "Run!"

Ellie and Millie ran on, for there was nothing they could
do to help Bonita. Fearfully she looked back, as arrows fell
all about her. The Paiute braves were coming closer . . .

11

Again Ellie and Millie paused, reluctant to leave the wounded Bonita.

"Come on," Don shouted.

"Cover me," said Mike. "I'll go get her."

Before anybody could object, Horton was over the arroyo rim and running toward the terrified Bonita, a blazing Colt in his hand. He cut down two of the pursuing Paiutes, and as firing from the arroyo grew more intense, the others dropped back.

"Oh, you shouldn't have," Bonita cried, when Mike knelt beside her.

"Hush," said Mike. "I'll have to carry you over my shoulder, so I can run with you."

He hoisted the girl over his shoulder, and with arrows zipping all around them, made his way back to the arroyo. There were shouts of joy from Ellie and Millie, as Don and Bob took Bonita and brought her into the safety of the arroyo. But it wouldn't be safe for long.

"We have to get out of here," Charlie said. "They're mounting up to cut us off."

"The rest of you get to your horses," said Red. "I'll hold 'em off long enough to give you a start."

"No," Don said. "We're all in this together, and we'll live or die together."

"Most of them are mounted," said Charlie, "and they're

splitting up. They're comin' at us from north and south, aimin' to trap us here.''

"Charlie, you and Red get the horses down here," Don said. "A few more yards, and this arroyo shallows down enough for them to get in and out. We're ridin' right through that Paiute camp to the river."

Without question, Red and Charlie obeyed, and even as they led the horses into the arroyo, there was shouting and the thump of hooves as the Paiutes closed in on them from two directions.

"Bob, you and me will lead the charge," said Don. "Bonita, Ellie, and Millie, you'll be riding double with Mike, Red, and Charlie, and you'll have to ride behind them so their hands are free to use their Colts."

Mike mounted his horse and lifted Bonita up behind him. Red positioned Ellie behind him, while Charlie quickly lifted Millie up in similar fashion. With Bob and Don in the lead, they trotted their horses far enough up the arroyo for the horses to climb out. While the majority of the Paiutes had mounted their horses and were seeking to close the jaws of a trap from north and south, a dozen of them still crept toward the arroyo directly from the Indian camp. They were taken totally by surprise when they found themselves facing five horsemen, each with a Colt in his hand. They scattered, and as the Texans galloped toward the distant river, only the squaws stood in their way.

"Don't shoot them," Don shouted.

But one of the squaws sprang at Mike's horse with a knife, and he slugged her with the muzzle of his Colt. The others offered no resistance, and with a pack of dogs yelping madly at their heels, they rode on. Reaching the river, they rode south. The band of mounted Paiutes, who had ridden south hoping to trap them in the arroyo, had changed course and were galloping their horses back toward the river.

"Rein up and use your rifles!" Don ordered.

No explanation was necessary, for they all knew they must dispose of this band, before the others rode in from the north and joined the attack. Expecting to find their prey riding for their lives, the Paiutes burst into the open and were confronted by a hail of lead while still too distant to attack with bows and arrows. More than half of them were shot from their horses, dead or wounded, before the others could gallop out of range.

"Now let's ride, before the rest of them get here," said Don.

The brief pause had allowed their horses to rest, and they continued south at a slow gallop. But there was no pursuit. Their comrades saw them coming from a distance, and there were glad shouts.

"You're hurt," Arch said, as he lifted Bonita from Mike's horse.

"It's nothing," said Bonita. "Mike saved me."

"I owe you one, amigo," Arch said.

Mike said nothing, for his eyes were on Rose Delano. There were tears on her cheeks.

Ellie and Millie were quickly lifted down, and they stood there, their faces flaming red.

"Damn it," said Don, "some of you bring some blankets. The Paiutes stripped them, and we didn't have time to go looking for what was left of their clothes."

"There was nothing left," Bonita said. "Squaws used knives. Clothes or not, I'm just thankful to be alive."

But Arch was there in record time with a blanket. With equal speed, Jim Roussel and Les Brown brought blankets for Ellie and Millie.

Bonita laughed. "We're in a fine mess, nothing but blankets to cover us from here on to California."

"But you got to wear it," Arch said angrily.

"I don't *have* to wear it," said Bonita, matching his anger. "After all I've been through, I don't feel like taking orders from you, Arch Danson. Mike, will you remove this arrow from my thigh?"

"Yes," Mike said uncomfortably. "Arch could do it."

"No, Arch can't," said Danson. "You won't see nothin' you ain't already seen. Go on, take it out."

Dominique and Roberto, understanding the need, already had a pot of water hung over the fire. From his saddlebag, Don took a quart of whiskey and handed it to Mike. Rose had already spread a blanket beneath a tree, where the others couldn't observe Bonita's ordeal.

"Here," Mike said, handing Bonita the whiskey. "Drink about half of this. We might as well take that arrow out and be done with it."

"Come with me," said Rose. "I've spread a blanket where you can lie down."

"While Mike's removing that arrow," Don said, "the rest of us are goin' to stand ready with our rifles. We hurt those Paiutes, but there's still enough of them to make it hot for us if they decide to."

When Mike went to Bonita, she lay on the blanket with a second one over her. There hadn't been enough time for the whiskey to take effect, and she spoke.

"What's wrong with Arch? I thought he would be satisfied that I'm alive."

"He is glad you're alive," said Mike. "I reckon he's got a burr under his tail because he wanted to ride to your rescue, and Don wouldn't let him."

"But Ellie and Millie were captured too," Bonita said. "Jim and Les didn't rescue them."

"Don wouldn't allow any of them to go," said Mike, "because they were half-crazy. He was afraid they'd ride in shooting and get the three of you killed along with themselves."

Bonita laughed. "He's a wise man, but I think there's something else bothering Arch. He said you could go ahead and remove the arrow because you wouldn't see anything you hadn't already seen. He's blaming you and me, because the Indians stripped me."

"I heard him," Mike said, "and I should have punched his ears down around his boot tops. That was a crude thing to have said, after all you've been through."

"You wouldn't have felt that way, if Rose had been captured, and was brought back like . . . I was?"

"No," said Mike. "I'd have been glad she was brought back alive. You'll have to overlook what Arch said. He's not a day older than eighteen, and I doubt he's ever had any talk with a woman except his mama. Besides Don refusing to let him go ridin' off, mad as hell, looking for you, he's got a bad case of jealousy bitin' at him. Right now, he's about as miserable as a cow caught in a bog hole, and he ain't got the foggiest idea as to what he can do to make things right. He'll come crawling around, and when he does, don't make it too easy for him."

Drowsy, her eyes slits, Bonita laughed. "I like you, Mike Horton. Perhaps I'll just tell him to go to hell, and fight with Rose over you."

Mike said nothing. When her eyes closed, he began rolling up his shirt sleeves. Rose arrived with the pot of boiling water and knelt down beside Bonita.

"This won't be pleasant to watch," Mike said. "You don't have to stay."

"I know," said Rose, "but I want to."

Mike punched the loads from the cylinder of his Colt. He then broke the shaft of the arrow, leaving just enough length to drive it on through. Because of the position of the arrow in Bonita's left thigh, she lay on her right side. To drive the barb on through, she must lie belly-down, and Mike rolled her over. Gripping the muzzle of the Colt, he used the butt of the weapon, striking the protruding shaft of the arrow. Even under the influence of the whiskey, Bonita grunted with pain. The barb advanced slowly. Even though there was a light breeze, and they were in the shade of a tree, Mike's shirt was soon dark with sweat, and it dripped off his nose and chin. The Colt became slippery in his hands, and he often stopped to wipe them on the legs of his Levi's. When the arrow's deadly barb finally fell free, Mike leaned back, breathing hard. Rose was ready with a clean cloth and hot water to wash the wound. She then poured some of the whiskey into it. She had prepared two cloth pads, and these she soaked in whiskey. One was placed over the wound where the arrow had gone in, and the other over the wound where it had been driven out. She then bound the pads securely, and covered Bonita with the blanket.

"You're badly in need of a fresh shirt, Mike," said Rose.

"I know," Mike said, "but I don't have one. This one will dry, and it'll be washed during the next rain storm."

"I'll stay with Bonita," said Rose.

Mike ducked his head in the river, using his hands to wipe his face and to squeeze the water from his hair. He then joined the rest of the outfit.

"How is Bonita?" Don asked.

"She'll be all right in a couple of days," said Mike.

"Bueno," Don said.

"Since we'll be here until Bonita can ride," Bob said, "I think we'd better see if those Paiutes are still around. I don't like this settin' on ready, not knowing if they're coming after us or not."

"I aim to do some scouting after dark," said Don. "This has been a bad day for them. They lost their chief and at least thirty warriors. If our luck is as good as theirs is bad, they'll want to get as far from us as they can."

There was no sign of the Paiutes. When supper was over, and the sun had dipped below the western horizon, Don saddled his horse. The men assigned to the first watch were already circling the herd. Dominique and Roberto had already cross-hobbled the horses the women rode, as well as the pack mules and the horse remuda. When Don was within half a mile of where the Paiute camp had been, he left his horse and continued on foot. While there was only starlight, he could see well enough, and when he reached the clearing, there was no sign of the Paiutes. Satisfied, Don returned to his horse, mounted, and rode downriver.

"Rein up and identify yourself," said Charlie softly.

"Don, comin' in," he replied.

The men on the first watch had all reined up, and when the rest of the outfit gathered around, Don spoke.

"The Paiutes seem to have pulled out. At least, there's

no sign of them beside the river where they were this morning.''

"Bueno," said Jim Roussel. "They've had enough bad medicine."

"I hope so," Don said, "but we can't afford to gamble. We'll continue with a five-man watch, but when you're sleeping, be sure your horse is picketed, and don't shuck anything except your hat. Dominique, you and Roberto move all your horses and mules close to the herd. Be sure they're all cross-hobbled, and they won't be goin' anywhere, even if the herd should run."

Don and the rest of the second watch settled into their blankets to get what sleep they could. On the first watch, Arch Danson dismounted, and walking his horse, approached the tree under which Bonita slept.

"Who is it?" Rose asked cautiously.

"Arch. How is Bonita?"

"Sleeping," said Rose. "You won't be able to talk to her until sometime tomorrow."

"I was hoping I could talk to her tonight," Arch said.

"Perhaps you talk too much," said Rose.

"I reckon I do," Arch said. "I don't rightly know *what* to say to her, when she's able to talk."

"You can start by telling her you're sorry for some of the things you said today," said Rose. "It wasn't her fault the Paiutes stripped her, and it certainly wasn't the fault of Mike and the others that they rescued her in that condition."

"It was her fault she got captured in the first place," Arch said. "She left camp with Ellie and Millie after Don had warned them not to."

"I won't deny that," said Rose, "but stirring up a fuss over it now won't change anything. Have you never disobeyed and felt sorry for it afterward?"

Arch laughed. "You got me there. Paw whipped me till my hide wouldn't hold shucks, but mostly I wasn't all that sorry. Just sorry I got caught."

"Bonita's been mistreated most of her young life," Rose

said. "She's been whipped and cursed, with never a kind word. If you want her, treat her decent."

"You done some of the whipping, so you don't practice what you preach," said Arch.

"No, I don't," Rose admitted, "but I learn from my mistakes. I've begged Bonita and the others to forgive me, and they have."

"If Bonita forgave you, surely she'll forgive me," said Arch.

Rose laughed. "Not necessarily. I'm not expecting her to sleep with me for the rest of her life."

"I reckon I deserved that," said Arch.

"I'm sorry," Rose said. "That was unkind. I'll talk to her some, when she wakes. Then you can talk to her."

"I'm obliged," said Arch.

When he had mounted his horse and ridden away, there was a giggle from beneath the blanket where Bonita lay.

"You little wench," Rose said. "How long have you been awake?"

"Long enough," said Bonita. "Since Arch first spoke to you."

"I ought to go after him, and make you talk to him tonight," Rose said. "He's scared and miserable."

"No more scared and miserable than I was, when the Paiutes had me," said Bonita. "Let him suffer some."

"From what Mike said, he wasn't all that angry with you," Rose said. "He was really angry with himself. When we learned the Indians had taken you, Ellie, and Millie, all of us were scared. But Arch, Jim, and Les started shouting about killing Paiutes, and Don didn't allow any of them to ride to the rescue."

"So Arch took it out on me."

"Yes," said Rose. "That's what it amounted to. It was childish temper. There are some things in life we all have to accept, not because we like them, but because that's how they are. You didn't see me giving Mike hell, when he rode in with you riding jaybird naked behind him."

"You could have," Bonita said. "Weren't you just a little jealous?"

"A little," said Rose. "You're fresh and unspoiled. I was used goods before I was taken to the mission school."

"I'm sorry," Bonita said. "I never knew."

"I never told anybody except Sarah," said Rose. "But I told Mike. He's a kind, decent man, and if he wants me, then he'll know what he's getting. I won't live a lie."

"I saw the way Mike looked at you before Arch helped me down from Mike's horse," Bonita said. "He would have rescued any woman, just as he rescued me."

"Yes," said Rose, "and you can't be sure that Arch wouldn't have done the same had he had the chance. He's young, with a lot to learn."

"But he hasn't been honest," Bonita said. "I ought to tell him I was had by some Paiute men, and see how he feels about used goods."

"Don't you dare," said Rose. "A spiteful, lying woman is nothing more than the devil's pawn."

While Jim Roussel and Les Brown were angry when Don had forbidden them to ride to the rescue of Ellie and Millie, both men had satisfied themselves with the safe return of the women. When Jim and Les went on the second watch at midnight, they managed to take a few minutes with Ellie and Millie.

"Don's hardly spoken to me or Millie," Ellie said. "He must hate the three of us for disobeying and leaving camp."

"He doesn't hate any of you," said Roussel. "I think he was mostly afraid for you, like the rest of us."

"You know him a lot better than I do," Ellie said. "I've never seen him when he looked the least bit afraid."

"Only a fool is never afraid," said Jim. "Despite what a Texan says and how he acts, he can be scared just like anybody else. The difference is courage. Courage allows him to go on when common sense tells him it may be his last trail."

Les Brown was having a slightly easier time with Millie.

"I was ready to ride off and kill every Paiute I could get in my sights," Les said, "but Don wouldn't let me."

"I wondered why you, Jim, and Arch didn't come looking for us," said Millie.

"Don was afraid we'd go off half-cocked and get all of you killed, along with the three of us," Les said sheepishly. "I reckon he was right, but it made me feel like a damn fool, settin' here in camp, when I felt like I should be ridin' to rescue you."

"Well, I don't think any less of you," said Millie.

The night passed without any sign of the Paiutes, and the outfit began to feel a little more secure. Don found Rose with the still-sleeping Bonita.

"How is she, Rose?"

"Better, I think," said Rose. "She had a fever at midnight, and I've given her whiskey twice since then."

"Bueno," Don said. "She ought to be sweating soon."

Arch Danson waited as long as he could. Immediately after breakfast, he was there beside Bonita.

"She's sleeping off a fever," said Rose. "You'll have to wait a while longer."

"Tell me when she's able to talk to me," Arch said. "That is, if she *wants* to talk to me."

Rose nodded, saying nothing. The sun was noon-high when Bonita finally awoke. She was able to speak only in a whisper.

"Water," she croaked.

Rose filled a tin cup four times before the girl's thirst was satisfied.

"Dear God," said Bonita, "I don't ever . . . want any more . . . of that stuff. My head feels like a rock."

"But you needed it," Rose said. "Your fever's broken. Arch was here a while ago. He wants to know when you're able to talk to him. That is, if you want to."

"I might as well talk to him now," said Bonita. "There's no way I could feel any worse than I do already."

"This might not be a good time then," Rose said.

"Good as any," said Bonita. "Send him over here."

Arch arrived, and Rose left them alone.

"How do you feel?" Arch asked, shifting from one foot to the other.

"Like hell," said Bonita, not helping him in the slightest.

"I . . . I'm sorry about . . . what I said yesterday," Arch stammered. "I shouldn't have said . . . what I did."

"Then why did you?" Bonita asked.

"I . . . I . . ." Arch looked down at the toes of his boots.

"You were jealous," said Bonita unmercifully. "Jealous because I rode in naked behind Mike Horton. Don, Bob, Red, and Charlie saw me naked, and so did every last one of the Paiute men. What are you going to do about that?"

"Nothing, I reckon," Arch mumbled.

"Well, I'm still naked," said Bonita, flinging away the blanket. "I kind of like it. I may never wear clothes again. So there!"

"Damn you, Bonita Holmes," Arch roared, "if you wasn't wounded, I'd . . . I'd . . ."

"You'd what?" asked Bonita, with a devilish smile.

"I'd take my belt to you," Arch all but shouted. "I won't have a woman behavin' like . . . like you are. I said I was sorry, damn it. Now you accept that, or tell me to go to hell, but stop beatin' around the bush."

"Of course I'll accept your apology," said Bonita sweetly. "Whatever gave you the idea that I wouldn't?"

For a moment, Arch just looked at her, unbelieving. Without a word, he retrieved the blanket she had cast away and spread it carefully over her. He then turned and walked back along the river, toward camp.

"Arch Danson," said Bonita softly, "before I'm done with you, you're going to become a man."

Sunset came early as the sun slipped behind a fortress of dirty gray clouds that had gathered on the far western horizon. Like crimson, mile-high feathers, the last rays of the sun reached far into the blue of the sky.

"There's a storm building up," Charlie said. "It'll hit us not later than tomorrow night, I'd say."

"I'd say you're right," said Don. "It's just as well we'll be here another day and night. At least we have some open space alongside the river, without any tall trees to draw the lightning. Maybe this won't be a bad one."

But as the night drew on, the clouds became heavier, and a rising wind was cause to doubt the storm would delay much longer.

"It's gonna blow before morning," Red predicted.

"Whenever it comes, and whatever comes," said Don, "all of us will be in the saddle until it passes. It'll come roaring out of the west, and if the herd's inclined to run, they'll run to the east. We'll move our camp, with supplies, pack mules and the horse remuda up river a ways. Every animal we're not using will be cross-hobbled. With the river behind the herd to the west, I want every rider in the saddle and blocking them to the east. It'll be our only hope of heading them."

"If they get scared enough to run," Bob said, "we can't hold them, unless you're willing to risk some or all of us being trampled."

"You know I won't risk that for every damn cow in Texas," Don said. "We'll form a line fifty yards east of the herd. If we can't calm them, once they surge to their feet to run, I want every man of you riding to get out of their path. Don't risk your life when it becomes obvious we can't head them."

By midnight, the sky was a mass of low-hanging gray clouds, rolling like waves on a restless sea. The wind moaned through distant pines, and thunder rolled far away. There was an occasional flash of lightning as it caressed the billowing clouds with jagged fingers of gold. Riders trotted their horses back and forth, seeking to calm the longhorns. When the rain began, it came in sweeping gray sheets, staggering both horse and rider. Thunder rumbled ever closer, and the blinding flashes of lightning became more frequent. Some of the steers had begun bawling nervously, and catching the fever, others joined in. The herd had been at rest, but when a few rose to their feet, the rest soon followed. It seemed they were waiting for something, and suddenly it came. Somewhere beyond the river, to the west, lightning struck. There was a crackling, an earth-shaking crash, and the leaden sky virtually exploded in a brilliant burst of light. For a few seconds, it was as though time stood still, while cattle, men, and horses were in shock. The longhorns recovered first. In a bawling frenzy of terror, they stampeded, the wind and rain at their backs. Riders drew their Colts, but the sound of gunfire was swallowed up in the fury of the storm.

"Ride," Don shouted. "Ride for your lives."

But his voice was lost in the roar of the wind and the rumble of thunder. He kicked his horse into a fast gallop, seeking to get beyond the far-reaching avalanche that was the running longhorns, hoping his comrades would follow. The rest of the riders gave it up, riding for their lives. Don looked back, and in a flash of lightning, he saw a riderless horse galloping ahead of the oncoming stampede. Wheeling his horse, he started back, but there was no time. In a brief flash of lightning, he saw a lone figure standing in the path of the thundering herd, his hands raised helplessly heav-enward. Then the pathetic figure was gone, swallowed up under twenty thousand trampling hooves. Sick to his soul, Don rode on, dreading what he knew must follow. The stampede roared on, until finally there was only the rumble of diminishing thunder and the howling wind. The rain slacked only a little, and it seemed hours before Don saw the first of the riders. Slowly they all came together, nobody speaking. When finally the wind and rain had diminished enough for them to hear, Don shouted his command.

"If you can hear me, sing out."

One by one, they answered, until only Eli Mills was un-accounted for.

"Anybody seen Eli?" Don asked needlessly.

"I saw his horse," said Mike Horton. "I started back to

look for him, but there was no time. I barely made it myself.''

''I saw the horse too,'' Don said. ''Eli didn't make it.''

''Oh God,'' said Les Brown, ''I talked him into comin' on this drive, when his family didn't want him to . . .''

His voice trailed off into a sob that was lost in the moan of the wind.

''We can't find him till first light,'' Don said. ''Then we'll do for him what's fittin' and proper.''

Sadly, in silence, they rode back to their camp.

12

The rain subsided and the clouds broke up, revealing a few stars and a quarter moon. As had become their custom, Dominique and Roberto had banked the cook fire with dirt, and with dry wood from within one of the canvas packs, the fire soon sprang into life. The coffeepots were placed over the fire, and soon there was hot coffee. It was sorely needed, for nobody slept the rest of the night. The tragic loss of Eli Mills had saddened them all.

"I feel just awful," Sarah said, as she sat beside Bob Vines in the darkness. "Eli was just a young man, with his whole life ahead of him."

"It's especially hard on Don," said Bob. "This is the kind of thing that can happen on any trail drive, but this time, Don feels responsible."

"But he wasn't, was he?"

"No," Bob said. "It might have happened to any one of us. It's a cowboy's job to head the herd, if he can. Don warned all of us not to cut it too close, to save ourselves if we couldn't head the lead steers. I think Eli's horse stumbled, pitching him off. It's just one more thing that can't be helped."

Don Webb had said nothing more after he had spoken to the outfit immediately after Eli's death. During the second watch, his rifle in his hands, he hunkered beside the river, staring into the dark water.

"I wish there was something we could do, something we could say," said Rose softly.

"There is nothing," Mike Horton said. "I have some idea how he feels. I could see the riderless horse, and in a flash of lightning, just seconds before he went down, I could see Eli with his hands raised. Maybe he was praying. I would have been."

After leaving Mike, Rose found Bonita awake.

"How are you feeling?"

"Just terrible," said Bonita. "I keep remembering how I treated Arch, and I . . . I can't help thinking it . . . might have been him . . . instead of Eli . . ."

"Like the rest of us, he's wide awake," Rose said. "Do you want me to send him over here, so the two of you can talk?"

"I wish you would, Rose," said Bonita.

It seemed the night would never end. Finally the gray of first light gave way to the golden rays of the sun, as it rose into a blue, cloudless sky. Nobody said anything about gathering the scattered herd. Although they knew it must be done, there was a sad duty—perhaps more a grim responsibility—that must first be done. Don spoke to them after breakfast.

"I'm going to look for Eli. Those of you who want to are welcome to join me."

"I'm going," said Les Brown.

Quickly, the rest of the men volunteered.

They soon found what remained of Eli's horse. It had been gored. The rain had created an enormous amount of mud, and only the buckle of Eli's gunbelt was visible. The pistol was gone, and when they found the mangled, broken body of Eli Mills, the weapon was clutched in his right hand. Eli lay in a shallow arroyo. For a long moment, they looked at what remained of their comrade. Then, to a man, they knelt and wept. There, but for the grace of God, might lay any one of them.

"We'll bury him here," Don said, when finally he was

able to speak. "Red, bring one of my blankets, the folding shovel, and the Bible from my saddlebag."

"I'll do it," said Red, "but what about the women? Do you want them to come?"

"Only if they want to," Don said, "and then only after you've brought the blanket and we've covered him. They shouldn't have to see him like this."

"The women are all coming," said Red, when he returned with the requested items.

Don carefully covered Eli with the blanket, and they waited for the arrival of the seven women. A blanket draped over her, Bonita limped along, holding to Rose for support. All of them wept over the blanket-draped body, and it was a moment before Don's voice was steady enough to read scripture. He opened the Bible to the Twenty-third Psalm, which he read. Closing the Bible, he spoke quietly.

"Lord, I can't tell you anything about Eli you don't already know. He was a good man, saddled with the same sinful nature as the rest of us, depending on Your grace for his salvation. May his soul rest in peace."

"Don," said Red, "the rest of you go on back. I'll take care of him."

"I'll stay and help," Charlie said.

Don nodded. Slowly they started back toward the river, as Red began shoveling dirt into the shallow arroyo.

"Give me a turn," said Charlie. "We'll pile it deep."

Three-quarters of an hour later, Red and Charlie joined their companions.

"Red, I want you and Charlie to remain in camp," Don said. "The rest of us are going to look for the herd."

The seven of them rode out, knowing the risk they faced. While the Paiutes had moved on, they might recognize the scattered herd as an opportunity to attack the riders or the near-defenseless camp. They had traveled almost five miles before there was evidence that the herd was slowing. There were occasional tracks where individual steers had broken away, and soon there were lots of three or four of the animals grazing.

"We'll ride on," Don said, "and gather these on the way back."

"Unless there's water somewhere ahead," said Mike, "these varmints will be going back to the river they ran away from."

"That's what happened the last time they ran," Bob said. "Can we be so lucky again?"

"Not for a while," said Don. "They can make it the rest of the day. But come sundown they'll be ready to water. A little wind out of the west will gather them quicker than we ever could. Right now, we're as much concerned with Indians as with cows. If those Paiutes know the herd's scattered again, they might decide to attack us or the camp."

The riders topped a rise, and below them was a shallow meadow with some graze.

"Must be a thousand head down there," Jim Roussel said, "but there's no water."

"We passed up another five hundred getting here," Don said. "I'm thinking we'd better take this bunch, and with those we'll gather along the way, drive them back to camp. The others may have drifted south, and if they have, our river will be the closest water."

They rode on down the slope with the intention of getting on the opposite side, behind the grazing cattle.

"I'd better ride up that other ridge and take a look," said Mike.

Horton was near the fringe of brush, when an arrow grazed the flank of his horse. It was all that saved him, for his horse began to buck.

"Come on," Don shouted. "Mike's in trouble!"

Drawing their Henrys, they galloped up the slope, arrows whipping all about them. But before they saw any of the attackers, it was all over. Only Mike's horse had been hit, and the wound wasn't serious.

"That answers one important question," said Bob. "The Paiutes haven't given up."

"No," Don said. "I was afraid of that. If Mike hadn't surprised them, they would have come roaring down behind us as we tried to bunch the cattle. Shooting down-hill, their accuracy wasn't all that good. Come on. Let's move those cows.''

"Once we get our gather back to the river, maybe we oughta go looking for that Paiute camp,'' said Mike.

"Not in daylight,'' Don said, "but we're not going to give them another chance at us or our camp. We'll wait and see if the herd doubles back to the river. If they come to us, we won't worry about the Paiutes. But if we're still missing a bunch, then after dark, we'll go looking for that Paiute camp.''

"Good,'' said Mike. "If we have to do some serious gathering in Paiute country, then I want to know where and how many there are.''

They gathered as many longhorns as they could and drove them back to the river. They ran some quick tallies, and the low count was 1,600.

"We'll see if any more of them show up before dark,'' Don said. "If there's not enough of them, then we'll have to do some serious searching tomorrow. But tonight we'll scout around and find that bunch of Paiutes.''

Many of the longhorns did drift in during the afternoon, seeking water, but there was still a great number of them missing.

"Charlie and me are give out from layin' around in camp all day,'' said Red. "Why don't you let us go lookin' for that Paiute camp tonight?''

"I'm trail boss,'' Don said, "and I figure that's my responsibility. How do you reckon I'd feel if the two of you was shot full of arrows and scalped?''

"That's downright insulting,'' said Red. "You think a few Paiutes can do what every Comanche in Texas ain't been able to do?''

"I'm trail boss,'' Don said, "but I'm willing to put it to a vote. What do the rest of you think? Should I allow Red and Charlie to go Paiute hunting?''

"I don't care,'' said Mike, "but if they get shot full of

arrows and their hair lifted, it's you that'll be breakin' the news to their kin.''

"If Charlie and me gets shot full of arrows and our hair lifted,'' Red said, ''the rest of you had better ride for your lives, because there'll be about a million Paiutes after you.''

It was cowboy boasting at its best—or worst—and everybody laughed except Molly Rivers and Wendy Oldham.

"Go ahead, then,'' said Don. ''But don't do anything foolish. All we want to know is where the Paiute camp is.''

As far as the riders were concerned, the matter was settled, but Molly and Wendy still had something to say.

"Why must you go riding off, looking for that Indian camp?'' Molly asked.

"Somebody has to,'' said Red. ''It's not fair, Don taking all the risk.''

"He's trail boss,'' Molly said. ''He admits it's his responsibility.''

"No matter,'' said Red. ''Charlie and me have a stake in this herd, and we aim to take our share of the risk. Besides, all we aim to do is find the camp and come on back.''

"Suppose you're discovered?''

"We won't be,'' Red replied. ''You don't know what it's like livin' in Texas amongst the Comanches.''

"I was hoping, once this drive is over and we returned to Texas, that I'd never had to look at another Indian,'' said Molly. ''Now you're telling me that Texas is full of them.''

"Not full of them,'' Red replied, ''but there are some. For God's sake, this is still the frontier. Where do you want to live, New York City?''

"Of course not,'' said Molly, ''and don't shout at me. Aren't you glad that I care what happens to you?''

"I reckon,'' Red replied, ''but don't try to hobble me. I won't have it.''

Charlie was having a similar conversation with Wendy Oldham.

"I care what you think,'' said Charlie, ''but you don't tell a man what he can and can't do. Hell, it ain't like I'm robbin' banks or holdin' up stages. There's some risk just bein' alive. The Paiutes could attack the camp and kill us all, but we don't aim to let it happen. Red and me can take care of ourselves. We're just goin' to look for the Paiute camp, not attack it.''

"All right," Wendy sighed. "If you're determined to go, then I suppose there's nothing I can do to stop you."

"No," said Charlie, "there ain't, but I don't like leavin' you with a burr under your saddle. You got a look on your face like soured milk, and I ain't wantin' to come back to that."

Despite herself, she laughed. "Go on then, and I'll try not to disappoint you when you come back."

Red and Charlie waited until after supper, when the last crimson rays of the setting sun had given way to the gray of twilight. As they saddled their horses, the first stars were in the sky. Despite the fact that the Paiute attack had come east of the river, they rode north.

"The varmints know by now that it don't take a lot to get a bunch of longhorns to runnin'," Red said.

"Yeah," said Charlie. "After that storm last night, they got a pretty good idea the herd was scattered from hell to breakfast, and knowin' the storm blowed out of the west, even a Paiute can figure the direction the stampede took."

"I'd bet my part of the herd that Paiute camp's somewhere along this river," Red said. "We already know there's no water east of here, or them cows wouldn't of come wanderin' back."

They rode on, and reaching the former Paiute camp, they rode more slowly. The light wind was from the northwest.

"I smell smoke," said Charlie, reining up.

"So do I," Red said, reining up beside him, "but that don't make sense. The wind's all wrong."

"The wind's all right," said Charlie. "They've set up their camp somewhere west of the river, and we're down-wind from them. We'd better leave our horses here."

They dismounted, tying their horses to a limb, and continued afoot. The smell of wood smoke grew stronger as they progressed. Suddenly Red seized Charlie's arm and pointed into the night sky. Charlie saw the tiny spark just before it winked out.

"They got a fire," Red said softly. "They ain't afraid of us."

"They may be, before we leave these parts," said Charlie. "Come on. Let's get closer, if we can. We need to know how many of them there are."

They crept on, pausing beneath a huge pine. Suddenly, without warning, a pair of silent shadows dropped from the branches above. Charlie and Red went down, each seizing the upraised arm of his attacker just in time, for the Paiutes were armed with knives. Using his free hand, Charlie swung his fist, smashing the Indian on the chin. Off balance, he went down, but like a cat, was on his feet again. Red had dragged his assailant to the ground, and they fought for the knife. The Paiute struggled free, and thrusting with the knife, raked it across Red's belly. But before the Indian could recover for another thrust, Red kicked him under the chin, and he tumbled over backward. Charlie's attacker lunged at him with the knife, but Charlie was ready. Swinging his Colt, he smashed the muzzle across the Paiute's wrist. The Indian dropped the knife, and pursuing his advantage, Charlie hit him in the head with the Colt. With both their assailants down, Red and Charlie tried to catch their breath, but there was no time.

"The rest of 'em heard the commotion," Charlie said. "We'd better get back to the horses, if we can."

Even as they ran, they heard the thump of horses' hooves. When they reached their horses, Charlie swung into the saddle, but Red could not. He clung to the horn, breathing hard.

"Red," said Charlie, dismounting, "what's wrong, amigo?"

"I been cut," Red replied, "and I'm weak. Bleedin' like a stuck hog."

"I'll help you into the saddle and take the reins," said Charlie. "You just hang on."

Charlie helped him to mount and he got his feet into the stirrups. Mounting his own horse and taking the reins to Red's, Charlie rode out. They splashed across the river and headed south, and when Charlie slowed the horses to a walk, there was no sound of any pursuit.

"We lost 'em," Charlie said. "You still with me, pard?"

"Yeah," said Red, "but I'm still bleedin' bad. Let's go."

"Rein up and identify yourselves," a voice said, as they neared their camp.

"Red and Charlie, and Red's hurt," Charlie said.

"Come on," said Don.

Red was clutching the saddle horn with both hands, and would have fallen if Don and Charlie hadn't helped him to dismount.

"Two of 'em jumped us with knives," Charlie said. "Red's been cut, and he's bleedin' bad."

"Bob, Jim, Les, Mike, Arch, and Felton, take your rifles and stand watch. Charlie, take a pot or pan, go to the river and mix a batch of mud while I get the shirt off him," said Don.

"I'm here," Molly cried. "What can I do?"

"Fill a pot with water and get it on to boil just as soon as Dominique and Roberto can stir up one of the fires," said Don.

Don removed Red's shirt. It had been slashed across the front from one side to the other, and was heavy with blood. Rose Delano had spread a blanket near one of the fires, and Don stretched Red out on it. Even in the starlight, they could see blood oozing from the wound. Charlie returned with a skillet of mud. Don knelt beside Red, and dipping his hands into the mud, began covering the bloody slash.

"The water's not hot," Molly protested.

"No matter," said Don. "There'll be time enough for that, after we've stopped the bleeding."

But stopping the bleeding proved difficult. Fresh blood crept out around the edges of the mud, and there was little to be done except use more mud. Nobody spoke, for they all knew the bleeding must be stopped if Red was to live.

"Let me have the skillet," Charlie said, "and I'll bring some more mud pronto."

"This may be enough," said Don. "There's no fresh blood."

There was enough light from the fire for them to see the truth of Don's words, and all of them breathed a sigh of relief.

"Are you hurting, Red?" Don asked.

"Some," said Red, "but not so much I can't handle it. Do what needs doing."

"Charlie, bring a bottle of whiskey from my saddlebag," Don said.

Charlie did so, and Don pulled the cork with his teeth.

"Here, Red," said Don. "We'll have to give that mud some time, to be sure the bleeding's stopped. Drink enough of this to knock you out, until we get you disinfected and a bandage around you."

Red drank a slug of the whiskey, shuddering as he did so. Nobody spoke until Red was snoring.

"I don't suppose you got close enough to the Paiute camp to learn anything," Don said.

"No," said Charlie, "and we didn't hear a sound. A pair of Paiutes dropped out of a tree with their knives ready, and we had to fight for our lives. They were expecting us."

"We didn't play our hand too well, or we would have been expecting them," Don said. "They know their bows and arrows are no match for our rifles, and they purely set us up in a situation where they had the advantage."

"I reckon you're right," said Mike. "They've come out second-best every time until now. They may have some more surprises in mind before we're out of their reach. Until that wound heals, Red will be so sore he can't move."

"So we'll be short-handed gathering the herd," Charlie said. "We can't leave the camp undefended. The varmints might attack in daylight."

"We'll leave two men in camp, and the rest of us will

make the gather," said Don, "and I think we'll avoid those Paiutes if we can."

"I feel like less of a Texan for sayin' it," Charlie said, "but I think you're right. With our long guns, we have an edge, but that's no help when they can come at us with knives in close quarters."

After several hours, the mud dried and flaked off, allowing them to better examine Red's wound.

"Not too deep," Don said, "but he lost a lot of blood. Molly, is that water still hot?"

"Yes," said Molly. "I'll bring it."

"I'll tend the wound, if you'd like," Rose said. "Molly can help."

"Go ahead," said Don. "You know where the medicine kit and bandages are."

Taking their rifles, Don and Charlie joined the rest of the outfit on watch.

"Red doin' all right?" Jim Roussel asked.

"The bleeding's stopped," said Don. "Rose and Molly are taking care of the wound."

"God," Felton Juneau said, "I'd as soon a man come after me with a double-barrel scattergun as a knife. It ain't the natural way for a man to fight."

"I reckon we can't much blame the Indians," said Mike. "We got an advantage with our repeating rifles. They have only knives or bows and arrows, so they got to get in close, or they don't stand a chance."

"Don't look for no sympathy from me where these Paiutes is concerned," Charlie said. "I've never had a tougher fight, and I don't expect Red has either. They was out to gut both of us."

"You and Red did well just escaping," said Don. "The same thing would have happened to any of the rest of us. Up to now, we've managed to outmaneuver the Paiutes, but they turned the tables on us. We'll try leaving them alone, and maybe they'll do the same for us. But just for the sake of our hair, we won't let down our guard."

"They won't leave us alone," Les Brown said, "or they

wouldn't have been waitin' for us when we went to gather the herd. That attack didn't hurt us, but it did make us mad enough for Red and Charlie to go lookin' for that Paiute camp.''

''Maybe they're not done with us,'' said Don, ''but they'll have to come lookin' for us from now on. They won't get another chance to gut some of us in the dark.''

Rose and Molly cleansed Red's wound, disinfected it, and tied a clean white bandage about his middle.

''I'll sit with him awhile, Rose,'' Molly said.

''We'll have to watch him the rest of the night,'' said Rose. ''There may be fever.''

Eventually, Wendy Oldham joined Molly.

''That might have easily been Charlie instead of Red,'' Wendy said.

''I know,'' said Molly, ''but they insisted on going. Cowboys are well-named, I suppose. They're as stubborn as the cows.''

The night passed without any sign of the Paiutes, and by dawn, Red had a fever. Rose and Molly began dosing him with whiskey. Molly washed his shirt, removing the blood as best she could.

''There's needle and thread in the medicine kit,'' Rose said. ''Why don't you get it and sew up that gash in Red's shirt? I doubt he has another.''

''I'll do that,'' said Molly.

After breakfast, Don called the outfit together. It was time to begin the gather.

''Arch, I want you and Felton to remain in camp,'' Don said. ''The rest of us will look for the herd.''

No further instruction was needed, for all of them were well aware of the Paiutes and what had happened the night before. They mounted their horses and Don led out, the six of them bound for the area where they had found part of their herd the day before.

''This river goes on and on,'' said Charlie, ''and you can't depend on a cow ever goin' in a straight line, even toward water. That bunch may have wandered back, but they might be ten miles downstream.''

''We'll consider that,'' Don said, ''but wherever they went, there'll be tracks. If they've doubled back toward this river, we'll know. We'll just have to trail them until we know for sure where they're headed.''

They rode cautiously, avoiding any brush or arroyos that might have provided cover for attacking Paiutes. They reined up on the ridge above the meadow, where Mike Horton had sprung the Paiute trap the day before. There were no cows in sight.

''It's odd that some of them stopped here, while the rest wandered on,'' Charlie said. ''It purely ain't like one of the critters to have a mind of its own.''

''The Paiutes may have headed some of them to get our attention,'' said Bob Vines.

''Maybe,'' Mike conceded, ''but I don't aim to ride across that ridge again. They know we'll be back, and they could be waiting for us.''

''All of you wait here,'' said Don. ''I'll ride down and look for tracks. The rest of them may have drifted south.''

Don trotted his horse down the slope. He rode part way up the farthest slope, looking for tracks. Except for those left by Mike's horse the day before, there were none. Turning south, Don rode slowly, and as he progressed, he found the tracks he expected. When he was again in the open, there was a wide swath of tracks, and virtually no graze. He rode back within sight of his comrades, waving his hat.

''The rest of them have drifted south,'' Don said, when they had caught up to him.

''That accounts for us not finding them along the river,'' said Bob. ''If they've drifted back to it, they're much farther downstream than we expected.''

''It looks that way,'' Don said, ''but we won't take any shortcuts. This time, we'll just follow the tracks.''

They rode almost ten miles before the tracks of the herd began to turn slowly west.

''The strides of them steers is gettin' longer by the minute," said Charlie. "That wind's brought 'em the smell of water."

"They should all be there," Mike said. "There's enough tracks."

Nearing the river, they began seeing grazing cattle. At first there were small lots of four or five, and then groups of a dozen or more. Finally they were close enough to see the river. With no brush to obstruct their view, they could see grazing cattle on both banks, strung out for a great distance.

"I have a feeling that's the rest of them," Don said. "Let's move them upriver."

They rode downstream until there were no more grazing cattle. Don, Bob and Jim crossed the river, and with three riders on each bank, they began driving the cattle north. The longhorns were easily driven, having grazed and watered, and the gather was going well, when suddenly there was a distant shot. Seconds later, there were two more.

"Leave 'em where they are!" Don shouted. "There's trouble in camp."

He kicked his horse into a gallop, his comrades following. There were more shots and then only silence . . .

13

Arch, Felton, Dominique, and Roberto were waiting,
their rifles ready, when the rest of the outfit rode in.

"We got here as fast as we could," Don said. "Anybody
hurt?"

"No," said Arch. "A bunch of Paiutes slipped in as
close as they could, along the far bank of the river. We cut
down on them, and they didn't come back."

"They expected us to come lookin' for them, after they
jumped Red and Charlie last night," Don said. "They're
still trying to draw us into a fight."

"For that reason, I think we should leave them alone,"
said Charlie. "I've never favored fighting when there's
nothing to be gained."

"I don't look at it that way," Mike Horton said. "If they
keep hounding us, we ought to kill enough of them to make
believers of the others."

"We should be able to finish the gather today," said
Don. "We'll only be here until Red and Bonita can ride."

"I can ride now," Bonita said, "and when the Paiutes
were here, Red wanted to get up and get his rifle."

"I'll be ready to ride tomorrow," said Red, who was
sitting with his back to a tree.

"When the gather's finished, we'll take a look at that
wound," Don replied. "We had a time getting the bleeding
stopped. I don't want to go through that again."

"We can stand off the Paiutes in daylight," said Felton
Juneau. "The rest of you go on back and get the balance
of the herd."

The six of them mounted and rode downriver. The longhorns were grazing along the river where they had been
left, and there was no problem getting them moving again.
By midafternoon, they were ready for a tally. The low
count was 5,150.

"We're still shy fifty head, but we may find them along
the river, before we get away from it," Don said. "If we
don't, we can live with what we have."

By sundown, there had been no further trouble from the
Paiutes.

"We'll go with our usual watch," said Don. "Since
Red's laid up, Les, I want you to go on the first watch with
Charlie, Arch, and Felton. Be extra watchful, because we
don't know for sure that those Paiutes have given up on
us. The pack mules and all the horses not being ridden will
be cross-hobbled."

After supper, when the first watch had begun circling the
herd, Molly Rivers sat down beside Red.

"I'm almighty tired of settin' here on this blanket," Red
grumbled. "I ought to be out there on watch."

"You were cut deep," said Molly. "I saw it, and I think
Don's right. You don't want to risk having it start bleeding
again."

"Damn Indians," Red said. "Why can't they wound a
man decent, without cuttin' him from one side of his belly
to the other?"

"Red Bohannon, can't you ever be serious? If that
wound had been just a little deeper, you'd be dead. For
heaven's sake, let's talk about something else."

"Then let's talk about Texas," said Red. "I want to go
back someday, but I'm thinking of stayin' in California
until the war's over."

"What war?"

"The War Between the States," Red replied. "The
North's fightin' the South."

"What are they fighting about?"

"Hell, I don't know," said Red. "That's why I ain't goin' back until it's over. Texas is sure to be dragged into it, and if I was there, I'd have to fight."

"Why would you have to fight in a war when you don't even know what it's about?"

"Texans stick together," Red said. "We don't always agree with one another, and we sometimes fight amongst ourselves, but let some varmint from the outside jump on us, and we're all of one mind."

Molly laughed. "I like that. It's like one big family."

"I kind of like it myself, but not where this war's concerned," said Red.

"I wouldn't want you going off to war. How long do you think it will last?"

"I don't know," Red said. "There's some that says it'll be over in three months, but I don't think so. That's why we're ridin' this God-awful trail to California. All the cattle trails to the north was closed, and Texas is broke. We had nothin' to sell but cattle, and it was our last chance to get our hands on some money."

"What do you intend to do in California?"

"I ain't thought much about it," said Red. "Between now and the time we get there, I'll talk to the rest of the outfit. We'll have enough money so that we don't starve. Maybe we can all stick together somehow. What would you like to do?"

"I haven't thought about anything, except being with you," Molly said. "What do you want me to do?"

Red laughed. "Just be with me, I reckon. I want to get you all dandied up, so that I can show you off when we get back to Texas. I want everybody that knows me—most of all, them that never expected me to amount to nothin'— to stand up on their hind legs and look. I want 'em layin' awake nights, just wonderin' how a ugly bastard like Red Bohannon ever got his brand on such a pretty girl."

"Hush," said Molly. "I don't think you're ugly."

"Depends on what you're comparin' me to," Red replied. "I'm a mite bowlegged, and when I ain't wearin' my boots and hat, I'm not even six feet. Once you skin me down and get in bed with me, I may be uglier than you think."

"Then I suppose we'll have to get in bed after dark and get up before daylight. Once you get me skinned down, I may not be all you expect."

"Huh," said Red, "you got everything in the right place, don't you?"

"I suppose, but I can't be sure. I've never spent any time with a man, except for Pa, and I was awful young, when he dumped me at the mission school. What does a woman do, when she . . . they . . ."

"I don't know," said Red. "I thought females was born knowin' what to do and when to do it. You mean they ain't?"

Molly laughed. "They ain't. At least, not this one. There's an awful lot you'll have to teach me."

"Then I reckon I'd better get busy learnin' it myself," Red said.

On the second watch, Les Brown finally found the courage to speak to Don Webb of what had been on his mind since the death of Eli Mills.

"It was me that brought Eli in," said Les, "and I feel responsible for what happened to him. It's me that'll have to tell his kin how he died and where we laid him. I know he had only a few more than a hundred cows in the herd, and now he's not here to . . . to do his part in drivin' 'em to market. With the war and all, his ma and pa are havin' a hard time, and I'd like to take 'em at least some of the money from Eli's cows."

"If, by the grace of God, we're able to deliver and sell this herd, you'll take it all to them," Don said. "Eli joined us in good faith, doing his share, and it's no fault of his that he's not ridin' to the end of the trail with us."

"I'm obliged," said Les. "With the war going on, what do you reckon will happen to us when we go back to Texas?"

"I don't know," Don said, "but before we reach California, I think all of us should do some thinking and some talking. I might just stay in California until the war's over."

"But you have a woman in Texas," said Les.

"I can send for her," Don said, "unless Mr. Lincoln blockades Texas ports and the sailing ships can't get in. Felton Juneau has a woman in Texas too. We'll have to see what can be done once we reach California."

"Maybe if Texas hasn't been closed to the ships," said Les, "I can send Eli's money to his kin, and some of mine to my kin. I want to go back to Texas, but I don't aim to ride this trail by myself."

"We'll have time enough to think about that before we reach California," Don said.

Dawn broke clear, but there was a band of gray along the western horizon.

"Looks like another storm building over yonder," said Bob Vines. "With all this rain in summer, the snow must be neck-deep in the winter months."

"I don't want to find out," Mike Horton said. "We got trouble enough when it comes down as rain. We've already had two stampedes from this same camp. I can't believe there might be a third one."

"This is a strange kind of place," said Charlie. "When the herd stampedes from here, they're lured back, because there's no water to the east. At least, none that's close."

"If they run far enough, there's the Little Colorado," Don said. "I just hope we can be long gone before there's another stampede in that direction."

"We ought to be on the trail tomorrow," said Red, who had been listening. "I refuse to set here another day, waitin' for them Paiutes to bother us again."

The storm held off. Though there was wind from the northwest, it was unbearably hot, a circumstance that didn't change much even after sunset. Thunder rumbled but came no closer. There was no uneasiness within the herd, and the four-man first watch included Red. Walking his horse, he stopped to talk to Wendy.

"After the Indians shredded my clothes, I felt bad, having only a blanket to wear," said Wendy. "Now I'm ready to get rid of the blanket. It's so hot."

"Shuck it," Red said. "It's dark, and it looks like the storm will rain itself out before it reaches us."

"I'd like to have the rain, but it always come with thunder and lightning. I can't forget what that last stampede cost us."

Despite the distant thunder and the gray clouds far to the west, there was no storm and no rain. The day dawned clear, and even before sunrise, the heat was terrible. There wasn't even a breath of wind, and the shirts of the riders were dark with sweat.

"There'd better be plenty of water close enough for tonight's camp," Jim Roussel said. "Hot as it is already, and with the sun comin', this bunch is gonna be stampede-dry."

"According to the map," said Don, "we can drive due west from here and reach the old trail, which follows the Virgin River on into Nevada. I'll be ridin' ahead just to be sure."

"I'm surprised that bunch of Paiutes didn't have another go at us," Charlie said. "They got to know that we'll be leavin' here pretty soon."

"I aim to look for sign of Indians," said Don. "We can't overlook the possibility they may circle around and get ahead of us with ambush on their minds. Compared to our Henrys, we laugh at their bows and arrows, but let them get close enough and they're deadly."

Southwestern Utah. June 15, 1862.

Griff and his band of renegades were camped near the bend in the Sevier River, just after it turned south along the Old

Spanish Trail. They sat around in the little shade there was, fanning themselves with their hats.

"I've never seen it so hot, with all that thunder and them clouds last night," Doolin complained.

Quando laughed. "Not near as hot as it'll be on the Mojave. After we take over that herd of Texas longhorns, we'll be drownin' in our own sweat."

"I can stand anything, for a while," said Lennox, "as long as there's big money waitin' for us in Los Angeles."

"It's about time we caught up to that herd and had a look at them hombres trailin' it," Oliver said. "How about it, Griff?"

"I want them into the desert before they learn we're on their back-trail," said Griff. "I reckon it ain't too soon to learn where they are. Rodriguez, you're likely the best tracker amongst us and you know this territory. Find out where they are without them seein' you."

"They oughta be in Nevada now, unless they've had Indian trouble," Bullard said.

"That's another thing, Rodriguez," said Griff. "Look close for Indians. Them Utes gave us hell, likely because they come out on the short end of the stick with them Texas trail drivers. We don't need another dose of the same medicine from the Paiutes."

"I know all about the Paiutes," growled Rodriguez. "You talk to me like I'm some kind of damn shorthorn that's never been down the trail."

They were all weary after many days of inactivity, and they laughed uproariously at the red-faced Rodriguez.

"Stay on bare ground, Rodriguez," Quando said. "Then you can always foller the tracks of your horse so's you can find us again."

"Just one more damn word out of any of you," said Rodriguez, "and I ain't goin' nowhere. One of you bastards that knows it all can scout ahead."

"All of you shut up," Griff shouted. "Get goin', Rodriguez."

Rodriguez saddled his horse, mounted, and rode south.

**Southeastern California. The Mojave Desert.
June 15, 1862.**

Elton Beavers and Arlo Dent had made their fortune in
California. Not by digging for gold themselves, but by mur-
dering and robbing other miners. But their past had caught
up with them, and they had been forced to ride for their
lives, just a few jumps ahead of the sheriff and a posse of
furious, deputized miners.

"By God," said Beavers, elated, "they've give up on
us."

"Their horses are played out," Dent said, "and ours
ain't no better. We'll be afoot long before we're out of this
damn desert."

"I'd rather be afoot in the desert than back yonder with
my neck stretched," said Beavers. "We can live like kings
in Santa Fe or Denver. We got near thirty thousand."

"Yeah," Dent said, "but it's in bank notes, thanks to
you. I don't trust banks. I wish we'd of left it all in gold."

"Too much weight and you know it," said Beavers. "If
we'd been carryin' gold, we'd of had to choose between
leavin' the gold and savin' our necks."

The westering sun beat down on them, and they yearned
for the little water remaining in their canteens. Not a breeze
stirred. Heat waves shimmered, and the desert seemed to
stretch on to infinity, where the desolate sand met the blue
of the sky. Buzzards circled high above, seeming to know
much that the humans on their dying horses did not. There
wasn't another living thing except an occasional yucca. Finally the weary horses stopped, their heads down, heaving.
No amount of beating and cursing would move them another step. They were finished. Beavers and Dent didn't
bother removing the saddles, leaving the poor beasts to their
fate. Taking their saddlebags and near-empty canteens, they
plodded on eastward.

"We got just one chance," Dent panted. "Tonight, without the sun suckin' us dry, we got to find water or get off this infernal desert. It has to end somewhere.''

Beavers, too near spent or not considering it worthy of a reply, said nothing.

Rodriguez rode carefully, for there were many tracks of unshod horses. If he were to encounter Paiutes, he must do so while he was still near enough to return to his renegade comrades. To seek help from the Texans would force him to justify his presence on their back-trail, which he dared not do. He followed the path the herd had taken, for there was no better way. Tracks of unshod horses were everywhere, and there was no way of knowing from which direction Paiute trouble might come. He heard their galloping horses before he actually saw them. Three hundred yards ahead of him, they burst from the brush along the opposite bank of the river. There were fifteen of them, and splashing their horses across the river, they came screeching toward Rodriguez. Wheeling his horse, he spurred the animal into a fast gallop. To his dismay, there were a dozen more mounted Paiutes riding toward him along the back-trail. Frantically he reined his horse around and galloped to the east, but the Paiutes were ready for him. Half a dozen riders split from each party and began closing in. Rodriguez rolled out of his saddle, his rifle in his hands, and fell behind a cluster of stone that reared up head-high. It was the only available cover, and it offered little protection. Already the Paiutes were circling, surrounding him. Rodriguez cut loose with his rifle and had the satisfaction of seeing one of the attackers tumble from his galloping horse. Quickly he accounted for two more. His only chance lay in the possibility that his comrades would hear the shooting and ride to his aid. But even had they been so inclined, there wasn't time. Rodriguez dropped his rifle, clutching the stone, as an arrow buried itself deep in his back. When a second and third arrow struck him, he lost his grip on the stone and slid to the ground . . .

* * *

"Listen," said Oliver. "Shots. Rodriguez is in trouble."

"Nothin' we can do," Quando said. "It's his funeral."

"What the hell we waitin' for?" said Doolin, angrily.
"Let's ride."

"Go ahead," Griff said. "He's a good ten miles away.
Maybe farther. He'll be done for long before we could get
there."

They listened, grim-faced, as the sound of the three distant shots died away. There were no more.

"Paiutes," said Lennox. "We still don't know where the
trail herd is, and we're another man shy."

"Worse, damn it," Griff said, "that bunch with the trail
herd may have heard the shots and they'll know there's
somebody behind them besides Paiutes."

"I reckon it don't matter what happened to Rodriguez,"
said Hernandez. "I knowed him a long time. He was my
amigo."

"You're welcome to ride out and shoot as many Paiutes
as you're of a mind to," Griff said. "Gettin' the rest of us
killed and scalped won't help him none."

"Since you don't care a damn what happened to Rodriguez," said Hernandez angrily, "I got a question for you.
Who do you aim to send to scout that trail herd now?"

"I reckon I'll ask for volunteers," Griff said. "What
about you?"

"I wouldn't take you a drink of water if you was in
hell," said Hernandez.

"Well now," Griff said, through gritted teeth, "how do
the rest of you feel?"

"Same as Hernandez," said Doolin.

Griff had his thumb hooked in his gunbelt just above the
butt of his Colt. But as his eyes met those of his renegade
comrades, he eased his hand away, dropping it at his side.
Doolin, Quando, Lennox—all of them—were seeing themselves in the position of the unfortunate Rodriguez. Seeing
the tide turning against Griff, Hernandez spoke.

"I reckon we'll all ride ahead if there's scoutin' to be
done."

"Hell," said Quando, "we can't do that. Them Texas trail drivers will know we're on their back-trail. Maybe Griff will volunteer to scout ahead. How 'bout it, Griff?"

"We'll ride as an outfit," Griff said. "Unless some of you have a better idea, we'll ride west into Nevada's great basin, and from there, south into the Mojave. We'll catch up to the trail herd there, and that will eliminate any problems with the Paiute."

"That makes more sense than anything you've said since leaving Santa Fe," said Doolin.

"Except that there ain't much water in the Mojave unless you know where to look," Quando said. "I ain't all that sure Griff knows where to look."

"We'll have to ride into the Mojave eventually," said Griff. "All I'm saying is that we'll be there a mite sooner, and I'd rather take my chances with the desert than with all these Paiutes. Anybody besides Quando feel otherwise?"

"Hell no," Doolin shouted. "What about the rest of you?"

"I'm goin' with Griff!" Bullard said.

Like an echo, the others joined in, with the exception of Quando. He said nothing.

"Then we'll ride west from here," said Griff, "going south when we reach the Great Basin. Water may be a problem, but not as much a problem as the Paiutes."

While Ben and Curt Pickford had agreed to follow Griff, their confidence in the ragtag renegade outfit had diminished. When they finally were alone, Curt spoke.

"This whole idea of avengin' Wiley has gone sour. Once we reach the desert and there ain't nothin' else between us and Los Angeles, I'm leavin'. With or without you."

"What about the herd?" said Ben.

"I got my doubts this bunch can take the herd away from them Texans," Curt said. "And even if they can, it won't put a peso in our pockets. We'll be paid off in lead."

"Maybe you're right," said Ben. "We can avenge Wiley after them Texans get to Los Angeles."

"Not *we*," Curt said. "*You*. I've already seen this Jim Roussel draw against you, with the promise to kill you if he does it again. Wiley's dead because he couldn't leave booze alone, was lousy at poker whether he was drunk or sober, and he was never the fast draw he fancied himself."

"All right, so I ain't fast enough," said Ben angrily, "but I ain't the kind that's got to play fair. If I want some bastard dead, I'll gun him down any way I can. I don't need you preachin' to me. If you aim to split and go on to California, I'll go with you. But once we're there, I aim to see this Jim Roussel salted down, one way or another."

"Then you'll do it without me," Curt said. "Roussel said he'd kill you the next time you go after him, and I believe he can and will."

Their conversation ended, for the band of renegades was breaking camp. They saddled their horses, mounted, and with Griff leading out, they rode west. Toward Nevada's Great Basin.

With the herd moving west, Don had ridden ahead, seeking the old trail and the river on the map. Red, Charlie, Arch, and Felton were riding drag, accompanied by the seven women. On their heels came the pack mules and the horse remuda. Roberto and Dominique never allowed any tolerance. Suddenly Red trotted his horse wide of the herd and reined up, listening.

"What is it?" Charlie asked, joining him.

"Shots," said Red. "Somewhere back yonder. Listen."

There was only one more shot, followed by silence.

"Somebody's run into that bunch of Paiutes," Charlie said.

"Yeah," said Red, "but who? I can't think of anybody who might be on our back-trail, unless it's the Pickfords."

"I can't imagine it bein' them," Charlie said. "Not just the two of 'em, anyway."

"Let's ride on then," said Red. "Whoever they are—or were—there's nothin' we can do. But I reckon Don oughta know."

They quickly caught up to the rest of the riders who were pondering the cause of the delay, and Red tried to satisfy their curiosity.

"I think we oughta know who's on our back-trail," Arch said.

"Not at the expense of ridin' back through Paiute country," said Charlie. "It couldn't have been more than one hombre. Not enough shooting."

"One hombre scoutin' ahead, like Don's doin' for us," Arch said. "There may be others followin' him."

"Not for long," said Red. "If the Paiutes got their scout, that should turn the rest of 'em around."

The women had ridden close enough to hear the conversation.

"Oh Lord," Molly said, "suppose that doesn't discourage them and they keep coming? Haven't we had trouble enough?"

Don Webb rode west, toward what the map called the Virgin River, which the old trail appeared to follow on into southern Nevada. There were no tracks except those of various wild animals, and Don breathed a sigh of relief. He had ridden more than a dozen miles, when his horse snorted, breaking into a trot. Soon he was within sight of the river, with its fringe of greenery. There was also evidence of the old trail that followed the river. Don rested his horse long enough for the animal to drink safely before allowing him to water. He then satisfied his own thirst, mounted his horse, and rode back the way he had come. The herd, moving at a faster than usual gait, had made good time. They were almost halfway to the new water when Don met them. He found Red loping his horse ahead of the lead steers, obviously waiting for him.

"We heard shots somewhere along the back-trail," said Red. "But not more than three or four. Sounded like one hombre in a losing fight with the Paiutes."

"How long ago?"

"A few minutes after you rode out," Red replied. "What do you make of it?"

"Several possibilities," said Don. "What do you think?"

"Charlie and me thought it might be them Pickfords that's after Roussel for gunnin' down that no-account Wiley," Red said.

"Maybe, but I doubt it," said Don. "When we left Santa Fe, it was no secret that we had a buyer for our herd in Los Angeles. What's to stop a bunch of owlhoots from takin' our trail with the intention of rustling our cows and sellin' 'em as their own?"

"Not a damn thing, now that you mention it," Red said. "From what we learned about Warren Blocker's murder, there was a bunch hangin' around Santa Fe that would likely be more than willing to bushwhack us. Of course, they'd wait until the hard trail's behind us, and we're within hollerin' distance of Los Angeles."

"Exactly," said Don, "and they must know something of this territory, since they seem to have had a scout riding ahead. It's just his misfortune that those Paiutes took their mad out on him instead of us."

"If we got outlaws on our trail, we need to know where they are and how many," Red said, "but this is no time to go scoutin' our back-trail, when it's likely full of mad-as-hell Paiutes."

"Time enough for scouting our back-trail when we're out of Paiute country," said Don. "Whoever's following us is in no hurry to catch up. That's proof enough that they're waiting until we're much closer to the end of this trail before making their move."

"Like in the Mojave desert," Red said. "That's when the herd will likely be dry, hard to handle, and cantankerous as sore-tailed bobcats."

"True," said Don, "but there are certain advantages in the desert. We can see for miles in every direction, and it won't be easy, settin' up an ambush."

Well before sundown, the herd reached the old trail and the river that it followed. Don again spread out the map while they waited for supper.

"After tomorrow, that map will be pretty well used up," Bob Vines observed. "I'd say we'll have about one day before this river drops off to the south, leaving us with nothing on our plate but sand and alkalai water."

"I'd say you're likely right," said Don. "After supper, I aim to have a long talk with Dominique and Roberto. We're pretty sure the lack of water is a problem as long as we follow the old trail as it's laid out, but who says we must follow the old trail? It's nearly a hundred miles across the Mojave, and there must be *some* water. We're goin' to find it."

14

A chill wind blew from the northwest, as Elton Beavers and Arlo Dent struggled on in the darkness, seeking to escape another day of unbearable desert sun. Distant stars glittered in the deep purple of the sky. There was no moon. Dent fell to his knees, panting with exhaustion.

"Get up," Beavers growled.

"I'm beat," said Dent.

"You'll be dead if we don't get out of this desert before sun up," Beavers said.

He slogged on through the sand, not looking back. With a sigh, Dent struggled to his feet and followed.

After breakfast the following morning, Don spoke to Dominique and Roberto. It was time for the Mexican wranglers to find water on the long trail ahead if they could.

"Arch," said Don, "I want you to help Roberto with the pack mules and the remuda. Dominique will be riding with me."

Don and Dominique rode west along the river, following the old trail. As expected, the river turned south after a little more than a dozen miles, while the Old Spanish Trail led west. Don and Dominique reined up, and Don spoke.

"We should be in Nevada, according to the map."

"*Si,*" Dominique said. "The Mojave is not yet."

"I'm figurin' two days to cross Nevada," said Don. "We leave the river in the morning, and we'll need water for tomorrow night."

"*Si*," Dominique said. Kicking his horse into a slow gallop, he led out.

There was little vegetation, and after fifteen miles, Don didn't trust his eyes. The patch of greenery ahead might have been a figment of his imagination. But as they drew nearer, their horses recognized the reality of it, for they broke into a fast gallop. Cool fresh water bubbled out of the ground, and there was a pool twenty feet across, but before their eyes the runoff disappeared into the sand only a few yards away.

"My God, it's a miracle," said Don.

"*Si*," Dominique agreed.

Assured of water for two days, Don and Dominique rode back to meet the herd. When they did, the drive was only about eight miles away from where the river turned south. Dominique again joined Roberto with the pack mules and the horse remuda, allowing Arch to return to the drag. As was his custom after scouting ahead, Don spoke to all the riders by riding along one flank of the herd and back along the other to his point position. They were all concerned with the scarcity of water, and Don reassured them. The herd behaved well, and they reached the bend in the river well before sundown.

"It's been nice, traveling along the rivers," said Rose.

"Yes," Mike agreed, "but this looks like the end of it."

"The water's there, just like Dominique and Roberto promised," said Don, "and I swear it's cooler and fresher than any we've had so far. What I don't understand is why anybody would draw a map of this trail, without showing a water hole or stream all the way from southern Nevada to Los Angeles."

"Maybe the hombre drawin' the map didn't want to encourage travel along this trail," Bob Vines said.

"That's enough to discourage damn near everybody but an Indian," said Red. "Not bad for the first try. Let's just hope Dominique and Roberto can go on drawin' all the right cards. We ain't reached the desert yet."

"They claim there's an underground river," Don said. "It could be our salvation, if it's the truth. Even an underground stream will surface occasionally."

"It kind of makes sense," said Charlie, "if our wranglers were with that sheep drive to California. I don't know anything good about sheep, but the varmints got to have water, just like our cows."

"Just wait until we reach that water hole tomorrow," Don said. "All of you will be as amazed as I was."

"Tomorrow," said Griff, when the renegades had stopped to rest their horses, "we'll be in Nevada's Great Basin."

"I hope you know where there's water," Quando growled. "I been through there once, and except for alkali holes, it was dry."

"Once we're in the basin," said Griff, "we can always ride south until the reach the Old Spanish Trail. There's always water."

"I know where that is," Hernandez said, "but suppose the trail herd's there? They can't be that far ahead of us."

"We'll just have to wait for them to move on," said Griff. "I didn't say this is the best way, but it's considerably better than fighting Paiutes."

There was little evidence that Beavers and Dent were free of the dread desert, for in the darkness the land seemed as barren as ever. But in the first gray light of dawn, all that changed. The two exhausted outlaws had fallen to their knees for a moment of rest, and as they looked eastward, they couldn't believe their eyes. They squinted, expecting the little patch of green to disappear, but it did not. Beavers and Dent stumbled to their feet, shouldering their saddlebags.

"I don't know how far away it is," Beavers croaked, "but it's there."

Dent again fell to his knees, got to his feet, and somehow

managed to go on. The last three hundred yards, the two of them were on hands and knees, for they hadn't strength enough to rise. Reaching the runoff, they dropped their heads into it, allowing cool water to flow over them. Finally, when they could, they drank. They then crept into the bushes near the pool, and in the welcome shade, slept the sleep of the dead.

"Tonight," said Don, during breakfast, "we'll reach the waterhole Dominique and I were at yesterday. Today, Roberto will ride with me, and we'll go beyond that waterhole, looking for water for tomorrow. Les, take Roberto's place with the pack mules and the horse remuda until we return."

Soon as the herd had again taken the trail, Don and Roberto rode ahead. Don allowed the Mexican to lead, for once they were beyond the known waterhole, all would depend on him. But when they were within sight of the vegetation surrounding the water, Roberto pointed south.

"We'll be leaving the trail then," Don said.

"*Si,*" said Roberto.

They rode south, and as far as the eye could see, there was only sand and sky. From the brush surrounding the waterhole they had bypassed, Elton Beavers and Arlo Dent were cursing their luck.

"If they'd just come close enough," Dent groaned, "we could of shot them and had the horses we need."

"Beats me why they didn't stop long enough to water their horses," said Beavers. "I'd bet they ain't another drop of water within fifty miles."

"Maybe they'll be back," Dent said hopefully. "Then they'll stop for sure."

"Maybe," Beavers said. "If they don't, come dark we'll fill our canteens and go on."

"You're crazy," said Dent. "We'll never make it to Santa Fe afoot."

"Without horses, we got no choice," Beavers replied.

*   *   *

Don rode behind Roberto, becoming increasingly conscious of the utter desolation that surrounded them. There wasn't a blade of grass, not even a weed, and no sign that the parched earth had ever seen rain. Far above them, buzzards drifted lazily, as though their ages-old wisdom exceeded that of the foolish humans below. The only change that Don could see in the endless panorama that lay before them was what appeared to be a hump. But as they drew nearer, the hump became a rock formation. Their horses, thirsty now, broke into a fast gallop. From beneath a lip of solid rock, water bubbled out into a stream that soon vanished into the sand.

"*Rio bajo,*" said Roberto.

"Underground river, fifteen miles off the trail, and no grass," Don said.

Roberto shrugged his shoulders helplessly and said nothing. There was no help for it, and wheeling their horses, they rode back the way they had come.

The sun bore down with a vengeance, and the longhorns were becoming thirsty. There were more and more bunch-quitters as many remembered the water they had so recently left and sought to return to it. While still more than four miles from the nearest water, a stray breeze brought the smell of it, and the herd stampeded. The drag riders, seeing all was lost, devoted their efforts to helping Dominique and Les hold the horse remuda and the pack mules. The sun was still an hour-high when the longhorns thundered toward the distant waterhole.

"Tarnation," Dent shouted, from his hiding place in the brush, "look yonder!"

"I am lookin'," said Beavers. "They'll trample us, if we don't get out of here."

The two outlaws ran, distancing themselves from the waterhole, as the longhorns converged on it.

"There'll be riders comin'," Dent said. "Maybe they'll sell us horses."

"Just keep your mouth shut and let me do the talkin',"

said Beavers. "We got to tell 'em something they'll believe. One way or another, we'll get some horses."

The longhorns reached the water well ahead of the riders, and some were hooking the others in a frenzied attempt to be the first to drink. Bob Vines, Jim Roussel, and Mike Horton were the first to notice Beavers and Dent.

"Who in thunder are they?" Horton wondered.

"Maybe we'd better find out," said Bob Vines.

The trio trotted their horses around the impatient longhorns, reining up before Beavers and Dent, who had retreated about three hundred yards beyond the waterhole. The pair had saddlebags and canteens slung over their shoulders. Neither made a move toward the revolver thonged down on his right hip. Beavers spoke.

"We're almighty glad to see you gents. Our horses give out on the desert, and we're needin' another pair to get us to Santa Fe. I'm Beavers, and this is Dent."

"You'll need to talk to our trail boss, and he's not here right now," said Bob. "But I can tell you we're shy some horses ourselves and need all we have for our remuda."

"We'll talk to your trail boss," Beavers said.

"Don and Roberto's comin' now," Mike Horton said.

Don reined up, while Roberto rode on to help with the pack mules and horse remuda.

"Don," said Bob, "this is Beavers and Dent. They were here at the waterhole when we arrived. They're bound for Santa Fe, and are needin' horses. I've already told 'em we're shy some mounts ourselves."

"Sorry, gents," Don said, "but I can't improve on that. How did you get here without horses?"

"We lost ours in the desert," said Beavers.

"I don't have any sympathy for a man that's afoot after ridin' his horse to death," Don said.

"We didn't have no choice," said Beavers hastily. "We been prospectin' in California and was tryin' to get away with our earnings when a bunch of thieves took after us. We had to ride for our lives."

"That doesn't change anything," Don said. "We still

can't spare you any horses, and if you had them, you'd
never reach Santa Fe alive. We've spent the last few days
fighting the Paiutes, and the Utes before them. The two of
you wouldn't stand a chance.''

"I reckon that'll be up to us," said Beavers. "Looks like
we'll have to waylay some of the varmints and get us a
couple of horses.''

Bob Vines and Jim Roussel only looked disgusted, while
Mike Horton laughed. It was Don who eventually spoke.

"Whatever you decide to do," Don said, "the two of
you are welcome to have supper with us.''

"We're obliged," said Beavers.

The women had just arrived and were dismounting.
Beavers and Dent eyed them with interest. The rest of the
riders had dismounted and were driving some of the longhorns from the water so that the horses and mules could
drink. Dominique and Roberto soon had cook fires going,
using wood they had gathered previously. Eventually,
Beavers and Dent were alone, and it was Dent who spoke.

"You done all the talkin', and I can't see it's got us
anywhere. We still got no horses, damn it.''

"We'll have some 'fore morning," Beavers said. "After
supper, we'll grab us a pair of them gals and put a pistol
to their heads. I reckon these hombres will saddle us a
couple of horses and be glad to do it.''

"You reckon they was tellin' the truth about Indian trouble?''

"No matter if they was or wasn't," said Beavers. "We
won't be lettin' no grass grow under our feet gettin' back
to Santa Fe. They had a trail herd slowin' 'em down. Anyway, we got to go on. We can't go back to California.''

But Don Webb didn't trust Beavers and Dent. He managed to speak to all the riders, as well as the women. He
specifically warned Dominique and Roberto to cross-hobble
and carefully watch the remuda horses during the night. But
Beavers and Dent didn't intend to simply steal horses in
the dark of the night.

"Beavers and Dent look like owlhoots to me," Jim

Roussel said, when he had a chance to speak to Don alone. "We have those two remuda horses that belonged to Eli. Why not sell 'em to these hombres and be rid of them?"

"Because they're not ours to sell," said Don. "They belonged to Eli, and when I return to Texas, they'll be taken to Eli's kin. As for Beavers and Dent, I don't like the looks of them myself, but I can't in good conscience leave them afoot. I'm going to offer them the chance to go on to California with us. They can ride those two extra horses that far."

Shortly before supper, Don approached Beavers and Dent with his proposal.

"If you want to go on to California with us, we have two horses you're welcome to ride. That's all I can offer because these animals belonged to one of our riders who died in a stampede. They'll have to be returned to his kin. You can ride back to California, or you can go on to Santa Fe, through Indian country afoot. What's it going to be?"

"I reckon we'll be ridin' back to California with you," said Beavers.

"Then we'll count on that," Don said. "Supper will be ready pretty soon."

"Damn it," said Dent, when Don had left them alone, "you know better than that. We don't dare go back to California. Why did you tell him we would?"

"To throw him off guard and ease his suspicions," Beavers said. "Didn't you see him makin' the rounds, talkin' to his outfit? He don't trust us. Once they bed down for the night, he'll have the horses and mules watched. After supper, we'll grab us a couple of them gals and get the horses we need."

"Soon as we're gone, they'll ride us down and string us up," said Dent.

Beavers laughed. "Not if we take them gals with us a ways. It'll be dark by then, and they'll play hell catchin' us. We'll have all night to get away, and by dawn, we'll be so far ahead, they'll have to give it up."

Dent said nothing. It seemed the only choice they had.

They were half-starved, having had little to eat while on the run. They ate heartily, and when they were finished, managed to work their way near where the women were helping Dominique and Roberto clean up after supper. Suddenly, Beavers seized Rose, while Dent grabbed Sarah. Using the women as shields, both men drew and cocked their revolvers.

"Now, trail boss," Beavers said, "you get us a couple of horses saddled. You make any wrong moves, and it won't go well with these ladies."

"Red, you and Charlie saddle two horses," said Don. "Bob, you and Mike back off."

Vines and Horton had their hands near their Colts, but realizing the futility of what they had been about to do, they yielded. Red and Charlie had each saddled one of their own remuda horses, using their own saddles.

"Drop the reins and back away," Beavers ordered.

Red and Charlie obeyed. Beavers and Dent, careful to keep their hostages in front of them, moved forward and took the reins of the horses.

"You have what you want," said Don. "Let the women go."

Beavers laughed. "I reckon you'll give us your word you won't gun us down. I don't think so, trail boss. We got somethin' better. These little ladies will be goin' with us far enough so's you hombres don't get ideas. But we won't take 'em too far. These horses has got to get us to Santa Fe."

Beavers and Dent caught up the reins, but rather than risk mounting, began backing away into the darkness, the horses following. When they were so far away that nobody could shoot without the risk of hitting Rose or Sarah, the outlaws lifted the women up to the horses and mounted behind them. Kicking the horses into a fast gallop, they rode away to the east.

"Bob, you and Mike saddle up and follow them," said Don. "Don't get too close and don't do anything foolish.

Just be ready to rescue Rose and Sarah when they're let go.''

"You got more confidence in that pair than I do," Mike said bitterly.

Bob said nothing. Quickly they saddled their horses and rode away into the night.

"Red and Charlie won't be much help from here on to California without saddles," said Les Brown.

"I hate you, Les Brown," Millie Nettles shouted. "You're more concerned with a pair of saddles than with the lives of Rose and Sarah."

"Yeah," said Red. "I should have used your saddle instead of mine."

"That's enough," Don said. "This is no time for bickering among ourselves. The first and most important thing is to get Rose and Sarah back alive."

"Maybe more of us should have gone after them," said Jim Roussel.''

"No," Don said. "Mike and Bob can bring Rose and Sarah back. There's nothing more we can do. Beavers and Dent will have all night to get ahead of us. By then, they'll be in Paiute country."

Beavers and Dent, after several miles, slowed their horses to a trot.

"That was easy," said Dent. "Why don't we just take these gals on with us, until we stop for the night? We can have some fun 'fore we let 'em go."

"Because we ain't stoppin' for the night," Beavers growled. "These horses can't carry a double load more'n two or three miles. Use your damn head."

"Please let us go now," said Rose.

"Shut up, woman," Beavers said. "I'll decide when we let you go."

But the added weight was beginning to tell, and soon the horses were heaving. Beavers and Dent reined up. Beavers dismounted and lifted Rose down.

''This is as far as you go, girlie,'' said Beavers. ''Help the other one down, Dent.''

Dent seized Sarah, taking some liberties as he helped her down.

''Keep your hands off me!'' Sarah shouted, slapping him.

''You damn wildcat,'' said Dent, going after her again.

''Leave her be,'' Beavers shouted.

Sarah stumbled away from him and Rose took her arm. The two of them disappeared into the darkness. After the horses had rested, Beavers and Dent mounted and rode on. The moon rose, casting an eerie light. An hour later, the outlaws again stopped to rest their horses.

''That trail boss was lyin' to us,'' Dent said. ''There ain't no Indians around.''

''Maybe not,'' said Beavers, ''but we can't afford the risk. Restin' the horses, we can travel a hundred miles before daylight. Indians ain't likely to be watchin' the trails after dark.''

But as the outlaws mounted their horses, a pair of shadows detached themselves from the ground. The moonlight was more than adequate, and each of the Paiutes drew an arrow from his quiver, nocked it and let it fly. Each of the arrows buried itself in the back of one of the outlaws, and they fell from their saddles. Spooked by the smell of blood, the horses galloped away into the night, back the way they had come.

Clinging to one another for support, Rose and Sarah stumbled along, stopping often to rest and to listen.

''Someone will be coming for us,'' said Rose.

''Perhaps we should just wait where we are,'' Sarah said. ''We may be going the wrong way, in the dark.''

Sarah's foot slipped off a stone, and with a cry, she fell.

''Are you all right?'' Rose asked anxiously.

''I turned my ankle,'' said Sarah.

''Then we'll wait here and listen,'' Rose said.

Mike and Bob had stopped to rest their horses. There

was no wind, and suddenly the silence was broken by a sharp cry.

"One of the girls," said Bob. "Let's ride."

"I hear horses coming," Sarah said. "Perhaps it's Indians."

"I don't think so," said Rose. "I hear the jingle of bridle iron."

"Here," Sarah cried. "It's Rose and Sarah."

The horses came on at a gallop. Mike and Bob left their saddles almost while their horses were on the run. Wasting no time with words, Mike lifted Rose to his horse while Bob went after Sarah. Within minutes, they were on their way. When they rode in, there was a shout from the rest of the outfit. Quickly, Mike helped Rose down.

"I turned my ankle," said Sarah, as Bob was lifting her down. "I can't stand on it."

"One of you fetch a blanket for Sarah," Bob said. "She has a twisted ankle."

With the arrival of Mike, Bob, Rose, and Sarah, the men on the first watch had come in. Red and Charlie were using saddles borrowed from Jim Roussel and Les Brown. From somewhere in the darkness, a horse nickered. Bob's horse answered.

"Somebody's comin'," said Don. "Let's go."

The horse nickered again, closer.

"Halt and identify yourselves," Red shouted, his rifle cocked and ready.

But then they could see the horse, and it was riderless. Behind it was a second horse, also riderless.

"It's our horses, with our saddles," shouted Charlie.

Charlie and Red caught the trailing reins of the two animals, led them in, and began unsaddling them.

"I reckon we don't have to wonder what happened to Beavers and Dent," Bob said, "and if anybody wants to argue that Paiutes don't strike at night, we can tell 'em a thing or two."

"I aim to find out what them jokers was carryin' in their saddlebags," said Red.

"Probably gold," Don said. "They claimed they were prospectors."

"They looked and acted like a pair of thieves, plain and simple," said Charlie.

"Maybe they were," Don said. "For sure, they had no intention of going to California with us. Open their saddlebags."

"No gold in this one," said Red, who had the saddlebag that had belonged to Beavers. "It's too light."

"Same as this one," Charlie said, who had taken the saddlebag belonging to Dent.

There was plenty of moon-and starlight, so they had no trouble seeing what the pair of saddlebags contained.

"Lord Almighty," said Red, "it's money, all in hundred-dollar notes."

"This one's full of it too," Charlie said. "Let's count it."

Swiftly they began counting.

"Fifteen thousand, five hundred dollars in this one," said Red.

"Fifteen thousand even," Charlie said.

"The varmints must have robbed a bank," said Jim Roussel.

"Not necessarily," Don said. "They stole our horses, but this money may be exactly what they claimed. Maybe they did earn it in the gold fields."

"However they got it, they won't need it now," said Bob. "Question is, what will we do with it?"

"Take it with us," Don said. "When we reach California, maybe the law can shed some light on this, and how they got their hands on it. If it's stolen, and there's some record as to who it belongs to, it should be returned. If the law has no proof that it's stolen, then it may belong to us."

"However it turns out," said Red, "I'm satisfied just to get my horse and saddle back."

"Same here," Charlie said. "Them Paiutes finally did us a good turn."

Rose had put on a pot of water to boil. When it was hot, she began bathing Sarah's swollen ankle.

"With Beavers and Dent showin' up, we never learned what Don and Roberto found," said Jim Roussel. "Will we have water tomorrow night, Don?"

"Water," said Don, "but that's about all. We'll be leaving the trail, traveling southwest maybe fifteen miles. The water, Roberto says, is from an underground river. There's not a blade of grass, no vegetation, and no firewood."

"Damn," Felton Juneau said, "them longhorns is strippin' the leaves and bark from the bushes now. Tomorrow, they won't even have that. It'll be as bad as no water."

"Not quite," said Don. "They may be racks of bones by the time we get them to Los Angeles, but after some decent graze, they'll fatten up. Water's the most important. We'll be as bad off as the herd. Without firewood, there'll be no hot coffee and no grub."

"That can't be," Charlie said. "I'm goin' to talk to Dominique and Roberto."

Following an earnest conversation with the Mexicans, Charlie returned.

"Well," said Don, "what's their answer?"

"In the mornin', they aim to consolidate our grub and supplies on four of the mules," Charlie said. "The other two will be loaded with firewood."

"There's no wood here," said Red.

"Dominique and Roberto aim to go back to the closest wood and load up," Charlie said.

"They're likely to find more than wood," said Don. "Beavers and Dent didn't have to ride very far to get themselves bushwhacked by Paiutes."

"Dominique and Roberto know that," Charlie said. "They aim for some of us to ride with them. I said for the sake of hot coffee and hot grub, we'd do it."

"There's never been a trail with danger enough to override a Texan's concern for his belly," said Don. "Now you and Red get back to the first watch. Midnight will be here, and none of us on the second watch have slept a wink."

15

After breakfast, Dominique and Roberto freed two of the mules of their packs simply by loading what remained of their supplies on the other four mules.

"Bob," Don said, "I want you, Jim, Les, and Mike to ride with them. Help them load as much wood as those mules can comfortably carry and get back here as soon as you can. We have to cover at least fifteen miles today, and we'll be getting a late start."

"Wood, three day," said Dominique.

"You think we can cross this desert in three days?" Don asked.

"*Si,*" said Dominique. "Sheep do."

"That's mighty good news," Charlie said, "but not so good for the longhorns. One day without graze will be somethin' to behold. But three days! My God."

"It's a shame they can't smell grass like they smell water," said Arch. "They'd all light out for California and they'd be there tomorrow."

Bob, Jim, Les, and Mike saddled their horses. When Dominique and Roberto rode out leading the mules, the four Texans followed. While he had time on his hands, Don sought out Sarah.

"How is your ankle?"

"Sore," said Sarah, "but it will be all right in another day. Rose is heating some more water."

Red was spending some time with Molly Rivers, and Charlie was similarly occupied with Wendy Oldham.

"If we're able to cross this desert in three days," Molly said, "we should be almost to Los Angeles in a week."

"I hope so," said Red. "It's been a long trail. We left San Antonio the first day of February."

Charlie's conversation with Wendy had much to do with the trail ahead.

"With the Indians behind us, what can harm us, except perhaps the desert?" Wendy asked.

"There's still time for outlaws to try and take the herd," said Charlie. "They'll wait for us to do most of the hard work."

"We can see for miles, here on the desert," Wendy said. "Will they attack us?"

"Not in daylight," said Charlie. "More than likely, they'll try to gun us down in the dark."

"Oh Lord," Wendy cried, "what can we do?"

"Try to get them before they get us," said Charlie. "I expect Don will have somethin' to say about that tonight."

Don Webb already was considering the possibility of such an attack. He stood facing the north, squinting his eyes. Nothing moved except distant buzzards drifting across the blue of the sky.

"The map says there's nothin' north of us but Nevada's Great Basin," Felton Juneau said, "and from what I've heard, it ain't much better than the desert."

"That's about the equal of what I've heard," said Don, "but there's no hostile Indians."

"There's likely some water in that Great Basin, if a man knows the territory," Juneau said. "Instead of followin' the trail, like we had to, we could have turned west long before we got into Paiute territory. Then we could have come south, pickin' up the old trail here in the desert."

"I've been thinking those same thoughts, Felton," said Don. "It's unfortunate that none of us knows the territory."

Not a breath of air stirred, nor was there a sign of dust against the blue of the sky. Yet, when Webb wiped his sweating brow, it felt gritty, and there was a smudge on the back of his hand. Somewhere to the north, in the Great Basin, men had been riding in the darkness, so there would be no dust against the blue of the morning sky. While Don Webb had no idea who they were, he had a Texan's eye for trouble. To his mind came a remnant of scripture. *Men love darkness, for their deeds are evil.*

Fifty miles north, in the Great Basin, the band of outlaws had made camp near a waterhole Griff had recalled. While there was water, there wasn't even a hint of shade, and the men were already sweating in the heat of the morning sun. Since breakfast, the bunch had devoted all their time to complaining about the day of inactivity and the unrelenting heat.

"Damn it," said Griff, "I've had about enough of your whining. I told you we'll ride at night and rest during the day, and all of you know why. If you can't live without shade, you can always ride back to Paiute country."

While they didn't like it, what they were planning demanded the utmost secrecy, and they settled down to wait for darkness.

To find enough firewood for the crossing of the desert, Dominique and Roberto had to ride back to the bend in the river, where they had camped the day before. They had four short-handled axes, which allowed four men to work and two to keep watch. In less than an hour, they had all the wood the two mules could comfortably carry.

"Why in tarnation didn't some of us think of this yesterday, before we left here?" said Les Brown. "We could already be on our way to the next water."

"We've had a lot of more important things on our minds," Bob Vines said. "Such as getting out of reach of the Paiutes."

When they returned to the herd, Don and the other riders had saddled the horses and loaded the pack mules. The outfit was ready to pull out.

"Dominique," said Don, "I want you to ride with me. We'll ride beyond tonight's water and go looking for tomorrow's."

"*Si,*" Dominique said.

But before the herd moved out, Don got the outfit together, for he had something to say.

"I have reason to believe we'll be having company, maybe as soon as tonight. They'll be riding in from the north. All of you keep your guns handy and your eyes open. Les, help Roberto with the horse remuda and the mules. Dominique and me will be back as soon as we can."

Don and Dominique rode southwest, toward the distant water that the longhorns must reach before dark. The rest of the outfit soon had the herd moving in the same direction. Mike Horton was riding drag. Rose had a question, and trotted her horse alongside his.

"There's nobody in sight and no dust. How does he know we'll be having visitors, and who are they?"

Mike laughed. "That's why he's trail boss. He's expecting outlaws who will try to take the herd away from us."

"If they come after us in the dark, what are we going to do?"

"I expect we'll be waiting for them," said Mike. "By the time he returns, Don will have a plan. You can be sure of one thing. We won't wait until they attack us to prove their intentions."

The other women, also among the drag riders, had ridden close enough to hear most of the conversation.

"They'll be shot without us knowing if they mean us harm?" Sarah asked.

"Sarah," said Mike, "when a bunch of men get together in godforsaken country like this, they're usually up to no good. If we wait to see what they have in mind, some of us will die."

"Early this morning, I saw Don looking toward the north," Millie Nettles said. "There was no sign of anyone, as far as I could see. How does he know they'll be coming from that direction?''

''They're riding at night,'' said Mike. ''You can't see the dust, but it's there. A good frontiersman can tell. Tonight, they'll reach this waterhole we're leaving behind. If they don't come after us tonight, they will tomorrow night, for sure.''

Dominique rode unerringly to the water bubbling from the rock, to which Roberto had taken Don the day before. Wordlessly, they dismounted. After their horses had rested, they watered the animals. Mounting, they rode out, Dominique leading. Again they were riding southwest, a considerable distance to the south of the Old Spanish Trail as shown on the map. Don said nothing. Having ridden more than a dozen miles, they reached a second outcropping much like the one they had just left. Again there was water but nothing else.

''Good,'' said Don. ''Tomorrow?''

He pointed to the southwest, and Dominique shook his head. He pointed more to the west, a direction that would take them back toward the old trail. Don nodded. Tomorrow they would be leaving the desert. Once again, the Mexican wranglers had proven themselves. Mounting their horses, they rode back the way they had come.

By noon, the longhorns had become unruly. The drag riders were kept busy, as increasing numbers of the brutes broke away, galloping madly along the back-trail.

''They're hungry,'' Arch said.

''Not as hungry as they'll be tomorrow,'' said Red

Arch, Red, and Mike were riding drag. While the women had no saddles and couldn't be of much help, they tried. A stubborn old steer, bawling his fury, charged the horse Bonita Holmes was riding. The horse reared, screaming. A horn raked its flank and she was pitched off. The blanket that she had been forced to wear had been blown up over her head. Arch dismounted and ran to her.

"Is anything broke?" Arch asked anxiously. "I don't think so," said Bonita, "but get me some clothes as soon as you can, and I'll not ask for anything more."

They struggled on, the herd settling down only when they became weary from lack of graze. They chose their own gait, refusing to be hurried, bawling like a demented chorus. They had traveled not more than five miles when Don and Dominique met them. Making his way along the flank, Don found the drag riders sweating and swearing. Tired as they were, three longhorns broke away, and Don headed them.

"They've been like that all the way, I reckon," Don said.

"Oh, hell no," said Arch. "They've been worse. They're tired now."

"They ought to be steppin' a mite wider," Don said. "We're still ten miles from water."

"They wouldn't move any faster if there was a rider behind ever' damn one of 'em with fire on the end of a prod pole," said Mike.

"Then don't allow them to go any slower than they are already," Don said. "As it is, I look for us to be after dark gettin' to the water."

"That'll be in our favor," said Mike. "The varmints will be so wore out, maybe they'll not get any rambunctous ideas durin' the night."

Don remained with the drag riders until there were no more bunch-quitters. While the longhorns continued bawling their displeasure, it seemed they had little strength for anything more than the steady gait they managed to maintain. As usual, near sundown, there was just a hint of wind. While the longhorns were hungry, they were thirsty too, and the smell of water prodded them into a shambling trot. The riders let them go, holding back the pack mules and the horse remuda.

"I hope we don't find half of 'em gored," Bob said.

"So do I," said Don. "There's plenty of water, but it's not spread out enough for them all to get to it at the same time. There's too many of them and too few of us. They'll just have to take their chances.''

"They can stand some wounds," Mike said. "Despite all the other problems we've had, I've seen no blow flies. Must be the altitude.''

When the outfit reached the waterhole, the longhorns were still pushing and shoving one another. The riders roped several who were standing in the water, dragging them away to make room for the others. While many had been raked by the horns of companions, it seemed none were seriously injured.

"Let them all drink," said Don, "and when they have, move 'em out to make way for the others. There'll be no coffee and no supper until the water clears.''

The sun had long since descended below the horizon when the last of the longhorns had been driven from the waterhole. Dominique and Roberto already had the supper fires going, waiting for water.

"Everybody pitch in so we can get the horses and mules watered," Don said.

While it was normally the task of the horse wranglers, nobody minded, for Dominique and Roberto would have been that much later getting the supper started. The women did their share, each watering her own horse.

"Now," said Don, when the horses and mules had been watered, "we'll cross-hobble all the mules, and every horse that won't be ridden on watch.''

Darkness had fallen by the time supper was ready, and they ate by starlight. Both fires had been put out, and when the outfit had finished eating, Don called them together.

"Thanks to Dominique," Don said, "we'll have water for tomorrow night, but still no graze. Another day should get us out of the desert, but there's trouble ahead, and I look for it sometime tonight. I have reason to believe there are renegades—outlaws—who will try to take the herd from us. They'll be riding in from the north, and I want every rider awake, with his rifle ready. We'll move the herd, the mules, and the horse remuda south of the waterhole, and position ourselves north of it. Tonight, that bunch should be at the waterhole that we left this morning, so when they ride in, it'll be from the northeast. We'll all be waiting, belly-down. Nobody fires until I do."

"Shoot to kill?" Red asked.

"Yes," said Don. "I aim to challenge them, and if they're who we think they are, their answer will be hot lead. I don't look for them until after moonset, and that's an edge, as far as we're concerned. Them firing first will provide muzzle flashes for us to shoot at, and as long as we're belly-down, their first shots will be high. There'll be eleven of us, including Dominique and Roberto, and there's no reason why each of us shouldn't account for one of them. They may have us outnumbered, but if we can cut down enough of them with a first volley, that'll make believers of the others. Any questions?"

"If we're that sure they're at the waterhole northeast of here," Mike said, "why don't we just ride up there and end it?"

"Because we could never be dead certain," said Don. "I won't kill a man unless I know he's out to get me and there's a gun in his hand. I figure if they ride in on us sometime tonight, and they answer my challenge with gunfire, that's proof enough."

"That's more than fair, and more of a chance than they'd give us," Charlie said.

There was quick approval from the rest of the outfit. While Texas justice was swift, it was fair. Each man took his Henry from his saddle boot, and they positioned themselves at ten-foot intervals facing the direction from which the marauders were expected to ride.

Soon as it was dark enough, Griff and his bunch saddled their horses and rode south, to the waterhole so recently visited by the trail drive.

"They were here last night, just like I planned," said Griff with satisfaction. "We'll wait until moonset before we go after them. We'll gun down every man on watch."

"They ain't likely to have the whole outfit on watch," Kenton said. "The rest of them could roll out with their rifles and give us hell."

"There'll be muzzle flashes, so you'll have targets," said Griff. "If half the outfit's on watch, and we cut them down, we'll have a two-to-one edge against the rest. If there's one of you that thinks that ain't enough, you're ridin' the wrong trail."

"You're right," Bullard said. "If them odds ain't good enough, then we'd all better get ourselves work at day wages."

But Ben and Curt Pickford had other plans and had separated themselves from the rest of Griff's band so they could talk.

"We'll stay behind," said Curt, "and before they get close enough for shooting, we'll lose ourselves in the dark. We can't be that far from Los Angeles."

"Yeah, and we'll be goin' there broke," Ben complained. "There's a chance Griff was levelin' with us, when he said we could share in the money from the herd."

"You and your damn Santa Claus ideas," said Curt. "That bunch of Texans is as mean and smart as a pack of wolves. I got my doubts that Griff and his outfit can handle 'em. Stick with me, and at least you'll get to California with a whole hide."

Ben said nothing. He had been much closer to his dead brother Wiley than he was to Curt, and he silently vowed to avenge Wiley by killing Jim Roussel. In a town the size of Los Angeles, he told himself it would be much easier to lay an ambush and then lose himself after the killing.

The bawling of the longhorns finally ceased, as the beasts became exhausted and bedded down for the night. Nobody slept. The men were awake with their rifles, and the women with their fears. Don had warned them to spread their blankets near the herd, far enough away so there would be no danger from stray bullets. To pass the time, they talked among themselves.

"After this," said Rose, "we shouldn't have any more trouble. There's water for just one more day in the desert."

"I have all the confidence in the world in Don Webb," Sarah said, "but there's shooting to be done, and we don't know a thing about these outlaws, or how many there may be. I can't help worrying."

"Neither can I," said Ellie. "For the first time in our lives, all of us have someone besides ourselves to worry about. If Jim were to be shot . . . killed . . . whatever would become of me?"

"You're still thinking of yourself," Rose said.

"Then so am I," said Millie, "because I feel that way about Les. He's young, with some growing up to do, but he's all I have. What in the world would I do in California with only a dirty blanket between me and jaybird naked?"

"You'll be no worse off than me, if something should happen to Arch," Bonita said. "All I have is this blanket, and when mounting or dismounting it's worse than nothing."

"I forgot to mention that," said Ellie, "but it couldn't be helped. We got away from those Indians with our lives. When we thought we were going to die, I'd have been willing to ride to California without a stitch, just to get away."

"So would I," Bonita said. "I don't mean to seem ungrateful."

"Neither do I," said Millie. "Instead of complaining that we have nothing to wear, perhaps we should be saying prayers that our men will live through this night."

"I have been saying them," Rose said. "I think they'll do more good than all of us just complaining among ourselves."

"We ought to be sleeping," said Sarah. "Us laying awake won't change anything. When the attack comes—if it does—I don't think any of us will sleep through it."

The night wore on. Midnight came and went, and when the moon finally set, the darkness seemed all the more intense for its absence. While the Texans were within speaking distance of one another, they said nothing. Each knew what to expect, and they all became more tense and watchful as the time for the expected attack drew near.

Five miles to the northeast, Griff and the ten men riding with him reined up.

"We can't risk the horses givin' us away," Griff said. "Pull your bandannas tight over the noses of your horses, tying a corner of it to each side of the bridle."

The men dismounted, following Griff's orders. It was a precaution they appreciated, for they dared not approach the cow camp afoot. Should their plans go awry before they were able to reach their horses, they might be ridden down by the vengeful Texans. When their horses had been effectively silenced, they rode on. They kept their horses to a walk, so there was barely any sound in the desert sand. But there was the ever-present breeze out of the northwest, and with the back of his hand, Don Webb wiped the grit from his brow. A cow bawled restlessly, and Griff strained his eyes, seeking the dim outlines of the riders who should be circling the herd. Bringing up the rear, Ben and Curt Pickford reined up their horses until the other riders had gone on. Then they carefully wheeled their mounts and rode west.

"Drop your guns," Don Webb shouted. "You're covered."

Startled, one of the outlaws fired at the sound of Don's voice, and the others, thinking it was Griff, also began firing. The Texans returned the fire, shooting at muzzle flashes. The fire was deadly, and seven horses galloped away riderless. Only Griff and Quando survived, for they had not fired. Wheeling their horses, they galloped away into the night. Don waited until the desert was again silent, before calling out to his comrades.

"Texans, sing out."

One by one, they called out their names. Nobody had been hurt.

"Stay where you are," said Don quietly. "That should

be the end of it. We'll take a look come first light."

The men dozed, all the sleep they were going to get for many hours. When the first golden fingers of dawn touched the eastern sky, they beheld a shocking sight. There in the sand lay the bodies of seven men. Gathered around the waterhole there were seven saddled horses.

"We didn't get 'em all," said Charlie, "but I'd bet my saddle them that got away won't be comin' back."

"Why don't don't you and Red saddle up and ride out a ways?" Don said. "Maybe you can find out how many of them were in the bunch."

Red and Charlie saddled their horses, mounted, and rode out.

"What about those saddled horses?" Rose asked. "Now that their owners are dead, who do they belong to?"

"Anybody who wants to claim them," said Don.

"I want one of them," Rose said. "While I appreciate the Indian horse, he's got a spine that's like straddling a corral pole."

Don laughed. "Now that we're practically in California, you have a saddle."

"I want one of those horses and a saddle," said Sarah.

The rest of the women quickly laid claim to one of the horses, and each of them began unsaddling their new mounts. After a few minutes, Red and Charlie returned.

"Wasn't but nine of 'em rode in on us," Charlie said. "Two of 'em hightailed it."

"Bueno," said Don. "They won't be bothering us again."

"There was eleven of 'em," Red said, "but before they got close enough for shootin', two of 'em backed out and rode west."

"It's not likely they'll come together with the two who escaped then," said Don. "The two who didn't come after us won't be on good terms with the others."

Dominique and Roberto soon had breakfast ready, and after they had eaten, Don called them all together.

"I want every last one of those cows to have a drink

before we move out. Mules and horses too. I'll want Roberto riding with me. Felton, help Dominique with the remuda and the mules until we return. We must find water *and* graze for tomorrow.''

The longhorns had begun bawling restlessly, and the last thing most of them wanted was water. They refused to drink, and despite Don's order, many took the trail without watering. The horses and mules drank gratefully, and the horses captured from the Paiutes were turned in with the remuda horses. Joyfully the women mounted their horses and the men adjusted the stirrups of their newly acquired saddles.

''What about the dead hombres?'' Arch asked.

''We'll leave them where they lay,'' said Don, ''but each of them had a rifle. Take them and return them to the saddle boots. If any of you want to search the bodies, that's up to you. I personally want no part of anything found on them.''

It was quickly decided, with the exception of their rifles and horses, the dead would keep their possessions. When the herd took the trail, Don and Roberto rode ahead on what they hoped would be their last quest for water on the Mojave.

Far to the west, free of the desert, Ben and Curt Pickford had stopped to rest their horses.

''Hell of a lot of shootin' back yonder,'' said Ben. ''You reckon they made it?''

''I doubt it,'' Curt replied. ''I think them first few shots come from Griff's bunch, but I think the rest of 'em come from that Texas outfit. I'll be surprised if any of Griff's bunch got out alive.''

''If they did, they'll be comin' on to California,'' said Ben. ''We better ride, or they'll be catchin' up to us, and I ain't wantin' to explain why we backed out on the fight.''

But there was little danger of the survivors catching up, for Griff and Quando had returned to the waterhole where the outfit had spent the previous night. Despite the darkness and his not having fired a shot, Quando had been wounded in the shoulder.

"The slug's out and it's clean, Quando," said Griff, "but that's all I can do for you. There was just a quart of whiskey left, and it was in Doolin's saddlebag. You'll be needin' a doc. We better go on to Los Angeles, while you can still ride."

"Saddle my horse," Quando growled. "If I can't set my saddle, tie me across it."

Griff watered the horses, saddled them, and helped Quando mount. Quando gripping the saddle horn with both hands, they rode west.

Only a few of the longhorns had the strength to break away from the herd. The others stumbled along, as though the next step would be their last, bawling only occasionally. The drag riders were hard pressed keeping the ranks closed.

"My God," said Mike Horton, "if they don't have graze tonight, they'll never be able to take the trail tomorrow. They'll fall and not be able to get up."

"I'm afraid you're right," Bob Vines said. "I aim to talk to Don when him and Roberto return. I think our only chance is to stop at the next water only long enough for them to drink. From there, we'll have to drive them until they reach graze, or until they drop."

"Dear God," said Sarah, "after months on the trail, after risking your lives, is there really a danger of them dying before you can get them to market?"

"A danger more real than any of us realizes," Bob said. "If we don't find graze for them by tomorrow, there's a fifty-fifty chance we'll lose all or most of them."

The longhorns stumbled on. With every step their weary heads drooped nearer to the desert sand that might soon claim their gaunt bodies and bleaching bones for all eternity . . .

16

Don and Roberto soon reached the source of water they had visited the day before, but of far greater importance was the distance the herd must travel to free them of the brutal desert. They dismounted, resting the horses before allowing the animals to drink. Lacking graze, they were gaunt. Placing his hand on his horse's flank, Don pointed southwest and then due west. Which way to the nearest graze? Roberto understood, pointing west. When the horses had been watered and they were mounted, Don pointed west. Roberto led out and Don followed. To the northwest, Don could see a distant mountain, and his heart sank. The hummock seemed many miles away, and from a distance, looked as drab and lifeless as the desert itself. But Roberto never faltered, and after what Don believed was ten miles, he could see what appeared to be a thin line of greenery. He reined up, rubbing his eyes, and when Roberto looked back, the Mexican was grinning. He kicked his horse into a lope and Don followed. The sand began thinning out, and the horses slowed, nipping at occasional tufts of grass. Ahead of them, the greenery became more substantial, and reaching a rise, they reined up. Below them, stretching to distant foothills, was a virtual sea of green grass that might have equaled the promised land. Pouring down from a higher elevation was a stream that fell to the valley floor and winded its way southwest, along the base of the mountains.*

"My God," Don said reverently. "My God."

"Mañana" said Roberto, pointing.

"Not tomorrow," Don shouted. "Today! We can't be more than a dozen miles from that last waterhole. We're going to push our horses, mules, and cattle onto that range tonight. Let's ride."

The desert sun bore down. The longhorns seemed determined to fall back to an even slower gait, but the riders urged them on. But when the outfit saw Don and Roberto coming at a fast gallop, they allowed the longhorns to bunch, bawling their misery. When the outfit had all come together, Don told them what lay ahead.

"Maybe a dozen miles beyond the next waterhole," Don said. "We're going to water this bunch and take them on to that range tonight. It's that, or lose them all."

"I couldn't agree with you more," said Bob Vines. "I'm just not sure they'll make it. I'd say we're still half a dozen miles from water. Lay another twelve miles on that, and it adds up to impossible."

"But we have to try," Mike Horton shouted.

"Try, hell," said Charlie English. "Let's do it. Once the sun's down, that'll help some."

Despite Bob's doubts, the rest of the outfit echoed Charlie's determination. Drag riders shouted, fired their Colts, and somehow got the longhorns moving again. Forsaking his point position, Don threw in with the drag, and somehow the weary herd picked up on the urgency that drove the cowboys. Just as the setting sun was feathering the sky with its crimson tendrils, the longhorns smelled water. Gaunt as they were from lack of graze, the desert heat had drawn the moisture from their weary bodies, and they broke into a lurching trot.

---

*The Sierra Nevada mountains. At this point, about a hundred miles from Los Angeles.

"Hold back the horses and mules," Don shouted.

The riders joined forces with Dominique and Roberto, heading the horse remuda and the pack mules, allowing the longhorns to make their way to the water ahead.

"Les, you and Felton stay here and help Dominique and Roberto hold the horses and mules," said Don. "The rest of you come with me. As soon as a cow's had a drink, drag her out of there and make room for another. We've got to get them moving again, while they still have the strength. If we can keep them on their feet, sometime before dawn they'll have graze *and* water."

Nobody mentioned supper, for there wasn't time. Swiftly the cattle were driven to the water, and after drinking, were dragged away. Finally it was time to water the mules and horses. Half the outfit kept the herd bunched, while the others watered the pack mules and the horses. The sun was down, and there was only a memory of its vengeance in the heat the sand had absorbed. Finally they were ready to again take the trail.

"Head 'em up, move 'em out," Don shouted.

The longhorns balked, for the day had ended. They had watered, now it was time to graze, to rest. But there was no graze and no rest. The riders swung their knotted lariats, swatting bovine hides, forcing the animals to move. Gradually, although unwillingly, they did. Darkness crept over the land, silver stars winked from their vast panorama of purple, and a cooling breeze swept in from the west. Riders shrugged off their weariness, further closing the ranks and urging the longhorns westward. There were few bunch-quitters, and the drag riders had only to keep the drag animals moving. Bob Vines was taking his turn at drag, and he rode his horse alongside Don's.

"Once we reach these foothills, how far do you reckon we'll be from Los Angeles?" Bob asked.

"I have no idea," said Don. "I made it clear to Roberto that we must have graze for the stock. I suspect we're not taking the shortest way to Los Angeles. I think, instead of crossing the Mojave in a straight line, we're only crossing a corner of it. That means we may be a considerable distance north of Los Angeles when we leave the Mojave."

"I don't care how much farther it is," Bob said, "as long as there's water and graze."

"I reached that same conclusion," said Don, "when Roberto and me arrived at that last waterhole. We'll need a week or so to fatten up the herd, and to get our pack mules and horses well-fed, so what does it matter if we spend that time on the trail?"

The water and the cool of the night seemed to make a difference. While the longhorns refused to be hurried, they maintained a steady gait. They were three-quarters of the way through their ordeal, when the herd smelled water. Despite their weariness and their gaunt condition, they stampeded.

"Let them go," Don shouted. "Let's hold the horses and the mules!"

The riders headed the horse remuda and the mules. They would be led to water and allowed to drink after they had rested. The outfit reached the ridge just a few minutes before moonset, and they could see the silver of the stream and the green of the grass as it stretched away to the foothills beyond.

"Dear God," said Sarah, "even if we didn't need water and graze, it's beautiful."

"It is," Don agreed.

"We ought to start our breakfast fire with that map, and double what we promised to pay Dominique and Roberto," said Mike Horton.

"Are we anywhere close to the Old Spanish Trail as it's drawn on that map?" Charlie wondered.

"I doubt it," said Don. "Dominique and Roberto took us some distance south of the old trail, getting us to water. I think if we'd followed the old trail all the way, we'd have gone through more of the desert. We must be somewhere north of Los Angeles."

"Wherever we are, it'll be worth the extra miles, gettin' us out of that desert," Red said. "All we got to do is start each day with the sun at our backs, and end it with the sun in our eyes.''

Reaching the stream, they found most of the herd had already watered, and had begun grazing. Quickly they removed the packs from the mules and unsaddled their horses. The remuda horses had rolled and already were drinking.

"Comida?" Roberto asked.

"Food?'' said Jim Roussel. "Roberto's askin' if we want food.''

There was a thunderous shout from the outfit. Dominique and Roberto took the rest of the wood they had packed across the desert and started two fires. They immediately filled both coffeepots with water and put them on to boil.

"What about the herd?'' Les asked. "They're strung out for a mile. Do we bunch them and keep watch as usual?''

"I don't think so,'' said Don. "They're not goin' anywhere. We'll hobble all the horses and mules, keep our rifles handy, and get some rest. I think we've earned it. Besides, it's only a couple of hours till first light.''

The meal—their first in twenty-two hours—was a gala affair. Tired as they were, after they had eaten, they finished the coffee and waited until more was brewed.

"Will we stay here a little while?'' Rose asked. "If I don't wash myself, I feel like I'll just crumble away into the dirt.''

"I think we'll remain here for three or four days,'' said Don. "The horses, mules, and cows need the graze. I can use the time to scout ahead and maybe learn how far we are from Los Angeles.''

It was near dawn before they finally settled down to rest. There were trees along the stream that would provide welcome shade. Despite their ordeal in the desert, Don was up and about well before midmorning. Dominique and Roberto looked at him questioningly.

"I know we usually eat only twice a day,'' Don said, "but we had breakfast mighty early this morning. I believe we could all stand another feed about noon.''

Long before the meal was ready, the rest of the outfit had been awakened by the welcome aroma of boiling coffee.

"I don't know if this is breakfast or supper," said Charlie, "but I'm ready for it."

After they had eaten, Don had something to say.

"There's no reason for us to wander all over the countryside with this herd, looking for Los Angeles. While the horses, mules, and cows are putting some meat on their bones, I aim to ride to Los Angeles to meet with the folks that's promised to buy our herd. And while I'm there, I'll have a talk with the law and maybe find out what we're supposed to do with the money we took from the saddlebags belonging to Beavers and Dent. I'll take Red with me, unless somebody objects."

"If we have money enough," said Bob Vines, "I think you should buy some decent clothes for the ladies, until they're able to go in and choose for themselves."

"It's a good idea," Red agreed, "but what do we know about choosin' female clothes?"

"I realize that," said Bob, "but who said anything about female clothes? I mean Levi's, shirts, and boots, like the rest of us are wearing. They don't need finery on the trail."

"Good idea," Don said. "You're in charge of making note of their boot sizes. Red and me can pretty well figure out the Levi's and shirt sizes. But don't waste any time. I aim for us to ride out pronto."

"Since you're goin' on into town, you'd better check out our supplies," said Mike. "We may be on the trail another week or two, dependin' on how far we are from Los Angeles."

"Good thinking," Don said. "While Bob's making his list, have a talk with Dominique and Roberto. Anything we're likely to need, write it down."

Mike soon had some interesting things to report.

"Three more days, and we'll be out of coffee, bacon, beans, and biscuits."

"Tarnation," said Red, "what's left?"

"Nothing," Don said. "We'd better take two pack mules with us."

"Yeah," said Charlie, "and you'd better get going. I get cranky and mean as hell when I don't have coffee."

"That's the gospel truth," Felton Juneau said, "but what's your excuse the rest of the time?"

It was noon when Don and Red rode out, each of them leading a mule.

"I hope there's money enough for all this," said Red.

"There should be," Don said, "thanks to Winkler buying those two hundred cows, back in Santa Fe. There won't be much money left, but we need grub to keep us going until we sell the herd."

"We're almighty lucky our grub held out as long as it did," said Red. "After we rode out of Santa Fe, we almost doubled the size of our outfit."

Don laughed. "You owe the Utes a debt of gratitude. If we hadn't rescued those seven women, you wouldn't have that perky Molly Rivers wearin' nothing but a blanket and of a mind that you're the grandest galoot that ever rode out of Texas."

"You got somethin' there," said Red. "Us redheaded, freckle-faced Bohannons usually end up with females ugly enough to stop an eight-day clock. When I'm finally able to take Molly back to Texas, there'll likely be a stampede of Bohannon men, hell-bent for Santa Fe or California."

They rode on, resting the horses often, and come sundown, Don estimated they had traveled almost fifty miles. To their relief and delight, the graze seemed plentiful, and there was no shortage of water.

"I've been hoping we might come upon a ranch where we could get directions and some supper," Don said, "but it seems unlikely. It'll be dark pretty soon."

"Then we'll just have to bed down wherever the night finds us," said Red. "I've never liked to ride into a strange place after dark. Good way to get a dose of buckshot in your brisket."

Eventually they reined up, listening. There was the distant barking of a dog.

"Last time we heard a barking dog, there was two hundred hostile Indians just about within hollerin' distance," Red observed.

"I doubt that will be the case this time," said Don. "Let's ride closer."

They reined up again, within a fringe of trees. From there, they could see the dim glow of a light in the distance. Again the dog began barking, and there came the distinctive bleating of sheep.

"Damn sheep," Red said, in disgust. "Locusts with hooves."

"We're not movin' in with 'em," said Don. "All we want is directions and maybe some grub. Come on."

The dog began yipping furiously as they approached the cabin. The door opened, and a bearded man in a sombrero stepped out on the porch. Don and Red reined up a dozen yards away.

"We come in peace, señor," Don said. "We ask only the way to Los Angeles and perhaps a little food."

"You are welcome to both," said the stranger. "You may step down."

Don and Red dismounted.

"I'm Don Webb and this is Red Bohannon. We are from Santa Fe, and we have a herd of cattle north of here. We wish to know the way to Los Angeles."

"I am Rafael Otero," said the sheepman. "Los Angeles is perhaps forty miles slightly to the southwest. I have meat, bread, and goat's milk, to which you are welcome."

"We're obliged," Don replied, "but Los Angeles is nearer than we expected. I believe we'll just ride on."

"*Buenas noches,*" said Otero.

He remained on the porch until Don and Red mounted their horses and rode back the way they had come.

"You don't like goat's milk and mutton?" Red asked innocently.

"I can stomach it," said Don, "but I wasn't sure you could."

"Gracias," Red replied. "Was you serious about ridin' on to Los Angeles?"

"Yes," said Don. "Resting the horses, we can be there in four hours. Do you reckon you can handle some town grub, a cold beer, and a soft bed?"

"I ain't sure," Red said, "but I'd like to have a go at it. Let's ride."

They were facing the wind, and after riding only a few miles, they were able to smell the ocean.

"That's got to be the Pacific," said Don.

"I aim to see it, sometime before goin' back to Texas," Red said. "Biggest pond I ever seen was the Gulf of Mexico, and I reckon the Pacific's considerably bigger."

"I reckon," said Don. "It reaches to the other side of the world."

Two hours shy of midnight, they reined up. Ahead of them was a scattering of lights.

"Sure don't look like much of a town from here," Red observed. "Santa Fe was bigger than this."

"We're seein' just the outlying part of it," said Don. "I was in St. Louis once, and the town itself didn't seem all that big, but there was little towns huddled all around it. That's likely the way it is here. With the ocean on one side, it'll be like an Indian camp strung out alongside a creek."

Saugus, California. June 24, 1862.

The village, when they reached it, consisted of a general store, a blacksmith shop, two saloons, a cafe, and a rooming house.

"Let's go to the cafe first," Don said. "I'm surprised it's open this late."

"Maybe it's Saturday night," said Red.

They tied their horses and mules to the hitching rail and entered the cafe. Even at the late hour, it seemed crowded.

There was just one available table, and they took it. It was awhile before the waiter got around to them.

"Pard," Red said, "what day of the week is it, and what town are we in?"

"It's Saturday night, and you're in Saugus, California," said the waiter. "If that's all you're here for, we can't spare the table."

"We're here for more than that," Don said. "Bring us a pair of the biggest steaks you have, well-done. Surround 'em with any other fixings you have, includin' plenty of black coffee."

While waiting for their food, Don and Red studied their surroundings. Hanging lamps lit the place up like day. The patrons were almost all men, and they appeared to have come from all walks of life. Some were miners, some— from their dress—were seagoing men, while others might have been sheepmen. Still others seemed strangers to hard work, for their complexions were pale and their hands soft. Almost without exception, their belts sagged under the weight of revolvers. Some had knives sheathed to their belts, while the others had shoved the blades of the formidable weapons beneath the waistbands of their Levi's or homespun trousers. Sweating Chinese gathered dirty dishes from the tables, and as quickly as men left the cafe, others came in to replace them.

"It ain't this busy in San Antone on the Fourth of July," said Red. "You'd think they ain't another eatin' place for a hundred miles."

"Settin' right on the Pacific, there must be ships comin' from all over the world," Don said. "I've been wondering how the war between North and South might affect everybody else. From here, it looks like everybody else aims to mind their own business while the rest of us kill one another."

"Damn yankee politicians," said Red. "Texas never would've become a state if old Sam Houston hadn't had some aces up his sleeve. Them varmints in Washington never has liked us, and I reckon if they needed an excuse to come down on us, slavery was good as any.''

Their food was brought to their table, and it was much like that to which they were accustomed. Their steaks were smothered in onions. Fried potatoes, biscuits, gravy, apple pie and coffee arrived, but that wasn't all. The waiter returned with a basket of fruit, some of which the Texans had never seen.

''I feel a mite guilty, settin' down to this, while the others are settin' on the ground, eatin' beans and bacon,'' Don said.

''I don't,'' said Red. ''They'll get their chance.''

Their appetites satisfied, Don and Red left the cafe. Mounting their horses and taking the lead ropes of the mules, they rode along the dirt street to the rooming house. There was a lighted lantern hanging from a pole over the entrance. The clerk had been leaning back in his chair, dozing. The opening of the door awakened, him, and he sat up, rubbing his eyes.

''Room for the night,'' Don said. ''Do you have a stable for our horses and mules?''

''Stable out back,'' said the clerk. ''Dollar for each of you and for each animal. That includes hay and grain.''

Don paid. Then he and Red took the horses and mules to the stable, such as it was. They unsaddled and rubbed down their horses, putting them in one stall, and the mules in another. After feeding the animals, they returned to the rooming house. Their room was on the first floor.

''Don't look like much of a bed,'' Don said, ''but I reckon it'll be softer than most of the ground we've been sleepin' on.''

They piled their saddlebags and Henry rifles in a corner, and sitting on the bed, drew off their boots. Their gunbelts and hats were hung on the bedposts. Red blew out the lamp, and just moments after stretching out on the bed, the two of them were snoring.

In the Sierra Nevada foothills, almost a hundred miles away, the rest of the outfit had settled down to await the return of Don and Red. It was a time to wash long-ignored clothing and blankets, and they all availed themselves to the opportunity.

"Do you suppose Don and Red will reach Los Angeles today?" Sarah asked.

"They should," said Bob Vines. "They'll need at least a day in town before they start back. We should be seeing them again in three days. Not more than four."

"Oh, I hope nothing goes wrong," Sarah said.

"I don't know what else could," said Bob.

For lack of anything better to do, the riders decided to run a tally on the herd. When the seven of them had finished, they compared results.

"Amazing," Bob said. "Every one of us is within a dozen head of tallying the same."

"That's because they're all settled down, grazing," said Mike. "Who got the low tally?"

"Felton," Bob said. "Five thousand, two hundred and ten."

"Considering we gave up two hundred and sixteen of 'em in Santa Fe," said Charlie, "I reckon it's close to a miracle."

"I'd have to agree with you," Bob said. "We started with five thousand, five hundred and twenty-five. That's a loss of only ninety-nine along one of the roughest trails I ever rode."

"Now that we've tallied the herd," said Felton, "what are we goin' to do until Don and Red get back?"

"I'm gonna sleep," Jim Roussel said.

It seemed like a worthy idea, and they all headed for the shade of nearby trees.

Despite their late arrival and not getting to sleep until past midnight, Don and Red rose at first light. They went immediately to the cafe and had breakfast.

"Which way to Los Angeles?" Don asked, when he paid for their meal.

"Keep goin' west," said the cook. "If you're ridin', you're half an hour away."

They then went to the stable behind the boarding house, saddled their horses, and rode out, leading their mules.

"What'll we do first?" Red asked.

"Track down Ellerbee and Sons," said Don. "I want to confirm the sale of the herd before we do anything else. Then we'll find a mercantile, buy what we need, and make tracks back to the outfit."

As they rode on, they soon were able to see the blue of the Pacific in the distance. It was of such magnitude, they reined up and just looked at it for a few minutes.

"We'll see more of it after we've delivered and collected for the herd," Don said.

The Ellerbee and Sons warehouse had enormous corrals on three sides, and all of them were empty.

"Looks like they're ready for us," said Red.

After stating their business, they were shown into the office of Dwight Ellerbee. When Don had introduced himself and Red, Ellerbee wasted no time getting down to business.

"I'll want to examine the stock before I commit myself," Ellerbee said. "Where are they?"

"North of here, about five days," said Don. "Grazing and getting fat. Will you stick to the sixty dollars you quoted us by telegram?"

"Yes," Ellerbee said. "In fact, I'll do better than that. If they're all two-year-olds or under, and they average twelve hundred pounds, I'll go sixty-five."

"We're perfectly willing for you to see them first," said Don. "You have cattle pens all around you. Are we to bring them here?"

"Yes," Ellerbee said. "It will take at least a day to get your money. I trust that won't be a problem."

"It won't," said Don. "We'll see you a week from now."

"Lord Almighty," Red said, "that extra five dollars a head will run my take up another five hundred dollars. That is, if I still got a hundred head when we get 'em here."

"I've already talked to Bob, Jim, Les, and Mike," said Don. "We've decided, since we own most of the herd, that we'll take any loss. You, Charlie, Arch, and Felton will be paid for all the stock you started with. Les will be taking Eli's share back to his kin in Texas."

Red kept his head down, saying nothing. Finally, after swallowing hard, he spoke.

"I've rode a lot of trails, amigo, but I've never trailed with a better outfit. I reckon I don't know what to say, except muchas gracias."

After asking directions, Don and Red located the office of Los Angeles County Sheriff Emery DeShazo. Quickly Don explained the purpose of their visit.

"So you believe the Indians murdered Beavers and Dent," said DeShazo.

"We're certain of it," Don said. "The horses they stole from us wandered back with the money in the saddlebags. If you were either of them, and alive, would you have allowed all that money to slip through your hands?"

"I suppose not," said DeShazo. "The trouble is, I have no proof they stole the money. The miners who claimed Beavers and Dent were killers and thieves were a mite hasty. Two other men have since been caught and charged. As far as I'm concerned, the money you're claiming was taken from the saddlebags of Beavers and Dent was theirs. Nobody in these parts had any idea where them two was from, and there wasn't a trace of any kin. So I'm in no way responsible for anything that may have belonged to them. The money is yours, as far as I'm concerned."

Don and Red left DeShazo's office, and it was Red who finally spoke.

"So now you have thirty thousand dollars."

"Wrong," Don said. "We're an outfit, and *we* have thirty thousand dollars. We'll tell the others what DeShazo told us. Then we'll decide what to do with the money."

Leading their mules, they reined up before a mercantile. They were anxious to complete their purchases and return to their outfit with much good news.

17

"We got out of there just in time," said Don, as he and Red loaded the mules with their purchases from the mercantile. "There's less than twenty dollars left of the money we got from Winkler in Santa Fe."

"It was the answer to a prayer," Red replied. "How in thunder would we ever have got to California without it?"

They rode back the way they had come, reaching Saugus an hour before noon.

"There's a chance we might reach the herd sometime tonight," said Don.

"I'm for that," Red said, "but we'll have to rest more often, with the mules loaded."

They rode within sight of the sheep ranch where they had asked for directions, but they had no reason to stop. The dog announced their coming, yipping for as long as he could see them. The cabin appeared deserted. They rode on, pausing hourly to rest the horses and mules.

"If we get there tonight, it'll be almighty late," said Don. "We have plenty of grub, and I'm of a mind to have supper."

"So am I," Red agreed, "but we got no coffeepot."

"I reckon we can manage just this once without coffee," said Don.

Lest their fire attract unwanted attention, they stopped well before sundown. The meal cost them an hour, but the delay served a dual purpose. They unsaddled their horses and removed the packs from the mules, allowing the animals to roll.

"If I'm any judge, we got fifty miles behind us," Red said.

"We're half way then," said Don. "That's the southern end of that mountain range up yonder."

"It don't look fifty miles away," Red said.

"It may not be," said Don. "We're guessing as to how far we've come and how far we have yet to travel. From the time it took us to reach Saugus, I believe we rode at least a hundred miles. Ten miles an hour is a comfortable gait for the horses and mules, even if the mules are loaded."

"We'll reach our camp before midnight then," said Red.

"After all those days on the trail, I never thought I'd get too much rest," Ellie said, "but I'm awful tired of just sitting here watching the horses, mules, and cows eat grass."

Jim Roussel laughed. "You haven't been on enough trail drives. You learn to rest and sleep when and where you can, and if you ever get too much of either, you don't mention it to anybody."

"I just hope Don and Red get here sometime tomorrow," Ellie said. "I'll be so glad to be rid of this blanket."

"They'd better ride in tomorrow with more coffee," said Charlie, who had overheard their conversation. "We got just about enough for breakfast."

Les Brown, Mike Horton, and Felton Juneau were taking the first watch. Bob Vines had joined Sarah, where she sat on the bank of the swiftly flowing stream.

"I slept most of the afternoon," Sarah said. "What am I going to do tonight?"

"You can join me on the second watch," said Bob. "There'll be a full moon later."

Sarah laughed. "I didn't know cowboys had any interest in a full moon."

"Oh, but we do," Bob said. "Sometimes, after we've had a snootful, we bay at it."

"That's one thing I haven't asked you," said Sarah. "Are you a drinking man?"

"Not since I was south of the border, maybe three years ago," Bob said. "I got myself a jug of that cactus brew. About a hundred and forty proof, I reckon. I come to about three hours before first light, afraid I was gonna die. Before I finally come out from under that hangover, I was afraid I'd live. Since then, I've never touched anything stronger than beer, and then never more than two."

"I'm relieved to hear that," said Sarah. "The only real memory I have of my daddy is of him being drunk."

Two hours before midnight, one of the remuda horses nickered, and from somewhere in the darkness, there was an answer. Cocking his rifle, Mike Horton issued a challenge.

"Rein up and identify yourself."

"Two ugly galoots from Texas, with pack mules bearin' gifts," Red shouted.

"Send in the pack mules bearing gifts," said Mike. "You two-legged varmints will have to wait for daylight, so's we can have a look at you."

Charlie punched up the fire, piling on more wood as Don and Red rode in. Roberto seized one of the coffeepots and went to the stream to fill it.

"I hope you brought plenty of coffee," Charlie said.

"Ten pounds," said Red. "That oughta last a week, even with you around."

Charlie and Arch took the reins of the horses and began unsaddling them. Dominique untied the ropes securing the packs, and when Roberto had the coffeepot hung over the fire, the two of them began unloading the mules. They concerned themselves only with the supplies, laying the other parcels aside.

"Ladies," said Don, "Dominique and Roberto have separated all the grub. The rest of those packages belong to you. There's Levi's, a shirt, and boots for each of you. I'd have liked to have done better, but our money was running low, and we needed grub. I'm sure that after we've sold the herd, these ugly varmints you've took up with will buy you some real finery.''

"Bless you," Rose said.

There were glad cries from the others as they ripped away the paper wrappings. The contents were exactly what Don had said they were. Ellie, Millie and Bonita cast away their blankets and got into their shirts and Levi's.

"They don't make those kinds of duds for ladies," said Red. "You'll just have to roll up the legs of the Levi's. They was made for long-legged hombres.''

The rest of the women had cast modesty to the wind and rid themselves of what remained of the rags they had been wearing. Soon they were all dressed in new shirts and Levi's. All the shirts fit very well, but Rose was looking with some doubt at the narrow-toed boots.

"I don't believe my big foot will go in there," she said.

"Sure it will," said Don. "I bought them all a size larger than what was on the list."

"Sit down," Mike said, "and I'll help you with them."

The rest of the women watched with interest as Rose sat down and poked the toes of her left foot into one of the boots. With only a little help from Mike, it slipped on, and Mike then tried the other one. It went on just as easily, and Mike helped Rose to her feet. She immediately stumbled and would have fallen on her face if Mike hadn't caught her.

"They'll take some gettin' used to," said Don, trying mightily not to laugh.

"Your turn, Sarah," Bob Vines said. "Sit down."

Soon they were all wearing the new boots, and unaccustomed as they were to such footwear, they finally were able to stand and walk without difficulty.

"I'm so excited, I can't sleep," said Bonita. "I feel like a real Texan."

"You look like one," Arch said approvingly.

"All of you had better get what sleep you can," said

Don. "I aim for us to move out tomorrow, and we're at least a hundred miles from Los Angeles."

"Whoa," Bob said. "We can't sleep, not knowing what you learned in Los Angeles. Is there water and graze along the way? Is Ellerbee still goin' to take the herd? What's to be done with the money that belonged to Beavers and Dent?"

"One thing at a time," said Don. "There's plenty of water and graze along the way. We passed only one place, which was a sheep ranch. Ellerbee still wants the herd, and they'll pay sixty-five dollars a head for two-year-olds and under if they're all a twelve hundred pound average."

There he paused, for the shouts of the outfit drowned him out. When they again were quiet, he continued.

"The money that belonged to Beavers and Dent now belongs to us. The sheriff had no proof it was stolen and had been unable to find any relatives. It will be up to all of you as to what becomes of it."

"You mean it'll be up to all of *us*," said Mike Horton. "What do *you* believe should be done with it?"

"I believe it should be split ten ways, with a full share going to the kin of Eli Mills," Don said. "Thirty thousand and five hundred dollars comes out to three thousand and fifty dollars a share."

"I like the idea of Eli's kin gettin' a share," said Les. "He's gone, but he's still one of us, and that's how it should be."

"Yes," Rose agreed. "Such feeling makes me proud to know all of you, proud to be one of you."

There were shouts of approval from them all. Dominique had put on a second pot of coffee to boil, and both were ready. Despite the lateness of the hour, Dominique and Roberto filled their tin cups with scalding black coffee.

"Don," said Bob, "we already have two watches lined up. You and Red have had a long hard ride, so you're both excused for the night."

"We're obliged," Red said. "Molly, do you aim to sleep

tonight, or will you be walking around in them new boots till daylight?''

"They're grand," said Molly, "but I think I'll give them a rest. But I'm not taking off my new Levi's and shirt."

"Damn, I was gettin' to like that blanket," Red said.

"Then I'll save it and give it to you for Christmas," said Molly.

Even with all the excitement, the hour was late, and at first light they would continue their journey. Those not on watch retired to their blankets, but when the full moon rose, so did Sarah. She found Bob leaning against a tree, near the fast-flowing stream.

"It's been an exciting day, hasn't it?"

"Yes," said Bob. "We've had some surprises. If Beavers and Dent came by that money honestly, then I'm sorry they didn't live to enjoy it."

"But they stole two horses," Sarah said.

"Yes," said Bob, "and that leads me to believe they stole the money too. Don offered to allow them to ride back to Los Angeles with us, but I think they had good reason not to. The extra three thousand won't mean that much to Don, Jim, Les, Mike, and me, since we own most of the herd, but it'll mean a lot to Red, Charlie, Arch, Felton, and the kin of Eli Mills. That will run their shares to almost ten thousand dollars each, if we can hold Ellerbee to sixty-five dollars a head."

"But there's some things money can't buy," Sarah said. "If you return to Texas while the war's going on, won't you have to fight?"

"I reckon," said Bob. "Some of us have been talking about staying in California for a while. At least until the war's over."

"Molly says Red plans to do that," Sarah said. "I hope we can too."

"I reckon we will," said Bob. "I don't mean to sound unpatriotic, but I kind of feel the way old Sam Houston did. He fought like a cougar to get Texas into the Union, and he saw no advantage to leaving it. He resigned as governor when Texas seceded.''

Dominique and Roberto had breakfast ready by first light. After a hasty meal, all the riders began gathering the cattle from along the stream. The good graze had done wonders for them and the horses and mules. Dominique and Roberto had all the pack mules loaded well before the herd was bunched. All the women were now riding saddled horses and were dressed like Texas cowboys. Don Webb looked at them approvingly. When the herd had been bunched, Don waved his hat.

"Head 'em up, move 'em out!"

The days of rest and good graze had made a difference, and the longhorns began with a long stride. The drag riders had only to keep up. Dominique and Roberto kept the mules and the horse remuda right on the heels of the drag. The women, dressed in their new cowboy garb, rode proudly. Having been to Los Angeles, aware that there was water and graze, Don kept his position as point rider. There would be no advance scouting the rest of the way.

"I'd say we did better than fifteen miles," said Mike Horton, after they had settled the herd alongside a creek.

"I think so too," Don said. "Another four days like this, and it'll all be over."

"It's time for us all to set down over a couple of pots of coffee and decide what we aim to do after we sell the herd," said Jim Roussel. "I think there's goin' to be hell to pay in Texas before the war's done."

"Some of us have already been talking," Red said. "It's mostly just a matter of us all gettin' together and seein' if we're headed for the same corral."

"Tonight's as good a time as any," said Don. "It's still early enough that after supper, we'll have a couple of hours before sundown."

After supper, well before dark, they settled down to talk.

"I reckon all of us can agree that we got no business

going back to Texas while it's neck-deep in war,'' Charlie said.

"We can all agree," said Don, "but Felton and me don't have much choice. We both have a woman waitin' for us, and they won't take kindly to settin' out the war in Texas, while we're in California."

"Mine won't," Felton said.

"Then go to Texas and bring 'em here," said Red. "Don, I seem to recollect you sayin' something about goin' back on a sailing ship to one of the Texas ports."

"I did," Don said, "and I'm not opposed to the idea, unless the Federals have managed to blockade the Texas ports."

"We should be able to find out in Los Angeles," said Bob. "If the ships are still sailing into and out of Texas ports, you should be quick to take advantage. You don't know how much longer you'll have the opportunity."

"True," Don said. "Does that suit you, Felton?"

"Yes," said Felton. "I sure don't aim to ride through Paiute and Ute country again."

"If you and Felton are able to get back to Texas on a sailing ship," Les Brown said, "will one of you take Eli's kin his share of the money and tell them what happened to him?"

"I reckon," said Don. "It's the least we can do for his kin."

"I hate to mention this," Mike said, "but we owe for some of the horses and mules we got from friends and kin. We promised to pay when we sold the herd, and with the war goin' on, they're likely to be in need of the money."

"I haven't forgotten," said Don. "Without their generosity, we never could have made the drive. All of you that's owin' for a horse or mule, write down who you owe, and how much. If I can get back to Texas by sailing ship, I'll see that every debt is paid."

"The rest of us ought to just pitch camp somewhere, until Don and Felton get back," Charlie said. "Whatever we aim to do here in California, I'd feel more comfortable if we done it as an outfit.''

"Am I allowed to say something?'' Rose asked.

"Yes," said Don.

"Speaking for myself, I'd like for us all to stay together, at least until we can go back to Texas. I've been through a lot with Sarah, Ellie, Millie, Molly, Wendy and Bonita, and I'd surely miss them if we were all to go different ways.''

There were shouts of eager agreement from the rest of the women.

"If everybody agrees," said Don, "we'll remain an outfit as long as we're in California.''

There were shouts from them all, including Dominique and Roberto.

"That's settled then," Don said. "Now we have only to reach Los Angeles.''

Ben and Curt Pickford had taken the most direct route to Los Angeles, straight across the Mojave desert.

"We'd best start lookin' for a way to get our hands on some money," said Curt. "We barely got enough to feed ourselves for a week.''

"That's about how long it'll take that trail herd to get here," Ben said.

"So you still aim to go after Roussel for gunnin' down Wiley.''

"More than that," said Ben. "When that bunch sells their herd, they'll have money. I'm of a mind to take some of it, and what better way than to bushwhack some of 'em, when they ain't got the whole outfit behind 'em?''

"Startin' with Roussel, I reckon.''

"Yeah," Ben said. "Startin' with Roussel, and I'll do the shootin'.''

Just two hours behind the Pickfords, Griff and Quando reached Los Angeles. Quando had been out of his head with fever the morning after he had been wounded, and it had been difficult for Griff to keep him in the saddle. In fact, honoring Quando's request, Griff had been forced to tie the outlaw belly-down over his saddle. Quando looked dead, and as they rode along the street, they received some curious stares. Griff knew the town well enough to find a doctor. The doctor—Otis Ballenger—watched Griff untie the rope and hoist Quando over his shoulder. He held the door open while Griff entered the office with his burden.

"We was waylaid by some outlaws," said Griff, without being asked. "He's had a fever for maybe four hours. I didn't have nothin' to doctor him."

Ballenger pointed to the next room. Griff entered. Easing Quando from his shoulder, he placed the wounded outlaw on the bed.

"I'll disinfect the wound and try to reduce the fever," said Ballenger. "He'll be here for a while, so unless you have nothing better to do, I don't advise waiting."

"I don't aim to," Griff said. "I'll be back."

At no time since leaving Santa Fe had the herd trailed so well. The second day after leaving the foothills of the Sierra Nevada, there was evidence of a storm brewing far to the west.

"Must be out over the ocean," Red observed.

"I expect it is," said Don. "We'll keep the herd moving, and maybe we can have them bedded down for the night before it reaches us."

Charlie, Les, and Felton were riding drag. There was little to do except to keep the ranks closed. Most of the land over which they traveled was grassed over, and there was almost no dust. All the women were in good spirits with their newly acquired clothing and saddles.

"I reckon you're ridin' a little easier," said Les, as he trotted his horse beside Millie's.

"I reckon I am," Millie said. "Try straddling a horse for a month, with nothing between his backbone and your bare behind, and you'll have more appreciation for your saddle."

Les laughed. "You're about to get your new duds and boots broke in proper. We're in for some serious rain."

"I don't care," said Millie. "I just hope there's no thunder and lightning. I'm so tired of waiting while all of you beat the bushes looking for stampeded cows."

"I reckon we're as tired of it as you are," Les said, "but we can do it another time or two if we must."

They kept the herd moving. By early afternoon big gray clouds had already hidden the sun. The wind rose, but there was still no sign of thunder or lightning.

"We'll bed 'em down early," Don said, to the flank and swing riders. "I'd say we're being spared the thunder and lightning, but there'll be plenty of wind and rain. This bunch will be wantin' to turn their backs to it, and there's no use running ourselves ragged trying to change their minds."

Water not being a problem, they bunched the herd near a stream. The storm held off long enough for the outfit to enjoy an early supper. When the storm struck, there was only wind-whipped rain.

"This is some surprising," said Felton Juneau. "I was gettin' the idea it never rains in this part of the world without thunder and lightning."

"God knows we've had our share of it," Bob Vines said.

There was no trouble with the longhorns. They grazed peacefully and might actually have enjoyed the rain. After about two hours, it slacked, finally ceasing altogether. When the clouds were swept away, the sun came out.

"Oh, look," Sarah cried.

Toward the west, there were many rainbows, some of them overlapping. Slowly, the more distant ones going first, they faded.

"I've never seen anything like that," said Mike Horton.

"It takes water," Felton Juneau said, "and there ain't that much water in all of Texas."

Wood was as plentiful as water and graze. Dominique and Roberto cut enough dry wood from the underside of fallen trees for a fire, and soon there was hot coffee. Within an hour, everybody's clothing was dry, and the rain might never have been.

"Seems like a waste," said Red. "We're settin' around drinking coffee, and there's two more hours of daylight."

"Hush your mouth," Charlie said. "A Texan don't hardly ever get to do this, and I aim to enjoy it while I can. It'll be somethin' I can tell my grandchildren."

Red laughed. "I didn't know about them. Have you told Wendy?"

"Has he told Wendy what?" the girl inquired, becoming aware of their conversation.

"Oh, nothing," said Charlie. "He's just bullyragging me."

"We was just talkin' about Charlie's grandchildren," Red said innocently.

"You ugly varmint," said Charlie, "why don't you get together with Molly and discuss your own grandchildren?"

"Yes," Molly said, becoming interested. "I'd like to hear about them."

"Settle down, all of you," said Don. "This is a time of rest. If nobody's tired, I reckon we can get the herd moving and keep them on the trail until midnight."

"I'm more tired than I realized," Charlie said. "Think I'll find me some shade and catch a few winks."

"I'll go with you," said Red.

Griff didn't return to Doctor Ballenger's place until after breakfast the next morning. Ballenger wasn't there, and when Griff went in, he found Quando sitting on the edge of the bed. Quando wasn't in the best of moods.

"Where the hell you been? I been settin' here six hours, needin' grub and a smoke."

"The doc told me not to come back for a while," said Griff. "You able to get up?"

"Why in tarnation wouldn't I be?" Quando snarled. "I ain't been gut-shot."

"I need to settle with the doc," said Griff. "Where is he?"

"How should I know?" Quando said. "Don't pay the bastard nothin'."

It was a good time for Ballenger to return, and he did so in time to hear what Quando said.

"Far as I'm concerned, you're free to go," said Ballenger. "There is no charge."

"I brought this varmint here, and I'll pay for him," Griff said.

He left ten dollars on the table beside the bed, and when he left the office, Quando was right behind him. When they were outside, Quando spoke.

"You don't hear too good, do you? He said there was no charge."

"He heard what you said about not paying him," said Griff.

"It bothers you, what a two-bit sawbones thinks?"

"It does," Griff replied. "I wouldn't want him thinkin' I'm the least bit like you."

Quando's laugh was ugly. "You're a damn thief, just like me, amigo. They don't come in different shades."

"I believe in payin' what's owed, if it's in money or lead," said Griff. "I don't even like you, but the doc was expecting me to pay. If I'm around the next time you get shot, I'll just leave you there."

"Then we might as well split the blanket, right now," Quando growled. "Last thing I want is some hombre watchin' my back that's inclined to get religion."

"Suits me," said Griff. "If somebody was about to back-shoot you, I reckon I'd have to wrestle with my conscience over whether you was worth savin'."

Griff had brought Quando's horse. When they mounted, Quando rode one direction and Griff rode another. Quando had money enough for grub, so he found a mercantile. When he had food to last him a week, he rode north. He needed money, enough for a stake, and when the herd was sold, those Texas cowboys would be flush . . .

But Quando wasn't the only one with robbery on his mind. Ben and Curt Pickford had taken a room not far from the Ellerbee stock yards, where they awaited the arrival of the Texas herd.

"I still don't feel easy about this," said Curt.

"All you got to do is cover me," Ben replied. "We'll wait until we know that bunch has been paid for the herd. Once they hit town, they won't stay together all the time. Soon as this Jim Roussel separates himself from the others, I'll gun him down. You just see that nobody bores me while I'm taking his money."

"I'll back your play," said Curt, "but when it's done, I ain't hangin' around here. Them Texans is likely more vengeful-minded than you."

The third day's drive after leaving the Sierra Nevada foothills brought the longhorns within fifty miles of Los Angeles. Well-fed and watered, the herd trailed well.

"Are we bunchin' 'em outside of town?" Mike asked.

"No," said Don. "Ellerbee has cattle pens, and when Red and me was there, they gave us permission to drive 'em right on into the pens."

"They're wantin' a twelve-hundred pound average," Red said. "You reckon they've put on enough fat?"

"I think so," said Don. "We haven't been driving them hard, and there's been plenty of good graze. They should be in prime condition."

The sixth day after leaving the Sierra Nevada foothills, they reached the little village of Saugus. It wasn't more than half a day's drive to the Ellerbee stock pens.

18

Los Angeles, California. July 3, 1862.

Not even during the glory days of Spanish and Mexican rule had the town seen the like of the Texas longhorns. They filled a street from boardwalk to boardwalk as far as the eye could see, and there wasn't a hitching rail left standing. Businessmen cursed the brutes as their massive horns raked doors and windows. Rain the night before had left water standing in the dirt streets, and they became a quagmire of mud after the passing of the herd. Don had ridden ahead and had opened the gates to the cattle pens. He waved his hat, and the riders kept the longhorns moving. When roughly a third of them had passed into the first pen, the rest were headed and driven to the other two pens. All activity came to a halt at Ellerbee's, as everybody hurried to see the spectacle taking place outside. When the gates had been closed, Don rode on to the office. He found Dwight Ellerbee waiting.

"We'll want a tally sometime today," Don said.

"I'll have it done immediately," said Ellerbee, "as well as an inspection. However, you may have to wait until the day after tomorrow for your money. Tomorrow is July fourth, and the banks will be closed."

"As long as we have a tally and a receipt," Don said. "I'll sign you a bill of sale."

"See me at four o'clock this afternoon," said Ellerbee. "I'll have a tally and a receipt ready for you."

Don rode back to join his waiting riders.

"I feel lost without a herd of cows to look after," said Red.

"Ellerbee will have us a tally and receipt at four o'clock," Don said, "but we can't get our money until the day after tomorrow. Tomorrow's July fourth, and the banks will all be closed."

"We could celebrate, if we had some money," said Mike Horton.

"I've thought of that," Don said. "We have the money Beavers and Dent left behind, and since Sheriff DeShazo said it's ours, we might as well divide it."

"I ain't so much wantin' to celebrate as I'm wantin' a decent shave, a haircut, and a bath," said Charlie.

Don wasted no time. He counted out equal shares of three thousand and fifty dollars for each of them.

"I'm keeping the share belonging to Eli's kin," Don said. "Now why don't we find us a good hotel that offers baths and has a dining room?"

"Good idea," said Felton Juneau. "I reckon you and me can share a room, Don."

Don laughed. "I reckon. It'll be up to the rest of you catamounts as to what you aim to do with your ladies."

"I got money enough for a room for Rose and one for me," Mike Horton said.

"Don't go spending money for an extra room for me," said Rose. "I don't think there are any secrets between us."

"I feel the same way," Sarah said.

Quickly the others expressed the same sentiments, and they went in search of a hotel. They found one appropriately named The Ocean View, for it faced the Pacific. There was a fancy dining room with a red-checked cloth on every table and a matching red carpet on the floor.

"Lord," said Bonita Holmes, "we'll be lucky if they let us in here."

But there was no difficulty. Don and Felton took a room,

paying in cash for the next two nights. The rest of the riders each took a room, also paying for two nights.

"Each of the ladies will need a bath," Bob Vines said.

"Two dollars extra," said the clerk.

Bob and his six companions each paid the extra two dollars. All their rooms were on the first floor. Four rooms were on one side of the hall, and four on the other.

"I don't know about the rest of you," Don said, "but I'm gonna find me a barber shop where I can get a shave, a haircut, and a bath all in one place."

"I reckon me and the rest of these galoots will be goin' with you," said Bob, "after we show the ladies to their rooms."

The others were quick to agree and began unlocking their doors.

"I'll stop at the desk and have them send up your bath," Bob said, when he and Sarah were inside. "When the rest of us are cleaned up and looking human, I think we all should go looking for some new clothes."

"But I already have new clothes," said Sarah.

"Cowboy clothes," Bob said. "We can do better than that. By suppertime, you won't look like a drag rider."

After leaving an order at the desk for baths to be sent to seven of their rooms, the men went in search of a barber shop with an adjoining bathhouse. They were gone almost two hours. When they returned to the hotel, the women had taken their baths and the tubs had been removed.

"I've never been on a bed the like of this," Molly said, when Red entered the room.

Her shirt and Levi's hung on the foot of the bed and her boots sat under it.

"You goin' to town like that?" Red asked.

"I didn't know we were going to town," said Molly. "Are we?"

"All of us was talking while we were at the barber shop," Red said, "and we decided it's time we all had some decent clothes. We ain't had these off since leavin' Texas, and it don't make much sense, gettin' a bath and then gettin' back into the same old ragged, dirty clothes. I want to see how you look without range clothes."

"Then take a look," said Molly.

"Damn it, you know what I mean," said Red. "Female clothes."

Eventually there was a knock on the door, and when Red poked his head out, Don was waiting.

"The rest of us are goin' looking for some new clothes," Don said. "Are you and Molly goin' with us?"

"I reckon," said Red. "Give us a minute or two."

Molly was already buttoning her shirt. Within seconds, she had on her Levi's and was pulling on her boots. She and Red left the room and found their companions waiting in the hotel lobby.

"We got three hours before suppertime," Don said. "We ought to get ourselves fancied up for a big day tomorrow."

"You have to be at Ellerbee's at four o'clock," said Bob.

"I haven't forgotten," Don said. "From there, I aim to ride down to the dock and talk to somebody about those sailing ships. Soon as we collect our money for the herd, Felton and me had better board one for Houston, if we can. Gettin' there is only half of it. We'll have to come back the same way."

"I wish you didn't have to go," said Mike. "It'll be a rotten break if you get there, and before you can return, the Federals close the Texas ports."

"We can't help thinking about the possibility of that," Felton said, "but it's a chance we'll have to take. You gents left Texas with nothing but the clothes on your backs, your saddles, and the horses you were ridin'. Now you got money in your pockets, a pile more comin', and a handsome woman by your side. A man don't often see a run of luck like that. All of you just say some words to the big boss up yonder that Don and me will go there and back without a Federal blockade of Texas ports."

It was a sobering thought, and despite the good fortune they had enjoyed, some of the hilarity had gone out of them. Los Angeles, with its sailing ships from many ports, had much more to offer than a mercantile or general store. There were stores devoted to the sale of clothing for men and women, and it was to one of the most prestigious of these that the Texans were attracted. They were met at the door by a handsomely dressed salesman, who looked at them with some disapproval. Don took notice and spoke immediately.

"We have ladies with us."

"Ah, yes," said the salesman smoothly. "In their . . . ah . . . attire, I might have overlooked them."

"Take the time to find a lady to see to their needs," Don said, "and then we'll talk to you about ours. If you're concerned about the money, then don't be. We're prepared to pay for their clothing and ours."

The look of relief that passed over the man's face was obvious, and as he rushed away, the Texans laughed.

"I don't like him," Ellie Andrews said.

"Neither do I," said Don, "but we have money to pay. He'll respect that."

When the uppity salesman returned, he had a gray-haired woman with him. When he spoke, his entire attitude had changed.

"I am Mr. Billington," he said, "and this is Mrs. Maxwell. She will see to the needs of the ladies."

With a friendly smile, Mrs. Maxwell took charge of the women, and they followed her up the stairs to a second floor. Billington raised his eyebrows and seemed about to speak, but Don beat him to it.

"Go about your business, Billington. When we find what we want, we'll holler at you."

At a loss for words, Billington nodded. The Texans wandered among the racks, choosing dark pinstriped trousers with matching frock coats. White ruffled shirts and red or black ties completed their outfits.

"I want some new boots," said Red, "but I ain't sure Billington would know a Texas boot from a busted calk horseshoe."

"Let's make do with what we have from here," Don

said. "We'll find a boot-maker for our boots. I want a new hat too."

Billington had been lurking about like a buzzard waiting to swoop down once he was certain the carcass was his. When Don nodded to him, he came in a lope.

"Are you sure the sizes . . . ?"

"The sizes are right," Don said. "We made sure of that. Tally it all up, a total for each of us."

One by one, they paid, and while they waited for Billington to wrap their purchases, Mrs. Maxwell came down the stairs. Her concern was plain, and when Don looked at her, she spoke.

"The ladies have made their choices, and I must warn you, the bill is quite large."

"Tally up a bill for each of them, and send them down here," said Don. "Their bills will be paid."

They came timidly down the stairs, their arms loaded with parcels. Molly was first, and she seemed almost afraid when Red took the bill from her. If he was startled, he failed to show it. He handed Billington the piece of paper and counted out a hundred and fifty-five dollars. The rest of the riders settled their bills with equal calm. They then left the place, ignoring Billington's profuse thanks and an invitation to come again.

"Dear Lord," Sarah said, "I had no idea it was going to cost so much. I'm ashamed of myself."

"Hush," said Bob. "You're worth it."

Dismayed at the expense, the others began protesting, but were quickly hushed, just as Bob had quieted Sarah.

"I still need some boots and a hat," Don said, "but I think both can wait for another day. By the time we get all this stuff back to the hotel, it'll be time for me to ride back to Ellerbee's."

"We'll all set tight until you get back," said Bob. "By then it'll be suppertime."

"We'd better decide pretty quick what we're goin' to do with all them extra horses and the mules," Mike Horton said. "Keepin' 'em in a corral at the livery and feedin' 'em hay will be the ruin of us."

"We can afford it through tomorrow," said Don. "We'll decide what to do about them before Felton and me have to leave."

Don arrived a few minutes before four and was quickly shown into Dwight Ellerbee's office.

"Our talley is five thousand, two hundred," Ellerbee said. "Is that satisfactory?"

"Completely," said Don.

"Good," Ellerbee said. "Like you said, they're prime, and I'm standing behind my offer of sixty-five dollars a head. Here's your receipt and a check. You may present it the day after tomorrow at the First National Bank."

"Get me some paper, a quill, and some ink, and I'll write you a bill of sale," said Don.

The items were brought. Don quickly wrote and signed a bill of sale. Unaware that he was being watched, he left the Ellerbee offices and rode toward the distant dock.

"He ain't had time to get the money," Curt Pickford said. "He'll have to get it from a bank, and it's too late in the day."

"I can wait," said Ben. "I don't aim to make my move until I know Roussel's got his share, and I got him away from the others. We know the hotel where they're stayin', and we'll follow Roussel when he leaves there."

"The banks will likely be closed tomorrow," Curt said. "It's July fourth."

"No matter," said Ben. "I can wait another day."

Quando had watched the longhorns being driven into the Ellerbee stock pens, and he knew the hotel where the Texans were staying. He would wait until he knew they had their money. Then he would choose a time and place to make some of it his own . . .

There was only one office that handled all the commerce into and out of Los Angeles, and it was there that Don made his inquiry about booking passage on a sailing ship bound for New Orleans that would take him and Felton to Houston.

"There's a sailing ship bound for New Orleans, leaving three days from now," Don told his companions, "and I just booked passage for Felton and me as far as Houston. As far as anybody knows, a week after we arrive in Houston, we can board another ship bound for Los Angeles. We'll have a week to tend to our business in Texas. Will that be enough for you, Felton?"

"More than enough," said Felton. "I got a feelin' we'd better go there and get out just as quick as we can. I went down to the hotel's dining room and bought a newspaper while you was gone, and it's full of nothin' but the war."

"I'll read it some other time," Don said. "I don't want to spoil my supper."

Despite the grim news of war, the outfit went to supper in the hotel's dining room. It was far more fancy than the cafe in Saugus, where Don and Red at eaten before. There was a huge table that would seat twenty, and it was to this that the outfit was taken. The waiters were dressed in fancy red jackets that bore the embroidered name of the hotel on the breast pocket, and three of them brought baskets of fruit to the table.

"We'll make this as easy as we can," said Don. "We're havin' steak with whatever kind of fixings you can serve with it. Make mine well-done. You can ask the others how they want theirs."

The order was taken quickly, and they began sampling the different kinds of fruit that overflowed the baskets. There were small printed notices on every table, announcing that the hotel would sponsor a fireworks display on July fourth.

"I've never seen fireworks," Millie Nettles said.

"None of us has," said Rose. "We never saw much of

anything at the mission school, except whippings and hard work.''

''We could ask around and see what happened to the place,'' Bob said. ''That is, if anybody cares.''

''I don't care,'' Sarah said. ''I wish I could put it out of my mind and never think of it again.''

The rest of the women quickly expressed the same sentiments.

''Enough of that,'' said Don. ''Let's talk about what we'll do tomorrow.''

''I think we oughta look for a place to pitch camp for as long as we plan to stay here in California,'' Charlie said. ''This hotel will gobble up all my money in three months.''

''Yeah,'' said Jim Roussel. ''Dominique and Roberto had the right idea. They're bunkin' down at the livery, with the horses and mules.''

''Oh hell,'' Red growled, ''we can do better than that. We been bunking with the horses and mules all the way from San Antone.''

Molly laughed. ''Don't forget the cows.''

A well-dressed, gray-haired man approached their table, tipping his hat.

''I couldn't help overhearing your conversation,'' he said. ''I'm Jeffries Butler, and I've a piece of property that may interest you.''

''We're not interested in buying property,'' said Don. ''We don't aim to be here more than a few months.''

''A sale isn't what I have in mind,'' Butler said. ''I have three hundred acres, with a twelve-room house. It used to be a horse ranch till the old gent that owned it died. Now his kin want to sell the place, but it's been on the market for a year with no offers. They are willing to rent it very reasonably, just to keep it all from going to seed, or possibly to prevent having the house burned.''

''On that basis, we might be interested,'' said Don. ''What's your idea of reasonable?''

''A hundred dollars a month,'' Butler said. ''There's a

barn large enough for as many as fifty horses. There's plenty of graze and water too.''

''Tell us how to find the place, and where we can find you,'' said Don. ''Tomorrow we'll ride out and look at it.''

''Here's a map I had printed,'' Butler replied, ''and my office is here, just off the lobby of the hotel.''

When Butler had returned to his table, the riders all looked at one another.

''With all of us payin' a little, that ain't much over ten dollars a month,'' said Bob.

''That's why we're ridin' out for a look at this old horse ranch,'' Don said. ''We don't know how long this war between North and South will last.''

The supper was an event to be remembered, and long after the food was consumed, they lingered over coffee, considering the possibilities of Butler's proposal.

''Suppose we rent the place, and he sells it?'' said Mike Horton. ''If he's willing to rent it for a hundred a month, maybe we could all just pitch in and buy it. Then we couldn't be put out of it. I'm bettin' we can hire Dominique and Roberto pretty reasonable too.''

''You're forgettin' one thing,'' Red said. ''Charlie, Arch, Felton, and me won't have the kind of dinero the rest of you will have.''

''I think we're gettin' the cart considerably ahead of the horse,'' said Don. ''Just wait until we've had a look at the place. Then if we think it's worth buying, maybe we can set it up so we can all afford a piece of it.''

''The fireworks display won't be until tonight,'' Don said, as they sat down to breakfast. ''I asked the desk clerk.''

''Then let's ride out for a look at that house Butler told us about,'' said Bob.

''That would be so exciting, having our own place,'' Molly Rivers said.

When they went to the livery, saddled their horses and rode out, several observers were more than a little surprised.

"Damn it," Ben Pickford said, "they're leaving. Where can they be going?"

"They'll be back," said Curt. "We been watching, and they ain't been to a bank. They still got to get their money for the cows."

But Quando wasn't so sure. He mounted his horse and followed at a safe distance.

The ranch was all that Butler had promised and more. Besides the ranch house, there was a bunk house. All the buildings were in good repair, and there were three fast-flowing creeks that ran across the property.

"That barn's plenty big enough for some serious horse ranching," Les Brown said.

"Let's look at the house," said Rose.

The doors were unlocked, as Butler had said they would be. The place had a natural stone foundation and was constructed from skinned logs, which had been painted a dark brown. The windows were large, with glass panes.

"That's the first log house I ever saw that was painted and had glass in the windows," Mike Horton observed.

They inspected every room, finding nothing amiss. Adjoining the kitchen, the dining room had a huge T-frame wooden table that was long enough to seat thirty. Finally, in the kitchen there was an enormous iron cook stove. Along one wall there was a series of iron sinks, apparently for dish washing. Mounted behind them was a pump. Don worked the handle a few times and was rewarded with a rush of clear, cold water.

"Water in the house," said Arch Danson. "I never seen that before."

"It's generally so dry in Texas, we was lucky to have a waterhole within walking distance of the house," Charlie said.

"I've seen enough," said Don. "Anxious as Butler is to sell this place, let's see what he has in mind, price-wise."

"This being the Fourth of July, he may not be in his office," Bob said.

"Then we'll see him tomorrow," said Don. "We can't cash our check until then."

To their surprise, Butler sat in the hotel lobby, reading a newspaper. Folding the newspaper, he got up.

"We're ready to talk to you about that horse ranch," Don said.

"Fine," said Butler. "Let's go to the hotel's dining room for coffee."

They were seated at the same long table where they'd had supper the night before.

"We don't believe in beatin' around the bush," Don said. "What's your askin' price for the place?"

"Fifteen thousand," said Butler. "Five thousand in cash, and the rest through the bank, over twenty years."

"We have nothing against banks," Don said, "but we don't like debt. How much, if we pay you all of it in cash?"

"Twelve thousand," said Butler.

"On those terms, I think we'll take it," Don said. "All of you have heard the offer. Is anybody unhappy with it?"

Nobody said anything.

"Draw up the papers then," said Don, "and we'll have the money for you tomorrow, when the bank opens."

"Fine," Butler said. "It will be then before I can have you a copy of the deed drawn up. To whom shall I say it's being sold?"

"You can use all nine names," said Don, "or just show it's being sold to the Circle 9-T connected. By ten o'clock, we should be ready to do business with you."

When Butler had gone, everybody wanted to talk at once.

"Why are we needin' a brand?" Les Brown wanted to know.

"When I get back from Texas with my woman, I might just buy the rest of you out, stay here and raise horses," said Don.

Mike Horton laughed. "Suppose the rest of us decide not to sell?"

"Then I reckon the rest of you damn stubborn varmints will have to stay here and raise horses too," Don said.

"When the dust has all settled, I figure the nine of us will each owe thirteen hundred and forty dollars," said Charlie. "I can afford that."

The following day, they were all waiting when the bank opened. Upon the suggestion of the banker, most of the money was left in an account from which they could draw as the need arose. They kept out enough to settle with Butler, and he was waiting in his office when they arrived.

"Now," said Jim Roussel, when the deal had been closed, "I aim to take Ellie for a walk around town before we ride to the ranch."

"I want to walk down to the ocean," Ellie said.

While the hotel overlooked the Pacific, it was still a good distance away. Jim and Ellie had to pass a vacant building, where Ben and Curt Pickford waited in the shadows.

"Nobody with him but one of them females that's been wearin' britches," said Ben. "I'll cut him down, and you cover me while I grab the money he's carryin'."

A single shot rang out, and Jim Roussel pitched to the ground, a growing patch of blood on the back of his shirt.

"Jim!" Ellie cried, falling down beside him.

Ben Pickford came on the run, his Colt in his hand. He seized the collar of the blouse Ellie wore, prepared to fling her aside, but the girl rolled away from him, gripping Jim's Colt with both hands. On her back, she fired once, twice, three times. Three slugs in his chest, Ben Pickford died on his feet. The shots had been heard. Don, Bob, Charlie and Red came running.

"That bastard, Ben Pickford," Charlie said. "Where's the other one?"

"I only saw this one," said Ellie, through tears.

"Let's get him back to the hotel," Don said. "Red, find us a doc."

The doctor came, dressed Jim's wound, and predicted he would recover. He had been hit high up.

"All of us had better stay in town another day or two," said Bob. "The doc will want to follow up on Jim's wound.

Besides, Don and Felton will be leaving for Texas some-time tomorrow."

"The landing is near enough for Felton and me to walk," Don said, as he and Felton Juneau prepared to leave.

"You want us to see you off?" Bob asked.

"I don't," said Felton. "I'd like to ride out to the ranch with the rest of you, so don't make it any harder for me to get on that ship."

"About the way I feel," Don said. "I have the money for Eli's kin, so I reckon we're ready to go."

The only warning they had, as they walked toward the dock, was the flash of sunlight off Quando's rifle muzzle.

"Look out!" shouted Felton.

He went down, drawing his Colt, as a rifle slug tore through Don's new hat. Drawing his own Colt, Don ran, zigzagging as three more slugs narrowly missed him. Felton was right behind him when Quando saw his cause was lost and started to run. Don fired, and the lead ripped through Quando's leg, dropping him. Rolling over on his back, he came up with his revolver in his hand but never fired a shot. Don and Felton fired together, the roar of their Colts merging like a drum roll. The shooting attracted attention, and men came on the run, one of them Sheriff DeShazo. Charlie, Red, and Mike were there too.

"Who in thunder was he?" Red wondered.

"I have no idea," said Don, "unless he was part of that bunch that tried to ambush us on the desert. Sheriff, we're on our way to board a ship, and we don't have much time. Our amigos can tell you anything you need to know about Felton and me."

The dead outlaw was taken away. Charlie, Red, and Mike stood there until the sailing ship drew away from the dock. They watched until it became a distant speck against the blue of the sky, and finally disappeared.

Here's an excerpt from Ralph Compton's

THE GREEN RIVER TRAIL—

the next exciting installment in
the Trail Drive series, available soon from
St. Martin's Paperbacks:

San Francisco, California. June 1, 1853.

*F*our men rode across the Sierra Nevada, bound for
southwestern Wyoming. Their pack mule followed on
a lead rope. At twenty-three, Lonnie Kilgore was the oldest
of the four. Dallas Weaver was a year younger, while Dirk
McNelly and Kirby Lowe were both several months shy of
twenty-one. They reined up on a ridge to rest the horses
and the pack mule.

"I'm glad I got to see California once," Dirk McNelly
said, "but I've never been so glad to be leavin' a place in
my life. It ain't natural, everything always bein' green. I
like to see the falling leaves."

"I reckon you'll be seeing plenty of them in Texas,"
said Kirby Lowe. "Remember, in just four years each of
us has come out of the California goldfields with more than
ten thousand dollars. Raising cows in Texas, starving
through the dry years, and fighting the Comanches, you
wouldn't see half that much coin if you lived to be a hundred."

"That's the gospel truth if I ever heard it," Dallas Weaver said. "Trouble is, what are we goin' to do with what
we've earned? A couple of bad years in Texas could break
us."

"Then maybe we'd better not settle in Texas," said Lonnie Kilgore. "Remember, on our way west, when we spent a couple of days at Jim Bridger's trading post in Wyoming?"

"Yeah," Dallas Weaver said. "Bridger's an old mountain man, and what he don't know about this high country likely ain't worth knowing."

"I'm thinking of something he said while we was there," said Lonnie. "He talked about that range along the Green River in northeastern Utah, where the grass reaches up to a horse's belly. He thought it would be grand for horses, cattle, or both. In the summer, herds of cattle could be driven into Washington, Oregon, Nevada, and California."

"That ain't all," Kirby Lowe said. "It'll be a while in coming, but the San Francisco newspapers was plumb full of stories about the building of the Union Pacific, a transcontinental railroad. It'll run across southern Wyoming near where Bridger's trading post is now. I doubt any of us will live long enough to see a railroad reach Texas."

"A railroad can be as much a curse as a blessing," said Dirk McNelly. "It'll bring in droves of sodbusters, and it'll mean the end of free range."

"Forget about free range," Lonnie Kilgore said. "We have money to buy land, and if the price is right, we can buy a lot of it. Once you got a title to it, nobody can root you out. That's my thinking."

"The farther we are from civilization, the less the land will cost," said Dallas Weaver, "but I'm not sure about this Green River range. Bridger was already having trouble with the Mormons when we was there four years ago, and he ain't even *in* Utah."

"Once we've filed on land and have a title to it, it's ours," Lonnie Kilgore said. "I'm not one to fight with my neighbors, but I won't be pushed around. I think we should talk to Bridger about this range, and unless somebody's already claiming it, we should consider buying four sections—or maybe eight—depending on the price."

"Eight sections!" said Kirby Lowe. "My God, that's more than five thousand acres."

"With the Green River running through it," Dirk McNelly said. "I like that."

"So do I," Kirby Lowe said, "but before we settle out here, I'd like to ride to Texas and see my folks. I ain't seen 'em since I was sixteen."

"I ain't so sure my folks will want to see me," said Dirk McNelly. "My old man called me a fool for wantin' to go gallavantin' off to California. I had to sneak off in the middle of the night."

"After we talk to Bridger, if all this still seems like a good idea, we'll be going back to Texas," Lonnie Kilgore said. "We'll need cattle. We may have to rope the varmints out of the brush, but we can do that, if we must."

"What about horses?" Kirby Lowe asked. "Even when it's hard times in Texas, a good horse can set you back two hundred dollars."

"There are some fine horses in California," said Lonnie Kilgore. "Once we've brought a herd of longhorns from Texas, we can bring in some brood mares from California."

"One thing we have to consider is the Indians," Dallas Weaver said. "From what Jim Bridger said, the Utes and Paiutes don't take kindly to whites coming into the territory."

"By now," said Kirby Lowe, "there ought to be enough Mormons there to keep them busy. At least the Wind River Shoshones are friendly."

"Yeah," Dirk McNelly said, "but they're too far north, in the Wind River Mountains."

"I think this is another case where we'll have to depend on Jim Bridger's advice," said Lonnie Kilgore.

The four of them rode on, still dressed as Texas cowboys, even after four long years in California. In each saddle boot there was a treasured Hawken rifle, and each of them had a tied-down Colt revolver on his right hip. Not until late afternoon did they discover they were being followed. Again, they had stopped to rest the horses, and it was Kirby Lowe who spoke.

"Maybe my eyes are playin' tricks on me, but I'd

swear I saw some dust back yonder a ways, along our back trail.''

''Whether you did or didn't, this is no time to gamble,'' said Lonnie Kilgore. ''There's always a horde of *hombres* around a gold camp who'd rather steal their gold than work for it. Remember last year, when three miners were bushwhacked when they rode out bound for home?''

''Yeah,'' Dallas Weaver said, ''and the bushwhackers were never caught. I think we'd do well to ride on a ways and then double back. This ain't the kind of country where a man rides unless he has to. We can set up a little welcomin' party of our own.''

''We'll ride to the foot of this ridge,'' said Lonnie Kilgore. ''There we'll leave the mule and our horses, doubling back on foot.''

They rode on, leaving a clear trail for their pursuers. Reining up in a thicket, they tied the mule and their horses.

''Dallas,'' said Lonnie, ''you and Dirk double back to the south and then west, keeping within range of the trail. Kirby, you and me will head north a ways, and then west. I'll challenge these riders, and since we'll be shooting from cover, we'll let them make the first move. They *could* be other miners on their way home.''

''Well, hell,'' Dirk McNelly said, ''if they are, we still may have a fight on our hands. They're likely to think we're bushwhackers aimin' to take their gold.''

''Maybe not,'' said Lonnie Kilgore. ''Bushwhackers don't shout a warning.''

The four men separated in twos, taking the north and south sides of the back trail. A vengeful sun bore down on them, and the armpits of their shirts were soon soaked with sweat. They waited for more than an hour, their patience growing thin, before hearing the distinctive sound of trotting horses. There were four riders, and they looked like anything but miners. They rode on, and when they were within gun range, Lonnie Kilgore shouted a challenge.

''Rein up. Identify yourselves and tell us why you're trailing us.''

There was a moment of shocked silence. Then, as one, the four went for their guns. It left the four friends from Texas little choice. Lonnie shot the lead man out of the saddle, while Dallas, Dirk, and Kirby accounted for the other three. Spooked by the shooting, their horses galloped down the ridge. There was dead silence, and none of the four who had been gunned down seemed alive.

"We might as well search them," said Lonnie, "and see what we can find. Then we'll go after their horses and search their saddlebags."

"Lord, I hope they wasn't miners on their way home," Dirk McNelly said.

"I doubt they were," said Lonnie Kilgore. "Bushwhackers wouldn't have challenged them, and if they didn't have mischief on their minds, they wouldn't have gone for their guns. They made the first move, and it was the wrong one. When a man pulls iron, it's evidence aplenty that he's up to no good."

Each of them searched one of the dead men, and it was Dallas Weaver who recognized one of them.

"This is Jake Doolin," said Dallas. "He's been hanging around for months, and as for mining, he ain't hit a lick. There's been some strong suspicions that he's one of a pack of coyotes who kill miners for their pokes."

"I've heard that," Lonnie said, "but nobody said it too loud. There was no proof."

"There is now," said Kirby. "Sure as hell, the four of 'em aimed to kill and rob us."

"Question is," Dirk said, "what do we do with them? I can't see ridin' all the way back to San Francisco to tell the law what we done."

"We'll leave them where they lay," said Lonnie, "and anything we find that we can use, we'll take with us."

Searching the bodies of the four men, they came up with more than a thousand dollars in gold coin.

"Unless somebody's hit pay dirt in Texas, that'll buy three hundred cows," Dirk said.

"Now," said Dallas, "let's round up their horses. We

can take them with us, and it'll be the start of a remuda for the trail drive from Texas."

They soon found the four horses grazing and caught them without difficulty. There was a rifle in each saddle boot. But the saddlebags were a disappointment, for there was only a change of clothing, clean socks, and jerked beef.

"They didn't aim to travel far from town," Lonnie said. "They'd ride just far enough to do their killing and robbing, and be back at the gold camp before dark."

"It'd be a shame, leaving these four good horses and saddles," said Dirk, "but there's a little matter of us having no bills of sale on any of 'em. They're all branded, too."

"Mex brands," Lonnie said. "They likely were stolen somewhere below the border, and as long as these four dead coyotes have been hanging around San Francisco, I doubt anybody's asked for a bill of sale. We'll take those four horses with us on lead ropes."

The four friends rode out. Three of the men had the newly acquired horses on leads, while Lonnie Kilgore led the fourth horse and the pack mule. They made camp for the night near a water hole in Nevada. They poured water on their small fire well before dark.

"I have some serious doubts about the direction we're headed," Lonnie said. "I think we ought to ride due north and take the Oregon Trail to Bridger's trading post. Remember, when we was there before, Bridger told us the Mormons was settling around the Great Salt Lake? If we ride a straight line from here to Bridger's, we'll be passing right through the Mormon settlements."

"It'll take us maybe a day longer," said Dallas, "and we'd come out somewhere in Idaho, I reckon."*

"Them Mormons has had four years to settle out here since we talked to Bridger," Dirk said. "There must be thousands of 'em by now. I kinda like that idea of ridin' north from here, and then taking the Oregon Trail to Bridger's."

*Near the present-day town of Twin Fall, Idaho.

"One thing wrong with that," Kirby said. "We'll have to cross South Pass."

"That won't be a problem," said Lonnie, "since we have no wagons. Horses and mules can make it, even if we have to dismount and lead them. If we settle along the Green, I'll gamble that we'll be in trouble with the Mormons soon enough. I think we'd do well to go north from here until we reach the Oregon Trail. Even with crossing South Pass, we can still make it in about six days."

"I like that," Dallas said. "Nothing but a fool fights, if he can avoid it."

"I'll go along," said Dirk. "We'll likely have all the Mormon trouble we can handle after we bring that trail drive from Texas."

"Count me in," Kirby said. "We got to claim the land, get us a herd of cows and some prime horses. Then will be soon enough to fight with anybody that don't like us."

They had reached an agreement, and there seemed little else to do except roll in their blankets and get some sleep.